City of Light

City of Light

A Novel by Cyrus Colter

THUNDER'S MOUTH PRESS
NEW YORK

Published by
Thunder's Mouth Press
632 Broadway, 7th Floor
New York, NY 10012

Library of Congress Cataloging-in-Publication Data

Colter, Cyrus.
    City of light / Cyrus Colter.
       p.   cm.
    ISBN 1-56025-059-3 : $22.95. — ISBN 1-56025-061-5 (pbk.) :
    $12.95
    I. Title.
    PS3553.0477C58   1993
    813'.54—dc20   92-38260
                                                       CIP

Design by Ultimo Inc.
Typesetting by AeroType, Inc.
Manufactured in the United States of America

Distributed by Publishers Group West
4065 Hollis Street
Emeryville, CA 94608
(800) 788-3123

To the memory of
Mary Imogene Mackay Colter,
wife, confidante, silent accessory.

City of Light

Chapter

One

Queen Saturn

Watchman, what of the night?!" It was his tipsy father's inscrutable war cry on leaving a fun party, say, a beaker of martinis under his belt, yet barring his pretty wife from any proximity to the steering wheel. It had all been routine, though, again, earning old Zacharias his friends' sobriquet "Watchman." He had laughed a lot, yet recently he had been slowing down—because of his son. It was almost biblical—the wish that his son would change for the better and finally come to love his father. *Ah, Absalom! Absalom!*

The afternoon was one on which a slow thin rain was falling as, alone, the son sat upstairs at a littered table, writing and talking, talking to himself, writing to Saturn Marie, his mother. "Sometimes," he was saying via pencil, "I feel you crippled me, my existence, without meaning to." The pencil was so inadequate. He wanted to hurl it to the floor or up against the wall, it was of such meager help to him. He felt he had a private mandate, however, to continue, if at all possible, not only to act but think rationally. He hoped he wasn't being childish these days even if he was sure he was dealing with crises. The pencil was an emblem of his attempts to reduce them to manageable proportions. Not the least of these tries, perhaps at the moment the most critical, was Cécile, the glowing factor in his present life; heaven-sent, he thought at times; at other intervals came speculation on the dangerous turn thereby his life had taken.

The pencil was moving again: "Never mind, Mother, you were good to me at times as well. It was just that your priorities were complicated, sometimes rash—to me, an only child, maddening. At last I feared insisting on my rights, only to find I had so few. I wonder if Father was aware, or if he just holed himself up in that big ornate office of his and concentrated on other things. Nevertheless, he was head of the house, wasn't he? Everything that happened, as they say, happened on his watch, right? Then, 'Watchman, what of the night?' To focus on the issue, someone failed to prepare me for my life. Not just any life. I'm not hunchbacked, or deaf; I don't have halitosis, or the clap; I'm not ugly (in fact, I'm said to be handsome); and though not exactly 'brilliant,' I am, through Father's largesse and the bevy of tutors he made available, a Princeton grad. Nor am I gay. Nonetheless, Mother, you brought, you *put*, me here. That happened on *your* watch. I didn't ask for it, didn't seek it—I didn't exist. You even gave me the wrong color. I'm not black. I'm swarthy, or beige, or saddle-colored. I am tall, though, and yes, handsome, they say. Big deal—at college even a few of the blondes gave me big smiles, and I hadn't ever made the football squad. It was you, Mother, no less, on *your* watch, and via *your* womb, who introduced me to rawboned Chicago. I think I would have preferred Lagos. I am therefore a NEGRO in the Western world, and you did not tell me." The pencil was scratching the paper now. He stopped and reached for a bag of peanuts. Finally he rose, went to the mansard window and through the drizzle peered down onto the Rue la Chatte, for him not a particularly exciting vista. He knew the remedy. He lifted his gaze, up, up, and father north, across the panorama of climbing housetops short kilometers upgrade, to the famed old landmark, the Deity's gift to Paris, the basilica Sacré-Coeur, in its majesty its three great Byzantine domes crowning that formidable hillock on which it rested and God viewed His equivocal universe. Suddenly then, alas, his be-dazzlement was broken, for at that moment back down on the Rue la Chatte, two painfully wailing, suffering dogs, male and female in furious, hapless copulation, had just hurled them-selves around the corner in his direction, the male of the pair all the while being dragged along the wet gutter by the taller, stronger, speckled bitch. Paul shuddered and started a retreat from the window, when below, a municipal streetsweeper, a husky woman, rushed up, her voice literally berating the whole scene, and began flailing the frantic dogs with her huge broom until they had suddenly wrenched themselves apart and, yelping in misery, went scurrying off down the street and around the corner out of sight. Paul stood trembling. He did not know why. As if exhausted, he finally sat back down at the table, reached for the peanuts, and then soon for another pencil: "No, you gave me no inkling, Saturn — none at all — then you went off and left me; into infinity, eternity, or wher-ever you now are. And me at the time barely out of high school. It was no fun and Zacharias Kessey ('old Zack,' or 'Watchman'), early on at least, wasn't much help. I think he sympathized with me, though, without really knowing my burden. But speaking of your own name, Saturn dear, I guess I thought about it most at Princeton. And I had studied so hard to get admitted — and with Watchman and his tutors on my trail all the time. He really wanted me in that place — and, I don't have to tell you, he's a real bulldog. Even hired two men and a woman to make sure I knew who Kant was. I got scared — it was worse than the later four years. But back to you, Saturn. I've especially thought of you today. Are you aware that this is the Ides of March? It's made me think of that classical mythology seminar I took by accident, but where I learned a lot about the Roman god Saturn — ha, who was arbiter of agriculture, vegetation, and fecundity. I've never forgotten that, Saturn Marie. Then — all of a century later, it seems — when I came to Paris, I was really in a bad way, drinking heavily for the first time; then I'd sit on the terraces along the Boulevard St. Germain, also the sidewalk cafes, and drink scads of strong coffee, trying to dry out. The trade name of a viscous, almost lethal, Sumatra java was Saturn. I'd sit there alone, knowing not a half-dozen people in town, lonesome 24 hours a day and night — thinking of you and blurrily watching the passing, oblivious Parisians. It was a bad time — for you would haunt me so. Yet, when you were with us, I must confess, you were most of the time a good Joe. I realize now I was unreasonable, a spoiled brat, which in turn would upset you and you'd then become cold and unresponsive. That's when I'd think you didn't give a damn about me. That's also when sometimes I'd almost want to kill you — especially when I thought of Father, to whom I was certain you gave all of your time. The truth is, and I see it now, you gave a lot of your time to me, too — which I'd woozily think about, acknowledge, sitting there on some Left Bank terrace imbibing Sumatra java by the carafe. I wanted to jump in the Seine, actually. Then Cécile came on the scene — another story, or treatise, or tome, in fact. Yes, more anon.

"But why didn't you school me on how to be black? That's what this sad ruckus we deal with everyday is all about, isn't it? But I have a theory on that. Could it be that you yourself turned away, refused to recognize the phenomenon? You recognized it, though, I recall, in the case of Jeannette Hall, who happened to be a black beauty. You recognized it with a vengeance. More anon, yes. But what about Father, the Watchman, your man? He's not all that black, true, but he's a long way from being white, or, ha, even sepia, or banana. Why is color so important, Mother? You didn't tell me about these things, or teach me to cope. I had tutors, all right — who, yes, taught me about the Magna Charta, and Erasmus (not a word, though, about Rastus), and the War Between the States. Nor did they instruct me on how to negotiate my relationship with beautiful Cécile. More anon."

There was a friendly knock on the door of his room. "Monsieur Kessey? . . ." It was his venerable, patrician landlady, his wise and spirited friend as well — Madame Natalie Theresa-Prue Chevalley. "Paul," she said through the door. "it's four-forty and time to suspend your African research. Africa will still be there tomorrow, even to eternity, and still a problem." He could hear her wry, mischievous little laugh. "*Quel quel, dommage.* Join me down in the parlor — although there is only a small bit of Campari left in the bottle. But enough. It's the talk and relaxation that counts. Besides, I need your counsel on a matter." He caught his breath. She knew Cécile. It made him wary. "*Oui, Madame,*" he said, though, "*avec plaisir.* Just give me a few minutes to become presentable." Thus it was arranged.

Shortly after five o'clock they were downstairs in her once-genteel little parlor. Through the streaked windowpanes they could see the slow rain still steadily falling. "They will take out my eyes first," said Madame. "It is true, Monsieur. My eyes." Paul winced. "I have already arranged for it," she smiled before giving a strange, lighthearted, though somehow now ghoulish, laugh. Then briefly she twisted about in her chair to be more comfortable.

City of Light

He looked away moodily. There were telltale hints of class, even elegance, about him now. In the brief interim, he had shaved and donned a tweed jacket and necktie. He sat on the sofa — across from her chair — beneath the large gilt mirror, finally edging forward slightly as if the better to study the pallor of her wizened yet painted face. They were sipping the modicum of Campari over ice in her pension in the Rue du Colisée on the Right Bank, where, eight months before, he had taken his two upstairs rooms in which, though, not only to sleep but to ply his tedious, and so-far-equivocal, African studies, but which he had convinced himself, as well as his already skeptical father, were his self-abnegating, high-minded reason for coming to Paris; where also, unbeknownst to his father, as half in penance, to write, then destroy, reams of scalding, nostalgic letters to his deceased mother, before then going off, out into the streets to meditate and lick his psychic wounds. Besides, in the picture there was his Waterloo — a beautiful woman. Paris thus had worked its will.

"Oh, it wasn't stressed," Madame was saying — about her eyes, her corpse as well — "I just stipulated that I wanted the university, the medical school, to have my body. *Tres bien?*"

His smile was dry. "You know," he said, "I've always told myself that, no matter what, you will live forever, Madame." He laughed then.

She went on obliviously. "I could not refrain from telling them about all the trouble, from years of punishing reading, I've had with my eyes, which, I'm sorry to say, haven't been much good to me for three or four years now." Her withered hand went up, touching her thick glasses, then stroking her lank, far-too-lavender hair.

He hesitated. "You . . . stipulated . . ."

"I did, yes. It's *my* body." Beneath her chin the lax throat muscles, as heavily powdered and rouged as her cheeks, turkey-waggled as she talked, though she could not now have weighed more than 105 pounds. "Of course, there was a lot of red tape," she said. "But they understood everything, my expectations and all."

His smile was irreverent now. "What were those, Madame?"

She waved him off. "Expectations, motives, rightness, wrongness, what have you—they're always complex, Monsieur Kessey. I, of course, could never explain my own to you. It all gets out of hand, and eventually into religion—which I'm helpless to deal with. Spare me." She proffered him her empty glass. "Be so kind as to pour me that little Campari remaining, will you, Paul? Ha, may I preempt you?"

"Of course." He reached for the bottle and complied, noting her trembling hand.

Although Parisian born, reared, and educated—her conservative father had been a prominent lawyer—Madame Chevalley spoke good English, if with an accent, yet also at times near idiomatically. For fifteen years, however, off and on, before retiring, she had taught French in private schools in Sardinia, the Orkney Islands, and the Isle of Wight. She had also at one time, many years before that—when she was young, pretty, and already through two husbands, plus repeated rifts with her father—been active in radical French politics. This was following the war and the Nazi occupation, when briefly she had been a fringe member of the Resistance and had had a nodding acquaintance with Sartre.

"Nevertheless," Madame went on, "the young woman at the medical school, taking down my information, was apparently impressed by my seriousness and determination—ha, my philanthropy. She avoided looking at me, though, when I spoke of my eyes. Oh, I had so trusted my eyes." There was both pride and exasperation in her manner. "In those days, way back, I was reading like a demented demon. I was extremely political, of course—as you are now, or, ha, claim to be—and was a virtual book carnivore. Trying to find answers . . . ah, what presumption." She fell silent. The ancient clock in the parlor's corner had just struck a late five o'clock, filling the room with its brassy gonging, as she sat gazing out at the traffic moving south in the rain toward the Seine.

After her health had failed, her three-story pension—a dozen or so rooms for guests and well-enough kept, though never overly ornate—had suffered moderate neglect, become slightly less attractive, yet never tacky or drab. And never less than expensive—this after all was Paris. Paul had had his second-floor two rooms, the best available in the house—with bath, television, and private telephone—longer than any other present guests their rooms, and even during a time when often a room or two went begging.

Madame again turned to him, her face blanched even beneath the harsh cosmetics, her smile both innocent and somehow now strangely demoniacal. "Does the thought of my head without any eyes in it shock you?" she said.

His mouth opened. At last he took a deep breath. "No," he finally said, though again repelled, inwardly shuddering.

"I don't believe you," she teased, tittering—"Oh it shocks you, all right."

He observed her warily, at last not answering.

Her ailing eyes, however, somehow now twinkled as she added, with spleen, "You black so-called militants are not so tough as you pretend, you know. Don't forget, I was a Communist Party member—in fact, for a time, a minor leader." The thought seemed sobering to her now. "I've known some really tough people—the women often tougher than the men—who would not have been a bit jolted by the idea of a shrunken white carcass, a gangrened cadaver, lying out on some dissecting table with a handful of medical students clustered around the professor, his protective rubber gloves on and a scalpel in his hand (now that my eye sockets were empty), and his other hand moving down, down, pressing, poking, probing, until, for a specimen, he slits off a sliver of my shaved genitalia, actually one of the vulvae, with an inquisitive, pedantic, supercilious wrinkle of his nose." Her eyes, though old and opaque, seemed now actually glowing. "Ah, you're terribly upset, really revolted, aren't you? You think me obscene, *d'accord*? Oh, Paul." She laughed weakly, crazily, as he gulped. "It's because you professed militants, blacks who can afford to come over here from the States for a year or two, are actually lacking in stomach. It's a paradox, but you are all bourgeois to the core. The real militants, the ones you left behind, don't have the money—or, as you do, a well-heeled father, who even sent you to Princeton—to come splurging over here ostensibly to study the conditions of your fellow blacks in this and other parts of the world, though to no sensible purpose that I've ever been able to see. You are very privileged, Monsieur Kessey, very. But how serious are you, how sincere? Does that question ever bother you, or your conscience?"

He bristled. "Madame, you mistake me. I don't happen to be just another of your light-headed, camera-toting tourists, you know—here for two or three days, then gone on to the next stop. I'm busy, very busy, and will continue to be—you've seen my cluttered rooms upstairs; they should tell you something about how seriously I take my work. Maybe, though, this has escaped you—the research I'm doing on the long-neglected culture and mores of the African people. Yes, we too have a culture, you know—apparently that's seldom occurred to you." He looked up—only to see her slow, caustic smile.

"Paul, did I hear you say that 'we'—meaning you blacks recently descending on Paris—are interested in Africa, in researching African culture? What I seem to see, though, is something quite different, which is that by no means has your diligent research entirely overlooked the beauteous French female gender, either. Ha! Am I right?" Suddenly then her hand flew to her mouth, apologetically, as if struggling to bring the words back. "Oh, I shouldn't have said that — forgive me, Paul. It's really nothing to take lightly — the other person involved, as we both well know, is certainly not having an easy time of it. Cécile has never, never experienced anything, in her wildest imagination, like this. Although no child, far from it, she is completely stymied, helpless, with no solutions whatever, about what's happening to you two — your relationship; and what you both are going to do about it."

At once Paul was desperate to sidetrack this unwelcome, and insoluble, issue. Rather, now, if by his mere behavior, he was insistent, on continuing Madame's former rude talk — it was at least an escape, an avoidance. Moreover, it not only dwelt on his "research" project but would almost certainly go on to the subject, also known to Madame, involving his other great venture (unknown, of course, to his father, nonetheless all at the latter's inevitable financial expense) having to do with Paul's recent founding of a somewhat strange organization, labeled, proudly, by its fledgling members as the "Coterie," whose mission, however, was by no means out of sync with its founder's research effort, i.e., the new organization might well launch a study on the present-day potential of Africa's possible role in, it was hoped, becoming a refuge, a haven, for confused and hapless world blacks who, with ample cause, thought Coterie members, considered themselves restless, roving casualties, historic victims of slavery and its grim twin, the black diaspora. Was there, then, even at this late date, went Coterie reasoning, any prospect at all of an African rebirth of the desire to bring "home" its scattered, ill-starred progeny and nurse it back to health? Harebrained? Not necessarily, thought Paul and his new organization. No matter, this is what, for obvious reasons, he now preferred to talk about. There was at least hope here, while the cause of Cécile meant only further frustration and heartache; it was definitely something to stay away from. "I know, Madame," he was soon saying, "that you were not making light, pointing fun, at my poor efforts to accomplish something that might help people. You did the same yourself at one time in your life and are to be commended for it. I realize it may sound corny, but I didn't come to Paris to have a good time but, I hoped, to get some things done that were needed, that would help certain people, my own people, whom nobody else seems interested in. I'm sure, as my friend, you weren't belittling this."

"No, Paul, I wasn't — or I hope I wasn't. Then I misspoke, and got into the really troublesome matter of you and Cécile. Naturally it's a difficult situation, and not only because she is married and has two young children, but because you both, in . . . I can only call it your driven ecstasy . . . seem to have lost all sense of direction, reason."

"Madame, I was talking about why I came to Paris — and it wasn't because of Cécile. I didn't know her then."

"Please stop trying to avoid the issue, Paul. It's not going away. It's such a thorny matter for a number of reasons, but one is that you are two absolutely unique people. It's something far, far beyond any relationship I've ever witnessed or even known of — that rare, wonderful exception, and involving an absolutely marvelous woman besides, all as if it were a union, a love, spread on canvas by Botticelli. And, just to think, it was through me — and a crazy, weird happenstance — that it all came about. Actually, because it's such a beautiful happening, I don't know whether to be proud of my part in it or to just go slink away. I do worry — it was I, remember, who introduced you two."

City of Light

Although wildly emotional on the subject, he seemed now only to grind his perfect teeth. He said nothing, though, keeping his stare riveted on a curlicue in the opposite figured wallpaper, even if soon moving his lips as if at any moment he might speak.

She watched him with a sudden compassion now. "Oh, enough, enough, of this difficult, impossible — yet utterly fascinating — subject," she finally said. "I'm sorry, Monsieur. I know how it irritates you. And worries you, too. But, my God, think of Cécile — it *agonizes* her."

He looked as if he might any minute spring up from the sofa — "What is it you're trying to say! . . . Excuse me if it sounds to me like pure gibberish — and I hope I'm not offending you, Madame. But why bring her up at all?"

Madame was unmindful. "It's your bourgeois background, I insist," she said. "I, of course, very well understand. Everyone doesn't, though. It's brand new to her . . . your family, and your upbringing, your education, and all."

"Madame, will you please tell me what any of this has to do with anything?"

"What kind of question is that? I'm being serious and assume you're following what I'm saying. I'm talking about family and class. The irony is that — oh, how wacky it all gets — none of what we're talking about would ever have happened had your background been different. Then, to complicate matters further, her family — forgive me — far excels yours in its considerable, and lengthy, history of accomplishments. Maybe they — the Cambons — weren't exactly famous before the war, but they weren't unknown, either. But had you been reared in, say, the Chicago ghetto, the slums, instead of in a townhouse on the sunny shores of Lake Michigan, Cécile wouldn't have looked at you once, much less twice."

Paul smirked. "Where did you get your information . . . about *what*? . . . townhouses on the sunny shores of the lake?

Please pay us a visit during the zero cold, ice, and snow of January, Madame."

She was wagging her forefinger at him. "Stick to the subject, Paul. I've never been to Chicago and don't expect to go now. But what about Cécile had you been shining shoes on the Champs-Elysées?"

"Of course, just as if I'd been white, she wouldn't have looked at me—once, twice, or three times. But I wouldn't have been in Paris in the first place. Where's your thinking cap, Madame?"

"Oh, maybe I *am* talking silly—you've got me confused. No, maybe you wouldn't even have been here—engaged in your fancy leadership role and your strenuous research. Instead you'd be in Chicago fighting it out in the streets with the racial bigots. What do you people call them?—honkies, crackers, white motherfuckers . . . ? Where do you blacks get all those weird epithets—they're not in the dictionary. I've looked."

Paul was shaking his head.

"Indeed, your whole life in the States is confusing," she said. "It terribly baffles poor Cécile."

"Have you ever heard me use foul language?" he said. "Or has Cécile?"

Madame's hand flew to her face. "Oh, heavens no! I should say not. And Cécile would faint."

"Madame, you're hardly your sharp self today—you speak about our fighting 'racial bigots' in the streets of Chicago. There is no such fighting—it doesn't happen. Unless it's blacks in the ghetto, fighting, shooting, each other."

Madame curled her lip. "Oh, listen to that—to the great activist for Negro rights. You could never be a member of the proletariat as I once was—black or white. If blacks *are* shooting each other in the streets, it's because people like you, and your father, have done little or nothing to help them. Then you vilify them."

Paul was shaking his head sadly now. "You're wrong, so wrong, Madame."

She was unappeased. "What do you know about, or feel for, the unwashed blacks? How can you possibly identify with them? You yourself certainly don't look so black—with your fine tawny-beige skin, and that hard, handsome, almost chiseled face of yours, with your jet-curly locks that you're so vain about. Even maybe, for all I know, that's a clipped Princeton accent you affect in your talk. Is there such a thing?" She finally threw her head back in a shrill, uproarious laugh—and then became contrite, again apologetic. "Forgive me, Paul—I've been too harsh on you. But you are sometimes the same with me—though you don't realize it. I know you're trying to do something big, meaningful, especially with the organization you've now formed, for your black brothers and sisters—if, *if*, Paul, you only knew specifically what it should be, what direction it should take. This is no small matter. I know, of course, you're serious, no poseur—that you really want to do good. But, believe me, it's no easy road to travel—I too was once a 'do-gooder' but have nothing today to show for it. I accomplished very little, if anything. Sometimes the people you're trying most to help will turn on you and hate you for it. *Homo sapiens* is a strange creature—God Himself, if there is one, hasn't yet figured him out. How can *we* hope to?"

Paul was silent, ruminative.

"I know what you're thinking about," she said. "Or, rather, *whom* you're thinking about." She too was grave now.

He finally turned to her, then shrugged, with the merest wisp of a sigh. "I find that thinking doesn't help much, Madame."

"Does she tell you how confused she is?"

"No. She doesn't have to. I don't have to tell her anything, either. We both know it — it's a mutual contagion."

"But, oh, Paul, it's so easy to see how she would absolutely lose her head. No, her heart. Never in all her sheltered life has she encountered such an absolutely unique man as you — though, as you must certainly know by now, she's a strong, very purposeful, person. She's not just beautiful, you know, but also a sophisticated woman, as well as one well born and knows it. Now she's come to this."

Paul was cool, indeed cold, at the remark. "Pray tell me — what is 'this?' "

"Oh, don't be so thin-skinned. Heavens, Paul. You brought it on — with my assistance, both of us unwittingly. And especially she. Oh, poor, dear Cécile. Now she's come to a point in her life when she's thoroughly bewildered, confused. It's a brand new experience for her, although she's mostly silent, especially when tears come to her eyes. And listen — though you may already know — she's suddenly become religious again. It's almost like she's reverted to her childhood, as we all have at one time or another, and prays devoutly and constantly, including going to Mass every day. It's mystified everybody, especially her husband and children — but not I, of course. I feel sorry for her. She's searching for some solution. Whether she will find it or not, or would know it if she found it, is altogether another matter and certainly beyond me. It's not at all a very pretty picture to watch. She's a troubled woman, Monsieur — catching hell. I'm sure you know, or definitely suspect, what it is, too."

He rose from the sofa and went over to the window. It was getting dark, but he saw the rain had temporarily slowed. His face was gaunt now, the symmetry not quite distorted, still somehow ambiguous and turbulent, before he was soon acting queerly, as if he were alone in the room.

City of Light

From her chair Madame pursued him with her weak eyes. "Can I be wrong," she said, "that you don't know, that you haven't yet diagnosed, her trouble?"

He was mute.

"You know, of course," she said. "Your silence confirms it. She's never in her life been within ten feet of a black man — and then on some crowded Paris street or boulevard where she hurriedly saw him but didn't see him. Moreover, historically, her senior family members have been staunchly conservative, or worse — in fact, an uncle, after the war, in the fall of 1945, was shot by a firing squad as a Laval, or Vichy, collaborator. But in her case it's all doubly complicated — for one reason, maybe the simplest, that Cécile herself is complicated. And if this were not enough — my God — so are you. When two people like that, for any reason, find themselves together — look out. A sudden, sometimes violent, kinetic energy is created, which, if released, can blow the roof off the place. It's because all kinds of things are going on, internally — *that* certainly fits you two. Yet at least Cécile's personality, her methods, and reactions are consistent — which can sometimes, when things are really up for grabs, be a plus. Your case, however — good Lord — defies any description at all. I can only say it's disturbing — I almost said 'scary.' Or, what do they call people like you? 'Loose cannons,' yes. For instance, today you may be one man, tomorrow very possibly, or almost surely, another. You don't know, Paul — I've watched these moods of yours, their sudden stops, starts, and changes, and I would say it becomes something almost reminiscent of Dr. Jekyll and Mr. Hyde. Only, of course, you're no criminal." She paused now, perhaps for a longer time than she was aware, before asking, quite soberly, sincerely, although now unable to bring herself to look at him: "Listen, Paul, have you ever considered putting an untimely end to this whole, strange, dangerous affair and returning home to the United States?"

Still standing at the window, his six-foot slender height a commanding presence, he remained mute.

Madame, though soft-spoken, humane, was relentless. "I know it's not fair of me to ask you such a question," she said. "You have feelings, deep feelings—especially in a matter so trying as this—and I think I can, at least partially, imagine them." He had finally turned around to her now, at the same time also noticing that her right hand in her lap was trembling. "You're as deeply involved in this as Cécile," she said. "Her stake is no greater than yours, and I acknowledge that. So, of course, I feel equally for you both." But she would not look at him and only gazed judiciously out the far, wet-streaked window.

At last he stepped over in front of the mirror and studied himself—as if with a strange, painful understanding of what she had said. When he turned and spoke, then, his voice was shaky and hoarse, yet also passionate, then soon fiercely supplicating. "Madame, Madame, the subject of your conversation is lethal. Also unproductive! It's chiefly drama, and I'd prefer to hear no more of it." Again he was grating his teeth. "*Please*, no more drama, Madame!"

"If you weren't so unjustifiably distraught by anything I've said you'd be able to see who has introduced the drama. Well, then, deal with this 'drama': When you next see Cécile, ask her, if you dare, her views on the average black or African person. Do that. It will enlighten you, Paul—until, that is, it begins to dawn on you that you may yourself harbor some of her own unpleasant views on race, or at least misgivings. Think about it for a moment. It's possible, you know; not at all far-fetched—considering your background, which we've already discussed. I sense it. Oh, heavens—if that were actually to turn out to be the case, that on this issue, you two more or less agreed, it would at least, almost automatically, solve many potential problems for the relationship. Ah, what irony. Think of it. You, the handsome, serious, would-be savior of the benighted blacks, she the lovely, white, conservative, devout Catholic, agreeing on this prickly subject like two peas in a pod. So, should I not consider withdrawing my suggestion that you break with her and go home? How does that strike you, Monsieur Kessey?"

He could endure no more of her taunting. The subject was deadly. Face ashen, unyielding, he faced her. "I of course understand all your inferences, Madame," he said, "the racist as well as the political and cultural, though they barely escape superficiality. Yet even on that level you are wrong. You know very little of my emotional life, to say nothing of my political orientation. You refer to me as a 'black militant,' which is not necessarily the case. Nor are you as informed, up-to-date, about what's happening in the world today as you think. The world has drastically changed, and is still changing. It's a historic fact, a thundering event, in fact — unprecedented. Even in the United States, just to take one aspect of the way we blacks see our new role, we are not, I repeat, fighting in the streets, as you — just because it's picturesque, and exciting, and idealistic, and takes you, Madame, back to your old Red days on the barricades — as you, yes, would probably prefer we were. But that's all passé. Actually, blacks did very little of it even back then — television exaggerated it. We have a more realistic, and effective, dialectic now. It came with the fight (not always in the streets) for the right to vote. We pursue the politics of numbers now. We do have numbers, you know. The concept's not Marxist, either, thank God — it wouldn't work if it were. Yet I notice you still use one of the old terms, clichés — you speak of the 'proletariat.' But communism, as you surely must know by now, is both a domestic and international — a notorious — failure. A scandal. A worldwide dud. You must admit that, Madame. It is finished."

She had already fallen into a deeply subdued mood of both reflection and dejection. "Yes," she finally said, "I do, I must, admit it. We failed." She heaved a heavy sigh. "We wanted — so badly — to make the world a better place. But is man really capable of this? . . . I often wonder now. But you go ahead — try your way. It probably won't work, either, but you too can say you tried."

Strangely, Paul brightened. "You discredit yourself too readily," he said. "It's a matter of pragmatism, logistics, canvasing, numbers — in the States, yes, it's our numbers now that count: the ballot box. It torments our enemies on the far right, of course — fills them with disgust, really. They hate our *numbers*, you see — claim that we breed like locusts."

Madame's eyes went wide, her feeble hand again to her face. "Oh, my heavens," she said. "I should think so. Aren't they right? You *are* a fertile people, Paul." Quickly looking away, her stress turning inward, she seemed momentarily frightened. "Oh, gracious . . . Locusts . . . blacks . . . yes . . . oh, heavens — it may be true . . ."

He watched her — fascinated. At last he smiled, saying, "You agree with them, eh? — like your countrymen in the last century, the French imperialists, colonialists, who tried to wipe out the hordes of blacks in upper west Africa. We survived, though. Ha, along with the locusts." He had turned grim now and soon showed his wish to depart. He said no more and stood staring out at the cold March rain. Nonetheless, as always, he was deeply in awe of Madame. And grateful to her, besides. Her inconstant, fragile, day-to-day notions were nonetheless pondered by him, never taken lightly, often even recorded in his notebooks. She had lived long, seen much, and was still charitable, humane. She had, moreover, been his sage confidante, advisor, confessor, in these past thrilling, blessed, but precipitous five months — when Cécile had entered his life.

He returned upstairs to his rooms and ate some sardines and crackers — pending a later modest meal to be had at a local restaurant down the Rue la Chatte. His real urge, though, was to sit down at his writing table, retrieve its pencils and notebooks, and, as usual, attempt to communicate with Saturn — her apparition — to whom today he had much to tell. Yet, not uncommonly with her, he somehow felt the exact time unripe, unpropitious, that he had best wait, indeed until his skin fairly prickled with, as it were, a kind of nervous green light's rays, for it had been his long experience not to take liberties with and thus rile Saturn Marie. Instead he took off his tweed jacket, sat down at the table, and tried to think about his current research commitments, hoping that while waiting he could somehow marshal his thoughts for resuming work on the historical problem of the Boer War and its aftereffects on the fortunes of certain African tribes in the Transvaal. He remembered only yesterday — she was driving him in her new Citroën — asking Cécile if she had ever been on the African continent. Turning to him, she seemed surprised at the question and said she had not. After an awkward pause she asked him if he had. He still recalled his embarrassment in having to say he had not, either. She inquired of him then why he had asked and, after some confusion, he confessed he was not sure but that in his research these days he was reading widely on Africa. Again she turned to him, with her sweet, truly innocent, smile. "Why?" she said. He hadn't the heart to reply, realizing how vastly she was out of touch with the efforts he constantly insisted to himself were crucial to his African mission in Paris. At once, caution to the winds, he reached for pencil and paper. It was the irony – of Cécile's innocent void about why he had come here and what he wanted to accomplish – that troubled him. Saturn's likely displeasure, even vitriol, about things in general, must therefore be brooked; the case, his plight, put to her – to test her willingness, even compassion, to vouchsafe needed advice. To this end, however – it was an intuition – he must first speak to her about the Watchman, and his heretofore unsuspected role in this maze of difficulties; for there could well be more than a possible, even dangerous, connection, he speculated, maybe not all that remote, either, entangling the presence in the picture of Cécile, i.e., the restless question of his father's volatile, unpredictable reaction were he ever to find out about her. But at this the pencil balked. He forced it: "The Watchman, Mother, seems in a pretty good mood these days," he, hopefully, began writing, "Yet we can't, knowing Father, depend on that. I did, though, receive a nice note from him Monday. He asked a few questions about how my various undertakings were proceeding, without getting too specific; then said he missed me, and you too, and wished me well; then enclosed his usual fairly generous check. It's not just the check, though, Mother – actually, I find his letters extremely interesting, especially coming from a businessman whose mind has more or less had to be on more mundane matters than he talks to me about in some of his letters. He's a good father, a good guy – and to think, Saturn, I used to dislike him. It's probably true, though, he's about given up on trying to bring me in as his successor in the cosmetics and hair-care business. He founded the company and, of course, would like to see it continue, yet, pragmatically, he knows I'm not the one to do it. He won't shed any tears, though – he's the resilient type. What a guy, yes. You must have been thrilled to marry him, even if you two were ages apart, and at the time of his first wife's death she was older than your mother. But now you were the new Mrs. Zacharias H. Kessey. (You later learned, you said, that the 'H' was for Hamilcar, the father of the Carthaginian — African — hero-warrior Hannibal, Hamilcar having been bestowed on Father by his own father, Jake, born a Georgia slave.)

"Ah, but now, Mother, you had entered Father's life. You thought you had really taken over, didn't you? And he let you think it, and go on thinking it. Besides, he really liked you; maybe, and probably did, love you; and I'm sure he liked the way you dressed — formerly, you, on a gym instructor's, then secretary's, tight budget. He didn't know of course, ha, that from now on your clothes were going to cost him a pretty penny. I don't think he minded, though. You were already very attractive, some would say chic — with your somewhat light skin and nice figure; you were vainest of all, though, about your breasts, which I thought, though, were modest, yet enhancing enough, I guess. But, oh, what an irony it was to turn out to be that in the hospital during the final throes of your illness, your ordeal — *breast* cancer metastasized — the agony, anguish, and all, your knowing you were going to die, that you deliberately chose to scream at me for, you said, my savage abuse of your breasts when still a feeding baby, all the while fighting (me fighting) every prospect of ever being weaned. The attending physicians, however, out of your hearing, literally scoffed at your charges as having no possible connection with their hopeless prognosis. I was crushed, of course, and cried, yes, like a baby. You were wildly hallucinating by then. Strangely, the doctors and nurses seemed embarrassed — though they were also soon administering even more medication for the pain. According to your wretched delusions, however, you had had not just the one child, me, but, even before I was born, three others — all girls! I was stunned. My heart sank at this pitiful untruth.

Cyrus Colter

Moreover, you adamantly claimed, the girls, unlike me, your disreputable last-born, were all, without exception, admirable, refined; also devoted and loving to you. One of them, the middle girl, Leila, you said, was part Scandinavian. Father, sitting there in the room with me, stiffened, froze, but soon then sadly shook his head in pity for you—in pity for us all. But this, the Scandinavian 'disclosure,' seemed, in your tormented apotheosis, to please you to no end. Helplessly, you tried to smile. You then, though—suddenly, as if you had almost forgotten—raised the question of the girls' present whereabouts, why they had not by now come to see you. What a dreadful experience it was for Zack and me—to have to sit there and undergo all this torture. At last, sadly, he got up and left the room—to go sit for awhile out in the corridor. It was of course not long, then, before you had again taken up your old saw, your diabolical theme—though always, as now, out of Zack's presence—your vile charge, yes, that I, as a mere suckling baby, had misused, defiled, as it were, your breasts. And although you did not then follow up by saying the words, your accusation was nonetheless clear, that, yes, the breast cancer had developed from my lust and savagery—that I had killed you, my mother. Ah, Saturn Marie, what a frightful charge for you to have made against me, your confused, helpless, desolate 'last-born.' I wept and tried to take you in my arms. I loved you—in almost an oedipal way. It shattered me—that's why I'm too prone to blame you for my present crippled existence, the malaise of my dreadful longings *to know! to know! to know!* the answers to what makes this fetid world go around, and the proper place, if one exists at all, of a black man or woman in it. When I was growing up, as I've said, you didn't even try to inform me about these absolutely critical matters and, although I love your very memory, I hold this terrible failure against you even today. It's not that you intended to do these things to me, you just had other, over-weening (no pun) concerns – clothes, parties, golf – that finally, sadly, made you a callous, or maybe careless, person. You never recovered, nor shall I – although, despite these foul things I've said about you, I've spent my days and nights trying to find a woman, *the* woman, to take your place. Maybe, who knows, I've done it at last – in Cécile. Ah-ha, you don't know her, do you? I haven't yet introduced you two. Ah, but I shall – in good time – to expiate for poor Jeannette, yes, for Jeannette Hall. Remember her, Mother? Or can you ever forget her?

"Yet, all of our times weren't bad – there were pleasant ones, when you demonstrated a true mother's love. But even then you were often guarded, though smiling. You were best when we practiced athletics, which you loved – baseball, football, golf, the latter in which you met Father and demonstrated you were a better duffer than he. Remember also those beautiful autumn Saturday afternoons when you and I would watch a football game on television, then go out in our big, beautiful yard and toss spiraling passes at each other, or even *punt* (you too) back and forth. Then – with a dinner party coming up somewhere – you would go in, shower, check your wardrobe to see what you were wearing that night, then come over to the chaise longue (we'd be in your and Father's bedroom) where I'd be sitting scanning the sports pages (and watching you out of the corner of my eye) and you'd sit down beside me and try to look over my shoulder at the paper. I was barely ten then, but your saccharine shower soaps, and now the hard-wafting perfumes of your slip and robe, gave me tremors I had not known before. I also remember that your pretty eyelashes were mascaraed. Yet, heavily sighing, I kept my eyes on the page – until, that is, you rose to leave the room. You, even the whole big bedroom, smelled like loud lilacs. (Ah, or – sad to say – a funeral parlor). But by now I'd forgotten all about the fact that you'd been doing all this primping for your husband, my father, not for me. As you stood before me then, I began pawing at you like the big baby I was not, reaching for your oyster-white slip, maybe worn over a dainty panty girdle, before coaxing you into rolling one of your stockings back down below your knee, whereupon I tickled the knee, maybe your tummy, too, or even, though just once, a little inside your leg, your thigh. But, good God! What did I do that for? . . . I'll tell you this, though, I'd never do it again. You slapped me so hard my face collapsed, my tongue clove to the roof of my mouth, and my ears rang like bells. I didn't cry, though – for I'd gotten even with you for the way, all that year, you'd been treating me: the neglect. I wanted to cry, though – my face, my head, hurt so. But, rather, I laughed. You were absolutely stunned, shocked, maybe terrified, too, at this. Your pretty mouth was open, and you couldn't get it closed. I never forgot that day – especially when I got older – and I'll bet you never did either. Have you therefore abandoned me, Mother? . . . Say, are you there? I feel I have lost contact. Do you and I still somehow exist on the same planet? It can't be, Saturn. Yet, occasionally, I think I still receive your very short messages, but they're so weak and garbled I get little from them. Sometimes I even think it's deliberate on your part – especially when I've insisted you make up for past deficiencies and advise me – if you know, and that's a big 'if' – how a black man, if he's got any sense, adjusts to a life among people most of whom have no respect for him, laugh at him, or, at best, patronize him. The rest would like to kill him, period. One night here in Paris, after I'd drunk two-thirds of a bottle of Kaiserslautern brandy, I came home and tried to make contact with you. It took about two and a half hours. Anyhow, I asked you the same old question, and expected the same old answer: 'Be more patient, Paul, and a *lot* more industrious. Cultivate the habit of making white friends, for they can help you; look what they've done; they rule the world, don't they? Black people are good people, and they will eventually achieve their reward for perseverance.' That's what I'd learned from you in the past, Saturn, and that's what I expected after trying all the time to make contact with you. But, lo and behold, you sobered me up, quickly. You said the greatest masses of blacks living — for whatever cause, even the past slavery — in the midst of Western culture ought to get out of there and return to Africa. That most of them could live for a millennium in the West and still be treated as third-class citizens because they *are* third-class citizens! That's the night I did something I had never done before and will never do again: I called you a 'No-good, black-hating, bitch!' Then I took you back into history — our history, yours and mine, Saturn's and Paul's — and used the unholy case of Jeannette Hall to prove to you that you were *in fact* a bigoted bitch. So let me refresh your recollection, recall a few things to your mind:

"We were a smug little Chicago family of three, and I was a student at Garrick High. I was a good student, not the best, but good, and you seemed pleased enough about it; not euphoric, not riotous, ha, yet at the dinner table, going by, you'd kiss me on top of my head and say something nice, which Father always joined in — to tell you the truth, I got an even bigger bang out of his supportive attitude than yours, but this was plain bias on my part and indefensible. What I didn't tell either of you, though, was that there was a girl in my room at Garrick whom I had big eyes for. She was terrific, but also made terrific grades, consistently. She was naturally confident, but was also really sweet. I not only admired her but felt sort of weak in the knees, or was moony, in her presence and could never figure out sensible things to say around her to keep me from making a fool of myself. So a lot of the time I'd just sit

back and watch her. She was tall, good-looking, and black — I
mean *black* — and had kind of strange sapphire eyes, which
often gave her a soft amatory gaze until one said the wrong
thing, which naturally, always off balance around her, I did a
lot. Yet I think she liked me — one reason was I was tall like she
was — or at least didn't dislike me; some of the girls thought
they liked me because they'd heard my dad, though no longer a
young man, was well-off. Jeannette never talked about personal things — although, because she was a star student, there
was occasional gossip about her family. They were poor, with
three children in the family, the mother an invalid in a wheel-
chair swilling Miller High Life beer all day, the youngest of
the two boys, Moss, a student at Platt Elementary School. But
he was so smart the kids had dubbed him 'genius,' yet his eyes
were so bad Jeannette, in addition to her own schoolwork, did
a lot of reading to him. She, though, never mentioned her
family except one solitary member of it, her father, Julius,
who was said to support the family by driving a municipal bus
in the day and a taxicab at night. True or false, Jeannette
practically worshipped him and would talk of no one else —
which in itself, I think, would support the veracity of the
rumors about this man's dedication to his family. I know
Jeannette was dedicated to him. Consequently it was somewhere along in here that I fell in love with her — head over
heels. But you know all this, Saturn, for later on — when the
violent crunch came between you and me — I told you, told you
everything, and was ready to commit murder over what happened. You cried, and so did I, but Jeannette knew nothing,
and never would, and I've always been glad.

"It all makes me want to recede, return to those far-off
better times for our little tripartite family, when we seemed
readying ourselves for good, even great, times. Father had
recently — as the uncanny judge of human nature that he was

and still is, and realizing even this early on in the game that he must, alas, count me out as his successor in the company he had founded (and labored in for now some 32½ years in order to make it all that it had become) — he had suddenly decided, with your eager approval, Mother, if not urging, to sell the business, lock, stock, and barrel, rid himself of all chronic management rigors, and have some fun with his family for a change while there was yet time. He therefore set about convening his expensive lawyers — himself, though, devising the intricate sale contract for his beloved, Memphis-founded, Kessey Hair-Prep & Cosmetics, Inc. — and now made himself a killing. During the legal procedures, remembering his lifetime struggle with hostile superior capital-financier cunning — plus race, always race — he was dewy-eyed throughout the process. Besides, in the early, dark days, he had also managed to stay out of jail despite, for success, the many legal (illegal) corners he'd had to cut. At home at dinner that night, then, our happy triumvirate drank champagne — except Zack, who drank his 94-proof gin — and sang songs, like 'Minnie the Moocher,' which Father still loves and sometimes sings when he gets high. It was the same evening, though, on the identical dinner occasion — may God forgive me — that I, inconstant, fickle Paul, your son, Saturn Marie, had been able to sit there and put completely out of my mind (no small feat) the dark, earnest visage of Jeannette Hall — no doubt at that moment, across town, reading *Ivanhoe* to her half-blind little brother Moss. Still, alas, I like to keep telling, and trying to convince, myself, though it's not easy, that my seeming temporary disinterest was the result of the many other distractions that night, the genuine jollity, the crazy talk, hilarity, all of which threw, and kept, my mind off track the whole evening long. And you, Mother, until I later said something you didn't like, were one of the ringleaders — I mean your gleeful chatter and laughter from the champagne, also Father's monkey business from his gin, olives, and clowning; then, to cap things off, even I had to get into the act, with my own callow, corny levity, congratulating you on what I claimed was your caginess, your shrewd know-how, in 'collaring,' landing, then marrying, this big-shot entrepreneur, Mr. Zacharias Hamilcar Kessey, a 'rich' widower, in fact, a real, honest-to-God, 'ty-*coon*!' You certainly recall what happened then, Mother — Zack, in his alcohol and merrymaking, almost had a stroke, throwing back his hoary head in great bellows of laughter, in the nick of time barely able to save his partial upper denture from flying out. You, though, Saturn, found in my congratulations far less hilarity than had Zack, or I, clearly for that matter, indicating by your frozen silence, also the blank mask now of your pretty face, that things were getting out of hand. But Father was still laughing. So it was these crazy goings-on, the loud tomfoolery, the celebration of the company's sale signifying in turn the great times now soon to come, all this, I still insist on telling myself, took my mind away from where, in seriousness and fidelity, it should have been — on wondrous Jeannette, her ideas, good deeds, her sincerity. There's only one word for it, I suppose — I was really, as yet, 'undedicated.' Yet have I ever been capable of dedication? — to anything or anybody? I think so, at one time — to you, Mother. But, to be sure, I'm susceptible to fickleness much of the time. I'm unschooled about some things. And who was largely responsible for that? But then, why didn't Father step in and take over, instruct me, or do something? How was I to know about such matters? Yet, maybe Father couldn't have done a good job of it. I have a hunch men aren't very good at such things, aren't as wise as women; less sensitive. Frankly, I can't see how a man could ever help me, 'school' me, etc. He's not cut out for such things vis-à-vis another man, or male. Ah, but it wasn't too long before I began to become aware of my own case, my individual situation — little by little. It was only later, though, alas, but not many years later, when Jeannette's short (indeed, as your own, her all-too-tragically short) time on the planet had elapsed, that I began to get a clearer view of things — far too often the way, the fatal error, of human beings, right? But if there ever was a woman — am I detracting from your role, your own contributions, Mother? . . . if so, forgive me, I'm sorry — yet if ever a woman, and she was so young (it wrenches the heart!), could possibly have straightened me out, squared me with myself, and the world, it was Jeannette. She showed such promise. Yet I have not given up. I still search for the Grail. I still hope to be shown the way, the true way, to understanding. But I can still see you just as if you were sitting across this table from me now, hear you challenging me, with a fiery impatience: *'Understanding of what?'* You are duly fed up with my situation — because I can't describe it to your satisfaction; you think me a crybaby, a chronic whiner, always trying to shift blame. I plead guilty to a certain extent. It's the complexities. I find the existence we live not only harsh but unfathomable. Why, then, are we put here? — I ask myself a million times. What the hell, Mother — and once we're here, what are we supposed to do? Whatever we want? Is that it? But they execute people for that. When Jeannette, way later, became a judge, though, she refused, absolutely, to impose the death penalty. More anon. But I constantly think of her life and death. Her case is powerful. Yet I can't tell you why. I only know that when I think of it, it makes me *feel*. Feeling, though, can also get you into trouble — you stop using your mind, and that's frightening, because the first thing you know is, although you're completely ignorant of why you were put here, also of what you're supposed to be doing while you're here, if your mind starts failing you you'll soon find you don't want to leave here. Then you're really in for a bad time — at least this can be argued. On top of this, then, you discover you're black — and no one has ever explained to you how this came about and why the penalties are so high, often so brutal, everywhere. Even in Africa! Mother, why didn't you, or Father, or at least some of those Princeton savants I had, explain this shit to me? It's bad, very bad — and then, as I say, it works on your mind till where you don't want to leave this crazy, weird scene. You want to stay till you've solved it. This last is the hardest of all to understand. Yet feeble-brained me, your wayward son, daily, nightly, searches for the Grail. Oh tell me, Saturn dear, do you happen to have a net with you? Drop it over my head, will you?

"To return: It seemed our triadic family now convened almost every hour on the hour, its sessions entirely devoted to travel, wide travel. You especially, Mother, were in your element — as planner, geographer, and worrier. Your first move, however, was to suggest to us that we go downtown and sign up for a crash course in French at the Berlitz school, reminding us that the language was spoken in most of the civilized world (which, it turned out, you didn't mean to go beyond). Father thought Berlitz a capital idea, and urged me to accompany you, but for himself begged off, saying that, especially at this very active juncture, he had neither the inclination nor the time. The upshot was that you and I went down and matriculated at Berlitz. It turned out to be great fun, studying, among all their other teaching paraphernalia, those little French glossaries. *'Voila mon passport.'* Little did I realize I'd later, in these present strange eventful days, and in Paris of all places, be making such serious, if imperfect, use of this your, and my, silly happenstance of foreign-language-learning. Now my peerless landlady Madame and my other French friends here, at this far distant date and time, understand me in almost any situation with minimum effort and without my having, too frequently at least, to repeat my words. It all began, then, with your taking me to Berlitz, where I'd sometimes, sitting there beside you in class, reach across and, gingerly yet stealthily, gently grasp your hand and just hold it, yes gently, so gently, until you'd get uncomfortable, or uneasy, with my brass and overbearance, or my puppy love, and pull your hand away. Now I can almost cry when I think of what you did to me later — about Jeannette. More anon. Yet, Mother, I somehow still love you and always shall.

"So we started traveling, widely, yes, spending Father's money — flying to western Europe first, but also, later, to the Caribbean, to South America, Egypt, Greece, and, oh, how you loved it all; you were in heaven and would send back, easily, a hundred beautiful postcards depicting your travels (while I was sending all of my cards to Jeannette). Somehow, though, Mother, you never mentioned to Father that we should possibly extend our itinerary, our grand pilgrimage, even if briefly, to, say, a few of the countries in sub–Saharan Africa, see the land from which, though in sorrow, utter disaster, often death, our black ancestors had come. I'm sure Father would have gone had you only mentioned it, hinted at it actually. But black Africa somehow never got on our list. Father, in fact, I recall, did bring up Ghana and Nigeria a time or two, but you eventually managed to nix them. So, maybe after another week at Cannes, or Monaco, say, and more — a rash — of the beautiful and expensive postcards were sent back to your bridge buddies in Chicago, we would leave and come home. But then — unbelievably — you suddenly stopped playing bridge. You told the puzzled, incredulous ladies that, since your wide travels, you were now going to read more — 'improve my mind,' as you put it — and, forthwith, began reading all the Michener books you could find in the bookstores — ha, heavy stuff, you thought. But even though I was just a growing-up kid in high school, I was already reading Camus, James Baldwin, Amiri Baraka, and even, in short doses, a little Thomas Mann now and then.

"But, Mother, no matter, you were riding high in those days. Your envious lady friends, I know, talked about you behind your back but coveted your dinner-party invitations. And your clothes—good God, they were out of this world. Father loved it, though. Even I enjoyed going places with you, just the two of us, although you wouldn't let me have a drink, not even a small glass of wine, if we, for instance, were having lunch downtown. You would say Father drank too much for his health and age and that I could inherit the same difficulty if I weren't careful. I thought about this during my dreadful early days in Paris, before the advent of Cécile, when I, often out of grief and loneliness for you—although you had long since left us—would frequent the bistros and terraces along St. Germain, the Rue Jacob, and Boul Mich. I could never forget, no matter how hard I tried, how you looked in your designer clothes, the ultra-expensive grooming you were getting in those days, and how it affected you—not always for the better, I hate to add. You were really good to look at, yet maybe not quite so good as you sometimes speculated. However, your manner of dress, though spectacular, was never gauche; there was always restraint, taste. True, you were light-skinned—good Lord, you would have had spasms had you been darker—light-skinned in the way of saffron, say, or peach, or even ocher, or whatever. Also, as I say, too, your figure was nice, very nice: trim, svelte, really eye-catching; especially now, in your new *haute* clothes. Yet, never forget, no one could have mistaken you for someone you were not. Ha, I mean Caucasian. In other words, you couldn't have 'passed'—you weren't *that* light. And your nose—it was sassylike and pretty, all right, yet still slightly pudgy. Not flat, but pudgy. Yet, by no stretch of the imagination, Saturn dear, could it have rightly been called a Roman nose, or a Thomas Jefferson nose, or a Marie Antoinette. Or even poor Mozart, dead at 35 and with certainly a less-than-perfect nose—it had the very slightest bulge, or undulation, midway its narrow bridge—could still never rightly have been said to have a pudgy nose. I guess, Mother, what you wanted was a nose which was proof to all and sundry that you were not part this and part that, that there were no bastards in your Mississippi bloodline, which of course is impossible and I, for one—just look at me—am living proof of the contrary. Unless you, and I, your son by Father, himself a dusky amalgam, are black as was Jeannette Hall (God rest her soul) we're *all* bastards, spawned by old Massa, or even his white trash overseer, either of them, feeling the orgasmic heat of his sour-mash bourbon, coming in the middle of the night down to the rough cabin quarters of our un-pedigreed lineage (man and wife by jumping through the hoop) where 'the man of the house' is told, in the presence of his 'wife' lying in the bed beside him—not necessarily ordered yet, no raising of the voice, no bluster, merely the suggestion that the 'man' get up and go down to the cistern, or the stable, or the pea patch, or, finally, with a little annoyance maybe coming into the voice, 'to *any* damn place, for about thirty minutes, then come on back and go to sleep.' So, Mother—are you listening?—I take it you like your nice light face, your fried hair, the pudgy 'pretty' nose. It's your bloodline, and mine, for what it's worth. It is Jeannette Hall who carries our *noble* blood! Ah, I see you bristle. 'What about your Cécile?' you ask me. 'What does *she* look like?' More anon, Saturn honey, is my present reply to that.

   "My memory is so vivid, Mother—too vivid. Garrick High—the only place outside her home where she, Jeannette, felt psychologically secure. This is important to remember. This is where she knew she was somebody. Even the teachers told her so. This was also the case when she got to pre-law school at the University of Wisconsin on a scholarship—but things were over between us by then, a circumstance, or calamity, you, Mother, are all too familiar with but that poor Jeannette would never know about. What I remember most, and most fondly, though, is Garrick High—and Jeannette in her beautiful (to me) but cheap (I was later told by you—how did you know?) dresses. In the Garrick days I would sometimes walk her home—an experience, however, doubtless because of her family adversity, she seemed never to relish—then catch a bus back in the direction of where I lived. I loved these walks, though. I could talk to her freely and she listened. Once she told me I should try to be a senator. She was always looking for ways to fit people into a career niche she thought right, and productive, for them. As for herself, she was sure the legal profession was right. What, silently, worried her was where the money would come from for an education in the law. One day during a walk she confessed to me to working so hard for good grades in order to enhance her chances for getting scholarship assistance after her Garrick graduation. She was sold on the law. She asked me one day, however, if I knew about a chief justice of the U.S. Supreme Court named Taney, Roger Brooke Taney, and she correctly pronounced the surname, something near 'Tawney.' I told her I'd read something about him in a history course, that he was a pro-slavery judge before the Civil War. 'I'd like to study him more,' she said. 'He was a real bastard, wasn't he?' I hadn't heard her use that language before and was both curious and entertained. 'A lot of people believed like that in those days,' I said. 'Judges ought to stand up for what is right,' she replied hotly. 'He claimed blacks had no rights whatever that other people had to respect.

City of Light

That's awful, and a chief justice of the United States said it. A man like that shouldn't be a judge. In fact, he should be tried himself.' She was angry, outraged. It was impressive, also moving, to watch her. Still in her late teens, she was already so righteous she was self-righteous. At such times she was admirable as well, I thought, and amusing — also sweet. I loved to try to make her laugh, though it didn't always work, yet this was when, trying not to be, she was sweetest of all. Good God, Mother, how attractive character can be.

"I thought about Jeannette all the time now. I was really a goner — enchained by love. But I also wanted to try to remain somewhere near her in my grade average — no small ambition — for I knew if I didn't continue to do well academically I would lose whatever respect she had for me, and I would be through. She was, of course, though, well aware of my ardor for her, yet seemed less than completely sold on it. I guess I failed to fit in with her other priorities, her hifalutin, outsized plans and ambitions, also — occasionally now — her shaky self-confidence. When I'd tell her how much I admired her, I'd try, feigning objectivity, never to use the word 'love.' But she saw through me — that I was crazy about her. She seemed at first embarrassed, then slightly irritated, at last distraught, vulnerable, as if she felt that only in a different, a better, world would my talk of the way I felt about her be in any way meaningful, but that under present conditions we couldn't afford that luxury of becoming closer than we were. This wasn't said, only left to be sensed. It was maybe my ego, Mother, but I think what she felt was anguish. Nor would she look at me as she talked. But, oh Lord — damn my soul — this actually made me happy! . . . I'm sorry, but it did. I was walking on clouds — my love had quadrupled. It seemed it did. It failed to occur to me that in fact 'change,' alas, was just around the corner. For weeks now Father's hired tutors had been hard at work on me, their mission, given them by the Watchman himself, being to make sure—no excuses—that I get into Princeton in the fall. Actually, of course, though later—after a semicomic intervening catastrophe (more anon)—I got in on my own good high school grades. All the while, though, hapless Jeannette was frantic to get her pre-law scholarship to Wisconsin approved. It was critical for her. Her family, which is same as saying her father, had no possible way of helping her. Things looked grim. Yet, in the final analysis, it was her terrific grades, plus her wide reputation for diligence, hard work, which weeks later would make the difference for her.

But I repeat—frankly with some pleasure and pride in the thought—that I ought not too much traduce my own grades. They were in fact highly respectable, not as good as Jeannette's, but good, very good. The Watchman was elated. So even were you, Saturn, though, as usual, less demonstrative. Alas, however, it was Jeannette's and my farewell to Garrick High. During this period, though, she must have been plenty worried, for it was too early for any rulings on her scholarship application to have been made. On top of all this—poor Jeannette—I now asked her if she would go with me to the Garrick High senior prom. What I really wanted of course was, on the way, to bring her by the house for you, Mother, and Zack to meet her. I was praying she would not refuse on either count—accompanying me to the prom after visiting you two. Knowing Jeannette, though, I was anything but sure. Still, somehow I could not bring myself to believe she would turn me down. I was later right—she did say yes, and even seemed glad about it at first—until, in a few days, I began to sense she was having second thoughts. Even maybe portents. Nevertheless, thought following wish, I felt that maybe my months of inept pursuit of her, the clumsy wooing, even an occasional faked aplomb to impress her and all, would finally have their hoped-for effect—for hadn't she at first seemed truly, genuinely, even if with her usual 'cool,' pleased to be asked? Soon, by this 'reasoning,' I had forced myself to become almost euphoric again. When, then, the great night had at last come around, and I had picked her up, Mother, in your pretty little Pontiac convertible, I told her the corny lie that, like the moron I implied I was, I had come to her house and left my wallet, with my money and driver's license in it, on the dresser in my room; that I'd have to return home and get it. This, though, you see, was a two-purpose ruse: I not only wanted to have her meet you and Zack, and, it was trusted, be much impressed, but, even more crucially, to have you two not only meet her, but *see* her. This I considered my trump card. I was sure you'd both be bowled over, for I thought Jeannette was absolutely beautiful. Which, God knows, she was. I was all agog, of course, to be presenting this lovely, brilliant girl, my prom date, my close friend, someone, moreover, I hoped might eventually be playing an even more important role in my life. So, yes, I was agog, Saturn—no question. I was also terrifically nervous, though, when I told this big lie to Jeannette about having to go home again and get my wallet. At once she fell silent. I could tell that this detour business back home had not been good news to her. Quite the contrary. Of course, her thinking was fairly obvious—she much preferred not meeting my parents. The very thought gave her feelings of insecurity, I was almost sure. I ushered her to the car, then, though afraid she might seek to thwart my nefarious plan by merely, politely, declining to come in the house. The upshot was that we both were very uneasy, tense, as I drove. I started talking about anything I thought was unimportant, an effort in which she readily joined. Soon we were both talking at the same time and at allegro rates of speed though often on quite disparate subjects— until she would finally smile and assure me that by right I 'had the floor,' etc., etc. Before we knew it then, we were laughing crazily, childishly, trying to fend off our fears and stress. Also, again before we knew it, we were suddenly pulling up into the Watchman's spacious driveway. At once I said, almost pleading, 'Come, go in with me, won't you? My folks have heard me talk about you so much, and they'd wonder about my manners in leaving you sitting out here in the car like this.' She made no reply, only brought her knees around at once and started climbing out, bringing me a stupendous sigh of relief. The weather was mild, and trailing her up to the front door I had the opportunity to get a better look at what she was wearing. Poor family or not, she was turned out beautifully—in a long scarlet(!) dress and pretty mauve shoes with lower heels. I'm sure, Saturn, you never forgot the color of that dress. I still never fail to wonder what her father had to pledge, or beg, or borrow, to get it for her. No wonder she idolized him. When we entered the parlor only Father was there, but I've never seen him more gracious. Smiling broadly, he rose and came straight to meet not us but *her*, lovely Jeannette. From that night he made himself my hero—he, too, I thought was beautiful, in his marvelous and, as I say, gracious behavior. I loved him for it, and do till this day. So far then that evening I was on cloud nine. Jeannette was more stunning than I had ever seen her, and her quiet entrance into the parlor with me can only, because of her dignity and general demeanor, be called queenly. Watchman now was grinning like a fox eating yellow jackets. I think it was because of me, his son. He was proud of me.

Finally, then, you entered, Mother—tentatively smiling. My heart was racing, for this was the test. In greeting Jeannette you held that dry, set smile as long as you could—though it seemed torture to you. I still had hopes, though. This girl meant a lot to me. Hell, Saturn, I was in love! And for the first time. Can you possibly have any inkling of how that feels? The first time, Mother! Goddamn it! . . . I don't want to start crying here! You held on until you had, with your piercing gaze, examined her entire pristine beauty. You could avoid it no longer. Somehow, then, you couldn't remove your eyes from her afterwards. Your mind was apparently telling you that you had not expected this—that conceivably, you had a real problem here. Finally, though, you looked at me—your gaze cool, controlled, yet also withering. You must then have gotten all your questions answered—and they were bad news. Love was flying on my face like a red flag. You finally then had to go over and sit down on your peach sofa with Zack, choking back your distraught sighs.

"The strangest thing then happened—trivial, comic, yet scary. I had forgotten the lie I had told. I realized suddenly that I must go upstairs, to my bedroom, as if to retrieve my wallet from the dresser top where I had said I left it. But I couldn't go now, I thought just at this crucial juncture, I must stay and protect Jeannette. I felt so sorry for her now. I was nonetheless watching you. Here you practically sat in judgment on my life—on the rest of my life. You knew this. Because you knew me. You knew, at that early time, that I hadn't the stamina, the guts, to challenge you. You knew I would fold. In fact, my knees were already knocking. It was the look on your face. It mattered little that you were willing to, and did, go through the ritual, the niceties, of polite conversation with both Jeannette and me for the few minutes we could endure the ordeal. Yet the clearer you saw that you had succeeded, the more you reverted to your reptilian poise. 'Have fun,' you said to us as you stood. 'It was very nice meeting you,' you told Jeannette. 'I repeat, have fun, after such a busy school year.' Zack, still smiling, was also standing now, making his manners. What, in my sweating anxiety, I had most noticed now, though, was that your glances at Jeannette's loveliness had become increasingly furtive, as if you might in the last two or three minutes or so be less certain of your 'victory.' Was it Jeannette's unfailing composure, self-possession? — for now you could hardly bear looking at her at all. She was, yes, that lovely — a bona fide goddess. Something you, Saturn, had always wanted to be — but of course a white one. Yet you saw that, instead, her color was a beautiful black, and you didn't know how to deal with that, did you? Ah, the larva had turned, had it not? Now, trying again, you couldn't miss an opportunity to stare at her. You also, I'm sure, now felt the depth of *my* feeling — but also that of your own. So it was then that we bowed out, left, and went to the car. I was in bad shape — a nervous wreck, and already with a bad headache. When I opened the car door to let Jeannette in I somehow, though, felt, psychologically, much better — freer, less afraid. Before I pulled off, she informed me that, for the second time, I had forgotten my wallet. But I somehow felt so secure — a grave mistake — that I readily confessed my lie, my transgression, to her and asked her forgiveness. The look she gave me is not easy to describe. It was something near horror. Now I felt much worse. I had never considered before this experience that speaking untruthfully was on a par with high crimes and misdemeanors. Here, Mother, we had a girl my own age, and from an almost indigent family, reacting to my white lie in this frightened fashion. I had thus learned something I had only cursorily been warned against in Sunday school, never at home. So it goes — so it was — so it is.

"Over the weeks, then, that summer, when apparently you thought you'd watched Jeannette and me enough, or for as many of our dates as you were going to watch, you told me one bright, balmy morning — you had summoned me into your boudoir where, in mules and a sheer turquoise robe over your sheer underthings, you were plucking your eyebrows with tweezers—you told me, and, yes, speaking rather peremptorily to boot, I thought, that it was time for me to break off the relationship 'with that girl,' was the way you put it. You then added, gratuitously, your drawn face (early, incipient, though you were unaware of it, your final illness was already upon you) your face, yes, stony-cold, also arrogant, you added that the 'relationship' had no future. I stood there. Then I think I kind of reeled. I remember wanting to grab the foot of your bed to steady myself. Partially coming out of it then, I asked myself: the relationship had no future for whom? I didn't have to ask you that, though—in fact, I had hardly asked myself. It was quite clear. You meant that it had no future for *me*. That was it. You cared not a fig for poor, quiet, self-effacing Jeannette's future. She, then, was the one scheduled to pay the price. Fate—in the guise of you, Saturn Marie—had decreed it. It was the ukase promulgated by your raw bitchery and my own scandalous, yellow cowardice. Your hold on me, though, was strange—was it not, Mother?—uncanny. Has that ever occurred to you? It was also evil, of course. Ah, maybe also sick. But how did it all come about, Saturn? Only since I've been writing these 'letters' to you—you, now a ghost in the memory—have I been able to muster not only the acumen but the courage to look at *our* (Jeannette's not in this one) relationship. It was a time when I was a mere rabbit. That was the measure of courage I'd been vouchsafed in my dealings with you, and that is the sad explanation of my behavior vis-à-vis the Jeannette debacle. When you made that awful statement to me, that there was no future in my relationship with Jeannette, it not only informed me of your ruling in the matter but—I do believe—sealed my fate. I hope and pray that's overly pessimistic, but we do know it sealed Jeannette's. And when I was fatuous enough to ask you to explain—which was a grave error—you did not flinch. You said she was too dark for me, that in fact, you said, she was almost coal black. Even though at the time I was just a kid out of high school, I should have felt the same 'horror' that Kurtz felt in *Heart of Darkness*. But I didn't. I do now, though, Mother. Now at times I want to jump in the Seine because somehow I can't get my life together. I've tried everything. No luck. I know it's cruel of me to charge you with much of what's happened to me – cruel and inaccurate – but that's probably why I continue to assail you with these hailstorms of letters, keeping you up-to-date on my daily goings and comings, my futile trying of this, then that; my fleeing from responsibility, my general torment. There's also the problem here with a woman – I may have hinted at it – that's real. I often look to her in your absence – and that's not good, for it remains to be seen if she can help me anymore than you've been able to. It's all because I haven't yet been able to free my mind of Jeannette and the way I failed her. As you well know the matter ended in a great disruption after you laid down the law to me about Jeannette as you did and after I fell in step, lockstep, thereby removing myself from Jeannette's life entirely. But I wasn't to get away with it that easily. Within the month I was so distraught, so filled with guilt and rage about my role in it all, and grief, then finally a wild vengeance, that I had forgotten all about having – despite Zack's expensive sta-ble of tutors – been duly admitted to Princeton on my own and where I was supposed to be by mid-September. So what did I do? You know that answer by heart. I completely lost control of myself. In my vow to get even with you, to make you suffer as you'd caused others to suffer, I embarked on the thoroughly maddened act of bursting into – God help me – a brand new courtship! I took out after little black Agie Thomas, my age, and crippled (her left leg was four inches shorter than her right), and after a fortnight of secret talks with her stunned, ne'er-do-well, but now almost-gleeful parents – who couldn't believe what they were hearing from me, or what a fantastic proposal, actually a 'deal,' that was about to fall into their laps – I, full of malice and reprisal, thumbed my nose at Princeton and was married to Agie early one Monday morning downtown in City Hall, by an unsteady resident black jackleg preacher whose breath, as he lectured us on the beauties of conjugal love, was an admixture of liquor, coffee, and cloves. Two hours later, then, out at O'Hare Airport, with wide-eyed, little ebony Agie in tow, I caught a vacation jumbo jet for Acapulco, where I spent the most hellish six days and nights of would-be-but-helpless sex it will ever be, I hope, my misfortune to experience. I was the culprit, though – not Agie. On my very first sally – up in our wildly decorated hotel room – my penis died, became silent, absolutely inert; and not only that – it stayed so for the remainder of our nuptial 'celebrations.' Her sad, unfortunate, crippled anatomy had undone me, undone someone already monumentally vulnerable, in the mind at least, even if, until now, spared in the genitalia.

One thing I learned, however, and on good authority – Agie's – was that she was by no means virginal, which moreover quietly filled her with anger at me for my duddery (my word, Mother, meaning I launched a dud), and on what she characterized as her first, and likely to be her only, honeymoon. Nor did the couple she described as her 'mercenary parents' escape her ire. They had even had the gall, she accused, to nickname her (their) 'Joy,' a frame of mind, she sobbed now, she had never known. I felt sorry for her of course, yet far more so for myself and, harking back, how I had sold out Jeannette. Suddenly then, for the first time, I realized, to my shock and remorse, that I disliked myself – grievously. This to me was the supreme penalty – for my craven misprisions against Jeannette. I felt low. Can you understand that?

Cyrus Colter

"Meantime, back in Chicago, Zack the Watchman, my strangest of fathers, was showing a side of his extremely complicated character about which we had always had suspicions but never until now graphic verification. He had entirely lost his equilibrium, gone mad, wild — if not murderous — on learning, finally, all that had happened; what, as he termed it in another violent seizure (yelling, I was told, like a madman), I had done to him. Ah, what *I* had done. He hadn't the slightest inkling, I'm sure, of what *you* did — but probably wouldn't have made a big issue of it if he had. That's how you had him wrapped around your finger. How were you able to do that, Mother? It was quite a feat. But indulgent Father, laughing, had always called you the 'Queen.' You acted the part, too. Yet, in the end, his letting you get away with your monstrosities cost him a lot of money. It all ended up wild. You even called it an earthquake — especially when you heard him cursing his feckless lawyers when it turned out that some worthless hustler like Agie's father, Dave Thomas, whom Zack merely knew *of*, was involved. For Zack knew what that meant — money, yes — and started raising hell all over again. Of course the lawyers had had nothing to do — yet — with Thomas, but, scared, scared of Zack, they, like they had some sense, asked the police in on the matter. This changed things, but not much, for they knew who Zack was and respected him for his long record of community philanthropies. They merely tried to calm him down but this was only minimally effective — until, that is, a black policewoman among them told him that if he didn't shut up he was going to have a heart attack and die. It was uncanny that she would say this for she had no way of knowing that Zack, at 71, was in inveterate heart-pill popper. But, as you told it, when she said this to him he started crying, yammering really, and said he never once imagined his son, his only acknowledgeable offspring in the world, would do

45

this to him. Then he let loose again. He wasn't cursing, you said. He was *cussing*. Few policewomen, or even men, had heard the likes of it—it was a one-man donnybrook. He's of an eerie breed, Mother, it's clear now, and, good God, I'm his inheritor! Yet, as I say, nobody even once mentioned what had been done to *me*—to make me do what I did. And the crazy irony, as I've said, is that poor Jeannette was never to know about any of this. She probably thought I had merely gotten tired of her, that there were a lot of girls ready to date me, well-dressed girls, girls prettier (that is, *lighter*, Mother) than she. All this. So, knowing her, I can see that grave, august chin of hers going up. Her solemn hauteur. Ah, Jeannette. She could be so serious, too serious, until she became almost comical. But not to herself—she was protecting her dignity, her accomplishments. She was serious because her life was serious, had always been so. But, as I've told you, what she didn't know was that to the people who really knew her, me for instance, the more serious she became, the funnier—and sweeter—she appeared. My God, Mother, this was a *sweet* girl! But she didn't know it. She thought she was tough. Can't you see *I* was the loser here? She could have helped me—once she wanted to, once she realized I was for real about her, once she had also discovered something new about herself: that she could truly love a man she had saved. But as it turned out, in *real* life—not in dreams, even frustrated ones—this was not to be. So if not Jeannette, then who? Cécile? you hint, from what I've intimated to you. That's a large riddle, Saturn. She is a fine, a lovely woman, certainly. A very different woman, too. She has also lived longer than I, by nine years, which maybe could be the real plus I think about. She is also from generations of people of class— though, yes, very conservative. What an irony. And I tell you, she is moral. Do you hear me, Mother? She is a moral woman. There are, alas, difficulties, too. But that will come later.

Cyrus Colter

"In closing, then, I must bring back to you the subject of still another unfortunate, and much wronged, player in the drama. I refer to my former little wife, Agie Thomas. Of course, it's I who has got to bear much, or most, of the responsibility for what happened to her, as well as the shame; it was a dastardly business which, even to myself, I've never lived down. First of all, *I* chose her for the role—chose her because she's a cripple. It was this, her body, that sent Zack up the wall; the humiliation of him, his family, he thought. Ah, but, Mother, she was also black—like Jeannette. This, I knew, would curdle your blood. Which it did, as I had wanted. Xosa, your evil maid, tittering of course, told me you drank a pitcher of daiquiris and kicked off a shoe through the window—like you and I used to practice punting. Zack himself, after having now heard the worst, had been on a gin 'rebel yell' binge for two days and three nights, but now, out of one eye, observing your dangerous daiquiri didoes, he became both sobered and alarmed. Finally able to leave his chair, he found his glasses and went and—as a last resort—fetched the big Bible.

There was also this development: Little Agie's father, Dave Thomas, had been on Zack's hit list ever since the latter had learned all the facts; now, the gin sidetracked, he was out on Thomas's trail with a pistol, thereby holding Thomas to the peril of being eliminated in the melee he had helped create—an outcome, however, about which, if I'm right, sad Agie would have shed few tears, for I had somehow caught the intuition, indeed the impression, in the hotel room down in Acapulco, that there was here some history, not at all negligible, of paternal insult. And though it may not entirely dispose of the charge, she, almost as if wishing to encourage me that she did not anymore fear the hurt, acknowledged, almost readily, to being no virgin. This could also have explained, I'm mortified to say, my consequent fiasco there, the pitiful dud I launched.

City of Light

Alas, though, I look back on the whole experience with self-reproach and loathing. No wonder, Mother, I've now come to so dislike myself. But much of it is your calamitous sin. You can't deny that.

"But now came a subact in the drama in which, trying for some semblance of damage control, you this time really came to the fore. High time, too, Saturn. Indeed it was a kind of miracle of contrition you now performed, or perpetrated. Making a string of direst threats, you almost bludgeoned Zack into calling up his fainthearted, overpaid lawyers again and directing them to begin, at once, round-the-clock negotiations with Dave Thomas and his wife for an immediate divorce for me from their daughter. There is no evidence Agie was ever consulted. (Speaking of contrition, my heart still goes out to her, as well as to myself. No, she is not destined ever to know 'joy,' and is well aware of it.) The negotiations began at once. Of course, Zack's lawyers (Trumpet, Trumpet, Trumpet & Stall) were at an impossible disadvantage. The wily, rascally, voracious Dave Thomas was in complete charge. Having less than a month ago taken my (Zack's) money, he now proceeded to tap the original source. The results were predictable. Next day, Zack, in bed with a cold, popping his heart pills, and occasionally shedding a tear, gave the negotiation proceedings an entirely accurate description. Said poor Father, according to your account, Mother, he still in tears: 'The bastard' (referring to Dave Thomas) 'swung me up by the thumbs, didn't he? Oh, my Lord,' he sighed, and, loudly snuffling, pulled the bedcovers up over his head. Next day, the only thing he said to me, and not in any anger I could detect, was, 'You've got to learn better how to take care of yourself.' As for you and me, Mother, we didn't speak for a month. No matter, I felt avenged — for awhile at least, until I began to moon again after Jeannette. There was no contact, no communication, between

Jeannette and me now, though. She went on to Wisconsin. I got into Princeton, though months late due to my sad, unfortunate, selfish, Agie escapade, and despite Father's tutors. I continued, however, to keep abreast of the student scuttlebutt from back home, for months, years — alas, even long after you had left us, Mother. Jeannette, into her books like an obsessed demon, later went on to law school, winning her share of awards and distinctions, among them the Order of the Coif, the highest law school honor there is. In the process, however — here is the irony, the tragic irony — she had changed, become an extremely complex person (as if there hadn't been signs of this before), and highly dissatisfied with the world she had now come to see, to know. Her disillusioning experience with me, of course, did nothing to reassure her. The result was to imbue her not only with anger, but with a deep sense of compassion for those 'feeling the whip of an uncaring social order,' as I've heard she once put it in a speech. The crassest irony of all, though, is that after becoming a lawyer she eventually ended up in, of all possible locations on earth, Africa. Yes, Mother, *Africa*. That's the place, you know, that we, our family, when traveling, somehow always managed to avoid. So at last we find the still-young — not quite 27 — Jeannette in Zaire, where, though, by then, she had been appointed to the bench, becoming a famous, fiercely committed, assize judge. Only, soon then — I hate even to think about it; it makes me so furious, and sad, also skewered by guilt — soon then, yes, to die in a dumb plane crash in the bush where she'd insisted on being flown on a mercy mission to some sick, starving, Luba children. So *that*, Saturn, was her reward for the life she had tried to live. It's disgusting — obscene!" Shaking his head feverishly, wildly — almost as if seized by a shock of delirium tremens and therefore unable to continue writing, Paul threw his pencil on the table as if trying to block, stymie, all further possibility of thinking.

City of Light

But this was not for long. "Saturn," he was soon saying, "do you realize, though, that, in a way, I have emerged victorious. There has come a great change. Now nearly everything revolves around Cécile. Am I not right? But I won't take you into that subject again for the moment—I know I've talked about her enough to make you want to scream. Yet I never fail to brood about Jeannette, either. She will always haunt me. She should you also, Saturn. Yet wonderful Cécile is alive and well. I can observe her, engage her in conversation, ask her questions—though my prying questions often puzzle her, sometimes irritate her as well. At times I wonder about this. Does it remind her that she is almost a decade older than I? I really doubt that, however—for actually she often acts like a child. It's you, Saturn, who seems not fully to have made up your mind about Cécile. This is hard for me to believe—after the bad time you gave Jeannette. I would have thought you would be shouting hoorays about my relationship with Cécile. You would seem to have had no problem about her. Besides, I can never marry her, even if both Cécile and I wished it— which, even race aside, we don't—for, as you very well know from me, she already has a husband, a highly successful one at that, plus two fine children, none of whom, of course, though, I've ever seen. Nonetheless, Cécile is very much a part of my life . . . ah, dangerous as this fact may be. Yet *life* is dangerous, Mother. You, however, should be very happy, absolutely thrilled, with no more Jeannette to worry about. And as for us, you and me, what has happened is nothing less than a miracle. It's ironic, but fitting, also strangely right, just, that in Cécile I may have, at long last, glimpsed the true light I've sought since Jeannette. Indeed, I may have found a brand-new mother, too. Best of all, though—for you—she, Cécile, is of the right culture, background, and, yes, Saturn, of the heavenly color you so feverishly cherish! I'm sure this must please you immensely. I can almost hear the rampant fibrillations of your heart as, somewhere up there, you thank the stars. So enjoy it all, Mother. Thank Cécile and her pure Western, Caucasian lineage for all this bounty. Listen, Saturn dear: No, she is not 'black,' not 'Negro,' not 'colored,' not even, God forbid, 'African American,' (that halfhearted, weak, vacillating excuse for a designation!); no, not any of these, Mother. Do you hear me? Do you follow me? She is not even an octoroon! – like you are. Not in her veins, her ovaries, her brain neurons, not even in her beautiful alabaster face; not, moreover, in her remotest well-born European ancestry, is she one scintilla BLACK! So there you have it, Queen Saturn. Be elated, proud, now, at this your self-fulfillment, indeed your vindication, here in beautiful Paris – City of Light. I have at last achieved for you your great aim, your purpose for me, your son, for my life. *Amen*, Mother! Ah, but what will it all bring?"

Paul was now trembling so violently he sat completely immobilized, with hardly any idea of where he was.

Chapter
Two
The Coterie Kaput

Next morning, after a bad night's fitful attempts at sleep, he found himself now, finally, again concerned about what he would say, the short talk he would make, at the upcoming fortnightly luncheon gathering of the Coterie, the nondescript organization he had only four months before founded but had yet to make some very basic decisions about. One example: What was the direction, ideologically, he should advocate that the presently small membership consider taking to end the drift to which the organization had already fallen prey? Yet he already knew, indeed repeated to himself, how the majority felt, viz., that the Coterie should at once mount a major effort to seek an African homeland somewhere on that continent for the growing numbers of drifting, wandering, or stranded blacks — many of them self-designated as victims of centuries of slavery, in turn responsible for the great diaspora of which they had now long been victims. It had always seemed to him, though, that throughout these past four months he had somehow been unable to get his jumbled thoughts organized, or reach any resolution of what he might do to get things started. Yet the original, the fundamental, idea had been his, he reminded himself, though it had been greatly motivated by the unhappy but powerful legend of Jeannette Hall. She had sacrificed everything and become a role model. But where now was his fervor? he asked himself. Where was his erstwhile glowing vision of Africa that had once sent a fervent zeal up his spine? This worried him. Where was his certainty, his sense of commitment, indeed the feverish mood of dedication he'd had after learning the strickening news of Jeannette's sacrifice? Blame for his change could not be assigned to Cécile, whose every thought and action, he was sure, would be warm, exemplary, once she knew what he had undertaken and why. Yet, he worried.

He worried, among other things, he presumed, because Africa—so it presently seemed to him in light of his most recent studies—was a strange, forbidding land; full of dangers and paradoxes; fraught with many unknowns. He therefore now had to ask himself if he, personally, would ever actually want to live there. Maybe in one of the larger cities, yes, he half-conceded, but what of the hinterlands? He remembered—in reappraising just one of his current research experiences—reading a short story titled "At the Well," in which its author, one John Temba, a Ugandan, had graphically, terrifyingly, depicted an African woman trudging through the forest-jungle with her four-year-old child at her heel. The child, stopping to squat and relieve himself, suddenly saw staring at him at point-blank distance—no more than five-feet—a huge twenty-foot python, which had just lumbered forward out of a large, dry well looking for some flesh-and-blood quadruped to instantly, violently, girdle, crush to death, then devour. The child, innocent, curious, transfixed, stared back at the monster snake in utter awe, fascination—just before the mother saw and screamed, screeched. Barely, then, in the split-nick of time, she dove and snatched the child away, running with him into a clearing where, hands and spittle flying, she railed at the soiled child on the vast, implacable subject of the unending mortal dangers abroad in the infested world of jungle, river, and six-foot-high grasses of lion prides, dangers abroad in the world in which he, the African child, and, hopefully, later the man, would have to live his life. The child, though, comprehending only his mother's wild anger and fright, began to cry, then squall, before the mother finally rushed him away to higher, clearer ground. The story had made Paul think.

The street-traffic noise and his growling stomach at last brought him to a consciousness of where he was—walking south on the Rue Colisée toward the Champs-Elysées. In quest of food—lunch. The day was bright, the sun high, the air chill, as, prim in hat, topcoat, and neck scarf, he made his way— trying, temporarily at least, to fend off the ever-more-pressing concerns about the Coterie and what should be his stand, his strategy, toward the members. These concerns, however, he was aware, were not of the kind to cause him to brood. Rather, his present agitated state, even if it sometimes included brooding, came from what these days, he realized, was his all-too-frequent disposition for excoriating the memory of his poor, tragic mother, Saturn Marie, which embraced his rare hubris and his harsh, phony letters to her. There was something horrible, ghoulish, about this irregular cruelty and he recognized, acknowledged, his recent inclination to continue it, even possibly to step it up, which nonetheless he admitted required of him much self-confession and endurance of guilt. It all, though, he realized, only pointed out his god-awful deficiencies, confusion, and dishonesty. He was indeed what he had feared all along—a blame shifter, a crybaby, a whiner, especially where his mother's truncated life and ordeal figured. It once more merely reminded him of, yes, the low opinion in which he held himself. Soon now his depressed feelings made him want a drink. He knew, though, that alcohol on an empty stomach—he had had only coffee near nine— merely made things worse. What, he knew, he needed was food. At once then he realized where he had been headed all along, from the time he had left Madame's pension: it was Jacques Valois's establishment, a modest yet very much alive and busy, especially now at noon, restaurant on the Avenue Franklin D. Roosevelt. He felt more oriented already and confidently quickened his pace, having even now decided what food he would eat—a small steak, no liquor, though, only a glass of red wine. It also somehow now occurred to him how much he enjoyed walking Paris streets in clear, bracing weather. It promptly brought to mind other magnificent, exhilarating features the famous city afforded—Cécile, for instance! Ah, this dear, sweet, generous creature, this beauty. His heart jumped at the thought of her. Then he smiled. How wonderful, stimulating, joyous, it would be to have her here with him today, talking, smiling, perhaps hanging on his arm (I must be dreaming, he thought, well realizing the latter had never happened and, no matter what, whether she were married or not, never would, so long as the lady was Cécile. It was not her way and contrary to her rank, her caste—she chose the clandestine mode; after all, she had much, indeed everything, to lose). Yet, were she actually here, she could tell him again what she had already told him, about, for instance, her taking her two beautiful daughters—Michelle, age twelve, and "Cutie-pie" little Zoe, age eight—to an all-Mozart piano recital at the Théâtre du Châtelet. Ah, Cécile, he thought, lovely Cécile, what was she to bring him? *Joy?* But not, he hoped, what it had brought little Agie Thomas. Or confidence?—a firmer grasp on life? Or absence of fear? Happiness?—even temporary

happiness? No? What, then, *will* she bring? He kept repeating
the question — imploringly. Do you know my needs? he asked
her — here on the Rue Colisée as he walked alone. What,
if anything, will you bring to them? What will you teach
me? What, Cécile? — what, for instance, makes this planet go
around? And why? I've got to know. After Jeannette now, it's
up to you, you know. You must somehow help me deal with the
fear. Yes, it's always the fear. So what will become of all
this? — and *us*? He sighed and did not want to know.

When he arrived at Jacques Valois's he was not at all
surprised to see the considerable number of luncheon patrons
queued up outside — though he also knew the line moved mod-
erately fast. When he stepped back to the tail of the queue he
found himself behind two neat women who, from what he
could hear, were talking French politics. He soon then let
his eyes rove randomly wherever they would; that, then,
was when, farther ahead up the line, he saw the man. And
the strange woman with him. Considering the restaurant
area's total human environment, the woman did indeed appear
strange — in both the Negroid color of her skin and her curious
mode of dress. Her dark skin, and the stubborn close-cropped
hair, and the extremely variegated bright-color makeup of
her long dress, under a short fur wrap — plus the prominent
gold-capping of her front teeth — all this brought Africa to
Paul's mind. He nevertheless — correctly — thought her strik-
ingly handsome. She was also doing her share of the talking.
Though having at first gawked, he soon now became only
casually intrigued by the pair until the man — white, well-
dressed — momentarily turned as he talked, and Paul caught his
full face. He had seen it somewhere before, he speculated — or
had he? He was unsure. Soon, then, the queue moved up a few
paces and Paul, though no closer to them than before, saw the
man, in making a point, quaintly spread the fingers of his right

hand for emphasis, and he remembered. He had met him in a television studio in Chicago — almost a year before. The man was a British journalist. Still, Paul could not recapture the name. The face, though, as well as the slight finger-spread, were unmistakable. He also now recalled, quite understandably, that the man, a prominent international journalist, was a well-known and highly regarded specialist, too. His specialty? African affairs. The surname came readily now — Lewellyn. Paul, seldom, if ever, a forward person, was now, for the obvious reasons of needing help, advice, on the Coterie stagnation, immediately seized with the urge to make himself known to Lewellyn again. At once, asking the people behind to hold his queue place, he went forward. On arrival in Lewellyn's presence, however, he found he had lost his nerve. Would the man remember him, he wondered. There had been three of them, panelists on a Chicago television discussion hour. The topic: "Survival Chances for Current Black African Democracies." Paul still well remembered his two nights of hard study preparing for the prospect, the challenge, of coping with this British expert who happened to be passing through town. Once the evening of on-the-air discussion was under way, though, it became evident that neither he nor the third panelist, a tall Norwegian professor, very young-looking for his title, with a long beard almost obscuring his flaming red necktie, was any match for the Britisher who frequently spoke, yet never excitedly, with all fingers splayed. Afterward, Paul recalled, the three of them, very amicably, repaired to a handsome hotel bar next door and, over drinks, reviewed their respective black African positions and forecasts at considerable length. For Paul it was a memorable occasion. He was astounded by Lewellyn's knowledge and grasp of the subject — also, despite his utter pragmatism, his seeming compassion and tolerance. Indeed, along with the powerful influence of

Cyrus Colter

Jeannette Hall's deeds and memory, the man, unwittingly, had played no small role in eventually turning his, Paul's, mind toward Paris and what had now, for good or otherwise, become the irksome, if not unfathomable, Coterie—the very entity, phenomenon, with which he was now hopeful Lewellyn could and would, while still in town, lend him a hand.

"Excuse me." It was himself he heard talking. At the interruption Lewellyn turned from the comely woman and observed him. "But aren't you Mr. Lewellyn?" insisted Paul, trying to smile. "I've forgotten your first name, but aren't you the journalist, the African correspondent, for the *Manchester Guardian*? We met last year—we were on a television program together, in Chicago, a discussion on Africa."

"Of course," said Lewellyn now. "I remember you—but not the name." He was smiling, though.

"Kessey—Paul Kessey," said elated Paul.

Lewellyn extended his hand. "Was that it?—Kessey." He laughed then—"One of the things I do remember is that in the question-and-answer period some of the hardcore Chicago blacks in the studio audience got on you quite a bit, wanting to know how you got up there, posing as an African expert, giving you the old sheltered-brat bit, et cetera, you know. It turned out, though, you knew quite a bit about 'the dark brooding continent,' as you put it. The heckling stopped. All told, it was a rather fun evening—I was on my way through to Montreal. We had a drink afterward, with the third panelist, the young blond chap, the professor, from Bergen." His lady companion was looking at him—expectantly. "Oh," he said, turning to her, then back, "may I present Mrs. Tosca Zimsu. Mrs. Zimsu lives here in Paris." The lady smiled, carefully, and put out, thought Paul, her rather rough-feeling hand. "*Enchanté, Monsieur Kessey*," she said, very seriously. Paul now got an opportunity, despite the scant fur wrap, to observe the outlandish dress close up in its wild quilt patchwork of colors and boundless variety of materials: vinyllike cotton, red silk, rayon, cellulose acetate, inflexible chiffon, cross-grained satin, denim, wool—all encompassed-about by a green-brown snakeskin belt, all this falling entirely below her unseen knees. Lewellyn—himself dapper, not tall, of ruddy complexion, wearing gloves, a russet trench coat, and black bowler— said to Paul, "Mrs. Zimsu is a widow and originally from Africa, from Copti, just north of Ivory Coast, before Copti, unfortunately, was overrun by marauding followers of a tribal leader, who insisted on being addressed as 'Mr. Zero,' known for his hatred of what he claimed was the then-current regime's attempt to 'westernize' the country's ancient African customs and mores. He said he meant to stamp all this out, then proceeded to do so, loosing much butchery and bloodshed, a ghastly tragedy. The country, in terrible shape ever since, is now, by Mr. Zero's decree, called Etavi. In the struggle, however, sad to say, Mrs. Zimsu's husband perished alongside her father. I had had the pleasure of once meeting her father, Dr. Auta, one of Africa's true statesmen—who also for a time had attended both Oxford and Cambridge." The queue was moving up again now and Lewellyn looked at his watch. "Kessey, come have lunch with us, won't you?" he said, then, giving Paul no time to answer, continued, "Mrs. Zimsu's young brother, her only brother, actually, who was also here in Paris for awhile after the coup, has, we fear—probably seeking some clandestine revenge—returned to Copti (or now Etavi) and she's of course extremely worried about him. I know quite a few people, Africans, from my travels over there—even during this trip of five weeks I've visited eight countries or regional territories on assignment for my paper— and Mrs. Zimsu here, learning from an African friend that I was leaving London to make this trip, and thinking I might possibly be able to learn something about her brother, had managed to reach me by phone just before I left London for Upper Volta, my first African stop. Now, having just returned to Europe after the five weeks, I decided to stop off here with what news, or lack of it, that I had, before going on home to my rather large but wonderful family—three boys, five girls, and a red-headed, Amazon-type, pretty woman for a wife—tomorrow, Thursday, I believe it is." Paul's heart plummeted. He almost winced. His Coterie luncheon meeting was scheduled for Friday—the day following. He knew now he was stymied. Of all the people in the world, he thought, whom the Coterie members should at all costs meet and hear . . . suddenly at this point Lewellyn's given name, "James," flew into his head . . . that person was certainly Lewellyn, James Lewellyn. But now, he told himself, that cause was lost. Glumly, almost grimly, he prepared to return back down the line to his old place in the queue—when, despite himself, his mind seemed doggedly at work again. Also Lewellyn appeared to have been observing him. "We'll save a place for you, Kessey," he said. "Join us when you return."

"OK," said Paul, only half-smiling, "I'll do that, assuming you'll allow me to be host." He left then—though followed by Tosca Zimsu's beautifully sad, yet longing, voracious eyes.

A half hour later they were eating. Paul's small steak had been brought with the others' orders and the conversation, in English, mostly between Lewellyn and himself, was on-going—as Tosca, whose English was hesitant, insecure, seemed again listening with those large, saddened eyes of hers, Paul thus surmising that Lewellyn's African tidings had been negative. What, however, Paul was most of all interested in was, somehow, telling Lewellyn all about the Coterie and what he was trying to do with it, if, that is, he thought, he himself could only make up his own mind on that slippery question.

City of Light

The dining room was large and well kept, cheerfully brown and orange, the waiters — men and women — constantly on the march. The table, at which Paul had found his guests seated, was situated off a picturesque alcove near windows with sturdy multicolored draperies which Tosca Zimsu, in her own elongated, patchwork, yet immaculate dress, watched with swift glances but piquant interest. Paul watched her as well — curious, fascinated. Although outside in the queue he had not been able to see much of her legs in this queerest of all dresses she wore, he nevertheless noted her pythonlike figure, which, still though, was somehow none too slender yet highly volatile, sexual. She saw him watching her now and quickly averted her gaze. Apparently Lewellyn, as he smiled, talked, and ate — and asked engrossed Paul if they might have more wine — had been beguiled as he watched the two. Again he soon smiled at Tosca, observing to Paul, "Mrs. Zimsu is perhaps quiet now — she was not earlier, before you came — because she is not quite as fluent in English as she is in French. Yet she gets along just fine, I think, and should be constantly reminded of that. But as for her French — and I never met her until I arrived here yesterday — her French is fully the equal of President Mitterand's. Ha!"

Tosca was still unsmiling as she finally spoke. "I have lived as long in Paris as anywhere. I was young. Most of my schooling was here. My father and mother even named me again — after the woman in the opera. My name before was Kowie. They came here many times to see it, the opera *Tosca*, by Giacomo Puccini. They loved this music drama very much, almost the same as they loved me. But my mother died — I was seven years of age. I did not know over the years I would lose more — my husband on the same day as my father. I have only my little son now." Suddenly her face became almost monstrous — "I hate Africa!"

Stunned silence followed. Lewellyn, rarely for him, seemed at a perfect loss of what to say or do. He said nothing, did nothing, except gaze at unhappy Tosca in a kind of wretched commiseration.

Paul, however, tense, eyes alert, saw an opportunity. "Africa," he said nervously, ignoring Tosca across from him in order to talk directly at Lewellyn, his quarry, at her side, "is a subject on the minds of many people these days, especially black people living in various parts of the world outside Africa, who are constant victims of all manner of abuses and bigotry. I suspect they think of the Jewish people, of their diaspora, and how you British were among the world leaders, including Harry Truman and the U.S., who secured for them — after the horror they had suffered from Hitler — a land of their own. But blacks, though for centuries casualties of their own special diaspora — i.e., a scattered slavery — know they have no such backing, never had, therefore can only look, longingly, to Africa, whence they came. This is what most of our Coterie members think."

"What do *you* think?" asked Lewellyn, though remembering to smile. "You're their leader, are you not?" Another smile.

"You're right — I'm aware of the leadership thing, the necessity for it," Paul said. He sighed and looked away, though. Then the waitress brought two more glasses of red wine — Tosca, from the start having drunk only water, had again declined anything stronger. "I do understand, though," Paul went on, "that blacks such as the people in my organization, with minds pretty much of their own, would want to know the truth — that Africa is altogether unique and presents a very complicated situation. No question, I should somehow make this clear to them. But considering their often chip-on-the-shoulder attitude sometimes when I get up to speak, it would have to be done carefully. Nevertheless, they should be warned—oh no, maybe not warned, nothing that serious, grave. It would be better if I just chatted with them for a few minutes—I certainly wouldn't want to do anything to rile them."

Lewellyn seemed to be watching him with a strange distaste.

"One must remember," said Paul, "that these people have been through a lot. That's why they're thin-skinned, touchy. We'd be the same." Lewellyn somehow seemed more understanding now. Paul, watching him, was almost elated, sensing he may have played the proper card, appealing to—what he, soon, felt certain was—Lewellyn's natural humanity, all of which now brought him to feel he may have begun to see some daylight, that he might be able to prevail upon Lewellyn to stay over and address the Coterie. He tried to keep his voice low now, not jittery. "Jim," he said, "give me just a minute or two to tell you a little about my organization. I founded it only a few months ago, right here in Paris, to see if such an organization could really do anything to improve the situation—here and elsewhere. It's pretty much made up of the kind of blacks, from all over, who, as I say, have been catching hell all their lives. I, of course, yes, head up the whole thing, such as it is—there are only a couple dozen of us, plus, always, the hangers-on, of course. I finance it, totally, but, I'm not too proud to say, all with my father's money. I haven't been able either, so far, to take it much of anywhere. That's the big problem, I guess—the members probably see it, too, although they treat me well; seem friendly. The fact can't be avoided, though, that I haven't been able to get the operation off the ground yet—even the name 'Coterie' was thought up by one of the members, not me. I feel somehow we're just floundering, haven't hit on a clear, precise objective. Yet, I don't take all the blame, Jim. The members themselves seem bogged down, confused, uninformed—all this on top of being sometimes sensitive and hardheaded. Really, though, they're all (with a few minor exceptions) good people at heart. But just think, Jim, what a wonderful thing it would be for them, and for me, if we were to hear a talk to us by a man of your credentials, your experience and expertise, on Africa. Think how much, afterwards, we'd know about Africa that we could never have dreamed of before! It would be terrific. It might show us the way to get our frustrated project really functioning. Isn't there some possible way you could accommodate us—put your departure back twenty-four hours—so we could learn some things we badly need to know? My members would benefit immensely— it might turn them around, let them see some hope, kill their lethargy. You'd be delayed only that short time, till Friday, when we have our regular fortnightly luncheon gathering. I wish you would think about that."

Throughout all of Paul's pleading, however, Lewellyn had sat shaking his head, no. "Oh, hell," he said, "of course not. I don't have to think about it. I can't do it—I don't have that kind of time." He emptied his wine glass. "I've been away from my family for almost six weeks. I salute you, though, your aims, your zeal—they're highly laudable. Under normal circumstances I'd probably oblige you, but not this time. Sorry, old man." His fork ascended to his mouth with the last morsel of his lamb chop, he then reached for his Burgundy glass—only to find it empty. He seemed hurt. Meantime, Tosca sat looking from one to the other of them as she slowly, decorously, masticated her food. Finally she spoke up in Lewellyn's behalf. "Monsieur Kessey, otherwise he would be home . . ." She nodded at Lewellyn. "He came here first . . . to bring me news. I had contacted him, asked him. He did not learn anything about my brother going to Africa. It looks bad. My brother may be dead. But Mr. Lewellyn should go home now to his wife and family."

City of Light

"Ah, how nice of you, Mrs. Zimsu," said Lewellyn. He turned to Paul. "Kessey, do you drink?"

Paul sat studying him. "Surely," he said. "As you saw, I've had two glasses of Burgundy."

"I mean whiskey, sir. Scotch.

Paul understood now. "I'd be glad to order you a scotch," he said. "May I?"

"I'd appreciate it to the fullest." Lewellyn fondled his wine glass, his mind, though, now seeming far away. When the waitress came he ordered a double scotch, afterwards addressing Paul: "Kessey, when he were earlier eating, you seemed puzzled about my interest in Africa, and therefore in Africans. 'How come, how come?' you asked. I see nothing complicated about it at all. We humans are sometimes driven to do certain things on our own initiative — often because of inner necessity — which itself in turn often comes from contrition, pure contrition. We British, for instance, back in the seventeenth and eighteenth centuries, caused many of the present-day problems. Slavery, slavery! We weren't the only ones, though, involved in that dastardly, that heinous, slave trade, but we were right in there with the others. It was the Americans who were probably the worst of all, though — despite, or because of, their so-called purists, like Thomas Jefferson and the others, all of them frauds, trying to have their cake and eat it too. We British, though, finally recognized the foul error of our uncivilized ways and set about changing things, outlawing slavery, for Britain. The U.S. instead chose to fight a bloody, a horrible war between their states to get rid of their slavery." Lewellyn's scotch came now and he abruptly stopped talking.

"Is that, then, why you took an interest in Africans, Jim?" asked Paul. "Because of slavery?"

"Damned if I know," Lewellyn said. "I'd like to think, I guess, it was for some kind of atonement. But I don't know,

really. Does it make me feel better? I don't know that, either."
He sipped the scotch and sighed. "Much of all this can't be
understood anyhow," he said. "What I am not, though, is a
bleeding-heart liberal. Hell, at home I'm a Tory!" He reached
for his scotch again.

Tosca's hand flew to her mouth. "Oh, what's that, Mr.
Lewellyn?—a Tory! Isn't that against the law?" Meanwhile,
she had risen to go to the ladies' room as nearby patrons stared
at her grotesque dress. Paul, though, thought her attractive,
indeed sensual, despite the quaint dress, or because of it. His
eyes followed her.

Lewellyn's face was fast becoming red as he imbibed the
whiskey. Soon the glass was empty. He turned to Paul with a
grimace. "Kessey," he said, "do you drink?"

After a pause Paul's laugh was nervous. "The same question," he finally said, "will get you the same answer. Yes, I
drink."

"Well, act like it." Lewellyn, half-smiling, shoved his
glass forward.

Paul at last understood why he was willing to get Lewellyn
drunk. He considered it his only possible chance to keep the
man in Paris. Soon he was waving for the waitress again—
as Tosca returned. "More *whiskey*?" she said. "Oh, Mr.
Lewellyn, you must not do that."

"I must not do what, Mrs. Zimsu?" Lewellyn, straining,
had brought his reddened face down almost to the tabletop, as
he gave Tosca a fishy look. "Tell me that, if you will, Mrs.
Zimsu. What?" He said it just as the new drink arrived.

Paul, though, was despondent now. He felt he had somehow been maneuvered off the trail. Soon he became grim.
"Jim," he said, resuming the battle, "except for those few of
our members who were born there, none has ever set foot on
African soil. Yet they somehow feel there is something there

that, for them, is redemptive. Africa, some of them think, will serve as a haven, a refuge, for drifting, maverick, benighted, black people who have no ties to anyone, or any place, or any government, or even to any set of beliefs or religion. What they're really after—although they may not realize it themselves—is a virgin, untried, freedom; a haut-Utopia of some kind, say; a new Canaan, as it were; actually maybe, yes, a vestal Shangri-la."

Lewellyn was laughing, tittering, his face now red as blood.

"You shouldn't laugh, Jim," said Paul, "without knowing, and understanding, what these people, every one of them, has been through—their forebears as well. It's for real."

Lewellyn, his chin now propped on his hand, was listening whenever his comatose eyelids were no more than halfway down.

"Are you still with me?" Paul smiled.

Lewellyn jumped. Then giggled. "Why, sure," he said, "where can I escape to?" He had not touched his drink yet. He turned to Tosca beside him, then jumped again, surprised. "Excuse me, Mrs. Zimsu," he said humbly. "You *are* still there, are you not? How jolly."

Paul finally blurted his distress: "Jim, can't we possibly come up with some way you could spend just a couple of hours on Friday with our Coterie? You'd be surprised how they'd react when they found out who you were and all about your accomplishments. They'd not only be interested, but grateful. We'd also, of course, be more than happy to meet the additional expenses of your one-day layover—that would be a pleasure and a privilege for us."

Lewellyn's behavior had changed. He was still woozy but, at least for the moment, not incompetent. "Kessey," he said, "I've booked a flight for London tomorrow, Thursday afternoon at four thirty-five, which will, however, permit me to see two of my old colleagues here during the morning and possibly have lunch with them. But I must catch my flight. I understand your situation and sympathize with it, but I can't do anything about it. I'm sorry. I've been away from my family for a long time. I plan to be on that flight tomorrow."

This was an ultimatum, true, but also a mistake—which wily Paul jumped on with both feet, as Lewellyn, his hand now shaking, lifted what would be his last drink of the afternoon and drained the glass. Already Paul was talking. "Listen, Jim," he said, yet trying to control himself, "a thought just hit me, a plan, even if it's one for emergencies. I'll call Fifi Mazisi, at once—she's a Coterie member, very faithful, and a go-getter."

"Oh, I know her, Mr. Kessey," volunteered Tosca. "She came to the world in Botswana. A pure African like myself. Her business is straightening the women's hair—in the Montparnasse district. She is a Coterie?—I can't believe."

Paul was concentrating on Lewellyn. "Fifi will get on the telephone, or out in the street, or even take the Métro, to get word to at least—maybe by word of mouth—to most of the members. Overnight, yes. We shall have the meeting at noon tomorrow, Thursday, at our usual place, the Chez Grenoble, instead of Friday. That will do it." He seemed grimly elated—having no idea yet of Lewellyn's reaction.

Lewellyn, however, was busy waving at someone. Paul looked up; then, just as peremptorily, waved the waitress away, leaving Lewellyn frantically flagging her vanishing back. Soon he was crying. "Ah, the blacks, the blacks," he said, "the Africans, yes. We shall all convene at the Chez Grenoble. I am black, you see—am I not? Look, look! . . . Am I not! Hey, hey!" He began slamming his chest with his fist—like a huge ape in the jungle. "We shall all meet at the conclave, eh? . . . Am I right, Kessey? Who will preside?" He looked around at Tosca, whose face had wilted in disappointment and displeasure. "Why so sad, Mrs. Zimsu?" said Lewellyn. "It is rather a time for merriment! . . . Tra, la, la — tra, la, la!" He stood now and began waving his red linen napkin around at the other, unentertained, patrons, then exhausted, flopped back down in his seat.

Paul was displeased, though only for a moment, for he felt better about his chances now.

But Lewellyn's shenanigans were not yet over. Remaining in his seat, he now undertook to brief them on his plans and his conceived responsibilities for the morrow. "At the hotel tonight," he said, "I shall work on my speech to your members at the noon luncheon gathering at that restaurant . . . Chez Grenoble, is that it? I shall have much to tell them, for I'm sure they're a very religious group, eh what? Are blacks not religious? He was soon pounding the table. "No retreat for *me*, though Governor!" he said to Paul. "I shall jolly well tell your would-be Africans how, yes, the Europeans 'evangelized' Africa. Sold them God. That was when the lights went out! *God* had gotten into the act now, you see. But where was He when they started bringing you people out of the bush and across the Atlantic, over to Europe and America, and of course for you-know-what. To finally work you — man, woman, and child — to death in the canebrakes and cotton fields, that's what. Eh, Kessey? . . . What about it, Mrs. Zimsu? Now, though, today — ha! — you folks are more Christian-religionized than the descendants of the abductors, your slave catchers, who brought you over here, are! Right or wrong?"

Tosca was crying.

"Don't cry, my dear Mrs. Zimsu," assuaged Lewellyn. "Never fear, I shall bring all these historic and theological matters out into the open for your members tomorrow in my

speech before that august Sanhedrin, that grandiose African
Coterie, when I disclose to them where the great Divine Presence was when the lights miscarried and you people were
shanghaied. Eh? Ah, God, yes—the savior of mankind, He's
called!" Suddenly frantically, though in vain, he waved to a
waitress passing carrying a tray of drinks. Again he looked
hurt as she shot up her chin and went on.

Paul stood to pay the bill, then led them out of the place—
though realizing as well now that he had more on his hands
than he had bargained for next day.

The Chez Grenoble, though a more-or-less working-class bar,
grill, and restaurant, was spacious, pop-colorful, and clean
enough—anything but seedy—and located over in the Latin
Quarter's Rue Jacob, where, particularly, its work-week noon-
times were crowded, busy, and often boisterous affairs. The
establishment also, in the deep rear of its premises, provided
private dining-room accommodations for varying numbers of
its patrons and their guests. It was in this latter area, then, that
every two weeks, at noon, Paul's Coterie members assembled
for their often loud, sometimes even taunting, laughter-filled
luncheon meetings. Today would be no exception.

Almost twenty minutes before the appointed hour of
twelve, and, as nearly always, the first Coterie arrival, a little
man (he was actually dwarfish, no more than five feet one inch
short) jaunty, alert—noisy steel plates on the heels of his
shoes—and gay, entered the Chez Grenoble and immediately
went over to the bulletin board at the end of the long bar to
learn the members' meeting-room, number 118 today. The man
was none other than the wiry bachelor Ari Ngcobo, a Zulu,
and a journalist, the editor of the fiery weekly newspaper
Réalité, a tabloid financed by the African National Congress
(ANC), and currently much involved with the many unhappy

third-world concerns, especially — stridently, bitterly — that advocating the violent overthrow of South Africa's apartheid regime. Not the least ambitious of Ari's present claims, moreover, was the work he professed to be doing on a graduate degree, never specified, at the University of Paris (Sorbonne) entailing, from him, a dissertation on colonial history which, he said, bore the title "Belgian King Leopold II and the Congo."

Soon now, close on Ari's loud heels, entered the redoubtable Fifi Mazisi, the Coterie's loyal pillar and staunch promoter — also articulate defender of its leader, Paul. Today Fifi, a tall, strong, self-assertive woman in her mid-fifties, African-born (present Botswana), and operator of an intermittently thriving beauty shop in the Montparnasse district, was today accompanied by her live-in boyfriend, Mango Mhlangu. Husky Mango, a Kenyan, whose stunted height, however, barely reached Fifi's broad shoulders, nevertheless claimed to be a son, even if illegitimate, of the late Kenyan Minister of State (post–British crown colony), Jomo Kenyatta. Ari, having warmly greeted the pair — they were still up front in the noisy beer hall — now escorted them toward the rear, the private dining-room area. "Why all the sudden change in our meeting date?" he asked Fifi, speaking a fast French as they walked. "I almost didn't make it — even though I got your message yesterday afternoon before five o'clock. *Je ne comprends pas.*"

"I don't know the whole story," Fifi said, "and didn't ask. It's got to be complicated, screwed-up, so forget about it. Maybe Paul's decided on something new."

"High time," said Mango, adjusting his pink-tinted glasses.

"We'll see here today," Fifi said, "what it is and whether it works. Don't write Paul off, though — he's smart as hell;

doesn't talk much, but he knows what's going on. Today's better than tomorrow anyhow, though — it's his birthday."

"What's the connection? — I don't get it," groused Mango. They had reached the rear, though, the private dining-room area, and, soon, room number 118. When they entered the room Mango whistled. "This is the smallest room they've ever given us," he said.

"You'd better wait first and see how many come," Fifi said. "Some weren't sure they could. We're lucky to have a room at all."

Ari, a chain-smoker, took out his fancy Egyptian cigarettes, offering them around to no takers, before lighting one up himself. He laughed then — "Do you think Paul is going to read us another of his African research papers today? He ought to get on a plane and go over there — see for himself. He admits he's never set foot on black Africa in his life."

"Why does *he* have to go?" said Fifi. "All three of us were born there, but I'll bet none of us knows as much about Africa as Paul."

They were joined now by three other members — two men and a woman. Meanwhile, Mango had taken it upon himself to more fully inspect the room he had adjudged too small. What may actually, though, have lent the impression of smallness was the huge circular dining table situated in the very center of the room. There were fully two-dozen chairs around the walls, with a variety of cheap yet attractively framed pictures hanging above them. The room was clean and inviting, even to the somewhat worn, wall-to-wall, bronze carpeting.

It was 12:10 now, and four more members, two of them women, arrived. Already a waiter had appeared and was taking drink orders. Two men and three women came next, one of the men the churlish Firestone Murphy. He was a large, slovenly, American black — restive, shifty-eyed, his trousers rumpled and almost dragging on the floor. His profession, or means of livelihood, was unknown. Ari, however, friendly, liked by all, greeted the newcomers with a fervent, eager zest — "Hey, *mon!*" he said to dour Firestone, whom actually he disliked, "always good to see you again." Whereupon the two men formally, ceremoniously — Firestone, however, somewhat aloofly — grappled, hoisting hands in the customary high, rigid, upright (elbows touching) handshake of world black militancy. Next a dumpy, middle-aged woman arrived carrying a shopping bag of groceries to take home later, followed soon by three men. It was clear now the number of people was swelling well beyond the formal roster of Coterie members. Fifi saw it and was not only alarmed but highly displeased. It was Paul's generosity, she thought, his tolerance, that were being violated, taken advantage of, by some members who had taken the liberty of bringing along a few uninvited relatives or friends. Whereupon angry Fifi got the waiters and instructed them to serve only hot dogs, hamburgers, and beer — as still even more guests arrived and Fifi fumed. Clad in a chic Parisian saffron wool skirt and bright-red sweater, the latter, however, embellished with a great necklace of African lions' teeth, she looked modish enough, and less than her true age. She turned to Mango — "What the hell's happened to Paul?" she said. "Why doesn't he come on!"

Almost at that very moment, as if it had been staged, a very handsome, dusky woman put her head in at the door. It was Tosca — in a long, patchwork, reddish dress. The next head appearing, at her left shoulder, was that of James Lewellyn, face pale, mien grave, austere. The third face, pressing in the background, was, of course, Paul's. Ordinarily a crazy, hilarious, maybe tipsy, shout would have come up from the members at Paul's appearance, but when now they descried his stern white guest, a hush, almost a pall, fell over the crowded room. Things then remained quiet, not so much tense, not

ominous or hostile certainly, yet strained and curious. Fifi
Mazisi, however, was speechless. What, she wondered, was
Paul up to? She knew the woman with him, though not well—
did not even remember her name, but had an impression,
typical of Fifi's prejudgments, that the woman was a screwball, wore the same (untrue) horrible red dress every day—as a
badge of some kind, it was said—after washing it. How did Paul
encounter the misfortune of coming to know her? Fifi sighed as
if she herself carried the weight of the world. What she wished
was that there was an opportunity to confer with other members, the level-headed ones, but in the present melee there was
no chance. Mango was gawking at her side, while she stood
watching Paul, interested now in only how, if at all, he would
meet this situation, this challenge, which no one but he had
created. She had not long to wait.

Indeed Paul had already begun—by first ushering his two
guests over to the great round table where he seated them on either side of himself, Lewellyn, symbolically, on his right. But
Paul remained standing to address the throng: "I see we need
more tables and chairs"—he smiled—"to be brought and, I guess,
placed around the walls. Will the waiters kindly attend to that? . . .
Thank you." Meanwhile, many members were elbowing their
way forward to get seats at the big table—Fifi and Mango in the
vanguard—from which they were all sure the action, which
they thought was likely to be exciting, would emanate. Paul,
still smiling, proceeded: "We have never had an attendance of
this magnitude before—although I do see some guests present I
have not met—yet we largely have Ms. Fifi Mazisi, whom I can
only call a magician, to thank for masterminding this turnout
on such short notice. It was an emergency, which she treated
as such, and, as always, delivered in fine fashion."

"What was the emergency, Paul?" It was bilious Firestone
Murphy, seated across the table next to little Ari Ngcobo.

City of Light

Paul tried to laugh. "We'll get into all that in due time — don't jump the gun, Firestone." He turned to the larger audience again. "So let me say that we welcome the newcomers and hope they will return as full-fledged Coterie members. For example, I invite you, as well as the others present, to give your full attention to what will be said here today."

Firestone leaned against Ari and whispered heatedly, "What I'm interested in is *who* is going to say it!"

"Me too," said Ari, frowning.

"I'll lay you a bet . . . ," Firestone began.

"No, you won't," interrupted Ari grimly. "It's going to be that guy sitting right up there at Paul's right arm. You watch."

"Sure, if he's permitted. What kind of brainstorm is Paul having? Jesus!"

Soon everyone was eating — which Fifi Mazisi now used as an opportunity to stand and say something: "Folks, I've got a secret to tell you. Guess what? Today is Paul's birthday. He didn't know I knew — that he'd once told us the date. Well, I didn't forget, and I think we ought to wish him well for all he's tried to do for our mutual cause." She turned to Paul and laughed — "How many is this one, Paul?"

Paul's smile could not, however, hide his embarrassment. He finally put down the hamburger sandwich he had been eating, stood, laughed, and tried to make a comic bow.

"How many, Paul?" insisted Fifi.

"Twenty-nine, Fifi, thank you."

There were smiles and applause all around. Even Lewellyn gave a partial smile, though he seemed in some kind of psychic pain. Tosca had sat stoically, silently — unmoved.

"What was the emergency you mentioned earlier?" It was Firestone again, sucking his teeth after having quickly devoured his sandwich.

Cyrus Colter

Paul paused. Suppressed anger had come on his face. "Very well, Firestone," he finally said, "you're rushing us a little, but I'll begin the program." Already Lewellyn had begun strangely, nervously, batting his eyes. "My friends," began Paul, "let me first identify for you the lady sitting here immediately at my left. She is Mrs. Tosca Zimsu and lives in Paris—has for some time. She even received much of her schooling here, although she was born and reared of an outstanding family in Africa, in former Copti. We are happy to have this estimable lady present at our meeting this afternoon." He paused again now. He seemed trying to control his tenseness. "To go on, then," he said shakily, "as it were, to the *pièce de résistance*. Folks, I've really been lucky in the last twenty-four hours. Yesterday, an unforgettable day for me, and, as a consequence, I hope, for you, too, I—just by accident, a fluke—ran into Mr. James Lewellyn, here on my right, and Mrs. Zimsu, at a restaurant over on the Right Bank. Mr. Lewellyn was merely passing through town, returning home from Africa to London where he's a foreign correspondent for the *Manchester Guardian*. I had had the pleasure of meeting him about a year ago in the States, in Chicago, so when our paths crossed yesterday at the restaurant, he invited me to have lunch with him and Mrs. Zimsu. I, then, of course, had the opportunity as we ate to tell him a few things, briefly, about our organization and what we are trying to do, et cetera; that is, assess modern Africa . . . for certain possible purposes, to see if it holds any promise at all for world blacks, blacks who make up their own huge constituency as a result of a worldwide historical diaspora. I'm of course talking about four centuries of chattel slavery. In other words, can Africa, or any part of it, ever, realistically, be considered our home; home for a new breed of blacks, who know nothing about the present, post-colonial, black African countries which, really, hold little attraction for us. We feel we are something different, new, and must therefore find new paths. This, then, if we, still sort of an ad hoc venture, can call it an agenda, is probably ours. We've even named ourselves. The 'Coterie' was our own choice."

Firestone Murphy was breathing hard now — trying not to interrupt again. Mango Mhlangu, too, was clearly uncomfortable, disenchanted with the direction in which he saw Paul taking them today. Little Ari Ngcobo, a loyal Paul supporter from the very beginning, nostrils flaring now, craving a cigarette, was reduced to noisily tapping both feet on the floor in unwitting protest of Paul's present "brainstorm" behavior. What was he really up to? wondered Ari, by bringing in this pale specimen of humanity as, apparently, someone to lecture them on the thorny problems which this purported "adviser" and his forebears, indeed his contemporaries as well, had historically helped to create. It made no sense at all, thought Ari. Paul was a good man, true, but Paul was also nuts, he vowed. Meantime, as Paul talked on and on, Lewellyn, sober, dignified, dressed to the nines, seeming taciturn master of all he surveyed, appeared prepared for whatever was to come. Tosca, mouth agape, was hanging on every word Paul uttered.

"Having heard, only last year in a Chicago television presentation," Paul was saying, "Jim Lewellyn's thrilling treatment of Africa today, its triumphs and tribulations, but, above all, its great potential, its real promise, if, that is, the right people — Africans, of course — are allowed to take charge and rise to the occasion, I have wrestled with his theories ever since. Oh, you should have heard him. I can only repeat that it was thrilling. And timely. In our own organization I think maybe we've too much tended to withhold from present black African governments their just due in order maybe to try something new, while there may be cause to believe we should rethink all this."

Firestone Murphy bristled. "Say, is he fish or fowl now?" he whispered to Ari.

"He's both, it sounds like," said Ari. "This is going to be interesting."

Paul warming to his subject, went heedlessly on. "Jim Lewellyn has just spent five weeks on assignment in sub−Saharan visiting a number of countries—though, unfortunately, not South Africa, from which he was barred. Five weeks are really a short time, he readily admits, but enough, in my opinion, to draw some of the conclusions he's reached from the data he did compile in the places he visited." Unruffled, Lewellyn again sat looking nowhere particularly—until there then came a slight distraction by the arrival of two more latecomers, both men and members, but who had no place to sit. The room was packed. They therefore merely stood just inside the door, leaned against the wall, and tried not to look surprised or disappointed. "I won't burden you," Paul continued, "with a long rehash of how I got him to come speak to us. Yes, Firestone, it finally developed into an emergency. It's quite natural that a man of his preeminence must operate on a tight schedule, so it's no surprise that he's got to catch a flight out of Orly for London this afternoon, at four-something, and we plan to see that he makes his flight as some kind of gesture of thanks on our part for his pains."

"What's the big deal?" muttered Mango Mhlangu to Fifi.

Fifi herself now looked worried, disappointed, but said nothing, only sighed.

"So before he goes out that door today," said Paul, "he will have had an opportunity to share with us valuable information from his African sojourn, as well as his own hunches or findings gained from this, as well as from many other past, and productive, forays into the motherland."

An increasing number of the members around the big

table and at the makeshift smaller ones around the walls were becoming ill at ease, some balky, at the tedium of Paul's introduction. Others, though, at least at this point, were merely curious about, if not yet suspicious of, the highly touted character of the coming speaker Paul was praising. Only Firestone Murphy, still hard-breathing, was clearly hostile, though now little Ari was not far behind. Soon, then, as Paul showed no signs of letup, more of the members were glancing back and forth at each other, some, on occasion, frowning, until Fifi began sorrowfully shaking her head at Paul. What, though, most riled Ari was what he considered Paul's crass presumption in bringing this man to their meeting at all, to say nothing of giving him (in, so far, a ten-minute introduction speech) the role of, as it were, keynote speaker. What, thought Ari, could such an interloper, and a "Britisher" of all things, possibly have to say of benefit to the Coterie?

"But, as I say," Paul went on, "Jim Lewellyn has a plane to catch later this afternoon and therefore won't be able to stay the whole time, yet maybe long enough after his presentation for us to put a few questions to him about what's happening in present-day Africa. There are bold new developments occurring over there in some of the countries he visited — some good developments, some not so good, if not actually disturbing. But I'd rather let him tell you, if he will, because . . ." He paused, as if he himself were now debating whether he hadn't said enough — too much.

The pause was unfortunate. It permitted, even invited, the first grossly irrelevant interruption of the meeting, in its near perfect execution almost as efficient as if it had all been — though it was not — elaborately prearranged by the members. Rather, it was a case of deft, if unholy, improvisation tracking a ready intuition on the part of a number of Coterie people present who were nothing if not geniuses of various degrees

of African aplomb — "cool." To what end? Simply, the pre-
vention of Paul's further introduction of his English guest
as speaker. They wanted none of Lewellyn. Therefore, surprisingly — and to Paul's astonished disbelief — the self-
assigned lead-off actress in the unrehearsed drama was none
other than Fifi Mazisi herself, who, like Ari, a chain-smoker,
had first mashed out her cigarette, then thrust even farther
forward her hairy chin and large bosom — the African lions'
teeth necklace loudly rattling — before speaking in a mishmash
of French, English, Dutch, and various garbled native-
African tongues. It was also then, though, that Tosca Zimsu,
by her curiously riveted stares around the room at the sundry
enigmatic but sinister actors, had become terribly, if at the
moment silently, involved. Indeed she had seemed talking,
whispering, to herself.

"Friends," began Fifi, however, watched by her "husband" Mango beside her, as she leaned in boldly toward the
center of the great circular table, "I remind you this is not only
the birthday of our friend and leader Paul, it is also the first
occasion in memory on which I have seen him somehow not at
his best."

"Wow — wait a minute there, now, Ms. Fifi." It was Firestone, faking loyalty and innocence. "How so, Fifi? What
are you talking about? Paul admitted it had turned into an
emergency."

"*What* had done that, sir?" It was Tosca, half-rising, and
speaking French. "You do not know about our emergency. I do
know."

Silence.

Lewellyn's jaw had finally dropped. He seemed now dispirited, spent by surveying the chaotic scene and hearing talk
defying both synthesis and comprehension. He turned be-
seechingly to Paul, as if his own words would not come.

City of Light

Paul, especially after having seen Fifi in her new (per-
fidious) role, was on the verge of panic, despair. "My friends,
my friends," he cried, yet his voice almost hoarse, "I do want
you to hear, firsthand, if only briefly, Jim Lewellyn's account
of some of the significant changes he saw in Africa. Having
over the years spent a lot of time there, he's a solid, cautious,
reliable expert. I told you about being on a television panel
with him in Chicago last year. It was about Africa. But it was
soon very clear that the other two of us panelists were pretty
much out of our league. Although a modest, courteous man, he
soon took over the show by default — before long the other two
of us had become merely occasional commentators. There's no
doubt in my mind — for I talked with him yesterday — that he
has some interesting, important, and very true things to say;
enhanced also, of course, by his own wise, experienced inter-
pretation of the data he's gathered. So you'll find out a lot about
what's going on over there — things besides just the South
African struggle — that you won't see in the Paris newspapers,
even in *Le Figaro*, for months to come yet, and then, depending on what paper, it might be a biased version. Much of the
Western media, as you know, is not averse to bashing black
Africa and Africans — and black leadership is a special target.
Yet, and I hate to say it — but Jim Lewellyn's recent trip there
sadly confirms it — that some of these black leaders merit bashing, when you look at the way some of them (note I say some)
run their countries and treat, or mistreat, their own people."

At this remark Ari, joined by Firestone, grunted disap-
proval, without uttering a word — merely grunted in unison —
yet everyone noticed.

"So, I'm surer than ever," said Paul, "that you'll all want
to hear what Jim has to say. Most of you remember our discus-
sions at these Coterie meetings. Many of them, you'll recall,
were, to say the least, inconclusive. We need to know more,

study that dark, brooding continent, and, whenever the opportunity arises, talk — as we have the rarest of opportunities to do here today — with the proven experts on the subject. The phenomenon of Mother Africa — even if it's not always a pretty picture — is something well worth our most serious study and thought, especially in light of what we're thinking about doing. Going there."

Little Ari bristled, before — with a respectful if bogus smile — speaking up: "Paul, my friend, also leader, why, in your thinking, must Mother Africa always present a 'pretty picture,' as you refer to it? Why?"

"Amen," said surly Firestone. "Why, leader?"

"Other governments don't always present a 'pretty picture,' " Ari said. "Then why must always Mother Africa? France has problems, doesn't it? The English" — he looked across the table at Lewellyn — "have problems, too. The Germans were until recently existing in halves, with a great ugly wall separating them. Trouble is easy to come by, Paul. Few escape it. Why, then, should not Africa — prostrate and bleeding, despoiled, its treasures and natural resources carted off in ships to Europe all these centuries. Why should it not have problems? But for us, here present today, in, if I may say so, this rather strange unripe" — he looked at Lewellyn again — "yet attempted collegial setting, the immediate goal, our great South-star, as it were, is to *re*-create a natural habitat for ourselves, a place to which we may all, free of Western scorn and insult, repair and call home. Is not this how we should view Mother Africa? We look around us and see, so clearly, how and why the concept grows increasingly urgent daily. And for reasons we see everywhere, especially here — I mean Paris. Or France, actually. But Paris, *mon*, is the hub. Because Paris is everywhere. It is a prototype. Forget about South Africa, Botha, de Klerk, and Pretoria for the moment —

ah, but only for the moment — and think of Paris. Then Africa! Do you not see how the concept grew? It's Mother Africa!" Ari paused now, oratorically, in order to raise high his right hand, as if, like John the Baptist, proclaiming, prophesying, the coming — somehow, from somewhere — of one destined to burn the chaff of Afrophobia inside a searing, unquenchable shielding fence of fires. Merely envisioning, his mind's eye descrying in the distance, such a haven, a glorious sanctuary — *Mother Africa, yes!* — he seemed now inspired, euphoric, eyes ablaze, lips in keening, spasmodic motion. He seemed transported, himself on fire. For a moment everyone at the table and around the room seemed likewise under his spell — including even Lewellyn and Tosca. "Africa, blessed Africa!" now cried Ari. "Where I was born! Our ineluctable mission! *Ad majorem Dei gloriam!*"

Finally Fifi Mazisi, hesitant, in utter confusion, turned to her man Mango and, *sotto voce*, inquired: "What in God Almighty's name is Ari talking about? . . . or trying to? He's demented, or having a stroke, or something — I don't get it. This stuff he's talking is horseshit."

"Quiet, Fifi!" said Mango, taking off his cerise glasses to clean them with his breast-pocket handkerchief. "Let him talk. What if he is crazy? — he's not the only one in this Coterie outfit that is. Besides, he's telling the truth."

"But Paris . . . it is everywhere . . . yes," went on Ari, though somehow now vaguely, almost weakly. "A prototype? . . . perhaps, yes. Or do I mean archetype? . . . In this situation aren't they nearly the same? No, they are not, I guess. Well, just let me say it this way: Paris is a dangerous place — for some people. Is this not so? *Vous apprenez?* — ah." Now he lapsed into silence, seeming far less sure of himself — soon bewildered, confounded, by the immensity of the ideas he apparently could neither quite prefigure now nor grasp. He looked around the table, then the room—blankly. At last his hand wandered down to the tabletop and for a moment he seemed vanquished, checkmated.

Paul was speechless.

The *mise-en-scène* itself, however, added to by all these unfathomable carryings-on, was clearly too much for guest Lewellyn. His face, no longer pale from yesterday's alcohol overindulgence, and now flushed ruby-red, somehow also looked pinched, craggy, rutted—as if he needed a week's bedded sleep—from the raw counterfrustrations of impatience and humiliation. Brusquely now be beckoned for the waiter and ordered coffee, black coffee.

But there was no letup—soon Ari, seeming revived, was speaking again: "Paul, my friend, here in Paris the devil takes the guise of the evil France for the French National Party (the FFF) and of course its scandalous leader, Monsieur Charles Poussin—who, as you well know, is France's rising Adolf Hitler without all the shrill speeches. Eh?" Hands once more in the air, stark fingers apart, he grimaced his macabre, toothy smile, which, despite the uneven teeth, yellowed by cigarettes, now fairly shown, glittered, in his cold vehemence. "I tell you, we must move out—before Adolf the second moves in. We need a new Marcus Garvey!—to *move* us!"

Untidy Firestone Murphy, ketchup on his necktie, had leapt to his feet, applauding. "How right you are, Mr. Ari! We need to get a-move on—time is running out. That ghoul Poussin, given the chance, would incinerate every one of us. I'm talking about every person of color—man, woman, and child—now here in France. Note, I didn't say Germany—no, no—*France*. Bear in mind this is the same France, if you will, of that now-dead blackguard-hyena, who some claim was a great writer, novelist, Louis-Ferdinand Destouches—'Céline' to most. Hating Jews as he did, you can imagine what he thought of us. But as for Poussin, if he couldn't exterminate us all, he would certainly ship us, body and baggage, out of the country. It's a certainty—he's repeatedly said it in his dour, phlegmatic speeches, promised it up front, like Hitler did about the Jews in *Mein Kampf.* Think about it—look out!—this is the man who could end up *president* of France. Then where are we? Maybe not in purgatory, but they'll sure need some kind of requiem, or whatever it is they call it, to keep us out of the hell of some concentration camp, every damn one of us—oh, except, that is, Paul's distinguished guest here, who is of course immune." Firestone, however, scratching under his foul arm as he talked, had let his gaze come to rest across the table first on Tosca, then Lewellyn—though strangely, almost politely, even with a hint of respect for the latter—before his eyes again began flashing their fire. "We've got to take stock, friends and colleagues!" he said harshly. "*That's* what we should be talking about here today—not about how black rulers over there are fouling things up. We should be offering them help instead of criticism—for it's they who are our potential saviors. If you want to get downright technical about it, the whole *world*—Ari touched on it—is f . . . , I mean messing, up. It's not just Africans, Paul." Firestone, from Akron, Ohio, was presently studying crucified Paul, until someone said, "Right on." Whereupon Firestone, handkerchief now out, wiping his clammy brow, once more looking, almost benignly, across in Lewellyn's direction, finally reached for, and, in deep thought, sipped from his stein of beer. Then he sat down, his tirade ended.

There were sighs of relief, even from the members, for Firestone—in his truculence and bombast, along with his slovenliness—was not the favorite constituent among them. No matter, the next obstructionist was already waiting—one of the very latest, tardiest, arrivals. Jack Chase, his name—a

consumptive-looking, whey-faced octoroon in his late thirties, wearing an unkempt black jacket and maroon beret.
Having just gobbled down the remnants of his sandwich before
addressing his beer, he had nonetheless expected Firestone
would be talking even longer than he actually had, but now
Chase hastily lit a cigarette and, in a hollow, rasping voice,
declared: "In addition to being black, my admired conferees —
as if that were not enough — we are also immigrants. You hadn't
thought of that, had you? So that's one more negative. Me, I
came here from Britain." Smiling, he glanced at Lewellyn —
whereupon Chase's thin, sallow face somehow cleared, though
almost convulsively, as if he were on the verge of laughing at
an option of ironies. "From, yes, Mr. Lewellyn's native is-
land. But for me, of course, Britain was merely a stopping-off
place. I was born in Bermuda. I am the precious offspring,
so they say — I knew neither — of a Scottish lord and a pretty
Saint Vincent chambermaid in the hotel there were mi'lord
was vacationing. I moved around, though, almost from the
beginning — from nearly the time I could walk and talk it
seems; but I was really twelve — going here, there, everywhere. On, on, on. To what? Or where? A child running from
the pederasts. At twenty then to Vietnam. Ha — but don't get
me wrong, don't kid yourselves, friends — to Vietnam to fight
alongside Uncle Ho Chi Minh, that's who, never that big-
eared Westmoreland, you can bet. Everywhere, yes — the im-
migrant black paleface, me, in motion, on the go — in *mobile
perpetuum*. (Guess where I learned that, friends — ha, when,
for a hot minute, I 'studied' at Cambridge!)" Chase still seemed
inwardly laughing — uproariously. But soon his wasted whitish
face grew grave, yet then impassive, as he sat silently, medi-
tating, occasionally flicking ash off his cigarette into the empty
beer mug. Although the room had become close, muggy, little
Ari, watching, sometimes frowning at, Chase, seemed still

trembling from the juncture when, in the midst of his own fiery speech (in which he had even invoked Marcus Garvey), he had, prematurely, he thought, yielded the floor to Firestone Murphy. Now he merely sat shaking, trying as best he knew how to control himself, step back from the precipice, quell the demons. The Coterie, he told himself, not Lewellyn, not even Paul, must prevail. He finally reached for and gulped some water, ignoring Chase, yet still agitated, wishing to speak again. Meantime, Lewellyn had turned to look, protectively at Tosca, then, hostilely at Paul, as if desiring to hurl his empty coffee cup at the latter.

But now, suddenly oblivious of everything, Paul was talking to them all again. His voice, however, was deliberately cool, patient, even if at times, inevitably, still edgy. "Why is it, my friends, that you refuse to hear Mr. Lewellyn? Oh, I know you've given random hints of your reasons, like Jim Lewellyn's, as well as my own, seeming—note I say 'seeming'—criticism of certain unnamed African heads of state. All that, though, is so fragile I wonder if you realize it's no reason at all—only a vacuous excuse. What I'm asking for is your real reason. It would help matters a lot if one of you spoke up—confessed, really." He paused. There was only silence as they studied their tablecloths. "Very well, then," he said. "Yet I want to tell you what you surely must have assumed all along, that Jim Lewellyn did not ask to come here. He is a busy and important man. I asked him, finally literally begged him, to come, and it was very decent of him to do it. There's nothing for him in meeting with us—we can't grind any axe of his. Your behavior toward him is passing strange." Lewellyn only turned and observed Paul glumly. "What we've all been about," said Paul, "almost our whole effort, has been Africa—the expectancy we've had of it. That's what has brought us all together these past few months. It's involved the concept of faith, trust.

We've all somehow been looking to Africa for hope." For a second his voice faltered, almost broke. "We've wanted *some* place on this earth that will have us, welcome us, not just grudgingly tolerate us." His voice was rising now, almost quavering with emotion as he fought for control. Ari was crying—silently. "Is it," said Paul, "that you fear the very fundamental things that Jim Lewellyn has to tell us?—that he somehow brings us bad news? Can it be that we fear the truth? Or that we wish to procrastinate—postpone, defer, hearing it? Or what? Will someone, yes, please speak up?"

Silence.

Suddenly then, on a gamble, he spun around to Lewellyn. "Okay, now, Jim," he said, his voice uneven, hurried. "The floor is yours. Give him a big hand, friends."

The instantaneous interloper this time was Fifi Mazisi's spouse-equivalent Mango. Even though Lewellyn had not yet moved, Mango's strong voice rushed in to fill the vacuum. "There are some things we should keep in mind," he lectured them—as Paul sat forlornly, weakly, shaking his head. "One is that there are considerations that sometimes outrank Mother Africa."

Little Ari bristled. "Name one." He hurled the words.

"*Sow*-Africa, for instance," Mango said, correcting in the process the common pronunciation. "We can't even claim it as an appendage of Mother Africa's. That's a bitter pill, but we presently have no alternative but to swallow it and hope it won't kill us. But we suffer. And from what? From our original blindness. Which, so to speak, was our original *sin*. It's our resulting diaspora syndrome, then, that, though we would, we cannot deny. Nor destroy. Then we confuse it with what we revere as 'Mother Africa.' But the problem is not there—it's more perplexing than that. Oh, I understand, of course, that we believe we are not at home in any place on 'the great globe itself,' as it were, except Africa. But it's the curse, the shame, indeed the very ghost yet, the roving, pillaging, gory specter of the diaspora that outstrips everything else imaginable. We let it happen! It is this ghost, then, that of our cruel uprooting, that is our everyday agony—our bone in the throat! We feel that ghostly—and, yes, ghastly—pain every time we are so rudely reminded that no one wants us. But can Africa now ease that pain?"

Ari surrendered to his demons. "*Yes*! . . . yes, it can!" he screamed, quivering as he rose from the table.

Tosca Zimsu, having withstood all she could, was somehow now struggling, flailing about, in her chair—trying to stand. Finally, on her feet, she hoarsely shouted, almost screeched it—in French: "No, it can't! That's a lie! I *know*!"

Paul sat incredulous at Tosca's wild behavior, also at Mango's surprising heresy. But Mango acknowledged only Ari, saying, "I must tell you, learned Doctor Ari Ngcobo, that that high degree you say you're on the verge of taking at the great Sorbonne, after years of grinding Western study, has nevertheless misled, deceived, maybe even stupefied you— has stunted your thought apparatus, your ability to ferret out the wheat from the chaff in the process of analysis. Not synthesis. *Analysis*. I must therefore repeat that Africa, per se, is a symbol—if not a ghost." Paul gasped. "It therefore cannot ease our trauma," said Mango. "What we need is a different God of some kind, a new religion—new to most of us at least. We need Islam—Allah."

"Oh, Jesus!" wailed Ari, slamming his forehead against the heel of his hand. "What next? . . ."

It was Lewellyn now who was aghast, yet, paradoxically, with the slightest, faintest, scimitar of a smile. Things were unraveling for sure now, he thought, and he felt a certain commiseration, also an understanding, and yet an astonishment. He found himself moved. Before he knew it he was on his feet, facing them all. A hush fell over the room. He glanced at his watch, then said to them—not loudly, even trying to smile—"Have no fear, my friends, I'm not going to make a speech. There's not time now, I'm due at the airport soon." He turned and looked at his trench coat and bowler hanging on the wall behind him. "But I think it's only fair for me to say 'thank you' to all of you for having had me here—even if I didn't speak. You'd have heard very little that was helpful. You've been dealing here with a monstrous subject. Earlier your leader, Mr. Kessey, very generously referred to me as an 'expert.' Maybe in a modest way I am—on certain peripheral aspects of African life, history, culture, et cetera. But I have not the slightest expertise on what I've seen and heard here today—I mean the wrenched human hearts in this room all in conflict with one another. What a phenomenon—it itself dissolves the heart. It is moving, my friends." He seemed suddenly awed by his own remarks and quickly, though awkwardly, cleared his throat before wanly smiling again. Soon then, briskly, he began circling the huge table, still smiling, and shook hands all around. Despite themselves, out of a kind of mute respect, they, too, were standing now, silently.

Paul meantime had turned into a vitual madman, reacting to the whole of an afternoon of pure evil, hell, and fiasco, he thought, and after all his 24 hours of frantic scheming, of effort, and artifice—the dogged stress of it all, too, yet somehow, no matter, with a confident hope—all that now, though, dashed to the ground by what he could not help regarding as these bullheaded, know-nothing Coterie members, all of whom he now totally disowned. He had not yet, of course, had time to consider any merit their solid, unanimous Coterie "votes" against Lewellyn (and himself) may, or may not, have had. His only thoughts now were that he had been miserably misused by his followers and their hangers-on. He was suddenly blazingly angry again and vowed that such a debacle as today's would be the last. This, though, he knew, could mean nothing other than that he was through with it all now, had washed his hands of his efforts. Yet he realized it all with a shock. Then almost at once he felt something else: a kind of felicity, a glorification, also a sense of refuge, a wonderful presence in his life—Cécile. It hit him harder than the other—than the vow, the anger. It was something very different—involving adoration, even a crazy ardor, and more, beyond precise definition. These matters were extremely complex, he knew. Yet he somehow yearned. There was not, however, he realized, any more equivocation about the Coterie. He felt sad.

At last, as he and Lewellyn—Tosca between them—left behind them the Chez Grenoble, exiting through the noise of its great front bar, Paul realized it was for the last time. Lewellyn, seeming to sense something, looked across at him. "I say, old man"—he smiled in greatest admiration—"perk up there, both thumbs perpendicularlike. It's no big secret that life is full of potholes. But we don't dare give up. Where would all the fun be?"

"Never—never again!" Paul, his fury suddenly returning, managed to say. "What a fool I've been all along. It's time for me to move on now, set my sights on some worthwhile new undertaking, though I have no way yet of knowing what it's to be. It will come, though—it must. But, in looking back, I had such high hopes—especially for today. It's all my fault."

Lewellyn seemed embarrassed, then irritated. "Oh, hell," he said, "you'll live."

Tosca, her long, red dress swirling below her jacket as they walked, had been looking from one to the other of them. She looked now, though disapprovingly, at Lewellyn until apparently remembering why he was in Paris at all.

Cyrus Colter

The brilliant afternoon sun seemed moving only slowly westward, the weather still gorgeous, the street alive with chattering pedestrians, as the three of them continued up Boulevard Saint-Michel. Lewellyn, smiling reassuringly, turned to Tosca. "The day was not entirely in vain, Mrs. Zimsu," he said. "You and Paul had occasion to meet. That's no tiny matter, really—two estimable people with at least one thing in common. Character."

But Tosca had not understood this last English word and looked at Paul bewilderedly. He translated it for her, then smiled at Lewellyn before reaching inside his jacket and pulling out an envelope, which he made remonstrating Lewellyn take. "It's the least I can do," Paul said to him, "for all the hassle I've caused you—it's merely taxi fare to your hotel, then out to Orly and your plane. Godspeed, Jim."

They were passing the inviting outdoor cafés now. Lewellyn laughed. "Paul, do you drink?" he said.

Paul laughed for the first time. "Yes, I do," he said. "And so do you. How do you feel?" Even Tosca had understood—including the context—and laughed with them.

Lewellyn was flagging a taxi now. "Don't forget what I said to you two!" he shouted, climbing in, before then turning to Tosca. "You keep on his trail, Mrs. Zimsu—do you hear? You both need each other!" He waved as the cab sped off.

Tosca looked lost, embarrassed, as they both continued walking. "What was he saying?" she said, now in French. "That I was to camp on your tail? . . ."

Paul laughed. "Not quite. He said 'trail,' meaning for us to be friends, I guess."

"We are friends already." She was adamant about it. "I would like to continue this friendship. I need it. So does my son, Gwelo. I think you are a good man, Monsieur Kessey—a kind man. I shall not give you my address, though—yet. You may give me yours, though, if you like." Paul hesitated. She understood, or thought she did. "I must go now," she said at once, stopping to go in a different direction. "Gwelo will need me. And, Monsieur Kessey, would you be kind enough to give me Métro fare. I have the fare all right, but I can save it to buy Gwelo food with."

"Certainly," Paul said and had soon given her ten francs.

"Thank you, thank you, Monsieur Kessey," she said earnestly. "I see that we shall be friends." She vanished into the crowd.

Chapter

Three

Dreams

It was mid-May now.

There were the three of them in the post-dawn chill — mother and her two children, daughters, all of them quietly dignified and smartly dressed — entering the little Church of the Blessed Ascension just off the tree-studded Place Blomet in the 8th Arrondissement. Outside the church, however, it had seemed hardly light, for the sun, still sickly and opaque, had somehow nestled down behind the ridges of purple cloud cover to the southeast where farther in the distance the great humps of the Louvre's roofs loomed awesome, umbrageous, as the streets lay silent, hushed.

But now mother and daughters were inside in the tender light of the church and Michelle, the elder child, age twelve, soft russet hair falling to her coat collar, suddenly found herself inhaling the acolytes' incense wafting down the nave as she grimly surveyed the scattered handful of seated or kneeling communicants. "I'm still sleepy, Mother!" she complained, whispering in the most agitated but cultured French. "Why did we have to come so early? *Je me couche tard.*"

City of Light

"*Shhhh*," uttered the mother. They had passed the rear of the nave now. "It's because," she went on in French, "that after taking you and Zoe to your school when we leave here, I must still be back at the hospital earlier than usual. I have two, not just one, silly women patients going into minor surgery who, with no basis in the world, dislike, or fear, their surgeons. But I thought I ought to be there to reassure them until the anesthesiologists take over. Besides, they are friends of mine—sort of." She was a comely, striking woman, a dark-haired beauty, but with an unhappy face—pale, drawn, preoccupied—yet, no matter, beautiful in a way to take the breath. It was also, however, an intelligent face—dominant over a body ripe enough yet lissome, shapely, almost sculpturesque.

"But why did Zoe and I have to come at all, Mother?" insisted Michelle.

The mother pondered the question, all the while playing games with her progeny, sad games, by which she hoped to veil her own misery. "I wanted you both here . . . ," she finally said, "in order . . . in order for you to pray with me."

"Pray for your patients—who are going to be operated on?" said Michelle.

"Of course not." Turning now and taking little Zoe, age eight, by the elbow, she steered them around to their right, behind and past the central pews, then to the left toward a small side chapel on the west wall of the church. "Your father is on a plane to Turkey," she whispered to them—her eyes darting nervously, deceptively—"where he has clients. Don't you want to say a prayer for him?"

"*I* do," said Zoe.

"Father said he'd be gone for eight or nine whole days," Michelle riposted. "He's always on a plane going somewhere and has little time for us—especially you, Mother. *C'est la vérité*." Even when, as now, merely whispering, Michelle's

French was precise, elegant, though her pronunciation, of vowels as well as consonants, was somehow attractively nasal. "*J'ai mal a la tête*," she added.

"Stop complaining, Michelle," said the mother. They had now arrived around at the little side chapel, situated beneath two puny, dusty light bulbs. "Come on, Zoe, honey — here," she said. "At least you want to say a prayer for your father. Let's all kneel." But momentarily, as she spoke, she somehow glanced away again, as if into some kind of black space, her tone uncertain, illusory, and once more faintly disingenuous. Zoe, though, was already yawning, while Michelle, feeling neglected, put down, and finally sorry for herself, sighed in resigned exasperation, as the three of them, crossing themselves, knelt before the small magenta statue of the Virgin Mary. The children's prayers were abrupt and brief. Their mother's supplications, however, were in soft, lengthy murmurs, the French diction delivered in deepest internal anguish and pleading.

"Dear God," she prayed, eyes tightly, fiercely, shut; cold, rigid fingers laced against quivering lips. "I have my innocent children here because they, too, even if indirectly, are involved. The drastic course my life has taken, if not changed, somehow curbed, will surely affect them — cruelly. And — oh, heavens — my husband, too. I cannot bear to think of it. I have never before needed Your presence as I do now. I'm still trying to get a hold on myself but it is difficult beyond any possible way I could describe it. It's as if misfortune, seizing on me, had shown me, as Mephistopheles did Faust, an utter bliss I could never have imagined existed — until it then turned on me, hurling me back into the darkest night of despair where I could no longer avoid facing the consequences of my acts, my sins. Then, like the devil himself, this wonderful bliss returns and mocks me in all of my agony and confusion. Now,

City of Light

except for Madame Chevalley, my long-time patient and now wise, honorable, and faithful friend—who does know more about life, though, than I ever shall—there is no one, absolutely no one, except You for me to turn to. I appeal to You, dear God! . . . It's the bliss, the bliss! I've never known anything like it before—this awful, this terrible, carnal love. I never knew such a powerful phenomenon existed. I feel like a dissolute junkie. I am hooked. Oh, how am I to contend with this affliction . . . this sweet addiction! It has utterly swept me away. Yet I call it a carnal love. But how can this be, when the other person is so upright and kind, so guileless, too, and sweet. He is a strange, hypnotic, young man—I say 'young,' for he is almost nine years my junior—and is as caught up in this frenzy as I am. And although he's never said it—for he's slow, deliberate, judgmental, about most things, and is very sincere—I truly believe he, as I, would, if he could, free himself, and me, in a split-second's time, had he, yes, only the power to do it." She paused now, however, as if to reflect on the statement. "At least I'm inclined to believe he would," she said, as though to convince herself of it. "For he, too, suffers. He did not force himself—or this calamity—on me. Oh, dear God, what has happened to me? It was I who was the aggressor—maybe not meaning to be, though. But he seemed curious only in a limited way. And certainly not sexually—he was a perfect gentleman. Yet he finally did everything but come right out and ask me about my immediate family and age. Why he would be interested in my age I've never understood— besides, I don't think I look my age, actually—but that somehow seemed to be certainly not the least of his interests. I've never understood this. Was he looking for a mother, a French mother, or what? Or was he looking for *anything*? He talked a lot about his deceased mother, back in the United States, which I never clearly understood. Dear God, this fine, attractive, young man is an enigma! Yet one I've come to think highly, passionately, about, even if I do wish I could truthfully say I was not the aggressor. Madame Chevalley, his landlady, however, seemed to recognize much of this before I did. She thinks he's really two people—if so, that may be why I'm attracted to him. Which also probably says something about me. At times, but not all the time, depending on how he feels, or what in a given interim has happened to him, he can indeed be one person one day and altogether another the next. Maybe it's foolish on my part, yes, but that trait in him has, I repeat, always intrigued me. This somehow seems to tie in with what I sense as his reluctant, and maybe unconscious, reliance on me. I'm not accustomed to that—even from my children, to say nothing of my husband. Oh, dear God, why am I burdening You with all this when, long ago, I should have gone to a priest and confessed everything. There's also the matter of Paul's passion—his physical passion. This, too, in its degree—and its timeliness—was new to me. It's something in his past that still affects him—maybe some kind of vague, indistinct (even to him) filial love. His mother died in her early forties, he says, yet he must have consulted her on a lot of things—just as he does me now. At times he seems constitutionally unable to control his thinking for long—i.e., about what he ought to be doing from month to month, even week to week, and what direction his life should be taking, indeed what he should, and should not, believe in. This is certainly the case—his strange, wavering composure—whenever he's in my presence. Sometimes he just sits there staring at me—whether I have any clothes on or not—as if hypnotized, or as if I were some grand sprite-goddess, or oracle, whose every word, to him, is bounden law. These are the few times when he seems to me to be slightly less admirable than he is capable of being. It's because at such times he seems so passive, so pliable, almost a weakling, as if he were virtually putty in my fingers — or over-whelmingly my inferior. Which of course he's not by any stan-dards one could possibly think up. He has an extraordinary mind, really — although you have to be around him for some time to see it — if, though, he only seemed more decisive. Dear God, he is a perfect mystery — I had not expected to encounter a man like this, ever. No man of any kind — I've thought only of my husband. I must repeat, though, there are often times when Paul seems unsure of himself — that's when he sits looking at me defensively, almost as if he feared me, but which I'm sure he doesn't. He may, though, fear what I represent to him — trouble. For both of us. I'm not one who is given to trying to see what awaits one in the future, but I do now wonder what will happen to Paul and me. The future does not augur well — I somehow feel it. Then why shouldn't I just walk away from it — if I have these strange premonitions, which I certainly do. He, though, seems lost also — that's when he sits looking at me defensibly, for then I have become the hungry, the greedy, aggressor again. Actually the possessor. He seems then, as I say, to have become a different man. He luxuriates in my possessing him, as if he's never had a friend in the world — since possibly his mother. I spoke of his different characters — well, now, he simply goes wild. Maybe, though, I shouldn't use that word, 'wild,' in Paul's context. He is an American Negro, You know, but comes from an excellent family, one of consider-able means as well. Accordingly, his education has been the best. I'm sorry to have to admit that I had never known there were so-called 'black' people of his, or his family's, caliber, or rank, to be found anywhere — especially in the United States, where their forebears had been brought over from Africa as slaves. He is extremely cultivated, genteel, when not in a silent, or morose mood, or feeling sorry for himself, which is sometimes the case. Yet somehow, to me — and maybe I myself am a more complex person than I'd imagined — those situations are when he is his handsomest and most utterly appealing. He takes my breath away. I forget about everything and thereby become my own worst enemy — sinning woefully, and unforgivably, in Your sight. Yet often, actually too often, when we're alone together like this, and have had a surfeit of one another, it's then he begins to put all manner of questions to me, and on the widest range of subjects — something he did, though, on the very same day we first met. On Africa, for instance — not a very pleasant, or profitable, matter for me — but on which he's perfectly daft. I know nothing at all about Africa. He knows everything — studies it day and night. Why then would he ask me, of all people, about it? But he's like that — beyond any understanding — and asks questions about everything, then sits there listening in awe as I try to answer them . . . ineffectually."

Cécile stopped now, temporarily, opened her eyes, and looked around her — for her children. They were nowhere to be seen. She refused, however, to forgo, or even shorten, this her brave but necessitious — and enraptured — bout with self-purgation as she genuinely sought help from none other than her Deity.

"I do my best, dear Lord, to remind myself of the enormity, as well as peril, of my present life. I have more than once gotten up the courage to at least start to do what would end my relationship with Paul. But then I eventually surrender to my need — I refer to a need far beyond the physical — for Paul. I feel for him deeply. I have even on occasion, when I couldn't sleep at night for thinking of my life with him — and when Georges, my wonderful and so successful husband, is in Borneo, or Sweden, or California, or some such place on business — I have telephoned Paul and told him it was time we became brave and stopped seeing each other. The alacrity with which he had agreed has surprised and saddened me. I would suddenly feel alone without him and wouldn't let him go—this from a woman with a vigorous, confident husband and two extremely spirited daughters. One night during one of these conversations Paul told me, only half-jokingly, that he was afraid of me. It was only when he sensed my shock and puzzlement over the telephone that he laughed, quietly. It unnerved me, though. I finally asked him why he was afraid of me. He said he didn't know—that it was just a feeling. Then he laughed again, quietly, and asked if I was afraid of him. I had never thought of that. I told him so, and that I didn't know. His only reply, with the same small laugh, was that maybe we both should be afraid—of each other. Again shocked, I finally asked him again why, and he made the same answer as before—that it was just a feeling. I wanted to cry, but I don't know why. Dear God, I need You more than I ever have in my life. I need not only Your mercy and forgiveness but Your guidance—in finding a way out. Would that You need merely say to me: 'Go and sin no more.' But that is at the very heart of the problem. I would long ago have eagerly begged Your forgiveness if only I had felt I could actually go and sin no more. I cannot, however, even today, truthfully say that I'm capable of that. Neither—despite his internal warnings, his 'feelings'—can I say it of Paul. Without each other we both feel utterly alone. He hasn't said this, and may not realize it, but it's true. That is what is so frightening about it! . . ." In her panic there was a tear on her left cheek. "Oh, dear God!—*j'ai des difficultés, j'ai peur!* . . . I am afraid!"

She opened her eyes again—only to see little Zoe standing at her side observing her curiously, anxiously. "What's the matter with you, Mother?" she said. "What are you crying for?"

Cécile came to at once—staring at Zoe, in fright. "Where is Michelle, Zoe?"

"She's asleep over there." Zoe turned and pointed. "In that faraway pew against the wall — see her? She studied late last night — she's sleepy. May we leave now, Mother?"

"Yes, dear," Cécile sighed. "I shall take you and Michelle to your school now."

"Michelle wants to go home."

"No, no — she'll wake up once she gets to school." Cécile took Zoe by the hand and led her over to Michelle, slumped in a far pew in the midst of the kneeling supplicants for whom a quiet mass was in progress. Cécile all the while was conscious of, familiar with, the two aisles leading up to the transept's intricate façade and statuary, the ornate ceiling rising above the stained-glass windows which now filtered natural light through the stilted images of holy martyrs. Little Zoe herself now yawned as her mother shook Michelle awake and escorted them both out of the church.

Outside, Michelle looked sleepily at Cécile. "Why do you look so upset, Mother?" she said.

They were headed down the street to their car. Cécile was irritated, but also still flustered, at the repetition of the question Zoe had asked. "I . . . I was thinking . . . of your father," she lied. They climbed into her sleet Citroën and drove away.

So went, immediately hereinbefore the omnisciently rendered showing, accounting, of what can only be described as severe cathartic fall-out. Two hapless humans, Cécile's and Paul's encounter, indeed collision, had borne a fiery fruit. One which in the future would be almost impossible to contain. Or would disaster strike first? Certainly a possibility. But how, one asks, did the intense heat of it all come to be generated — originally? Quite simply. And at no great length in the telling. Nor can, this time, the cause be dubbed "fate." There was rather a kind of lethargic meandering, and therefore all the more sinister stacking of cards, as it were—when, on that memorable bleak wintry midday some five months before, Madame Chevalley had, willy-nilly, been cast, as a wild card so to speak, in the role of crisis-patient. Crisis indeed. But the patient of whom? Of one Dr. Cécile Stephanie Cambon-Fournier, age 38, respected internist and professor, wife of the international steel-works design engineer, Georges Fournier, also professor.

Then, however, had occurred that prophetic meeting, born of sudden emergency, signaling the entry in the drama of this strange and striking man, age 29. A man, yes, a man mostly silent and, it seemed, habitually grave, an alien omnipresence of blurred African lineage (and lodger in Madame Chevalley's not quite shabby-genteel pension) who, though, bore the handicap, of a strange set of vagaries—e.g., a seeming adolescence, hesitancy, crypto-dependency, even sonlike worship of women older than he (almost a stipulation), often not without the bizarre, subtle, if near-compulsive, cachet of libido. It seemed the same deep Saturn complication all over again.

But now came the overhanging "emergency," consisting in what was at first thought to be a coronary event—Madame's. That wintry day, then, complaining of dire chest pains, she had been brashly, ineptly, rushed by her gloomy, taciturn, if very caring and frightened, lodger to her physician's office—nearer than any readily available hospital—in a frantic ramshackle taxi painted or splashed a rusty burnt orange. However, in short, Madame's "coronary" turned out to be a false alarm—rather a massive acid reaction to an overdose of Prussian turnips. That, though, was amply enough to change the history of two already off-center lives searching for something—they knew not what—which they both thought likely, though, to transform their very disparate existences into a new Golden Age, an Eden, a sunny Garden of the Hesperides. It was in fact, then, fate after all—riding like the stallions of the Apocalypse in an old, grimy, rickety, orange-spattered taxicab bearing down on the encounter of the two "star-crossed" ingenues, who were never to forget this day.

But now, alas, five months later, the piper had arrived—so soon, already?—to collect his miserable payment and Cécile now heard, and felt, from within the biblical verdict: "Physician, heal thy self." (Luke 4:23) It was not only an admonition but a challenge—this well after all her attempts at psychic self-treatment had failed, utterly. She finally then, *in extremis*, had gone to Dr. God himself, now repeatedly, even, at last, once with her two children, to His office in the little Church of the Blessed Ascension. It was here, throwing herself on the mercy of the court, as it were, that she candidly admitted to Him that her malady was no longer a matter of life and death but of flesh and the devil. There, yes, she, unburdening her soul, had confessed all, everything, to this the tribunal of her last resort. To no avail. The Throne's response—silence.

It was two days following her passionate encounter with God that the shock of Cécile's hopeless predicament had finally metamorphosed into a kind of groping, dazed, tedious ennui. After a forenoon with patients at the hospital, she was now in her beautiful dark Citroën on, perforce, a mission of high family duty, responsibility, if not mercy, one, however, she in no way relished, particularly at a time of mute crisis in her own life. Yet it was an obligation—so she regarded it—that she could no longer defer, one she felt that had been imposed on her, maybe unwittingly, even in absentia, by Monsieur André Cambon, her late father. So today it was his, and her family's, business she was about. Alone, driving the car up Boulevard

City of Light

Saint-Michel, headed over to the city's 7th Arrondissement, she would have preferred being on her way home. The afternoon was overcast, but the May air balmy, the moving traffic aggressive, if not slightly mad, even if it would soon jell into a study in solid immobility. By now, though, she was already into heavy thoughts — and, at the moment, not about Paul. The pressing question today involved her harried, irascible, old Aunt Lili.

Yet, she thought, wasn't she, Cécile, really making too serious a matter of someone else's hardships, someone who, in consanguinity, was no closer to her than her aunt — Lili Cambon — her father's brother's widow? Indeed, even now her thoughts of Aunt Lili were already perilously close to drifting. Drifting to make way for her own more pressing, hazardous problems. She would have much preferred, from this day on, spending the rest of her life, literally, in her own household, with her children, with her husband, too, had he only been able to find more time for his family and less for the professional demands, attainments, honors, he so regularly received. Yet she knew Georges loved her — because he often told her so. She believed him, too. Why, she thought, wouldn't he love her? She of all people fully realized her pluses, strengths — beauty, mind, profession, breeding. Had not other men, men of culture, means, station, for as long as she could remember, looked at her, sighed, and shaken their heads? She had, moreover, yes, married exceptionally well — to the gifted and still ambitious engineer Georges Fournier, seven years her senior and once divorced. But until now it had only been when she thought of her children, her two daughters, that she grew wistful with love — putting aside an occasional longing, when daydreaming, that she might have a third child, a boy, but now this was no longer as wise as in former years, her obstetrician had said, and she had, if pensively, accepted it. Once, however,

106

afterwards, she had mentioned her erstwhile wish to Georges. He seemed interested and sympathetic, kissed her eyes, cooed in her ear, but the subject never rose again, even in their love sessions. It made her wonder about his real feelings. And then her wondering ramified: Had he ever had another woman since their marriage? She would never believe it, she told herself. Besides, she was not the jealous type, she thought, and certainly not spiteful. Moreover, she was positive — though in grave error — that she knew Georges. He was clear-headed and straightforward and, in their lives together, quite uncomplicated as well, though extremely intricate, she was sure, in his highly abstruse profession and business dealings. He was also proud and admitted it — a stout, blond, good-natured man (so he seemed) who liked food, wine, and the musical theatre — he would say, "Why should I be falsely modest?" He would laugh: "My wife is the most beautiful woman in Paris, who, besides, has given me two lovely, and very bright, daughters whom we both adore, and I've made, and am making, money. Ha! — lots of it. Why, then, shouldn't I be a proud man? In fact, I'm so proud I still quote my dear old papa who said, when he was rich, he'd gotten where he was by struggle and that's exactly what it would take to get it away from him. Ha, ha! Ah, but too bad, too bad — he was afterwards wiped out in the absolutely ghastly market plungings after Hitler and the war. He lived twenty more years and died bitter. *But still proud.*"

Cécile, now stopping the car for a red light, wondered why her mind was dredging up all these strange and not particularly happy thoughts. She stubbornly denied any problem with Georges. He loved her, she loved him, so why did she insist on sensing difficulties? she asked herself. It certainly could not be Paul. He and Georges — with all of Georges's accomplishments — could not possibly be mentioned in the same breath. In no way could they be considered on the same playing field. In her mind they were even two wholly separate concepts. Then why was it she never thought of Georges when she was with Paul — but, almost to the exclusion of everything else, invariably, constantly, thought of Paul when she was with Georges? How could this be? she asked, plagued. She doubted now she would ever answer the question to her satisfaction. The only clue that occasionally came to her was her feeling that Paul needed her, somehow depended on her. But for what? This was as far as she ever got. It was not, she was convinced, her silly answers to his silly questions. She had never even been sure it was solely her answers he sought, but rather a testing of himself by the intricacies of his questions, questions whose answers he possibly knew better than she ever could. Besides, they were even sometimes put to her in the throes of one of their trysts — an experience, alas, in which she was almost always the vulnerable one, her mind in cruel spasms of delirium, ecstasy, when she herself, aloud, piteously cried out to *him* for answers. At such times she knew, yes, confessed, that Georges was somehow cordoned off in an innermost and sequestered cranny of her mind — or, worse, temporarily forgotten. It was a state of things she disliked acknowledging to herself, yet knew it to be the truth. In addition to all this, now God had abandoned her. She was certain, and shaken, appalled, that this had happened to her. Her pinioned mind seemed in a vise, unable to function, as, almost by rote, she continued driving the Citroën west — with the sun now in and out of the clouds — on the Avenue de Tourville, where she slowed, then stopped, for another traffic light. At last, though, out of immediate necessity, her thoughts began to deal with what she must face upon arrival at Aunt Lili's. At best she considered it an irksome chore, at worst a further pitiless assault on her already overloaded nervous system. Nonetheless, it was an obligation which had, at least for the moment, to be attended to.

Cyrus Colter

She was actually coming to see her venerable aunt, who was soon to leave Paris, to say good-bye. The way, though, the enfeebled, churlish, old lady was remonstrating with anyone who would listen, one would have thought she was departing her beloved France to go spend the balance of her days among the Hottentots. Instead she would be going a mere one hundred and fifty kilometers, ninety miles, from Paris – to Reims. But there, alas, she would live with an erratic, ne'er-do-well, divorced daughter, Blanche, whom she had always loved, yet seldom admired. But old Lili's misery went far deeper than that. It was the course, and the curse, of history, the twin scourges of her life, which now, in her final phase, she must face. Indeed even Cécile could at least partially visualize, as well as feel, the weight of it, conjuring up memories of her own girlhood in her parents' handsome Paris household in the late fifties and early sixties when André Cambon, her father, would often talk of the terrible war times and their immediate and vengeful aftermath. She could never forget the grisly episodes recounted and the opinions expressed, many about Aunt Lili and what André Cambon had described as "the great tragedy of Aunt Lili's life."

Lili Cambon, now 86, and in religion extremely devout, had, for the last forty years and more, well known her share of desperation, sorrow – a time, according to André, when she had been made to suffer "a particularly harsh and ignominious widowhood." The beautiful child Cécile had learned much of the larger history as well, this often at her parents' dinner table: Aunt Lili's husband, Hugh Guy Cambon, who had begun his spectacular rise, an astonishing career, as an ambitious young French lawyer, now seemed to old Lili in retrospect – over the span of nearly sixty years – a virtual god no less, who had risen in pre-war conservative French politics to become, in the mid-thirties, a cabinet minister in Pierre Laval's second premiership. But the highly dramatic, and simultaneous, rise of France's next-door neighbor, Adolph Hitler's Third Reich, instead of filling Monsieur Cambon and his rightist colleagues with apprehension, if not downright fear, for their country, somehow imbued far too many of them with an almost obsessive admiration, even envy, for the disciplined, jack-booted Germans and their splenetic führer. When war finally came, however, and Hitler's great *Wehrmacht blitzkrieg* struck France, Hugh Cambon at once enlisted in, of course, the French army, fought valorously for his country, and was wounded twice and decorated three times. Yet when the temporarily victorious Germans established the new puppet Vichy government for France, they elevated former premier Laval to head it (always of course subject to their own harsh oversight) with still-considerable dictatorial powers. At once then, Laval brought to his side many of his former aides and colleagues, including his brilliant protégé Hugh Cambon. The rest was adamant, immovable history. Three years later, on the eventual defeat of Hitler by the Allies and the overthrow of the Vichy government and its record of ghastly crimes against the French people, Laval was, at once, tried for treason, convicted, and shot. Inevitably, of course, in this inexorable process, his stellar lieutenant, Monsieur Hugh Guy Cambon, now exhausted, despairing in his incarceration, and ill, was soon, as he well realized, to follow his leader, for it was Judgment Day, and the verdict, predictably, was death. Yet the carrying-out of death was unseemly, botched. When at long last, fettered, then tied to the execution stake, listening to the hollow roll of the military drums, Cambon was shot by the firing squad, he first lurched forward, then slumped, yet somehow though still conscious, writhing, moaning, at last whispering his wife Lili's name, all until he was finally, mercifully, dispatched by an officer's heavy pistol at point-blank range in a grisly *coup de grace.* Thus Madame Lili Cambon was left destitute, forever denounced and stigmatized as the widow of a traitor, with a family comprised of a fourteen-year-old son and three daughters scarcely older. Therefore to this day, indeed Cécile's present visit, old Lili remained as embittered, unforgiving, as ever, savagely unrepentant as well, as she had been from the very start, especially against all those who (and, as she put it, the "effete" political philosophy they preached) had brought her husband down. Now soon *she* would die. And she knew it.

Having been driving the car almost in a state of abstraction, Cécile became suddenly aware that she had arrived in the Rue Blois, her Aunt Lili's street and location, and she needed a place to park. This eventually accomplished, she found herself on foot making the trek up the steep sidewalk to a drab, yellow, apartment building on the north, hilly intersection of the Rue Fontaine and the Rue Blois. Her dear father, she thought, in whatever rolling Elysian fields he now dwelt, must be watching and pleased at her faithfulness. She was fulfilling his implied assignment, mission, that Aunt Lili not be permitted to leave Paris without this proper, well-wishing visit with promises of future ones to come, no matter wherever the old lady might be. These thoughts somehow strengthened Cécile, remembering, as she did, her beloved father just now as she stood at the door, the threshold of Aunt Lili's musty parlor, to confront the never-failing inquiry about the "darling" children, their absolutely unaccountable absence, etc., etc. ("Why, why, Cécile dear, did they not accompany you? *Comment vont-elles?*") It was almost a ritual; whereupon Cécile, ever forbearing, indulgent—her father always in mind—would be obliged to withhold the truth, viz., that, although it was a Saturday, both Michelle and little Zoe, but especially Michelle, had expressed a definite preference not to come. They invariably found the scrawny, white-haired, old denizen—who, moreover, to them, did not always "smell nice" — not so much boring, or unintelligible, as she was downright scary. It was her constant wild-eyed fury, her ranting about her life, her misfortunes, and those, under the present and foreseeable governments, of "poor, disastrous France."

So now the old woman, tall, gaunt, frail, withered, seemed somehow out of breath as, her cane in her right hand, she faced Cécile in the door of the darkish second-floor apartment, seeming only now to realize that the parlor window shades were still down at 2:20 in the afternoon. "Oh, do come in, dear Cécile," she said, her voice raspy as she extended a quivering left hand. "It's so dark in here, isn't it? *Qu'est-ce qui se passe?* Let me go lift the blinds, too. Oh, I'm so pleased to see you! I was elated to get your telephone call that you were coming." Then came the unfailing question, indeed demand, about the children, all as she hobbled around the room raising the ancient window shades.

Cécile, earnest, restrained, lovely to look at as she tried to smile, wore a chic turquoise tweed suit with a Chinese-red scarf at the throat. But today no jewelry except her wedding ring — of heavy diamonds.

Old Lili had soon finished with the shades and, pointing now, said, "Sit there on the sofa, Cécile dear. I'll go back in a moment and make tea for us. Oh, you look so lovely — and your marvelous figure, it's perfection. Do you diet?"

"No, Aunt Lili — although I try to be careful. Georges might notice."

"Oh, you perfect couple — it's a marriage made in heaven. And then those beautiful children. Ah, how fortunate you are, Cécile — some, I'm sure, have expected it would spoil you, but it hasn't. You're as sweet as you ever were — and that's since your birth." She sighed. "Your father idolized you so, as well he might. How sorry I am Michelle and sweet little Zoe couldn't come. I may not see them again soon. I shall be going to Reims, you know—possibly in two weeks. How sad, very sad, it makes me to have to sit here and tell you what is the truth: that I have no idea whatever my life will be like there." She was near tears.

"I know how you feel," said Cécile, seated on the tattered sofa, "but I'm sure Blanche will be very glad to have you there with her now. She must worry about your living alone. And Reims is not far."

"Oh, no, no, Blanche does not want me." Feebly, Lili retreated to a straight chair. "That's the reality, dear. No more than I want to go. Oh, it's true."

"Aunt Lili, it's the best thing, the only thing, for you to do. And Reims is so close, actually. You're not leaving for Marseilles, you know." Cécile tried to laugh. "It's not the end of the world!"

The remark caused old Lili a swift intake of breath. "End of the world—my God. My world ended years ago—with the death of my martyred husband. Wait till you attain my age, Cécile honey." Inexplicably then, using her cane as she sat, she began poking at a naked spot of sunshine on the frazzled carpet. "But poor Blanche—yes, she still puts up a front and insists that I come. What's got into her? But in going to Reims to live I shall no longer have my privacy, my solitude. Maybe, though, I'm only looking at my own troubles—a mother shouldn't do that to her children, for they have their problems, too. I do hope I won't be too much of a burden. Blanche has had a very hard time—luck has been heavily against her—so she can't really afford, no matter that she loves me, and I know she does, as I do her, an additional burden on her. I have a definite suspicion she moved to Reims for possibly a better job, and also lower prices—Paris is so expensive. And she has no husband now. That blackguard lives in Le Havre with the strumpet he took up with — she *must* be one — who has a child of her own. Probably by him. Oh, poor Blanche — she's so gullible; how could she have ever taken up with a creature like that? Life has dealt badly with her. Much of it, though — I dislike to say — is of her own making. Her poor father would cry out from the grave."

"We shall miss you, Aunt Lili," said Cécile. "And I hope you realize you have a friend in me — I won't see you suffer. We shall keep in touch — so don't worry about being a burden on anyone. You won't be. Father would have me see to that. I'm also going to bring you into the office before you leave Paris and give you a thorough physical examination. So rid yourself of the feeling that you're alone — you're not."

Old Lili was crying. "You sweet girl — you're an angel, that's what you are. I shall never be able to thank you enough. Oh, bless you — your father, dear André, my Hugh's younger brother, is looking down on you from heaven and approving your great heart and your loyalty to the Cambon family." Old Lili stood. "Now would you like to come with me to the kitchen where I shall brew us some tea?" Cécile rose and followed her, all the while wishing she could escape and go home to her own children.

By the time they had returned with their tea and gingersnaps to the parlor, old Lili had launched into a diatribe against present-day French politics, comparing it, harshly, negatively, with former times and her husband's zealous involvement in it. "Just think, Cécile, dear," she said, nibbling on a cookie, "I was already a widow when you were born. And there has never been a single moment since my husband's death that, by deed or even thought, I have ever betrayed him or what he stood for. He was no Nazi! He was a French patriot — wounded and decorated in battle against the Germans when they attacked France. But after we lost to the Germans,

Laval later pressed him to return to government and help get a better deal for the French people. My Hugh was a conscientious and idealistic man — thinking only of the welfare of France. He wanted so badly to help restore the country after all it had been through. He had the highest hopes, indeed expectations, for France — this whether the Germans won or lost the war. He thought only of France — was motivated solely by the deepest, purest, patriotism. Oh, dear God, rest his tired, noble soul! . . ." Again she fought tears.

Cécile stumbled for words, finally, though sympathetically, saying nothing.

"And those vengeful scoundrels — disguised as a French court of law — who ordered his death, every one of them now dead and in hell, God be praised" — she crossed herself — "cared nothing for France, nothing at all, but only for themselves and their warped, misguided prejudices, their blindness, and cowardly hearts. These, mind you, though, were the same people whose children now run — that is, *ruin* — the country. And this includes many of those who now mistakenly consider themselves French conservatives! Holy Jesus. Look at France today if you have any doubts. Actually, by and large, the French people no longer rule their country. They have abdicated to the huge raft of outsiders, aliens, the non-French, who have descended on the hapless country like swarms, a plague, of deadly nightflies. Look how the Jews have come back in hordes. There are seven-hundred thousand of them now! This of course was to be expected — when all the restraints went off and they were once more loosed on the poor French people. Oh! It's too frightful to think of. Add to that, then, the Algerians and other North Africans. And the Arabs. The Turks, too. Plus the Bulgarians now. The government must have let all this variegated mass of lower humanity come in on some kind of open-ended work visas, I presume, that gives them

access to jobs which ought to go to French citizens. And then—
oh, my God!—there are the blacks, the heinous blacks, the
scourge of the earth! Hordes of them—not only from sub-
equatorial Africa, but from all over the world. It's frightening! They of course are the worst of all—dirty, ignorant, lazy,
shiftless, who breed like flies and have absolutely no moral
instincts whatever, which also means, of course, that many, if
not most, of them are infected with that dread disease AIDS.
All of them, by their very nature, their genes, are thieves and
murderous criminals. Holy Father!—help us. It's terrifying!
Poussin and his French National Party have been trying to
awaken the country to the perils of this unholy influx of the
world's biological lepers, misfits, and riffraff; but the liberal
politicians, and, as I say, even some of the so-called 'conservatives,' plus all their various factions and camp-followers—
always abetted, of course, by the ever-present Jews, their
influence, money, and other ill-gotten gains too numerous to
mention—have made it almost impossible for Poussin, a truly
farsighted and courageous politician, to get his message, his
dire warnings, across. They've cursed and vilified him—even
called him the new Hitler, the French Hitler—until people are
now really beginning to believe it and are turning a deaf ear to
what he's been trying to tell the country. The French public is
so credulous and apathetic that it will tolerate almost anything. The streets and boulevards of Paris furnish more than
ample proof of this. It's a tragedy—or a deadly comedy. It's
nothing any more now to see a beautiful French girl strolling
down the Champs-Elysées on the arm of a big, smug, grinning
black with a bright-red beret slanted off his bullet-bur head.
And you well know, of course, that things are not just going to
stop there—when they get to where they're going. I'm sure
you've seen it yourself, Cécile—it's not at all an uncommon
sight today, French women horribly degrading themselves

beyond all possible redemption. And imagine *sleeping* with one of those black apes. How can women, white women, bring themselves to do such a thing? Something must be done! . . .The people should rise up! I know, because I lost my husband, a wonderful man, a selfless French patriot and hero, in the struggle to make France free and all it is capable of being. But France turned on him — yes, yes, it was the French *people*! — and destroyed him. Therefore — and I hate to say it — they deserve what they're getting. But the time will come, and it's not far off, when things will have gotten so bad that they'll finally wake up, come to their senses, and radical changes will occur in this potentially great country. I won't live to see it, but you, Cécile, will — you can even help bring it about. You owe it to your great family and its history to become active in the struggle to change things, save France, save it for the new French people — who will have created it!"

Frightened Cécile's face was white as a sheet.

Old Lili was oblivious. Reaching for her cane now, she fought to rise from the chair, before pulling herself to her full, somehow indomitable, height and, speaking with a harsh, hoarse, quavering voice, laden with all her pent-up emotions, she said: "I shall soon go to meet my husband, but I remain adamant in my prophesy that he did not die for nothing, for no purpose! He died for what France once was and for what it is capable of becoming again! *Demain, demain — ou apres-demain!*"

Cécile panicked. Yet she was so weak, aghast, so stricken by what she had heard and experienced, it was scarcely evident — except in her lovely, tormented face, which was still deathly white. For a moment she did not even try to — could not — speak. At last then, however, she too rose, though glancing furtively, evasively, at old Lili, and, hands fearfully shaking, took her purse up off the sofa where she had sat. "I must go now, Aunt Lili" — her voice a tremolo, almost trilling — "Good-bye, good-bye. . . .I shall tell the children you asked about them. Good-bye. . . ." She wandered, drifted, almost floated, to the door, but then, as if suddenly awakening to reality, opened it and fled down the steps for her life.

Later that evening, she was still in shock. Yet somehow, in a longish, rambling, incoherent, mental retrospect, she was trying, as best she knew how, to make out, at least at this distance in hours to descry, the point of her whole life through the wild prism of the afternoon just spent at Aunt Lili's. To no avail. Nothing responded. Was it her own thunderclap of fright and surprise at the experience undergone? she wondered. Soon her mind was vacant altogether — before, again, she began her spasmodic trembling. She had been trying, straining, to assuage the fears, then, by embarking on this present harried study of her own strange life — strange, that is, in the last five months — only, yes, to find it all an exercise in a kind of hollow, drained, phobia of frustration. She felt as if her private vista had taken on the bizarre likeness, of, say, the barest Arabian plain or the white sand treks to a Buzaymah. Or a Hindu Kush. Or even the vast towering steeples fixing the grandeur of the Himalayas. Chaos. Such were the disjoined, yet apparently valid, puzzlings which had assailed her hourly since her return from what could only be referred to as that hellhouse up on the Rue Blois occupied by one frightful old harridan euphemistically called "Aunt Lili." Cécile, in bed alone, began to pray now, at 9:50 P.M., then remembered her unavailing pleas to Dr. God and felt as if she had been excommunicated. Yet, at least, she insisted on praying for blessed sleep.

She therefore now reached under her pillow, brought out a strange, mystifying object, and minutely examined it. At last, as if duly expecting some onslaught by Genghis Khan, she, still quite painstakingly, fitted the object onto her beautiful head. She had thus, in fact, donned a deceased great-grandmother's white silken nightcap—though it was formed more like a Trojan helmet—for which she had spent most of this ominous evening searching, and finally unearthing, having heard it said in the Cambon family, even if apocryphally, that the "dainty" headpiece brought instant drowsiness, "lassitude," until then came sleep and "most pleasant" dreams. One such saying, then, conveyed to her mind a second one, also from a past Cambon generation, viz.: "We are very near to awaking whenever we dream that we dream." But soon she began to feel some deft, subtle locomotion of, as it were, the total brain issue—just as, she remembered, vaguely thought of, the children, Michelle and Zoe, whose bedroom was far down the hall of the large, lavish apartment. She realized, and she was glad, that for them sleep was no object, no issue. It just came—often—with a child's heedlessness and for-granted-taking, like a freshet in spring or a huge snow drift in winter. Ah, bless them, she thought. As for Georges, he was—if she remembered correctly—somewhere in Turkey.

But already now something had begun to stir, gestate. As she lay on her back in the bed she soon found herself shifting, slightly, her lovely legs around, as if they sought—in expectation of some fierce upheaval, or difficult and challenging athletic feat—improved, stabilizing positioning. But, strangely, it had already begun—the "lassitude," duly predicted, yes, had already arrived, and there now seemed—a paradox—a complete absence of athletic strain or imminence of upheaval. Her mind, rather her blurred cognitive functioning, seemed already to have moved, unobtrusively, away from her, even if in no recognizable direction, then, like some great last gasp on earth before surrendering, it slid gently to-and-fro, all the while retreating, as if softly on tiptoes withdrawing, from

City of Light

what could only have been solid terra firma. Then it was, at long last, though she still could not have told how long, hardly maybe at all, like some guileful narcotization, or perhaps a whole thirty minutes in the process, that she finally began to sink — with no intuition whatever, no presaging, certainly no merciful warning of the dream-dire events to come. No matter; it was now she plainly saw him, as well as, especially, his grim, jutting jaw. Yet somehow now he was behaving almost nonchalantly, until, as if suddenly about to bare his fangs, he approached their table, hers and Paul's, in their familiar, often-frequented, little indoor café on the Rue la Suisse in this beautiful, sequestered, little town of Fantes only a 45-minute drive out from Paris in her Citroën. Now, her dream-heart congealing, recoiling, she recognized him in a flash, which was all the time she had, yet all she needed, although never having seen him in person before, but, now quickly, close up, he was the very spitting image of his bold likenesses in the newspapers and those, as suddenly, thrown on her evening television screen. Yet, now in the flesh he was somewhat less tall, though not squat either, but clearly well-tailored even with his slightly bowed legs which, however, in no way detracted from his average solid heft. It was the countenance, though, which was memorable — heavy, beefy, darkly reddish, most always harsh, the eyes never still. So, she thought at once, her heart crazily drumming, this was the famous (or, depending on one's politics, infamous), Hector Duquesne, No. 2 man, or chief deputy, to none other than the quiet, contained, yet fanatically, savagely, determined leader of the France for the French National Party by means of which he, its leader, daily vowed to become the "savior" of France — Aunt Lili's idol, yes — Charles Poussin, Hector Duquesne, then, was his sworn vassal, Cécile well knew, and now the vassal was approaching their table. *Why?* She felt numb.

But to go back. The usual relaxed atmosphere, as well as the desirable attractiveness, of this "their," Cécile's and Paul's, café had apparently somehow swum up inside the white silken nightcap of Cécile's dream-consciousness long before the present moment, for she had not only not recognized but had not even seen Chief Deputy Duquesne sitting at a table across the room with another man, perhaps one of his FFF party cohorts. Nor, of course, did she or Paul notice the reaction of the two men upon their entrance or as Paul pulled out her chair for her before the smiling waiter, to whom the lovers were no strangers, reached their table. Duquesne and his tall, spruce companion looked on with shocked, sulphurous gazes, which soon turned to hateful stares. Cécile and Paul were, of course, oblivious as they ordered their usual fare—a croissant apiece and hot chocolate. Paul seemed in some kind of quiet but wrought-up ecstasy—head high, lips slightly parted—even as now, when not talking or smiling, his eyes first smoldering, then alight, watching her. Finally, though, he looked around the cheerful room, but as if he had never seen it, before seeming to succumb to the grip of some exalted euphoria—Duquesne and the other man, like two diamondback rattlers in the grass, watching; deadly dream actors in a preternatural dream. Soon Paul, his eyes searching Cécile's face, said, "Sometimes, especially of late, you seem reluctant to talk about many of the questions I put to you . . . pester you with, I should confess." He tried to smile. "Why is this?"

Cécile was serious, almost grave. "I don't know the answers to most of them," she said. "I don't think many people would. They are not really questions—they're invitations to render a disquisition on whatever subject you've chosen: like, 'What makes the world go around?' If we weren't serious friends, real friends, I'd think you were having fun at my expense. I'm not unaccustomed to questions, Paul, dear—

from patients and students – but most of them are answerable, if not by me certainly by someone who knows more on the subject than I do."

"And there aren't many of those." Paul laughed.

"What do you mean when you ask, 'What makes the world go around?'"

"I'm not sure." He pondered the question briefly. "I know that makes me seem like an ass. But I guess I'm mostly interested in who's in charge of things; so, the person or thing who controls the world like that must at least have something to do with some of the things that happen on the earth he's spinning like a top. There are some unusual things that go on. Do you know there are people born on this earth who hardly ever – I mean *ever* – have one single day or night of happiness. Then they die and rot into nothingness. Who's in charge of all that? Maybe we ought to want to find out who it is that's spinning this earth around like clockwork – *if* that's what really happens. In Christopher Columbus's day, you know, most thought the earth was flat – but if we knew who can do, or does do, these things, maybe that would give us a clue to something else. I don't know what – but perhaps something would happen. Are you unhappy a lot of the time? *I* am. Ever since my mother died. But I can't say I was happy as a lark even when she was here. I didn't like some of the things she did, some of the things she believed in. She even thought light-skinned blacks were better than the dark-skinned. What do you think about that general proposition?"

The waiter arrived with the croissants and hot chocolate. But Cécile seemed unaware of the interruption, her confused, equivocating eyes staring in Paul's face.

"Do you see what I mean?" he said when the waiter had gone. "How do you react to what my mother thought?"

Cécile began shaking her head, impetuously, in great

irritation. "Oh, I know nothing about those things, nothing at all. Paul, why do you ask such vexing questions!"

They were speaking French, and he could not translate 'vexing.' "Let me ask my question differently," he said. "Suppose *my* skin were jet black instead of tan, or sepia, or copper, or bronze, or whatever — what would you think? . . . What would you think of *me*?"

Cécile was angry, furious. "Paul, your questions are unfair! . . . I know nothing, absolutely nothing, about this subject. Why you brought it up, I don't understand — you were talking about your mother. I'm not versed in those things. That's why you should not discuss them with me — it's not fair, I tell you. *Si la tête me tournait comme une toupie!*"

Paul gave ground at once. He had never seen her so excited, aroused, or vulnerable. "I beg your pardon, Cécile, honey," he said at once. "I'm sorry about these nutty subjects I bring up, and far too often, but I'll try to be more careful from here on, honestly I will." He was clearly contrite.

At once she melted, became penitent, embarrassed. "Oh, forgive me," she said. "I'm sorry I overreacted. Please forget it — will you?"

"Of course, of course. But you've done nothing wrong. Really, do I bore you?"

She smiled and blushed in the same instant. "How can you say that? What a question — after today. I shall be thinking about today for a long time — until there is another day. Do you understand me? I'm sure you do. I shall be thinking about it even as we go home — with you still in the car right there beside me."

"Bless you," he said, gazing out a far window of the café. Today, dream-day, there was the lightest dusting of snow in the adjacent vacant lot. Also an intercity bus was slowly climbing the sharp street incline. "I need you," he finally added, even though it seemed apropos of nothing.

She smiled. "May I, then, turn the tables and ask *you* a question? You speak of your needs — almost as if that's peculiar to you. I need help, too, though. I have no one to advise me. Except possibly Madame Chevalley. And, appreciating the stakes, she is loath to do it and I don't blame her. It's also clear by now that God doesn't hear me — or is so offended by my life that He no longer cares. What are we eventually to do about his liaison of ours? Paul, it can't go on forever. Think of how I daily betray my family. How shameful of me. Tell me, does our relationship, especially what has been my hungrily aggressive part in it, seem to you something showing me in a not-very-sane light?"

"No, I don't quite think that," he said. "I could ask the same question of myself, you know."

"Please do, then." Her face was anxious.

He took it for a joke, though, and laughed outright — as across the way Duquesne sat observing, with his upper lip in a perfect vaudeville-villain's snarl. "Indeed," said Paul, "there are times when I can claim no sanity whatever."

But now Cécile's mind was somehow already far away, even if only a mere two city blocks, for on such occasions as now she could not avoid a feeling of dread at possibly having left some personal (identifying) article, say an item of clothing, or some jewelry trinket, in the hotel room of their tryst, though, realistically, there was little such peril. Paul, noticing her deep absorption, became himself momentarily silent as he sat watching her and trying to ready her mind — which was still back in the hotel room where, two hours before, agitated, almost out of her senses, her upside-down mind, greedily expectant, and not for food, she had been, even for her, extraordinarily demanding of him. So much so, in fact, he was still, here in the café, all but exhausted.

Yet, like hapless, fleeing orphans in a storm, they had both, perforce, become enamored of the lovely little municipality of Fantes. It was here, whenever possible, they came, almost as on a pilgrimage, to the quaint, though quite fancy, little hotel, The Achilles, up the street, where, for their passionate, if fearful, purposes, Paul, who could ill afford it, maintained a tiny, modest suite — furnished, equivocally, with a strange amethyst-purple wallpaper design unforgettably depicting the Palm Sunday incursion of Jesus Christ astride His tiny, stunted, humble jackass entering through the gates of Jerusalem. The petite suite also afforded an aromatic (hyacinth blossoms) closet were Cécile was wont to hang her stockings, dress, and underwear — if, that is, on the first entering the room, and in the early mad onrush of their passionate libidos, there was still time for such amenities. Now today, slightly more than two and a half hours following the onset of another such tryst, they, the two "orphans," as was their custom, sat more or less silently, uneasily, indeed portentously, eating in this orderly, well-patronized, little café.

It was, then, as aforementioned, at this fateful juncture — in the chimera-dream-drama — that Cécile looked up and saw him. Coming. Yet she was most of all frightened by this face, the present rendering of which she had never seen, or even imagined unless, yes, in vaudeville, as he now suddenly stood over them. The visage, however, miraculously, was now somehow pulverized, swollen, a scabrous dark blood-red. It was, yes, a chimera's face. She was able also to just glimpse the hands, which were large, red-freckled, and grasping. Paul sat first galvanized, but then merely curious, until, with lightning speed, the large chimera hands reaching down, Duquesne clutched the tablecloth and with all his might yanked it straight, horizontally, toward himself, sending cups, saucers, silverware, flying, clattering, across the hard floor, all as, still in one motion, he wheeled around to them, eyes bulging, well-kept and attractive teeth bared, and, in English, first hurled his words at Paul: *"Pimp Nigger!"* he yelled. Then at Cécile, if possible, even louder: *"Paris Whore!"*

Paul, in leaping, vaulting, up at him, overturned the naked table, but then, again springing at him, clumsily slipped and fell on the wet floor. Duquesne, however, had already stepped back, free, and now, followed by his tall companion, was heading for the front door — not running, though, not even loping, only briskly walking. Yet Paul, finally up from the floor now, was, like a streaking demon, pursuing them toward the door. The shocked patrons, some now standing, napkins in their hands, had heard, then seen, what had happened, and also recognized the issue involved. Soon, though, they seemed hesitant, nonplused, inconclusive about their own roles, if any, until the café owner burst out of the kitchen, which seemed to relieve them no end.

Suddenly Cécile, from the shock having at last found her voice, was already crying out, wailing, indeed almost keening, in Paul's direction: *"No, no,* Paul! . . . Come back, come back! . . . Let them go! . . . *Please!* . . ." She had nearly reached him now. "Paul, Paul — do you know what you're doing? Our pictures could be in tomorrow's newspapers. Paul, listen to me! . . ." She seized his arm and began trying to pull him back.

"I'll kill that bastard! . . ." was all, over and over, Paul kept saying as he finally wrenched free again.

"Oh, Paul!" she cried. *"J'ai raison, mais!"*

Finally free, he was soon at the door, the panting café owner at his elbow cursing the miscreants, who now, however, had disappeared up the street and around a corner. Gone.

In the dead of night now, the large, elegant bed and its sole occupant seem tossing like a frigate in a wild, north Atlantic gale, all upheaval, turmoil, strife, worsened by a continued flailing about of her beautiful limbs and accompanied by a frantic moaning even before the muffled outcries, muted shrieks, sure to come, finally resume. The result is, alas, that sometime during all this mattressed melee the white silken nightcap has come off. With, then, her trembling hands groping in the darkness, the eccentric headpiece is at last retrieved — from halfway under the same pillow whence, hours ago, it had come. At last, it is restored to the perspiring, tousled, now-unattractive head of hair, as her hot breath comes up in short gasps. The white silken chin strap this time, however, she loops and ties securely. She lies there, then, still quivering, between a pair of luxurious, perfumed sheets, inwardly reeling from the Fantes café dream-cataclysm just experienced — though sadly unaware of what is yet, and soon, to come, this time, though, with no forewarning, no prescient expectancy, only the sudden blitz. But now there is nothing more than her heavy breathing, soon accompanied by light seizures of nerves and palpitations, until at last again come the twisting and turning between the elegantly scented bedsheets. It is not, then, until the elapsing of a time period she could not possibly have particularized — actually at 2:25 A.M. — that she at long last begins to experience the slow, undulating lassitude again; as it were, the perfect and family-heralded drowse; finally, then, a gradual immersion in what seems something more or less as if her pillows were a pair of fleecy, cumulus clouds. She is consequently unable even to recall, or, if vaguely so, construe, the Cambons' nightmare stricture, to wit: "We are near to awaking whenever we dream that we dream." So now, the nightcap tightly in place, as, exponentially, it had best be, she is once more free, buoyant, airborne; unknowingly, though, in the direct path of the tornado furiously impending, the dream ordeal soon to be unleashed captioned as Hector Duquesne's revenge: gang ravishment, sodomitic crucifixion, extraction of body wastes, fellatio, cunnilingus, the whole terrifying present, all beyond her faintest, crassest possibility to grasp or visualize. Nonetheless, her hardly justified assurance that she is now safe at last is paramount in her psyche—confident there will now be quietude, rest, relief, her slumber unharried, whole.

The curtain once more rising, then, we see a new silvery moon, as sharply convex as it is concave, which has been shining down brightly on the Place de la Concorde for over an hour now. In her agony, however, she could take no notice of it, of anything, for since her abduction she had worn the same filthy, unsightly garments which now felt to her also somehow greasy, though they were not, quite—only putrid, rank, in odor. Moreover, in one of the gang-action melees, the dress had been splashed with cheap red wine of which it now also reeked. And her foul stockings had so many fissures and runs—from the violence of the gang sex—they made her once-shapely legs seem now gaunt, pale, cadaverous. She also no longer wore underwear—it has been stripped from her by one of her many attackers—bringing her now to feel the ironic truth of what Monsieur Duquesne, in his stormy rage in the café, had labeled her: *A whore*. Moreover, a scruffy one. So tonight, in the limpid moonlight shortly before nine o'clock, they—she and Duquesne—were on their way again. But before getting behind the steering wheel of his two-door Peugeot, to drive off with her, he had first, as always, somehow climbed in the backseat where he had her sit and securely tied her wrists and ankles with a heavy twine. Once more, for the n-th time, she piteously begged him to kill her. He only seemed not to hear her. She had been his abducted prisoner now for six days and five nights—if, that is, she had reckoned the harrowing, interminable time correctly—and she was sure, or at least she prayerfully hoped, she would soon die, mercifully. No human anatomy, she knew, could much longer withstand the animalism, brutish force, the unspeakable horrors, including her untimely menstruation, of the ordeal she had been through. Ironically, the June night was mild and lovely as they drove past the Rond Point and on up the brazenly lighted Champs-Elysées from which the Arc de Triomphe was so plainly in night view. She had once—since a girl—thought this a breathtakingly magnificent sight but now the Arc seemed a horrible, stupendous guillotine looming ominously at the top of a hill.

In her body-soreness, then, her pain and misery, her hoarse voice pleading—she could no longer cry—she said to him: "*Oh, Monsieur Duquesne! . . .S'il vous plait! . . .*I wish to die! Instead of taking me back to that dreadful, unmentionable house of horrors, please kill me. Where did you find so many blacks in Paris? Or why couldn't you have had just one — *at least one*—white man among them? Shoot me! You have a gun, a pistol, for I saw it! Use it, then! . . .I beg you, in the name of my family, my children, *kill me!*"

Duquesne raised a sardonic eyebrow—as if surprised. "*Pardonnez-moi, Madame Fournier,*" he said. "Why would you want to die? Look at all you would be missing. Prior to when I, a true French patriot, stepped into the picture, that is, having one afternoon, but only by sheerest accident, encountered you in this small-town café with your nigger paramour, prior to that, as I say, your greatest pleasure was no doubt derived from being fucked into absolute, utter ecstasy by this handsome buck of yours with you that day." The car had reached a red light now. Momentarily holding his foot on the brake, he turned around to the backseat and observed her, at last adding: "Well, I dare say that in the past week you have had as many niggers, each with a different disease, as you will ever want for the rest of your life, eh? Some nights there have been, literally, a queue of them on the stairs and outside the bedroom in which you receive them, and where you will do so again tonight. Ah, but now, at long, long last, you have finally experienced what one might call, for want of a more apt expression, a *surfeit*. Eh? — am I right? A surfeit, yes, of all the things they've done to you and made you do to them — these wild, filthy, diseased African brute niggers right down here from the wharves at Le Havre where, to France's everlasting shame, they are employed as stevedores. But now, it really does seem, that you've finally had enough of them, so your crying, sobbing, would at least intimate. Can this actually be true? . . ." He feigned concern, almost anxiety, then even commiseration for her, at last asking, mock-innocently, "Am I not correct in this, Madame Fournier? . . ."

"*Kill me!*" She pleaded hoarsely, her voice now actually a croak. "Don't take me back to the fiendish, hellish, that inhuman, place again tonight. Have mercy on me, I beg of you. Shoot me, yes, with that gun in your pocket. Use it — kill me!" Her attempts at sobs were futile — she had cried as much as she was capable of. Now she could only lapse into childlike whimperings before then coughing up the strange, hollow sound of a lonely caterwaul. At last — the car had gone three more blocks now — she went into a benumbed, listless silence, then closed her eyes. Fifteen minutes later then — she could somehow sense it — the car was finally nearing its hated destination. She knew it. She opened her eyes and, to her right, saw, and well remembered, the scraggly stand of horse chestnut trees along this outlying and narrow street beyond the Clichy district, up in the 17th Arrondissement. The trees, however, partially hid an unsightly, but familiar, building which she had always, even in her tortured misery, noticed to be some kind of unpainted, or flaking, warehouse. Yet all these indicia told her it would not be long now — possibly less than five minutes — before her arrival in hell, triggering in her a violent trembling as if she had suddenly been seized by some convulsive, fatal ague. All this while, though, Duquesne had driven in silence — since taunting her about her final "surfeit" of black debauchery. The mere thought of all she had been through brought her yet another violent seizure at which she — well knowing what she was soon again to experience — began to pray. Ah, yes, but where was God? she thought. Was there, though, in fact, a God anymore? she asked herself. If so, was He, as was said, even contended, both omnipotent and good? If He was indeed omnipotent, or even omniscient, then He knew all about her plight, her terrible, pitiable ordeal. But if He knew and had done nothing to help her, could He be said to be good? Or if, on the other hand, He knew and did, very much, want to help her, yet, for some reason, any reason, whatever, could not — that is, lacked the power — could He then be said to be omnipotent, all-powerful? Though she longed to, she could not bring herself to say yes to any of these postulates and was promptly plunged into a new, gigantic, despair.

Soon now Duquesne, as if somehow deliberating on how he might accomplish it, very slowly turned the corner — onto a street even more seedy than those they had just traversed — and she saw the familiar run-down apartment building, its faded, despoiled, dingy red-brick façade reaching three stories up. Suddenly then, before she realized it, he was carefully, almost fastidiously, parking the Peugeot.

She knew they had arrived now and her hoarse, trembling voice came up out of her hollow chest in another rattling croak — "Oh, Monsieur! . . . have mercy on me! . . . Don't take me up into that ghastly hellhole, that bedroom of unspeakable horrors, again. Let me die, I say. Your satisfaction will be just as complete."

"No, it will not," said Duquesne, almost matter-of-factly. "I beg to differ with you on that, Madame Fournier."

City of Light

"But by my death you shall have shown me compassion. Can you not feel that at all for another human being? . . . no pity? . . . *nothing!* . . ."

"Nothing, Madame. We are trying to save France — our country. No half-measures will do. I venture to say that if you survive what you've been through, and have of course maintained your sanity, you, for the rest of your natural life, will be another, a changed, person. You will see the world differently — you will see it for what it actually is, Madame. You may, for all I know, thank me."

Again she was trying to cry, sob, yet could not — when just then three ragged, filthy, loud-talking-and-laughing black men, African dock laborers, came drunkenly staggering up the sidewalk toward the front of the car but headed for the wretched red-brick apartment building she knew all too well.

"*Get down!* . . ." whispered Duquesne breathlessly. He had already thrown himself beneath the steering wheel — to prevent the men from noticing the car. She, though, had not moved. Unaware, he then said, as, miraculously, the men passed on, "If those drunken black animals had seen us, especially *you*, they would not have waited to get you up in that bedroom but would have come to this car and fought each other to the death over who would take you first, right there where you sit in the back of this car. Be careful — they might yet come back. Keep your head down, Madame!" She did not move. "Of course, though, in the bargain," he said, "they would have tried to kill me, but naturally I'm ready for them. Ah, sad, sad, that this is what France has come to . . ." and, as if to reassure himself, he felt in his jacket pocket where the pistol was. But by now the three men, still laughing boisterously and using the full cache of their foulest language, had entered the run-down red-brick building and were climbing its stairs. At once, Duquesne climbed in the backseat with her, his purpose being to untie her wrists and ankles preparatory to their following the men in.

She had already begun a frantic moaning before pitching and threshing about on the seat, all as, in her spent guttural voice, she repeated her plea to him: "I beg of you, Monsieur Duquesne, humbly, prostrate, with no longer any wish to live, to have at least enough mercy on me not to take me up there again! For almost a week now you — and France, as you say — have had your revenge. Please don't take me up in that room again! . . ."

"I'm glad, Madame, to hear you mention France — that's a good sign. But I wonder if you've ever realized that your handsome, debonair, princely nigger-paramour is, in actual reality, no different from those black apes you just saw entering that building. They are all roving animals, come to France, our country, yours and mine, to do their hellish mischief — steal, murder, rape our women, raise general holy havoc in our country. Roving beasts — yes, that they are — from deepest black Africa, who are not at all human beings, but primates, vicious anthropoids, despoiling our land, our beloved France. They should be rounded up, all of them — including, yes your mauve princeling — and first interned, then castrated, and finally burned alive. Who can argue that they're fit to live? — it's like Hitler and the Jews — certainly no *sane* person." He was breathing stertorously, vehemently, as if on the verge of a stroke. Having at last untied her wrists, he was leaning lower to free her ankles.

She still found herself able to say: "If you try to take me up there again, I will resist."

"Oh, you will, will you?" he said, quickly, though smothering his grisly smile.

"I will make you kill me first," she said, "right here . . . now!"

City of Light

But, bent forward in a strain, he was still trying to free her ankles.

It was then, suddenly, she saw his bulging jacket pocket. Unaware, he was still trying to unknot the stubborn twine on her left foot. Under the feeble streetlight, however, she had already deftly extracted the pistol, then, raising it above his back, leveled it point-blank behind his large right ear, pressured, then squeezed the trigger. Nothing happened. She was near to fainting. Suddenly then her ankles came free to him—she felt it, and knew now he was rising. Frantic, desperate, she began rubbing the butt of the pistol with the two middle fingers of her left hand, feeling, testing, despairingly searching for the safety mechanism. Miraculously, a finger found it—just as, his head coming up, eyes staring, he saw the gun and lunged for it. It went off in his unbelieving face. The grooving slug went straight in slightly above the right eyebrow, as, dark gore already percolating, he fell forward into her malodorous lap. It was then she let out two, long, bloodcurdling screams as—the white silken nightcap on her head wildly askew—she propelled herself bolt upright from the elegantly perfumed sheets of her very own bed.

Almost at once, then, she heard Michelle and little Zoe running, stampeding, down the hall toward her. Both—in their pajamas, fright in their eyes—burst in the open door and over to her bed. "What's the matter with you, Mother!" demanded still-sleepy Michelle. "What's that on your head?"

Cécile, crazed, aghast, eyes dilated, staring fiercely from one daughter to the other, seemed totally unaware of where she was.

"*Ma-MAH!*" cried Zoe and, sailing up into the bed, threw her arms around her mother's neck. "What were you screaming for, Ma-MAH? . . . Is something hurting you? . . ."

"She was having a nightmare," opined Michelle loftily. "I have them occasionally. Mother, what's that you've got on your head? It looks like an old aviator cap without the goggles. You were dreaming badly, weren't you?—screaming and all. I don't think I scream, though. What was all the fuss about, Mother?—did you dream that Father had gone down in the plane coming back from Turkey or something? Why don't you sit up in the bed, Mother? Here, let me put those pillows behind you." Michelle leaned over the bed where Zoe's vicelike bear hug was close to throttling her mother's breathing.

"Ma-MA!" cried Zoe. "Are you sick? . . . Do you want us to send for a doctor?"

"*She's* a doctor, Zoe—heavens. Take that crazy cap off her head."

When at last, though, eyes still staring around the bedroom, Cécile finally realized she was in her own home, her bedroom, safe and whole, she broke into a fit of wild crying and sobbing, before then yammering like a calf. Meanwhile Michelle, reaching over and around Zoe, was trying to untie the chin strap of her mother's preternatural white nightcap. "Mother, where did this come from?" she persisted. But Cécile, unassuaged by little Zoe's loving ministrations, was still yowling. Whereupon Michelle reached for the tissue box and gave her three Kleenexes before trying someway to smooth down her frightening hair. "Look, Zoe—look here," she said, "Mother's got two gray hairs already." But Michelle was, as usual, forlorn—she was convinced of it—she was also sleepy and bored. "I wish Father were here," she said, "instead of always on the go—this time somewhere in the Middle East, where they're fighting all the time. Don't cry anymore, Mother. It will only make Zoe and me cry. What were you dreaming about? Tell us, so we can get excited, or sad, or scared, too. Anything to pep things up a bit. It must have been interesting—to say the least. Gosh, and, yes, scary. Nothing exciting ever happens to

City of Light

Zoe or me — and Father's always away in Timbuktu or some place. So what were you dreaming about — come on, tell us. In the dream did you have a lover? It would have been exciting." Michelle stood up from the bed and, stretching, then yawning, only casually observed her mother now.

Cécile was soon quietly sobbing, as her two loving, confused, harried daughters looked on helplessly. "Go run a tub of hot water for me, will you?" she finally said to them.

Michelle's eyes went big. "You took a bath just before you went to bed, Mother!"

"You put on perfume afterwards, Ma-MA," added Zoe. "You smelled so good."

Wretched Cécile, still trembling, eyes red, pretty face wet, streaked, only stared desolately across at the far wall.

Almost thirty minutes later, then, when at last Michelle and Zoe had returned to their room, Cécile got out two huge bath towels, a large, heavy bar of soap, and a long-handled bath scrub brush. She then went into her and Georges's great white marble bathroom and ran a tub of scalding water — all the while, finally, frighteningly, speculating on how tonight had changed her life. Forever, she was sure. Now she wanted only to call Georges, in the middle of the night, and wherever he was, in Turkey — or was it, yes, Timbuktu? — to tell him how much she loved him, and of course their children, and France. Yes, yes, she thought, shuddering. Noble France. It was her country, her dear country. She was its thrall — now forever. Duquesne, she all too well remembered, had said as much, that henceforth she would be a changed woman. How right he was — even perhaps psychic. Soon she let her fingers, gingerly, touch the water in the tub. It was still scalding. But she would wait. She would wait for her own scalding life to heal as well, to change, become whole — for her family, for France. It was a mission now seared in her flesh. The past, the past, the culpable, derelict past! she thought — she was trembling now, shivering, over the scathing-hot water — yes, how wrong had been the past. It was God, though, who had rescued her after all. She vowed this — her dear God. He, in His unearthly wisdom, had all along understood everything, had put her through this ghastly time, this hell, this test, for His unerring purposes. She was certain of it. Thus had she been saved. "May God's name be praised, exalted . . . ," she kept saying, again and again. Now the tears returned, yet only briefly, and soon she was fiercely whispering: "I am saved! . . . I am saved! . . . God did not abandon me at all. He changed me." She leaned over now, opened the silver tap again, and let more water, thermal, seething, in steaming billows, run, gush, to escape its boiling source. She felt reckless. Then afraid. "I'm saved, yes," she began whispering, however, insisting on it again, her deliverance, her redemption. "Saved . . . ," she whispered it again, doggedly, adamantly, bent on convincing herself of it. It would be a struggle, she told herself, momentarily wavering, her own lonely struggle, almost requiring she keep herself locked in her house, her very bedroom, as if it were some fetid dungeon.

"Paul, oh Paul, do you hear? — I am saved! . . ."

It became a wild repetition.

Chapter
Four
Quo Vadis Speaks of Missions

It was the first week in June, a Thursday afternoon, with Paul upstairs at his writing table hurriedly scribbling in a notebook the last pages of another letter to his mother, Saturn. Then, as it was his invariable practice, he would destroy, or seek to do so, everything he had written, perhaps trying in the process to help himself forget, and forgive, all he had just said. "But I must stop now, Mother," he wrote. "I've gone on too long as it is. Besides, I've got to go out and get some food, which these days, though, I have little appetite for. Only vodka, in the last couple of weeks, has enabled me to weather this strange tempest lately swirling around me. I feel more confused and insecure than I ever have. Let me tell you before I leave of one more thing I've done: Believe it or not, I have closed down the Coterie. It's true—completely. It had finally gotten out of hand, though. Father will be shocked, of course, but soon I'm sure he will be very pleased also—he thought the idea of the Coterie was nutty from the beginning. 'But what next?' he'll now ask himself, sighing. What he'd actually like

me to do, no question, is to come home and get a job. Doing
what, though, Mother? I have an A.B. degree from Princeton
University, but what is there that I can really do? Can you
think of something? Oh, the times I'll bet old Zack has wished
you were back with us again — you the all-time problem solver.
For he doesn't know what to do about me — any more than I
know myself. So, being the good, caring father that he is — up
to a certain point, that is, as long as one doesn't get him riled —
he sends me fairly generous checks and hopes in the interim
the problem of my general disorientation, from birth actually,
certainly since you left me, will eventually solve itself, right
its course, or just go away. Actually, though, to be absolutely
pragmatic about it, I see very few signs of any of this happening. So now, wouldn't you know it, along comes the great
mystery of mysteries — yes, I refer to my dear Cécile. What
happened? you want to ask — climb aboard, please. That's all I
ever ask myself, day and night. What happened, yes. I give up.
I sometimes find myself thinking of wonderful Jeannette instead. For what, though? — would you please advise me on
that? For what, I ask — maybe merely to have one more person
to lean on — one, ha, who won't remonstrate with me so impatiently, as you-know-who did and still does. So let me leave
you, sweetheart Saturn Marie, for today, only today, my
inconstant friend, supervisor, and scold. I must stop now. You
take it easy." Whereupon, strangely, he reached across his
worktable and picked up another five-and-dime notebook; but
then seemed not at all eager to start writing in it. Instead he
lifted his left foot up onto another chair, leaned back, chin
aloft, and sat quietly for nearly five minutes — ruminating.

Jeannette was, indeed, back on his mind. He wanted to
tell her about the sudden demise of the Coterie. He realized
then, even had she been in that very room, she would not have
known what he was talking about. Or it would have required

some fabulous ESP on both their parts to achieve the needed comprehension. It was not to happen, he told himself. Such communication was possible only between himself and Saturn Marie. Nor, because of this, did he find himself at all unhappy. He, yes, never tired conversing with Saturn. But was that what it really was? . . . Did he ever hear her voice? He knew he did not. But his inner feelings insisted he did. And, she, without exception, spoke of matters important to them both, even when she was disappointed, or sad, or, sometimes, wildly furious with him. He invariably looked forward to their wireless, mystical, countertalks and "handholding." Something struck his consciousness then. Cécile again. What of Cécile? Where was she? What a mystery, yes — disappeared entirely off the radar screen. What an irony it was that Saturn, so inclined to admire a Cécile, had turned out to be jealous of her, maybe from the very beginning, he thought. Maybe, moreover, she was glad Cécile, for whatever strange reason, was now giving him a bad time. Maybe, as a result, Saturn was gloating. Weird, weird, he thought. Cécile was weird. Though at times lovely and sweet, as well as often quiet, contemplative, she was not the most predictable of women. Nor the most stable, he was now persuaded to believe. Moreover, she was now religious again — in fact, devout. What the upshot of this was to be he had no way of knowing, or foretelling — even if little of this was any longer germane to what had recently happened. Cécile had, yes, recently, abruptly, broken off from him — disappeared, absolutely, from his sight or knowledge. Yet he knew she was not ill, or even out of town. A number of times, in fact, though very circumspectly, he had telephoned her office, though no longer leaving his name merely to have it again ignored, and asked when Dr. Fournier would return to her office from the hospital that day. The answering office girl, he so well recalled, had assured him it would be in early afternoon. No, he knew, Cécile was alive and well. He must, then, he told himself, have done something terrible to her. But if she would only give him, as it were, an audience and tell him what it was, things might be better for him. He also knew now she no longer telephoned Madame Chevalley. Cécile would even no longer return Madame's phone calls. Strange, strange, he thought — for Madame was not only a friend of Cécile's but a patient. Refusing to take, or return, a patient's call, he knew, was no idle matter.

What, then, was to come of all this? he wondered now. But, even more curiously, how had it all happened? He could only sigh and think of Saturn. Would would she say? The question completely stumped him. He wanted to cry out: "Mother, Mother! . . ." as he had as a child. Instead he reached for a pencil.

"Oh, hell," he wrote, "I hate letting you go, dear. But we've been through all this before — how long you could stay, when you should go, and all that. If I had my way you would never go, you would always be here — with me. I'd rather have you here, if for nothing other than to talk to me — you surely must know that by now — than to have any kind of communication imaginable with any other human being on earth. Why is this? — since you've not always been nice to me, you know. But I won't go into a long rehash of all that. Besides — sometimes I really think this — you're not due all the blame, the abuse, I've heaped on you. In every situation, I've finally convinced myself, you've only acted as you were born to act. There was no other way. For awhile, when I was at the university, I became really wacky over the writings of Thomas Hobbes, the 17th-century British philosopher and determinist, who insisted that we really don't have a lot, if anything, to do with the way we are, the way we came here; that these matters were settled by other forces that we can't even imagine or grasp. Mother, I do wish you could have read a few things like that — instead of Michener all the time."

The pencil went bad on him now, and he picked up still another. "But you know," he kept writing, as if with a fever, "I can't help wondering if you wouldn't also by now have found some reason to dislike Cécile, despite all the things you heard, from me, about her solid background, her good looks, and her other accomplishments — like, for instance, her medical profession. But I also told you, and I'm sure you haven't forgotten it, that she's nine years older than I. And, Saturn dear, what do you think about the fact that she and I can't marry, even if that seemed desirable to us, which I have no indication either of us wants. She of course, yes, is married, to a very successful man and has two children by him. And all this says nothing yet about the matter of race. This, of course, wouldn't phase you, Mother, but it certainly does the two of us, the interested parties. There, however, *is* an aspect of this matter involving Cécile and me that I'm sure has given you much thought. I can, bless your heart, envision you in a situation where you're in constant fear, fear for your son's life — fear that he might get shot by a jealous husband. I know this must worry you. It's the kind of thing that makes anyone think. But especially someone like you — and when a person is involved whom you deeply care about, I know you, Mother, I've known you in all kinds of situation. Oh, but I must go now — to get something to eat. I'm starving."

No matter — despite his growling stomach — he now pulled open the drawer in his worktable and took out a flat bottle of vodka, from which he twisted off the cap and took a gurgling swig. He shivered then before drawing his shoulders together. "Ah-h-h-h," he uttered, "I needed that," recapping the bottle and returning it to the drawer. "Did I tell you," he resumed scibbling, "that you were very wary of me at one time? It's true. Didn't I tell you this? I think so. Well, anyhow, you were—very much so. You didn't trust me—that's the heart of it. Yet I trusted you. It should have been the other way around, though, Saturn." He pulled open the drawer again, gingerly placed his hand on the vodka bottle—as if it were a warning pistol—yet did not bring it out. "I've been aware for a long time, though, that you were wary of me. But why? I've also had my wary moments about you, too, Saturn Marie dear, I need not tell you—which, I might add, is fitting and proper; altogether so. I remember, for instance, that one night here in Paris I dreamed (the truth is, I'd gone to bed half-drunk) I dreamed you were cheating on Father (to say nothing of me), seeing, I dreamed, of all people on earth at your disposal, this big, black, handsome chauffeur of Father's (who, by the way, had a luscious vocabulary of 'deez and doze'), some guy who in real life you wouldn't have spat on. Yet, I dreamed you were seeing him. I pondered the matter in this dream with great gravity. I considered it a toxic, virulent, affront—not only to Zack but especially to me. Soon I became apoplectic. Before long I was bent on killing you for your unthinkable perfidy. That's when, thank God, I abruptly awoke, finally dressed then (at three in the morning), and went out to walk the streets and try to get myself together." His hand was trembling so as he scribbled that he finally gave up and, nauseated, revolted, sickened to tears with loathing, he let the pencil drop into the wastebasket. "Oh, Mother," he groaned.

Five minutes later he had somehow unearthed a cheap fountain pen and resumed writing, his hand calm, purged, resolute. "Did it every occur to you, Saturn Marie, that, although your young son, your recruit (your 'cruit,' as Father, laughing, would put it as he watched me meekly trailing you around), did it ever, yes, dawn on you that I was watching you, too—everywhere, as you, grim, self-possessed, captivated, read ('devoted yourself to' would be a better way to put it) read, yes, all those fashion magazines you subscribed to and stacked in various places around the house. Father tripped on them so much that you told Xosa, the maid, to put them in your bedroom — where Father then tripped on them more frequently than ever. Finally you had a few put in my quarters — that's how, in time, I came to know something about *haute* fashion. Then before long, as I watched you, I began to notice what it was that had so enamored you about these society-drawing-room types of periodicals. It was one lone woman. That's all. But she was something to write home about — a bona fide, breath-catching, *baux veux*. It was she who modeled the clothes you yourself most liked — ah, liked, yes, because it was she who modeled them. But this your 'lady of the magazines,' shall we call her, modeled with such divine regality that her viewers, certainly more than a million strong, dubbed her 'The Queen.' I'm sure no zealot-devotee of the lady's was more in accord with this action than you, Mother. You had gone absolutely bonkers. Soon the magazine publishers, no fools, came up with the final accolade for their illustrious lady. Who, pray, could have flubbed that guess? It was a crown, of course. Your lady, Mother, was henceforth called Queen . . . Queen Somebody or other. It will come to me. I was some Hungarian title — or Rumanian maybe. But you would sit there, Saturn dear, dreaming, yearning, over this magazine, utterly enthralled, idolizing your 'Queen.' Then one day (we were in your bedroom) you came up with something that stuns me till this day — your gravely concerned, and almost secret, confession of sin. You said that we (meaning you and I) were spending too much time on sports, athletics — following golf, baseball, football, far too much. That our attitude was getting vulgar. Then you showed me one of your magazines and its picture of the Queen. It wasn't anything new to me, though — for weeks, unbeknownst to you, of course, I had been checking on the particular issues of the magazine that you yourself had been so madly (and, to me, sadly) taken with. I was disturbed, though I didn't let on, and sat there that day, in your lovely bedroom, and watched as you virtually got your kicks showing me the different magazine displays of your Queen Helena Turnu-Severin, yes (or some such names as that), who, no question, was a lovely creature to behold. The only thing she lacked was a golden scepter. You came over to me then, though seeming very moved by Queen What's-Her-Name's tender, charming, trace of a smile, and bent and kissed me on the cheek before whispering in my ear that I should always remember that your mother was a Queen also. I was happy as hell to hear that—because I thought so, too. You were certainly *my* Queen, and I told you so. You virtually glowed. Honest to God you did, Saturn. You leaned toward me again, then, and do you remember what, as you faced me again, you whispered? *Do* you? *No?* You softly whispered, 'Thank you.' I was happy beyond words. I later went out and bought you the only think I had money for, not much—a bunch of a kind of worse-for-wear daffodils. No matter, you were the *Queen*. I was proud of you." His pen wavered. "You . . . were my mother, too," it finally said and ceased.

Paul's Xeroxed letter to the Coterie membership, informing one and all of his decision to withdraw from the organization, had created little less than a fire storm. Only a few of them had his telephone number but active, aggressive, Fifi Mazisi was one of these. She even called Paul early one morning, before he had risen. He was not pleased, though, and talked in clipped sentences, also sourly, to the person who had most helped him in his attempts to make something significant out of the enterprise he had founded—with his father's underwriting. But Fifi now was both angry and on the verge of tears. "Paul, what in the world has come over you?" she shrilled into the phone. "Why would you do this to us? Oh, God."

"Why would you and your friends do to me what you did?" Paul said in a kind of sleepy snort. "You've got a helluva nerve waking me this early to complain about something that's over and done with, moot—and largely precipitated by you and your thankless cohorts. I'm sick of all of you—and did what was best, for *all* of us."

"Paul, listen to me." Fifi's voice was lower now. "Do you realize you're cutting off your nose to spite your face? What are you going to do now that you no longer have your organization, your plaything, to give you the feeling, on your father's money, that you're doing great things for the good of mankind—black mankind. Come clean, now, and tell me. What will you do with yourself?"

Paul fumbled with a few unintelligible words, making no sane reply of any kind. "Stop talking to me like I'm a child, Fifi," he said, at last.

"No, Paul, you're no child, but you act like you are sometimes. Even little Ari, except for me your best and staunchest friend—who, by the way, is sick these days—gets fed up with you. And that's something that should make you stop and think—for Ari has been one member (me, the other) for whom you could do no wrong."

"He's sick, you say?" Paul, wearily, was climbing out of the bed now, the telephone in his hand. "What's wrong with him? I've noticed myself he's lost weight and is not his ordinarily spry self these days."

"Would you believe me if I told you, Paul, that Ari is fifty-one years old."

"He certainly doesn't look it. What's he sick about? For one thing he smokes those damned Egyptian cigarettes, the strongest made, one right after another, like he's nuts."

"One more thing, Paul, before I let you go. That attractive African woman, who came with you and the white guy, the Britisher, Lewellyn, to the meeting—came to see me yesterday. She was asking, though, about you."

"Her name is Tosca Zimsu," Paul said. "I only met her the day before the meeting. What did she want?"

"I don't know the answer to that. I do know, though, she was out to learn whatever she could about you." Fifi laughed ruefully. "That's nothing new. Show me a woman who's been around you for five minutes and I'll show you one who, too, would like to know more about you than she does. Some people have even claimed I'm one of those women."

"Fifi," Paul interrupted, "I've got to stop now and go out—will you excuse me? We can talk later maybe." Whereupon the conversation soon wound down and Fifi hung up.

An hour later, near nine, Paul left the house, first to get breakfast down the street at The Derby, before then going by the local public library for a quick scan of the American newspapers. But by eleven he had returned home, only, however, to find awaiting him, alone—in Madame Chevalley's cozy little parlor—none other than Mrs. Tosca Zimsu. Tosca stood up at once on seeing him. Clad in another of her long, strange, reddish dresses, she smiled wanly before finally greeting him: "*Bonjour, Monsieur Kessey. Comment allez-vous?*"

Paul, though still surprised, at last—in his insecure French—told her he was OK, thank you, but then he could think of nothing else to say. Yet he was unable to keep his eyes off her wonderfully lithe body in its bizarre garb, until then, greatly embarrassed, he summoned the smiling and interested courtesy in order to inquire: "What brings you here, Mrs. Zimsu?"

"Oh, I'll tell you soon," she said as she looked around her, plainly coveting greater privacy for them to talk.

Cyrus Colter

Almost at once then, he had taken her upstairs, where he sat her at his littered worktable. Yet, when ascending behind her on the stairs he had still been unable to avoid an insistent wonder at her body and her manner of dress. Everything was African — which brought Paul to wonder if this was the same Tosca who had vowed she hated Africa. But, by far, the most astonishing item of all her fantastic getup was her headpiece — which had shocked him from the first moment. It was what presumed to be her hair, which up until now, the few times he had seen her, had been worn somewhat short and very neat. Today, however, she had apparently clapped on her head what appeared to him to be huge, outlandish, "reggae" wig made of long rough braids, plaits, or "dreadlocks," reaching down her shoulders and her back, fully to her waist. It was a habiliment, certainly not unknown to him from his African and Caribbean studies, worn by the so-called Rastafarians, a religious cult among black Jamaicans which teaches the eventual redemption of blacks and their return to "Mother Africa." This had also, however, for him at least, an untimely symbolism — for the continent of Africa was no longer an allure for him.

"Please excuse this untidy room, Mrs. Zimsu," he said. "It's where I work, though."

"What are you working on, Monsieur Kessey?"

Paul's tongue stumbled. "Oh, it involves . . . the numerous things I have to do . . . from time to time." He quickly changed the subject. He thought of what Fifi Mazisi had said — that with his killing the Coterie he now had nothing to do with his time. Even now the thought jarred him and the ordeal, he knew, had only begun. He inwardly sighed and finally returned to Tosca again. "May I get you something, a soft drink maybe?"

"A soft drink would be fine," she said. "You wouldn't also have a sandwich of some kind, would you?"

"I'm sorry — I haven't any food. I eat out most of the time. I do have a few crackers, though, I think. Maybe some peanut butter."

"That would help a lot, Monsieur Kessey. I had to feed my son, Gwelo, this morning before school, and there wasn't anything left."

Paul looked quizzically at her before going over to the tiny refrigerator against the wall and getting out what little was available, which he gave to her, with a cold Pepsi Cola. She was profuse in her thanks.

"I can't get over your hairdo," Paul finally said.

"It's not my hair, it's a wig." She smiled.

Paul laughed. "I know that, I have eyes."

"You mean you don't like it. Neither does Gwelo. I have a purpose, though. These dreadlocks are sometimes helpful when things are not going well for Gwelo and me — as now. But it all depends on the phase of the moon."

Paul's quizzical look returned, suddenly.

There was a pause then, during which Tosca quickly disposed of her crackers and peanut butter, before now asking, politely: "May I use your bathroom?"

"Of course — in there." Paul pointed to his bedroom adjacent.

On returning she seemed more relaxed. "I'll bet you're still wondering why I've come to see you like this," she said. "The man whose flat Gwelo and I live in suggested it."

Paul looked lost again.

"He's heard about you, Monsieur Kessey, and of course the Coterie, about the sincerity and the humaneness of your views and your conduct, et cetera, and admires what you stand for. I also told him about your giving me the Métro fare to get home that day of the final Coterie meeting."

"You say he suggested you come see me. What for? But I'm already beginning to see the light. Indeed, in the bargain, you might want to tell *me* a few things. I of course know all about your tragic misfortunes in Africa—from James Lewellyn. I sympathize with you—who wouldn't feel compassion for you and your family, especially for your son. Yet how did you come to choose a beautiful but hard-boiled city like Paris to make a way in for you and your son with no one to help you? Was that very smart?"

"I'm not sure," said Tosca. "But what were my alternatives? I knew nothing about the world—certainly nothing, or very little, about the low regard people of color were held in. As for Paris, I had gone to school here off and on for six and a half years. I wanted my son, whom one of his teachers right here in Paris only four months ago called a genius—I wanted him to get an education commensurate with his gifts. This seemed to me to be a career in the law, as my father had done in England. Then I fell on bad, on tragic, days. My Paris schooling, in languages and the arts, hadn't prepared me for a respectable job in Paris after the deaths of my father and husband (I should say after their heinous murders), so I was cut adrift with very, very little to sustain two people only one of whom, one an unproductive child, yes, could contribute to the expenses of our lives. I've never experienced such a barren, frightening time in my life and hope never to again. So, to make a long story short, about nine months ago, we were rescued, so to speak, by this man I mentioned a minute ago—with whom Gwelo and I live for the present. He charges us nothing. He's a man whom we've found to be honest and upright in every way—an American, a black man, a *huge* man (who, though, I'm sorry to say, doesn't bathe as regularly as we would like), originally from Atlanta, Georgia. His unlikely name is Quo Vadis Jackson."

"*Well*," said Paul, "Interesting."

"I could write a book about him, one of the most unique

human beings I've ever — *ever*, I repeat — met. The extraordinary thing about him, though, was, and is, that he has very little money than we have — he makes a very narrow living by washing municipal motorbuses way out at the trolley barns. Yet he has a college education and gets his greatest pleasure from daily, also nightly, reading — having his head in some really no-nonsense book. Well, this was the man — good Quo Vadis — who took us in, opened his dark, dismal, little flat, over in the Latin Quarter, to us, and virtually saved our lives. What did he want from us, you might be thinking. I'm convinced he wanted absolutely nothing — at least so far as we can tell — nothing more than our company in that desolate flat of his. Of course it's strange, but this is a strange, and a very unique man. My son, who will soon be eleven, and I owe our lives to Quo Vadis, as I say, and, further, Gwelo has come to idolize him almost as a surrogate father. But Gwelo also knows about his and my straitened circumstances. My father and my husband each left me a few French stocks, which are now, though, poor, very poor, producers. I also work three days a week at a fruit-and-vegetable market down the street from Quo Vadis's place. That's all, Monsieur Kessey. Quo Vadis lets us share his flat but, as I say, won't take anything from us — except that we buy some of the food. How could he be more generous? He's a wonderful man — some evenings he even helps Gwelo with his schoolwork. I can only say my son and I, all things considered, have been very fortunate. But somehow now Quo Vadis, almost as if his life were soon to take a sharp, a drastic, turn, one in which, for some reason unknown to us, Gwelo and I cannot be included, has, though very circumspectly, mentioned you as someone who might conceivably take his place. That's how he came around to quietly suggesting that I come and size you up, talk with you, find out what you're like, for it's his impression that you are indeed a man of principle and humanity, who, for the uncertain future might be someone it might be wise to know better—especially after I had told him of the circumstances under which you and I had met when Mr. Lewellyn was in town. Quo Vadis showed definite gratification at what might be our prospects. Even I somehow-felt buoyed up."

"Do me a favor, will you?" said Paul. "Please get that horrible thing you call your 'dreadlocks' out of my sight. They interfere when I'm looking at you, trying to hear what you're saying. You are an attractive lady, really good to look at, when you're not wearing that god-awful wig."

"What do you care how I look, Monsieur Kessey—as long as I'm clean and respectable? You don't like my dreadlocks because otherwise I'd look better to you, is that right? I didn't realize you thought like that—toward me. I'm not particularly proud of it, either. A minute ago you were also looking at the 'dress of many colors' that I have on. You didn't seem displeased by it, though. You were trying to look through it, it seemed to me. Which was impossible, though. But again I was not proud, nor pleased. Nor would Quo Vadis be."

Paul, seated across the table, tried to laugh but failed. "I certainly beg your pardon," he finally said, "if I seemed to be undressing you. You don't like to be considered sexy, is that it?"

"That *is* it, Monsieur Kessey. If you knew more about my life you would understand."

"Again I beg your pardon, Mrs. Zimsu—profusely." But Paul was smiling. "Now, back to your Mr. Jackson," he said. "What did he expect you to accomplish by calling on me? And, incidentally, unannounced."

"Frankly, although he didn't say it, he wished me, yes, to engage you in conversation. But I had already done that—when we were with Mr. Lewellyn that day. But Mr. Jackson wanted to get some idea about how you felt about philanthropy, whether or not you took it seriously, or ever felt a real duty, under certain circumstances, to give, just give. I still feel that you do, in a given, or special, situation—but one where something in return might be expected. Or at least hoped for."

"May that still be properly called philanthropy, though, Mrs. Zimsu?"

Tosca paused. "I'm not sure," she finally said. "One would have to find that out in advance, probably. Mr. Jackson sent me here to merely look you over, hoping, however, I guess, that you might feel some compunction for Gwelo and me in what might be ahead for us."

"Look, Mrs. Zimsu, I've never had a job in my life. I subsist entirely on my father's largesse. How would Mr. Jackson regard that?"

"I have no idea," Tosca said. "I only wish you two could talk sometime—for instance, like this evening, at dinner, at Mr. Jackson's."

Paul's laugh was discourteous, almost mean. "I see this whole thing has been rehearsed. No, no, count me out of that. Did Mr. Jackson tell you to invite me?" Another laugh.

"Heavens no," said Tosca. "There's little, if any, food in his flat today. I must go now, Monsieur Kessey. Thank you for talking with me. Would you be kind enough to walk me to the Métro. I don't know this area well."

"You seemed to find out where I live all right," Paul said.

Tosca acted as if she had not heard, and together they started to leave.

Outside the day was sunny and pleasant. Within less than ten minutes they had walked to the nearest Métro station— Comite d'Accueil—where Tosca said suddenly to Paul: "I'm sure, at a time when I'm so hungry I can hardly stand, that you will not abandon me here and just walk away. It would be so unlike the caring and dedicated leader of the Coterie, a man whom I met in a luncheon queue one day. I refuse to believe it." She was soon biting her lip — before her eyes began welling tears.

"Come on, follow me!" Paul said, irritably. Soon they were on the station platform, where he stopped. "How about this . . . where are you going?" He seemed momentarily disordered.

"If you go with me," she said. "I'm going to a large food mart not too far from where I live. There we shall get the groceries for our dinner — Quo Vadis is a master cook, you know — you'll see. But, Monsieur Kessey, I can't wait that long for a sandwich. I shall keel over."

"Here," he said, pointing, before going in his pocket for coins. He went over to a candy-vending machine, returning with a large chocolate bar, and thrust it at her. "*Here*," he repeated.

"Thank you, sir," she said humbly, at once tearing off the candy wrapper. As she stood there like a child, masticating the chocolate, neither of them said anything. Anything, that is, until again he was aware of the dreadlocks. "*Oh!*" he uttered. Then said no more. Nor did she. She was eating.

More people were entering onto the Métro station platform now where already a crowd was waiting in the slanting sunlight for the arrival of the next train. It was not long in coming. Whereupon there was a great surge toward the car doors in the sunlight. "Don't expect a seat!" warned Tosca breathlessly, yet as best she could she was pushing ahead. In the interim she had pulled off the harried wig and stuffed it in her baggy purse.

Suddenly, then, it occurred to Paul he was already on the train and the train was moving. He was not unhappy — she had taken off the horrid dreadlocks. Behind her now, he was merely trying to keep the two of them from becoming separated.

City of Light

Already now a gray, rat-faced, little man had managed to squeeze himself in between them, although to Paul he seemed innocuous enough. Paul even seemed unfazed when a minute later a second man, nondescript, tieless, somehow wedged his way in between the tiny rat-faced man and Paul. The only clues Paul could use now for identifying Tosca were her singular, reddish dress and the baggy purse jammed under an arm. Five minutes later, then, the train began to slow for its next stop. That was when Paul heard Tosca's bloodcurdling scream. It came, though, only a split second before the tiny rat-faced man who, having been wedged against Tosca, and now having perfectly synchronized his psychopathy with the slowing of the train, managed to dive among three straphanging riders and, eyes rolling, mouth chattering, drooling, as the train stopped, frantically elbowed his way to and through the exit door and onto the platform outside, then ran, scurried, like the wet rat he resembled, out of sight. Meantime, as the train pulled away again, Tosca was still screaming and rubbing, almost kneading, her left buttock as if to make sure it was still intact from the culprit's furtive but compulsive probing and fondling. "That little bastard!" she cried out, still in French, to muddled, confused Paul as well as to all the others in the car. "The little sickie was feeling me up! . . . honest, Monsieur Kessey! If Quo Vadis had been here that little bug, instead of crawling off this train, would by now have been dead, stomped to death, completely obliterated, under giant Quo Vadis's two huge feet! Ghouls like that little pervert should be boiled in oil, Monsieur! . . . Oh, it's awful!" There were tears in her eyes. "I'll bet anything that right now that little insect is somewhere in a toilet closet jerking himself off!" Bewildered, Paul was also now astonished at her indecorous language—he never imagined her having such words, or knowledge, for that matter, in her lexicon. Now he began talking to her quietly, trying to assuage her anger, depression, and humiliation. She paid him scant attention, though — until, discouraged, he finally asked her how far yet they had to go, which at once brought her back to their original intentions: going to the food mart. Biting her lip, she soon became quieter, more self-possessed, and, staring out the Métro window, told him it would be another ten or fifteen minutes before they reached the Saint-Chelles station, their destination. Paul stood firmly beside her now, even put his arm around her waist, which, however, apparently caused her mental discomfort, and she slightly moved her body away from him. Thus, haplessly, they stood, saying little, until she remembered how ravenously hungry she was and began to talk rapidly about food, especially what was to be gotten at the food mart where they were heading. "I think I shall get lamb kidneys," she said. "They are a specialty with Quo Vadis and besides are not so expensive as some other meats. How does that strike you, sir?"

The question seemed not to have reached him. He had instead descried a woman seated near the front of their coach who had eyes and a complexion — though, by far, not the style or class — of someone the mere thought of whom made him gasp for breath. Cécile. She was talking, laughing, to another woman, a friend no doubt, standing over her and he saw her, the seated woman's, bad, almost blackened, teeth. Thinking of Cécile's beauty, her vogue and generally distinguished manner, the sight almost made him shudder; it also filled him with a wrenching sadness. What had happened to him? he wondered — his life, plans, his kismet. Then he remembered, sorrowfully, that he had never had any of these — instead, for the shortest of times, he had had Cécile, a beautiful woman, who had now, to quote the Bard, "melted into air, thin air." Where was she, what had happened to her — what had happened to himself? He realized now he was wretchedly unhappy — not alone for Cécile, though that was a large part of it, but for what she represented. What was it she represented, though, he wondered. It was something that dwelt, existed, far beyond anything he had known — or possibly anything he would ever know. Yet he yearned for her — but was it really for her? Or for what, in his shilly-shallying mind, he thought her to be, or to stand for. But now he was aware of Tosca's eyes on him. "You did not hear my question, Monsieur," she said. "You were daydreaming."

Paul did not smile. He was grim. "We are on our way to buy food, as I understand it," he finally all but sneered. "And how mundane that can be."

Somehow, though, even this response had come, yes, tardily. It seemed indeed to have hardly come at all. Neither of them could be sure. They only glanced ineffectually at each other now — as if perhaps some kinder rejoinder might eventually show its head, anon. It never did.

Seventy-five minutes later a taxi pulled up in front of the dingy little three-flat building where Quo Vadis Jackson lived with his sheltered mother-and-son guests, and Tosca and Paul, laden with groceries, plus a jug of red wine, slowly, cumbersomely, climbed out and at last made it up to the second-floor furnished flat. As for Paul, his faint, apprehensive heart had been pounding ever since they had left the swarming food mart where he had, of course, paid for the groceries and wine. But now he was to meet Quo Vadis, and he was nervous, if not plain scared.

"Hello! . . ." cried Tosca, panting now, when they were inside the flat, her voice echoing throughout the small, dark, cramped quarters. "Anybody home?" Silence. "Quo Vadis and Gwelo must have gone out for their walk," she said. "Let's lug these groceries back to the kitchen." Paul, out of breath, too, followed her — relieved, however, at having gotten a reprieve from the coming dreaded meeting. They started to the rear.

"That's Quo Vadis's bedroom there," she said, nodding to her left. "But I wouldn't dare peep in. He keeps the door shut, as well he might. I can imagine how it looks, like a tornado just struck." She looked to her right now. "That's my bedroom, such as it is; it's clean, though. And Gwelo sleeps on a cot outside my door." They had reached the tiny, drab kitchen now, where they began putting their impedimenta down. "I'm tired," Tosca said. "We've covered a lot of territory today, I more than you." Suddenly then, as if most unpleasantly reminded, she began feeling, kneading, her left buttock again where in the Métro car she had been fondled by the little gray rat-faced man. Pitying herself, she uttered a strangely tearlike sigh, yet somehow kept her eyes on Paul, who, however, had not missed watching and understanding her silent travail—and more. "Stop looking at me like that," she said. "You see, you're doing it again. Quo Vadis would never do that, and he would not like it that you did it. Your eyes were practically undressing me." Paul, though guilty, quickly if tardily looked away, his libido, however, already having soared. No matter, he somehow also felt hurt, not necessarily only because of her harsh words but especially because she had cruelly and negatively compared him with Quo Vadis. He was angered. He felt demeaned.

Finally, trying to keep from exploding, he managed to say, "Tell me this, will you—what's going on between you and Quo Vadis? Is he some kind of stinking saint? That's right, isn't it—you say you wouldn't marry him, that his hygienic habits leave much to be desired; also that he's not exactly of your class. That doesn't keep you and your son, though, from living free of charge in his scruffy but welcome flat. Does it ever occur to you that there still may lurk in his mind the wish to marry you?"

"No it doesn't. He couldn't marry me if he wanted to. Not even if *I* wanted him to. He's already married. To a woman in

City of Light

Atlanta. He walked out on her, though, and then soon came here. He could easily have qualified as a member in good standing of your Coterie — blacks on the move, trying to live down, forget, atone for, as someone said in that final Coterie meeting that day, the scabrous truth of the black diaspora. He also came here, though — after walking out on his wife — to, he says, escape her three brothers, who were looking for him. To kill him. I don't entirely believe this tale, however. Quo Vadis fears no man alive and I'll bet his wife's brothers knew that. I think he really came here to change his whole life, make a fresh start, foil, rout, the anathema of the diaspora. So what so far has been the outcome? Why, he has a job scrubbing and hosing down (for dear life, and to pay his rent) many of the passenger buses of Paris. But that by no means keeps him from having great dreams about his future — and for the future of others, black and white, similarly situated. Yes, in his generosity, his, as he calls it, 'world view,' he's taken on himself the cause of — his word — *mankind*. Some people might think he's got a lot of crazy ideas swirling around in his head, but I'm not one of them. He thinks everybody should have an even break in life. And if they don't, they should take it, by any means at hand. He's got a head full of ideas like that, which are wonderful on paper, or when you hear him discussing them, and often impress you as being mind-boggling. He's always thinking, thinking, thinking, whether he's sitting down, standing, or walking — even, most of all probably, when he's in the bathroom sitting on the toilet. He's also always got a book of some kind in his hand, and they're not books for birdbrain readers. I think I also told you he had three years of college, before he was expelled. He even talks about a lot of his ideas to Gwelo — which I don't particularly care for. I'm the one who should be shaping Gwelo's mind, but, you see, I'm caught in this dilemma that I've so far been unable to escape. How shall we live? . . . What about Gwelo's education? Even Quo Vadis, good man that he is, sees this and, although trying to hide the fact, really wishes I could find some way out. He even told me one day that he prays for me. Actually, you wouldn't think a man like him would be religious but he is. That's one area in which he's good for Gwelo. His genuine interest in what's going to happen to Gwelo and me inspired me to tell him about you — all I had heard about you, all of which, by the way, was good, until I learned the truth on my own: that despite all the nice things people say about you, that I've found you are by nature prone to be a panting skirt-chaser. Of course I didn't know this when I told Quo Vadis all the wonderful things I had heard. As I say, he became very interested, hopeful for me, and encouraged me, as Mr. Lewellyn would have put it, to start camping on your trail. But then I began to think about it. And the more I thought the more I began to see this perhaps was only another harebrained idea of mine. Yet, as you see, it still hasn't prevented me from trying to somehow bring it off. Tell me this, though: earlier today up in your rooms, when I so bluntly, out of the clear blue, told you why I had come, why was it that you didn't merely tell me, just as bluntly, that I must be crazy and for me to go get lost somewhere. You didn't, though. Why?" She tried to smile but it turned into a frown, then a grimace. "You know very well why, Monsieur Kessey — that if you weren't too quick in slamming the door in my face that you might eventually be able to cajole me into having sex with you. Well, let me say that you're not the first man to be attracted to me sexually. I'm aware I attract some men that way. I even thought at first this was what was motivating James Lewellyn, until I remembered that when he detoured to come here he had never seen me before in his life. He had genuinely come to give me the bad news about my brother, that he had been unable to learn anything about him.

City of Light

Nevertheless he had come to see me personally, to tell me, then ask if there was any further way he could help me. He therefore in my mind turned out to be one of the most upright of men. Do you agree? Wouldn't you yourself like to be able to say you regard me in much the same light — platonically?"

Paul eyed her dubiously. Then said nothing.

"The truth is, Monsieur, that I have had absolutely no interest in sex since I lost my husband, since he, with my father, was so cruelly, so brutally, murdered by a pack of wild animals posing as men, as human beings, when actually they were mad dogs. These are the circumstances under which I lost my wonderful husband and now, for more than likely the rest of my life, I am militantly antisex. My poor martyred husband was the only person I ever felt warm and giving about like that, and he still is."

Only now, there in the dismal little kitchen, did they realize how tired, spent, they were and, in their utter absorption, how little they had thought of even briefly sitting down. Still absorbed, and also riled, Paul said hotly, "You're an intelligent woman, Mrs. Zimsu. That's why I can't see how you could say such an absolutely radical thing about sex to a man you're at the same time trying to get closer to. It's almost laughable if it weren't so pathetic. Maybe you're not all that intelligent after all."

"Maybe I'm not," she said ruefully, and looked away.

"But forget sex, Mrs. Zimsu, and let me ask you this: Are you aware that I haven't a dime to my name except what my father gives me? I've moreover never had a job in my twenty-nine years and wouldn't know what to do with one were it imposed upon me by some unthinking person. Considering all that, then, I'd have to be on my way to an insane asylum to get close to a woman who has less than I have — and even fewer prospects — no matter if she is as attractive as you and . . ."

There was suddenly talk outside the front door. They then heard a key in the lock. Tosca jumped and started trying to put the groceries away. "Don't move!" she said hoarsely. "Stay where you are. It's Quo Vadis and Gwelo."

The door opened then and Paul looked — Tosca did not look — to see Gwelo, skinny, brown, tallish for his age, bolt through it, followed finally, though almost solemnly, by a huge, bearded, stygian black, slightly stoop-shouldered giant.

Tosca spoke first: "You fellows must have walked all the way down to the river and back." She was still in the kitchen out of their line of sight and they did not respond. At which juncture, however, Gwelo glimpsed Paul's face poked around at him from the kitchen door frame and his romp ceased. Mouth open, he stood gawking. The bearded black colossus behind him, though, came up and stood appraising nervous Paul. Tosca, now finally visible, repeated herself: "You two must have gone clear down to the Seine." The newcomers seemed too amazed to reply. "Meet Monsieur Paul Kessey — from the United States," Tosca said. Paul, now standing in the kitchen door, smiled weakly and proffered his hand to Quo Vadis who, however, took it gingerly, tentatively, as if having no alternative. "Pleased to meet you," Paul said in English.

"Same here," said Quo Vadis at last.

Now Tosca had turned. "Monsieur Kessey, this is my son, Gwelo." Unhesitatingly, Gwelo stepped forward crisply, like a young adjutant, and put out his hand. Paul took it as the great panjandrum Quo Vadis Jackson, to Paul still an unknown quantity, coolly looked on. But, it was to Quo Vadis that Tosca next turned. "I'm sure we're all as hungry as can be to still be standing around at the kitchen door talking," she said. "I was earlier so famished on our way here that Monsieur Kessey had to buy me a chocolate bar. But listen to this: He also accompanied me to the food mart and bought the food for our dinner." Tosca turned around and waved at the groceries. "The menu is as follows: Lamb kidneys (which you love, Mr. Jackson), boiled potatoes, fresh vegetables of two kinds, crusty Rivoli bread, and a big green salad. How does that sound? And, for you two men, a jug of robust country red wine—a hearty Gamay Beaujolais." Tosca was beaming. "I can sense your mouth watering already, Gwelo."

Gwelo, however, had by now observed Quo Vadis's relative coolness, his aloofness so far, toward the entire proceedings. Gwelo, his staunch apostle, was therefore accordingly affected, negatively; his childish face soon taking on a phony composure, almost a disinterest, in events all its own.

Wily Tosca, though, had missed nothing. "Mr. Jackson," she said, "no matter what an illustrious cook you are, you don't seem in the mood this evening; your mind seems elsewhere. Would you prefer instead that I cook, while you and Monsieur Kessey get acquainted over some wine?"

Frightened Gwelo's hand flew to his face, his mouth, before he could prevent it. He well knew his mother to be an execrable cook. Quo Vadis, already fulfilling Tosca's, yes, wily aims, had all but burst into laughter now. "No, thank you, Mrs. Zimsu," he said. "I'll manage." The uptight atmosphere had thus that quickly been dissolved, Tosca at the same time secretly congratulating herself—except for her one misgiving: How was she to hint to Quo Vadis that he first go wash, scrub, his hands?

Even Paul now felt better, though, having seen Quo Vadis in a different light, even if he was uncertain about how long the black giant's "era of good feeling" might last. There was, however, another aspect of Quo Vadis's presence, his mind-set, and their expressions, that Paul, in all the talk and greetings that had so far been rife, had until now overlooked. It was Quo Vadis's strange voice. It was somehow high at certain times, occasionally even strident—especially for a man of his great size, weight, strength, and apparent aggressiveness. No matter, the voice was somehow fully masculine, no tilt, lilt, or melody; yet, for Paul, it was still an octave too high. He thought it only served to make this already extremely interesting man even more so still. Soon then, when the general talk would permit, Paul, almost as if staging a test, and again speaking English to Quo Vadis, smiled and said, "At least a couple of times today on our way here Mrs. Zimsu spoke of what a great cook you are. How did this ability come to you?"

Quo Vadis, pausing, did not look particularly pleased. At last he said, "I was a chef on an Amtrak train for awhile after I left college after three years." But, to Paul's astonishment, the voice was now low, quite low and measured, perhaps even ominous, too, and altogether free of stridency. So the man had two voices, Paul concluded immediately. It was therefore when he was at ease, agreeable, or maybe even laughing, Paul was almost sure now, that the voice seemed high—*was* high— when it should have been just the reverse. He was puzzled. But soon he was flattered to hear, to his surprise, his own name being spoken by both Tosca and Quo Vadis in a mishmash of broken French and English, freely participated in as well by alert and precocious Gwelo.

"Quo Vadis, let's get going," said Gwelo. "I'm hungry."

Quo Vadis ignored him and spoke to Tosca. "Mrs. Zimsu, I wouldn't dare show a lack of respect for the estimable Monsieur Kessey here after he has gone to all the trouble and expense of furnishing us with the makings of sumptuous meal, especially when we're all so hungry. As you say, I love lamb kidneys, and not only because they are less expensive than most meats, but because of their succulence and especially their hardy tang when properly prepared with olive oil and garlic. We are unanimous, then, in saluting our esteemed visitor from the States who has without doubt come to us bearing timely and welcome gifts." He stepped over and began rummaging through the numerous bagged grocery items on the kitchen table—before Tosca politely but nervously intervened.

"Mr. Jackson," she said, "let me right quickly go get a clean towel and put it in the bathroom for you. You'll feel more relaxed then. . . . I mean your hands."

"Why, that would be nice, Mrs. Zimsu," said Quo Vadis. "Thank you indeed." Although still addressing Tosca, he had now turned his unrevealing eyes on Paul. "I also hope and trust, Mrs. Zimsu, that you have had a pleasant—and productive— day's visit with Monsieur Kessey. I construe this lovely food, and especially the luscious wine, as tidings of negotiations well had by you both."

Tosca almost gasped.

"What negotiations, Quo Vadis?" said Gwelo.

"I think we're getting the cart before the horse." Quo Vadis smiled. "It's time for me to start cooking first, Gwelo my man."

"I wholeheartedly agree," Gwelo said.

But Paul had been listening to Quo Vadis's voice. Paul, however, was still unsure, even puzzled yet. What would that voice be like with its owner on one of his reputed warpaths? Paul was fascinated by this. He was fascinated by the man, Quo Vadis Jackson; one, thought Paul, whose secret may well be authority—such as that of Achilles, Patroclus, Odysseus, Nestor; also Hector, even though from the enemy. Authority, yes, sought to be wielded now by a black American titan who washed and hosed down Paris's buses but not himself. Paul, though, at this early time, could only surmise. He had been in the presence of the man not ten minutes; his conclusions were therefore obviously underripe, overhasty, he knew; yet he sensed here a being, staunch and virile, who was somehow outside the pale; probably; maybe, that is. The man with at least two voices, who — Paul was leaning on what Tosca had said of this black soapless mammoth who had given her a home — who, yes, it was hoped, meant to use those voices in some goodly cause. Paul knew he himself had tried, and met defeat, because he knew not authority, the concept of it. This man, now, was therefore worth studying — for both the voices, the strong one and the weak, from this black behemoth, yes, who hadn't time to bathe.

"Are you hungry, Quo Vadis?" Gwelo said in French. "*I* am."

"Then everybody must leave the kitchen," said Quo Vadis, "while I go get in my house shoes and tie on an apron — and also deplug that wine."

"I've already put your hand towel out for you, Mr. Jackson," Tosca said, a bland yet somehow worried expression on her face.

Whereupon Quo Vadis said innocently, "Why is that, Mrs. Zimsu?" and promptly laughed in the high, raucous, strident one of his voices, of which Paul took serious, captivated note. "I shall, yes, now go wash up," Quo Vadis said. "And remember, I must then have the kitchen to myself. I owe our generous guest here, Monsieur Kessey, the tribute of the best meal I can put together." Before them all, then, he began peeling off the musty maroon turtleneck sweater he had been wearing under a dingy corduroy jacket. The T-shirt underneath all this, however, looked reasonably clean as Tosca gave a somehow stealthy sigh before they all now dispersed.

Up front the small living room of the flat, with its ancient sofa and three mismatched chairs, nonetheless contained the dining table around which they would all later gather. This was the area to which Tosca now took Paul and Gwelo, pointing them both to the sofa, while she took a chair not quite facing them. This, of course, was where she had in mind trying to keep Paul preoccupied with random shoptalk, while Quo Vadis back in the kitchen drank Paul's red wine and made dinner. What, though, she had apparently forgotten was her son—captious Gwelo's utter impatience with shoptalk.

"Earlier, Mother," he was not long in asking, "what 'negotiations' were you and Quo Vadis talking about?—negotiations today between you and Monsieur Kessey. You remember that when I asked Quo Vadis about it he brushed me off, said I was getting the cart before the horse. What cart, what horse?" Now Gwelo rubbed his nose vigorously, almost angrily, then looked sideways at Paul on the sofa at his elbow.

Tosca, her eyes moving left and right, her brain working feverishly, seemed no longer afraid of the question, rather regarded it possibly as an opportunity. She feigned a deep sadness now, though directed less at Gwelo—whom, however, her eyes still pointedly held—than at Paul. She said to Gwelo, "Dear, it's a subject—although you are very much involved—we can't fully discuss at this time. Some other, maybe. But it's very important to us both. Even to Quo Vadis—who had a perfect right to broach the subject to me when I returned with Monsieur Kessey. You well know what a terrible time you and I have had in merely having a place to sleep, food to eat, to say nothing of what it's been like to try to continue your education. Yes, Quo Vadis as well has been as concerned about it as you and I—the man has worried about us almost as if we were his family. Look what he's done for us as it is, with hardly any more money than we have. I hope in some way, at some time, God will repay him for his generosity. But he, realizing he is not the answer to our difficulties, has encouraged me, or us, to get out in the larger world, forage about, as it were, meet other people, people, if possible, of standing, substance, character, to see if any of them would recognize our plight and help us. Otherwise our future is bleak, Gwelo."

Paul had a wry, not quite contemptuous, smile on his face. "But, Mrs. Zimsu," he finally said, "what, in such an arrangement, would be in it for such a kind benefactor? Does he come in for any consideration at all?"

Tosca bristled, knowing his meaning. "Yes! . . . Yes, he does," she said. "He experiences the glory of God, Monsieur Kessey."

Gwelo's eyes seemed popping from his head as they went from his mother to the man at his left, then back, only still to return. He, of course, understood nothing about what they were so seriously — his mother heatedly — differing. He wanted, though, fiercely, to join in on her side but he could not fathom what they were talking about. It riled him and tears came to his eyes.

Tosca finally noticed now and sought to assuage him. "Gwelo," she said, "You mustn't think Monsieur Kessey and I are having a misunderstanding. The truth is . . . oh, I may as well tell you, that it's about Monsieur Kessey and me. Quo Vadis thinks maybe Monsieur Kessey might be able to help us, take up sort of where he's left off; when, that is, he's going to be unable to do any more than he's doing already. He thinks, as a matter of fact, that you and I deserve much better."

Gwelo's childish face was still innocently gyrating from one to the other of them. Paul, seeing the boy's agony, wretchedness, in understanding nothing of the talk that his mother, Paul thought, had so dumbly and inconsiderately opened up, was deeply touched, contrite, and furious with Tosca for what he deemed her thoughtlessness, almost callousness. He then, however, soon began to think about himself, his own condition, his plight, vis-à-vis the boy's headstrong, capricious mother, and began to hate himself. Why, he thought, was he spending all this time and energy — and money — with this admittedly good, but crazy woman, especially when he had no thought on earth, ever, of marrying her? The very thought was laughable, yes. He would be better off staying to himself, no matter how lonely he was in his rooms at Madame Chevalley's, than, in trying to deal with the recent emptiness in his life (Cécile, the Coterie) than, yes, taking up with someone like this, regardless of the fact that she was a good woman, educated, physically appealing, with valid class, and a poignant love and ambition for her young son. But this was not for him, he told himself; he must get out of it, at once, indeed after this very evening. Soon he was no longer angry with himself. Now it was only pity.

It was almost an hour before Quo Vadis — again in his high gleeful voice — summoned them to put the plates and silverware on the table, then get ready to come help him bring in the food. Gwelo, having gotten few if any of his crucial, nagging questions answered, had finally gone off to sleep on the sofa. Meanwhile, Tosca and Paul had taken pains to stay off topics, subjects, that would try their patience and thus their tempers. She told him in tedious detail about her part-time job at the nearby fruit-and-vegetable market, and he talked of his mother out on their big lawn punting footballs to him in the clear, bright, chill of autumn. Nothing more happened then, which was what they both wanted. Yet they could feel the strange, inexplicable tensions between them, Paul's, however, mostly libidinous. Tired, hungry, hectored Gwelo was snoring. Finally, with the coming of Quo Vadis's summons, they agreed on letting Gwelo sleep the remaining few minutes while they went back to help transport the food. As they stole out of the dank living room, Tosca turned and asked Paul in French, "Do you like me any better now, Monsieur?"

He slowed, cleared his throat, then for a moment studied the dusty ceiling. "I'm afraid not, Mrs. Zimsu," he finally said.

To herself she smiled.

The little kitchen smelled heavenly as they entered, conjuring up as their reward all manner of wholesome and succulent things for starving people, who had at last won a kind of coveted alimentary prize conferred by a 260-pound chef-in-charge. They found Quo Vadis, heavily perspiring and the red wine jug (three-liter size) over a third empty. Paul also now saw in his host a new, even stranger, yet a more graphic human being than he only an hour and a half before could have imagined. But this time it was Quo Vadis's face that astonished him. Not one of the dual voices. The face-syndrome now played an almost startling role in a vastly different likeness, coupled with a whole new presentation of self. First of all, this face was not only large, and somewhat misbegotten, also, of course, jet black, but in shape and contour somehow more rotund, less graven and symmetrical, than Paul had earlier perceived it. There was also, to Paul's surprise, and self-embarrassment, a dark, almost maroonish sheen to this face somehow intermixed with the jet blackness, which now, though, seemed a kind of hybrid shimmering of rose-blush on black and, potentially, could, when the subject was angered, much less furious, with brazen teeth bared like fangs, could, yes, change into something frightening, horrific. This, conceivably, was the new message on his face—another Quo Vadis, who was not talking now. Was it the wine, the third of a jug, he had drunk as he cooked? Paul wondered. The hot kitchen? Or what? It was also quite noticeable that his formerly white apron was smudged with food particles and various heavy seasoning substances he had apparently used in the troubled throes of his cooking, all evidence of the thoughtless, over-wrought use of the apron as some mammoth hand towel. Paul was awed. He also awaited the opportunity to hear which Quo Vadis voice would soon go into action at dinner, thereby signifying what mood would reign. He somehow felt on the eve of discovery.

"Oh, you must be very tired, Mr. Jackson—standing on your feet all that time," said Tosca.

"It's not my feet, Mrs. Zimsu," Quo Vadis said.

Paul wished she had kept quiet. Besides, he was already communing.

But Quo Vadis was calling on him now, softly. "You may take in that plate of kidneys there, if you will," he said, pointing. "And, God, don't trip."

Ah, it's the low voice now, not the high, thought Paul. Paradoxically, he was glad. He had no idea yet why.

And it was Quo Vadis, not Tosca, a few minutes later when they were all—Gwelo still rubbing his eyes—seated at the table, who apologized for the coffee stains on the table-cloth. Waiting then for the perfect quiet, he, *sotto voce*, said the blessing: "Dear Lord, we thank Thee for merely another day. There is no law that says we had it coming to us, except Your great, and settled law, which takes precedence over any edict by man. We especially thank You for answering prayers— in this case ours, Mrs. Zimsu's and mine—and accordingly sending into our midst, hopefully into our lives to come, this good man Monsieur Paul Kessey. We consider him Your personal emissary, for he has unquestionably been endowed with Your own humanity and generosity. Witness but the food on this table this evening. It is his work through Yours." (To Paul's utter fascination, Quo Vadis was speaking hardly above a whisper, soon bringing him misunderstanding and impatient frowns from his acolyte Gwelo across the table.) "So we praise Your intervention, dear Lord. There is much at stake—not only Mrs. Zimsu's life, a great part of which, of course, has already been lived, but also that of her young and adored genius of a son, who is just beginning the slippery business of life, one of the most precocious minds, and promising futures, of any young person I have been privileged to know well. Monsieur Kessey, a man who by his record, even here in Paris, has shown he understands, and accepts, the duty we all have to others less fortunate than ourselves. So far, then, dear Lord, You have looked down beneficently on our present plight and at the very time of certain important, indeed crucial, negotiations aimed at saving the lives and hopes of two people whom I've come much to admire since they joined me here, sharing my dark, humble quarters and, in doing so, making a little more pleasant, endurable, the rocky life it seems my lot to live. But now all this must change, hence these timely negotiations I've mentioned. Our trust is in You, Lord—in Your wisdom, saving grace, Your mercy most of all—the trust that You will do what only You know to be best. Please, then, bless this food—in the name of Jesus, Your Son. Amen."

Gwelo, eyes wide, alight, his wiry body straining forward on the edge of his chair, finally said, impatiently, to Quo Vadis: "For the second time this evening—*what* negotiations?"

It was Quo Vadis who was patient—and still, to Paul's continued captivation, hardly letting his voice climb above a whisper—patient in replying to Gwelo, his voice low, caring: "How about waiting till tomorrow, Gwelo. We'll talk. At present I know little more than you." He turned to Tosca now—"Would you please pass the lamb kidneys to Monsieur Kessey?"

Thus the dinner was finally launched—Quo Vadis pouring Paul a brimming glass of the heady Gamay Beaujolais, himself then as well; Tosca, though, remaining the teetotaler, while Gwelo still smarted under the maddening "negotiations" mystery. Quo Vadis's voice was still low (Paul took note), yet, somewhat now buttressed, strengthened, by the wine, was rising in intonation by the minute as he, Quo Vadis, almost at once opened the conversation (the meeting) thus: "Monsieur Kessey, what brought you to Paris originally?"

The question was not unexpected, yet Paul took his time, was earnest, deliberate, speaking his broken French to be sure Tosca and Gwelo were included. "In Chicago I was at my wit's end, I guess you could call it," he said. "My mother had died, and the marvelous girl I had been in love with, Jeannette – a lawyer, later a judge in Africa, in Zaire – was killed, in Zaire on a mercy mission, in a ghastly plane crash. So I was about wiped out after all that."

"Oh, I should imagine!" said Tosca sympathetically. But Quo Vadis, masticating his salad, sat watching, waiting.

"I admit," said Paul, "that I chose Paris back then for its romantic reputation – the culture, a haven of the arts, a very literary place, et cetera. But another reason was – because of Jeannette, whom I regarded as a martyr, a symbol of giving one's life to help others – I suppose I wanted to do something on my own (not to lose my life at it, of course) but something that would give me some stature, in my own eyes if in no other's; a belief in myself, that I was worth something after all and . . ."

A high, now almost soprano, voice intruded. Paul's ongoing fascination, however, made him glad to give way. "Ah-ha!" said Quo Vadis gleefully. "You were looking for a symbol. Right? Nothing wrong with that – if, that is, it doesn't take youe eyes off the main prize." Paul, bewildered, could only observe him and say nothing. He waited for Quo Vadis to continue, but he did not and merely poured himself more wine before forking his hot, buttered potato. Finally, with Paul still silent, Quo Vadis added: "Now don't get me wrong. I don't demean you. In fact, you speak with authority. So much so – considering your relatively high-class background – that I sometimes have the urge to address you differently. Not as 'monsieur,' necessarily, but still in some way that accords you some title of the crown, say, or something very near it—ha, like 'Your Lordship,' or at least 'Your Grace.'" Now Quo Vadis's spinto voice spiraled ceilingward in highest delight. Paul could only conclude his host was drunk. This gave him anxieties. He continued to observe Quo Vadis and finally, rather, thought himself to be wrong—it was something else. He vowed to test the man now. "Mr. Jackson," he said, "you are a religious man, and I was wondering if . . ."

"Aren't *you*, Your Lordship?" Quo Vadis intervened.

Gwelo giggled. "Nobody is but you, Quo Vadis," he said.

"I was asking him," Paul said, "if there was any dogmatic, or canonical, conflict between praying and imbibing alcohol."

"None whatever," said Quo Vadis. "But I have no problem with alcohol. I'm always in complete control of myself, Your Grace." He reached for the jug, and Gwelo giggled again, causing Quo Vadis also to laugh, stridently. "I am religious, of course," he said. "What nigger in his right mind, with all we've been through, is not religious? But I don't let it interfere with having a little fun occasionally. Like now, with his Lordship here, who has set us up to such a lovely meal— and which I had the honor of preparing . . ."

"Oh, what a wonderful job you did of it, too, Mr. Jackson." said Tosca. "You're entitled to a glass of wine; a wine, mind you, that I selected with you in mind."

"Thank you, Mrs. Zimsu," said Quo Vadis. "The Lord will bless you."

Paul still could not make up his mind—was Quo Vadis drunk or was he demented? He felt uneasy nevertheless. No matter, he was inclined to admire the man—in fact, very much inclined.

City of Light

An hour and half later found Gwelo, his stomach full of food, his mind, though, groggy from sleeplessness and fatigue, making his bed on the cot outside his mother's bedroom door, after which she herself retired for the night to her room inside not knowing, however, whether her dreams were to be the terrifying nightmares she so dreaded or the blessed revisit to the halcyon days and nights of her tender youth. As for the two men, Quo Vadis had brewed a pot of coffee which now stood on the dining table between them as they talked and argued — seriously.

"You asked the question," Quo Vadis was saying, "and I'm going to answer it. But I had interrupted you almost before you could ask it — about my praying and drinking on the same occasion. I think I said, in effect, there was no problem, no conflict. Then I got off into something about religion in general, but soon about the nice food you had brought — ha, or did I say 'bought?', which was also the truth — and also that I had cooked so successfully, et cetera, et cetera."

It was now Paul's assessment, once more, that the wine had taken Quo Vadis over completely. Soon, though, he was once more equivocating about this complex giant, especially the kind of education he'd had, and his mind. Or was he plain nutty, or, yes, trying to confuse him, get the better of him? He was uncertain about it all and elected merely to sit and listen.

"And even before that," said Quo Vadis, "I had already interrupted you when you were telling about your sweetheart Jeannette who was killed in that horrible plane crash in Zaire after all the good things she was trying to do for others, et cetera. It was extremely interesting, also touching. I can't conceive — and certainly can't recall — why I was carrying on so like this; the interruptions, et cetera. Maybe I was afraid you had upstaged me — which, ha, is something I've never been able to abide. It's my ego, of course—I have one hell of an ego!" His voice, Paul noticed, was now fast reaching the strident range. As always, Paul's captivation and curiosity rose apace. What an extraordinary human being, he thought—even if he did in fact turn out to be a nut.

"The reason I came to Paris, though," Quo Vadis went on, "had nothing about it, unlike in your case, so noble as trying to do good. Oh, Lord, no. I was on the run. Not from the law. From my wife in Atlanta, Georgia. And there were other reasons—actually a lot of them—but I won't go into all that at this setting. But I hope we shall have other sessions. I can help you. I've sized you up here this evening and I'm impressed—that's the truth. You do need help, though. I know. I did myself at one point in my life. So besides running from my wife, Glade, and her outlaw brothers, my own main reason was to get away from those American niggers so that I could think. Just think; that's all. Or maybe even learn *how* to think. Hear me, that's a big deal in itself—just learning how to put on your thinking cap. So here I was—back in the days when, like you now, I was looking, searching, reading, even spying on other people's lives, trying to get a hold on my life—as you so aptly, and kind of pitifully, too, I thought, put it—so I'd win some stature for myself. Even if nobody else agreed, *I'd* know I was a man of substance, and character, and humanity, a guy who cared for other people sometimes. One of my two great helpers in all this was of course religion, the church—I was born again. I did then, and do now, take Jesus Christ very seriously—*very*. My other helper was books. Weighty books. That's how I learned how to think, Monsieur Kessey. It changed my life."

Paul, however, in his mind's eye, could not refrain from envisioning Quo Vadis the very next day in the act of scrubbing, then hosing down, a jumbo municipal bus. He did say, though, "Tell me, Mr. Jackson, how did you happen to meet Mrs. Zimsu?"

"That's a long story but not a very important one. The important story was when, at her daily insistence, I began to see Gwelo's outstanding promise. He's a real whiz-kid. He didn't say much tonight because he was tired and hungry — and also resentful that we didn't explain what we were talking about when we mentioned 'negotiations.' We'll get to that later. It's a big problem, though, and the first chance you have — meeting Mrs. Zimsu — of really doing something spectacularly good. You came over here to do good — like the girl in Africa. These are two very fine people — people of our own race. This latter is important. As blacks — you and I — we know what a rough road they've traveled, but how much rougher, with Gwelo coming into his own, it's now going to be, for her; even if she is a smart, and feisty, woman. But she has no breadwinning skills — that's the tragedy. She worries all the time about Gwelo's education, but I worry about *her*. And maybe so should you, Monsieur Kessey — although you've known her for only a week or two."

Paul said coldly, "If you were I what would you do? If you were I, yes . . ."

Quo Vadis exploded. "Hell, I'm *not* you, Your Grace. I'm a man who makes his living by the hardest manual labor imaginable. I did not go to Princeton, but for three years to a little black college down in Tennessee. You're asking me a moot question: 'What would *I* do?' I'd do what I've been doing for the past few months — keeping a roof over their heads. That's all I *can* do. Yes, your question is moot — I almost said ignorant, Your Lordship."

"You know, Mr. Jackson," Paul said, "I don't necessarily appreciate those comical, or meant to be comical, titles you've cavalierly given me. I don't exactly consider myself a clown. Apparently, though, you do."

"Monsieur Kessey, sad to say, we all somehow qualify for that 'title,' as you call it. That's sad, of course. But, rest assured, I wasn't placing you apart from the rest of us. You can't get your life together, despite the fact that I hear you're already twenty-nine, so you are one of those people in the king's court, a joker, a harlequin, who would have others laugh at their, the jester's, sorrows, failures, ineptitudes, and at times almost feel glad, for at least you can say, as indeed you've already said, that you seek 'stature.' So you have stature, Rigoletto and Tonio style, but you are a clown, a very solemn clown, yet a clown, and you chose the identity just now yourself. But, as I say, you are not alone. We are all clowns!"

Paul felt his eyes stinging, then, momentarily, they watered over. Suddenly then he was angry. "Tell me," he said, his teeth almost grinding, "what is it you want of me?"

"First, some information," said Quo Vadis after sipping his coffee. "Was Mrs. Zimsu forthright today in telling you why she had come to see you?"

"Yes, in a way."

"What did she say?"

"Well, let me paraphrase it. It was something to the effect that you had said, sir, or at least intimated, that you might have other future plans for yourself, plans that did not, perhaps could not, include her and her son, and that you had thought of me as a possible successor to you in trying to help them."

Quo Vadis was watching him now. "What happened?" he said.

"We talked and I told her the truth—that I'd never had a job in my life, that I subsist entirely on the largesse of my successful father, a businessman; that I, sir, was not your man."

"So that's what happened, eh?" said Quo Vadis. "You made her shoot a blank. Well, you'd never have guessed it by watching her high spirits tonight."

City of Light

"Who knows?" Paul said. "She may have been glad about the outcome. I think she sees me as a very sex-oriented guy and she would probably want no part of that life, I gather."

"Ah, how sorry I feel for her," Quo Vadis said. "I think it has to do with all she's been through, possibly with some of the horrible experiences she had, for all we know, that terrible time when both her husband and her father were slaughtered, and now the same may have happened to her brother, her only brother, who made the probably fatal mistake of returning there on a revenge mission. Who knows, maybe if — and it's only a guess, a surmise — as women we had been through such an experience, we too may have had the same abhorrence of sex. The marauding soldiers, you know, may have raped her."

Paul was so shocked he could make no comment.

"Plus the fact . . . or I mean the possibility," stuttered Quo Vadis, "that she may in some way sense that she looks good, indeed, very good, to you, as well. Now, don't get me wrong — I'm not saying that you should be taken out somewhere and shot for that. Still, Mrs. Zimsu is a chaste and sensitive lady and she may be reading your mind — ah, like *I* am."

At once Paul tried to finesse what was apparent in Quo Vadis's thoughts, saying, "She does have a strong reaction, negative of course, to anything she considers even hinting at sexual intrusiveness. For instance, coming here this afternoon on the Métro, one of those weird little sallow-faced sex freaks who often, to get their pleasure, ride the crowded trains, apparently got close enough to fondle her. By her frantic screams you'd have thought he had drawn a knife to cut her throat. It was scary. But I wasn't close enough to grab the sick little bastard before, perfectly timed, he scooted off the train at the next stop. My failed attempts to get to the guy, however, didn't keep her from reminding me that had you instead been on the train the little malefactor would quickly have been dead, stomped to death by you. It told a lot, though, about the fear and violence of her sex reactions. One can only feel sorry for her."

Throughout, Quo Vadis had sat studying Paul, trying to read his true mind, with presumably negligible results. Finally he rose, went in the kitchen, and put the coffee pot on again. He returned then saying, though as if he had just thought of it: "She has a strong sense of self. Actually a high opinion of herself. That's of course admirable. Nevertheless, she also has considerable admiration for you. She tells about observing you pulling all the tricks in the book to get that white man, the British journalist, to come speak to that organization you had. Apparently the man sobered up and came the next day. She thought that took a lot of savvy, also a lot of courage, even if your members did later turn you down. They're the kind that made me want to get out of the States—you can't help people like that. I learned that years ago, even when I was a student down at Gladstone College in Tennessee. I was trying to do something roughly similar to what you were doing and I got thrown out of school on my ass for it. Oh, I could teach you a lot of things—I know all about the hard knocks involved in trying to help our folks. They think they know everything, when actually they don't know their asses from a hole in the ground much of the time. As I say, that's why I got the hell out of the States."

"I think you're too hard on blacks," Paul said. "Dealing with them is a lot more complicated than you make it out to be, in my opinion. Sure, I resented what they did here to me. But, in looking back, a lot of it was due to my own ineptness, wishy-washiness, inability to make decisions, et cetera. They lost confidence in me—although they did not dislike me."

"That's what I hear. Well, it's too bad. My case was different, though. Down at Gladstone College, where I was most of the time an honor student, the students, or ninety percent of them, were solidly behind me in what I was trying to do—get a monument erected to a former student who was lynched, back in the 1940s."

Paul was impressed, and curious. "That *was* a big deal," he said. "No, I've never been in on anything like that." He stopped to think. "I don't know, but in such a situation I might handle myself better than in some smaller matter, like, say, the Coterie."

"If that's true," Quo Vadis said, "and it might well be— for I don't see you as any coward—you would have gotten thrown out of Gladstone just like I did, or sooner. But that was a great ordeal for me. I've never forgotten it—how could I? Have you ever been in the South?"

"No," Paul said.

"Some years ago that would have been a handicap, but no more—much of the South now is better for us than the North since Southern blacks got the vote. So I'm sure you never heard of a little town in southwestern Tennessee called Valhalla. That's where Gladstone College is located. And of course, I take it, you're not aware of a guy, a student back then at Gladstone, by the name of Lee. Rollo Ezekiel Lee. The other students were crazy about him. He was also the type they could poke fun at, tell anecdotes about: like the brawl he got into with the local white police (which is funny, but I won't spend time on it tonight) for which the students came up with a nickname for him—'Cager.' The town of Valhalla back then was a real cracker town—mean and dangerous for blacks. Remember this was during the time of World War II, and Cager spoke the student's language, as it were, about the rampant discrimination, bigotry, and antiblack violence in the town. On the other hand, he worked, did house chores for an aristocratic old white woman who in the main was good to him.

Cyrus Colter

Meantime, in his rather crazy though well-intentioned zeal, he got himself in an impossible situation in which he was having all kinds of visions, glimpses and glimmers, about what blacks went through in slavery and — good God! — finally worked himself into such a state that he took all his miseries out on the old woman, ran her through with an ancient Confederate bayonet, killing her. All hell erupted, of course. Cager was lynched, naturally — burned alive — and Valhalla plunged into a period of bloody riots in which many from both sides were killed and the courthouse burned to the ground. It was a catastrophe that was still being talked about by Gladstone students when I arrived there twenty-five years later. I — my rash self — soon got very much interested in the whole matter, its history and aftermath. I studied everything about it I could get my hands on. At last, then, despite the heinousness of Cager's crime, I began to see and better understand much of what had been on his mind and in his heart. It was both hair-raising and poignant. Right or wrong — I was yet only a junior — I soon began to see Cager not only not as a murderer but as a hero. I talked many of my student friends into agreeing with me, getting them interested in his life and tragically short career, until he almost became a campus idol. It was not long then before I took up leadership in behalf of an effort to raise the money (not only from students and their families but from the Valhalla black townspeople) to do something really great, even if expensive — that is erect an imposing statue of Cager on the campus lawn in front of the library. This of course started a big turmoil in town hardly less acrimonious than the original havoc a quarter of a century before. Naturally, the black president of Gladstone, John Glass, ordinarily a pretty nice guy, declared war on me and many other students active in the enterprise, but especially on me, the instigator of it all. It was hell. The upshot of it was that they expelled me and two of my lieutenants. I never got over

that, yet I learned more about life, and good, and evil—
mankind, in short—in that struggle when I was a college
youngster, than probably I've learned in all this time since.
One of the main things I learned, though, was that there are not
good or bad people in this world necessarily, but people with
agendas. Be careful, keep your eyes open, steer clear of them,
for they will destroy you if you're not able to save yourself by
destroying them first. This is what it's all about and almost
all the books I've read—and, Monsieur Kessey, if I may say so,
that's a goodly number—have merely corroborated it. I've also
learned a helluva lot just on general principle, just by keeping
my eyes open and my mouth shut, all of which I'll tell you
about sometime, things that will help you yourself to unravel
all those tangled threads in your life, so that you'll soon be
able more or less to follow a road that has few detours, that
is going someplace, and will bring you out at a destination
which generally equates with one thing only—victory." Paul,
though, could only think of the municipal bus wash. "Yet,"
said Quo Vadis, "these are all things, thank God, that can be
taught—taught, that is, to intelligent people who are trying to
straighten out their lives. The effort's not all that complicated
either, really. The main thing that's required—but it's a must—
is guts, courage, stamina, even, if need be, the willingness to
die. You can't live forever anyhow, you know. It's not how
long you live, it's the quality of your life while you are
living. What I mean by the quality, of course, is the success
you achieve in helping others; people who would otherwise
have long fallen by the wayside. I learned a lot from Cager
Lee's life and history, his martyrdom also of course, and
I shall always have faith in what he stood for. Not murder.
But in having visions about improving one's life and that of
others—in his case that of his fellow blacks who are to this day
catching hell in this world, in this 'veil of tears,' as my father

used to call it, and trying to find the high road to eventual deliverance."

Paul was watching him carefully, closely, as he preached; not only out of curiosity but in an effort, a feel for, the basic premises he spoke from. Could there be, possibly, Paul wondered, the slightest chance that any of the folderol he had been listening to had any efficacy — any at all? Was it the man's genuine orientation that fueled all this fervor in his now-high-again voice, gesticulating fingers, the wild gleam in his eyes? There was one thing, however, thought Paul, that without doubt was convincing, viz., that Quo Vadis himself believed, utterly, in what he was saying. To Paul this was apparent, and not without its own importance, its inclination, yes, more or less to convince. But he somehow now wanted to leave, return to his rooms back at Madame Chevalley's, and himself for a change engage in his own rigorous thought process. His host here claimed one was capable of — ha, — thinking one's way to "victory." This man had to be nuts, thought Paul. What had his thought regimen done for himself — Quo Vadis, that is. Nothing which could be detected — indeed nothing except exhortations, homilies, prayers, which often had a facile, hollow ring. Yet, it occurred to Paul, there was also the possibility, slight or not, that they had the ring of truth.

Quo Vadis suddenly cleared his throat, as if importuned by some insistent higher order that he indulge himself with just one more afterthought: "It is an absolute necessity," he said now in his highest, wavering, yet most sanctimonious voice, "that the strong protect the weak. It's God's own edict. We die for it or else overcome."

Paul looked at him. He so wanted to believe him. He thought of Jeannette, thought of her now as a saint, no less. But this huge, hulking, jet-black man before him, with the slightest stoop, the yellowish teeth, and extremely small eyes, like an opossums's, with great rough hands—was it vouch-safed to this man to lead him in the almost-sacred ways of a Jeannette? He could not abide the pregnant thought.

"It's no secret," said Quo Vadis, "that what I speak of here tonight—I'm sure it's not lost on a man of your penetrating intelligence—deals almost directly with your involvement, consciously, willfully, or not, with Mrs. Zimsu. It's God, no less, who has assigned you this mission. You can shirk it only at your own peril. Therefore, where she is concerned, you can no longer let your mind dwell on sex. Your assignment is a high, not a low, one. She does not appreciate your wayward-ness. Yet I don't think I've asked you your opinion of Mrs. Zimsu. Would you care to venture a comment on that?"

There was a pause. Paul felt cornered. Finally: "I'd prob-ably agree with her on her rather high estimate of herself. But I'd also probably agree with her on what she thinks of me, if that makes any sense."

The penetration by Quo Vadis's beady eyes told Paul he had not been clearly understood, that his statement, especially about what Tosca thought of him, was somewhat enigmatic. Quo Vadis pondered it, however, for a moment, then at last desisted. Instead he reached across and shook Paul's hand. "Well, enough said," he lied, his changed voice somehow now guttural, then again edgy, all at the same time. It was apparent he was struggling with another idea, even if ancillary, but did not quite know how to put it. "It's your background," he finally said. "You yourself, I warrant, understand that with Mrs. Zimsu this is a matter of the highest order. Not necessarily to me, who is in charge here, but to people like her, and you—it is important. She sees her son coming to manhood under the influence of a high-born black man like you, who, though, is still hardly black—yet black enough, for her. Whether, in the long run, this is good for Gwelo, I don't know. I must not let my prejudices lead me into miscalculation. She almost faints when she hears me inadvertently say a 'bad' word or two (I of course had no inkling she was around—I respect her, so I'd never have said it), but Gwelo is another matter. I know, more than anybody, I think, about his precocity and what it means for his future—for hers too—if he is properly influenced. But this can mean many things to many people. I, for one, believe that you handicap a kid like that if you shield him too much from the sordid, the shitty, side of life. How can a man help the downtrodden—and that's what I'm trying to talk Gwelo into becoming interested in—when he has no knowledge or experience about the terrible lives some of them have to live, and with no relief in sight. Just suppose, for instance, Cager Lee—who was the son of a dirt-poor Virginia sharecropper—had been brought up the way Mrs. Zimsu wants Gwelo to be. Could he ever have felt as he did for the illiterate, unwashed blacks?—and finally give his life for them."

"Mr. Jackson," Paul said uneasily, "when you say 'unwashed blacks' do you mean that literally? . . ."

"No, I don't mean it literally. It's a shorthand way of isolating that class of people in any conversation dealing with them and their plight. Yet, Monsieur Kessey, when you get right down to it, there's a limit anyhow to the number of baths you can take in a day. Even Queen Elizabeth the First, and later, Queen Marie Antoinette, of France, took baths only when they felt like it—which wasn't always often. Sometimes they wore all those fancy floor-dragging dresses and smelled to high heaven at the same time. This is no earth-shattering issue, believe me, especially when you've got people, even poor little children, starving to death. And let me add, the people who perpetrate or permit it should be brought to book for it—and by that I mean by the knife or firing squad."

"But, Mr. Jackson," said Paul, "one can still be a leader

for all these things you're talking about, the improvement of the lot of less fortunate people, et cetera, and still take baths." Paul smiled.

Quo Vadis grimaced malevolently. "I see what you're trying to get around to, all right, Mr. Princeton. I guess you'll soon be wanting to know how frequently, or infrequently, *I* bathe. Huh?"

Paul almost gasped. "I want to know nothing of the kind . . ."

"Well, then, I'll tell you anyhow. Just like those two queens, I bathe whenever I feel like it — unless, that is, I begin to itch. You see, with me it's a kind of badge. It, inside my brain at least, identifies me with, yes, other unwashed people. What's wrong with that? I'm not going to the Opéra when I leave this house, you know. I'm going to wash city buses. My French colleagues out there don't come to work, either, smelling like a bunch of daffodils. Ah, but that's another grim subject — how long any of us emigrants, especially blacks — will still have a job in another month or so; a job of *any* kind. It's a bleak picture, Monsieur Kessey, and deals with the very same subject — tyrants putting their jackboots on the necks of the poor and underprivileged. Yes, Monsieur, poor people like me, even. I, for instance, am now feeling the hot breath of the oppressors, the French oppressors, led by the Adolph Hitler of present French history and politics. This man — whose name somehow I can never recall (there's something probably meaningful in this fact as well) — declares he is out to save France for the French. This doesn't sound too heinous as long as you don't take a look at the proposition close up. I won't tax you with all this tonight but the truth is that if this man and his absolutely devoted followers — estimates vary on their numbers, but they are huge and mounting — continue to have their way, we'll all be leaving here in relatively short order."

Quo Vadis suddenly snapped his fingers—"Poussin! . . . that's his name. Charles Poussin. He's the leader. He founded the organization—it's really a party, a full-fledged political party, called 'France for the French National Party.'"

Paul nodded his head. "Yes, we're all acquainted with FFF. But I wouldn't give it the same high danger marks that you do. Yet it's not something that should be taken lightly, I agree."

"If you've known about it all along," Quo Vadis said, "why haven't you tried to do something about this man, this Poussin?—you yourself were the head of an organization. Maybe your members were right—you were apparently asleep at the switch. What an irony it would be if Mr. Poussin came to power and designated you as the first black to be made an example of. If he merely shipped you out of France—to say nothing of what he might do to the rest of us—you'd be damn lucky. Why, a bastard like Poussin is not fit to live—don't you see that, Monsieur?"

"Well . . ."—Paul could not find a response. Finally—"I wouldn't want to overreact," he said.

"You're damn right you wouldn't," said Quo Vadis. "Not in public."

"I wouldn't want to overreact, period." Paul's tone, though, was less adamant than his words. He seemed nervous; he fidgeted in his chair.

"Some way must be found, however, Paul. . . . Oh, excuse me—I didn't mean to call you by your first name. . . ."

Paul shrugged. "I much prefer that to your insistence on 'Monsieur.' I'm not French—especially to another American. 'Paul' is fine."

"Fine indeed. I was influenced by Mrs. Zimsu. And of course my given name is 'Quo Vadis,' if you will." At once, then, he returned to his sternness. "The thought of Poussin naturally takes me back to my younger days, my time at Gladstone College, and all that happened to me there — including my fervent study of the martyred life of Cager Lee. He became my hero (and of course still is) but he, too, had a hero. You see, I could write a book on nothing but heroes. They are not only important, they are crucial to us. They prepare, set the stage, for what is to come and in so doing make possible the heroes of the future — in other words, stone built on stone, granite on granite. It was the same in Cager Lee's case. His hero, yes, was a black slave, named Ofield Smalls, a man who could not write his name yet led — and died in — a bloody slave rebellion that as Cager read about it, studied it — it seared his soul. And at that very moment, you see, Cager himself, two hundred years later, became a hero. When I would read and reread about him as I sat up there in the dorm at Gladstone in the wee hours of the night and morning (neglecting my assigned studies in the process) I would cry, blubber, like a baby. I couldn't help it. That was when, then, I conceived the idea of honoring his memory by trying to raise the money to erect a fittingly grand statue commemorating him, smack in front of the library on Gladstone's campus. And then — *good God!* — within three weeks I was *expelled* for it." There were tears in his eyes as in his now-wild paroxysms he stamped his huge feet on the floor and beat his herculean breast.

Paul, aghast, quailing backwards in his chair, reminded at the same time of some great infuriated black Congo ape before him, was shaking like leaf. "I'm frank to say, Mr. Jackson," he finally managed to get out, though groping, unsure of himself, "that, although you frighten the hell out of me, I nevertheless deeply sympathize with you and your heroic experiences back then. That Gladstone must have been quite a place. In fact, the whole scenario even further complicates the questions, put on both our parts to each other, of why, originally, we ever came to Paris. In my own case, I'm surer on some occasions than on others about why. Sometimes I'm more or less guessing. Things get complicated. Is that the way it is with you?"

"Oh, no, no, no," said Quo Vadis. "I don't see any complications at all in my situation. I just happened to come here but it could have been any place — London, Madrid, Rome, or Istanbul, even Baghdad, who knows? The place was unimportant. I only wanted to get away from those crazy, violent, drugged niggers in the States. They paralyzed me. I couldn't think around them, my mind stopped functioning, especially when I'd consider how wild and stupid they were in thinking that whenever they saw one another they were seeing the dire enemy. Right now — think about it — they're gunning each other down wholesale: limping old people, housewives with their food stamps, kids on their way to school, even little babies slavering in their high chairs at the window. *Zoom!* — in come the fatal shots. It's mad! Drugs — crack — have completely taken over. That's what I was facing there in the States as I tried to plot out my coming life of service to the downtrodden — all this, then, in addition to my wife, Glade, and her flaky, dangerous brothers. I couldn't take it any longer. So I stood in line a couple of hours downtown and applied for a passport to France; then a week later in the middle of the night I tiptoed out of the house and caught a Greyhound bus to New York. A month later I was here in Paris, trying to figure out this damn language and get some kind of a job, any kind — that's another hellish story. Then less than a month after I got this job washing buses, I — God's hand must have been in it — encountered, in the most outlandish situation you ever heard of (which I'll tell you about sometime), Mrs. Zimsu and her poor son Gwelo in the most terrible, pitiful straits. God told me I had no choice; I had to help them. Then I almost fell in love with her. I didn't quite, as a matter of fact, but I admired her so, her brains, her purity of character, her willingness almost to die in order somehow to get Gwelo the best education — good Christ! How impressive it was! I have great admiration for this woman — she is extraordinary."

Paul sat engrossed, mesmerized.

"Well, time went on," said Quo Vadis, "and with the Lord's help the three of us have somehow managed to make it. But now there are black clouds gathering. I have problems here. The question now is, how long is the FFF going to let me keep my job?" His swollen face had taken on a horrible, manic frown. "When they come to power — and they will; nobody's out to stop them — they will drive us all into the sea, us foreigners, especially blacks. Ah, that blackguard Poussin!"

"But you had alternatives," ventured Paul. "You say there were no complications surrounding your departure from the States, yet did you ever consider staying there, staying put, and trying to help those blacks on drugs you've just been assailing, the ones hooked on that terrible crack especially? Did this possibility ever cross your mind? . . . to make a great effort to get them off drugs and try to do something positive with their lives? That was a complication which apparently you didn't see as such. You could have stayed right there. Am I right?"

"No, you're not," Quo Vadis replied almost heatedly. "I didn't overlook anything. I made a judgment: It was that these people were beyond helping, by anybody. They can only be written off."

"I believe, from what I've seen and heard," said Paul, "that you are a praying man. Did God sanction this write-off?"

"I don't even bother Him with such trivia," Quo Vadis said, but then fell into another deep study, self-study, saying nothing more for a minute or two as he kept his eyes well away.

"And why," asked Paul, "do you refer to these people as 'niggers'? Isn't that a little cruel, also biased, and overlooks their appalling backgrounds? Have you ever checked out any of this with God?"

Quo Vadis's great lips, even if still silent, were nonetheless frantically moving, almost in fervent whispers, as if he were heatedly conferring with himself, not God, though to no avail. Suddenly then, as if having thought up some make-do answer, he almost blurted it: "I call them 'niggers' because they *are* niggers! You can't help people who don't want to be helped. What they want is more and more crack so they can kill more of each other, more of their own kind."

Paul said wryly, "Is that you talking? Or does God go along with you on that?"

"Why are you asking me all these questions?" Quo Vadis frowned. "They're not quite as brilliant as you may think. Maybe I shouldn't say this, but the revealing mark of a haphazardly educated person is that he or she is always out to show how perfectly the world and its functions are put together, how perfect God is in everything He says or does. You ask does God go along with me on some of these things. How would I know? But I'm not one who sits back and waits for orders, not even from God. I try to do what God, long ago, has generally set out to be the path I should follow and do the rest on my own. Very few things on this earth work perfectly—there are many mistakes made, much pain, suffering, as the result of some massive blundering; yes, even by God Himself. He doesn't take us around by the hand each morning when we pile out of bed in order to protect us, for us to ask for answers for every little thing that pops in our minds. Some of these things we're supposed to figure out ourselves and go on with our lives—which should be dedicated to the task of helping people less gifted than we are to do the best they can with their lives—*that is*, if, as I say, they want help. But if they don't, there's much to be done for those who deserve help and are thankful to get it. So, yes, God goes along with me — *in the abstract*. The rest is up to me. Sure, I make mistakes. But there's one mistake I haven't made, which is that I do not live a life that is purposeless, has no meaning, which makes me hate to get out of bed in the morning. Ofield Smalls and Cager Lee were *doers*. They didn't sit around with their fingers up their asses and look the other way when benighted people, people who don't understand the world they're living in and are thus ready prey for the lousy predators operating all around them; no, they don't wait to be told what their mission is — the Olfied Smallses and the Cager Lees — for they know, God has given them the broad outlines, and that's all they need. So, no, Monsieur Kessey, I can't say that I've checked out everything I do, even what I *propose* to do, with God for His OK. I know right from wrong. I also know what's wrong in God's sight: it's to sit around, in the face of all the suffering in the world, and do nothing. On this subject, if I may politely say so, you could profit by some well-meant tutelage. And I'm in the posture and frame of mind — though not without my motives, which in themselves, though, are upright and pure — to help you. If, that is, you will help me. I think, indeed I'm positive, that you are a good man. I was much impressed by what little you told us about the wonderful young woman — Jeannette, was that her name? — who went to Africa, to Zaire, to do good. No wonder you so admired her, maybe loved her . . ."

"I did, I did!" suddenly cried Paul.

"Do you see?" Quo Vadis said, as if proud of himself. "You are a good man — I saw it from the beginning. I'm sure Mrs. Zimsu did too. But, for a moment going back to Jeannette, do you realize that her death, and its manner, may not have been quite so tragic as you have led yourself to believe it was. This is because her life had purpose and she knew it. This makes up for many things. For instance, since I myself have found my bearings, I no longer fear death. Did Ofield Smalls, who couldn't read or write, knew nothing of the world or its history, did he fear death? I doubt it. Did Cager Lee fear it when he did what he did? He well knew it would be the most heinous kind—lynching by being burned alive—yet he did the deed, the accounts say, 'with unruffled dignity.' These three people, whom I would die for before called *them* 'niggers,' were protected by one thing—each of their lives had a worthy mission. It's no more complicated—your word, Monsieur— than that. God was not the only one who taught me that. I've always somehow known it—as Jeannette must have, and Ofield, and Cager. They died and entered the pantheon of those we not only most admire (and they were black), but whom we most wish to emulate and thus redeem our own sorry lives."

Paul was upset, demoralized, yet also moved by what he had heard. He also now, however, wanted to leave, to flee. Quo Vadis instead poured them both more coffee. Ignoring his, Paul rose to go, his face ashen, confused, almost appalled. Quo Vadis, across the table, watched him, all the while batting his beady eyes, whose stare Paul did not return. "You must help me," Quo Vadis finally said, "and I shall in turn help you. Moreover, you need my help—if you're not going to continue your present rudderless life. I need yours, however, just as desperately. We must help each other. Although I'm a foreigner here, I don't plan to see my little job wrested from me by some French neo–Nazi. It's because my little job is the avenue to far greater things—all in behalf of the luckless suffering people, both black and white, who have no one to help beat back the horde of voracious scoundrels bent on sucking their blood into lifelessness. There is much to be done.

City of Light

My life will be full, all in behalf of the people. Meantime, I shall teach you much, very much. Or, stated in another way, you shall learn much from me — firsthand. Soon your life will no longer be without purpose. I repeat, however, you must in the bargain help *me*. You must take Mrs. Zimsu and Gwelo off my hands. They are wonderful human beings, whom I have come almost to love, yet they also constitute impedimenta. How, with them in my life, can I pursue my mission . . . my obligation . . . my most crucial work. Cager haunts me as Ofield Smalls haunted him — and as Jeannette haunts you."

"Oh, God!" Paul whispered inaudibly. His tawny-beige face was somehow wreathed in both his distress and perplexity. He stood gazing at the far wall as if it were a prison barricade.

Quo Vadis's tiny bloodshot opossum eyes still watched him. Finally he, too, rose from the table and escorted Paul out past Gwelo's cot — the sleeping child's left hand was almost touching the floor — to the front door. "*Bonsoir*, Paul," he said as, parting, they shook hands.

Though trying hard to, deeply absorbed Paul could say nothing as he stumbled through the front door and down the stairs into the street. It was Saturn whom he wished to speak to now.

Chapter

Five

The Niggerines

On her way to the Crillon to meet with Cécile, Madame Chevalley found herself thinking now not so much about her imminent rendezvous as about her late father, Emile Chevalley, a successful lawyer, a jolly cardsharp to his friends, and an avid tennis player. She often wondered, now late in her life, what her life would have been like had she lived it as he had wanted her to. Her mother, Leonie, though in awe of the rigorous Emile, took no stated stand on the issue, although the daughter had always known what, in fact, her mother's stand was: that every person should live his or her own life, with a minimum of advice or exhorting from others, especially the family. There would be mistakes of youth, of course, sometimes costly and regretted, yet forced parental advice could often be far worse — as she was sure would have been the case had she, a tender 21 years of age at the time, married the lawyer Jules, a favored and ambitious young man in her father's firm, who, though handsome, was to young Natalie Theresa-Prue as romantic as a telephone pole. Instead she married another young man, Maurice, daring and charming, and, above all, an activist in "the movement," the far-left political movement. Natalie's father, Emile, never quite recovered from this deed except for one short hopeful period during her divorce from Maurice, which, however, was only to be followed by her marriage to the brilliant but unstable contrabassoon player in the Opéra orchestra. This union did, though, last for almost five years. Her next liaison, however, involved no marriage at all—the man, in his late forties, a fairly well-off businessman, Freudson by name, was, as young Madame well knew, already married, indeed, she would learn, almost happily married. Then, hardly a year later, Freudson became terminally ill with lung cancer. Nevertheless, unobtrusively, he had his lawyers pass along to her a somewhat generous sum of money with which she later bought her present serviceable pension for lodgers in the Rue du Colisée. In the meantime, after Freudson's death, came a number of years of sporadic French-language-teaching chores abroad after which she returned to Paris in equivocal health and—her parents now deceased—with only two friends on earth: an inconstant niece and the now-suddenly-mysterious Dr. Cécile Fournier. But it was the latter she was finally on her way to meet now, for a private luncheon at the famous Hôtel Crillon, a meeting, however, Madame had almost brutally forced on her unfathomable physician-friend.

But it was the splendid hotel—located on the Place de la Concorde, in the busy, sprawling, famous district which, even at considerable distances, was dominated by both the Etoile and the broad historic Champs-Elysées, with Maxim's and Fouquet's marvelously situated along the way. It, yes, was this venerable hotel, then, which in the rain her taxi now approached, which invariably caused her to think of her father, whose habit it often was in the early days to take his family of five there for dinner, especially after, say, he had just won a case in court for a particularly substantial corporate client. Sighing, she thought of him now, an honorable, at times even tender, father who had so wanted his youngest, but headstrong, daughter Natalie to have a happy, child-bearing, comfortable, bourgeois life. This was not to be, she knew, contrary to the good fortune pére Emile had had with her two sisters. Yet at his death the bequests they had all received were identical down to the franc, in her case substantially exceeding Freudson's largesse to her. Her mind, yes, today was on her father despite the critical encounter she was soon to have with Cécile. Would her life, she wondered, have been markedly different, better, happier, had she followed his advice, his wishes? She knew she had no way of knowing this, ever, but even this made her sad. The greatest happiness she had known in her earlier life had come from her mother whose memory, along with her father's, she still blessed, revered, recalling them both with deepest affection and emotion. Again, she could only sigh, then remembering what she herself had insisted on; she must now confront the strange Cécile Fournier who until recently she somehow — daydreaming, fantasizing — vaguely thought of as her surrogate daughter. Now she felt betrayed; also dispirited, and stern.

Peering through the wet taxi window, she suddenly now realized the Crillon was almost upon her — already the driver was turning into the Place de la Concorde. Soon then they were at the entrance of the great hotel, where one of three available liveried footmen, his garish uniform reminiscent of a Napoleonic hussar, came scurrying, his umbrella up, to open the door of the taxi. Madame now, as she paid the driver, found herself dreading to climb out but realized there was no alternative, even though her heart was pounding. Soon, however, the footman hovering over her, she entered the grand lobby — only soon to descry fifty feet away a seated woman who looked, yet did not look, familiar, until, on seeing Madame, she smiled and quickly stood. Madame could not believe her eyes. Cécile was fat! Or almost so. She had gained at least twenty-five, maybe thirty, pounds, Madame was sure. Beautiful Cécile — fat. Madame still could hardly believe what she clearly saw and at once somehow felt a deep, unassuaging pity. Nonetheless, they approached each other and were soon embracing, though with tears in Madame's eyes which Cécile saw at once and was both miserable and contrite about as she held frail Madame in her arms. "How are you, dear Madame?" she said, her voice unsteady, almost husky, and full of emotion. "It is so wonderful to see you."

It was then Madame lost control of herself — her eyes angrily flashing fire. "I cannot accept that," she said, "cannot accept it at all. Please don't say it again." She twisted herself free of Cécile's arms.

"I'm so sorry, Madame." The voice was still husky but it also now verged on the hysterical. "I'm really sorry!" Petulantly then she turned and walked two or three steps to her left, almost as if she were lost, or did not quite know what to do with herself. "It's been nearly six weeks . . . hasn't it?" she finally said, "Or maybe more. Oh, I've lost count completely. . . . But let's go to the rear, the dining room — I need a drink."

Madame did not — it seemed could not — move. Nor had she ever before heard Cécile speak so crassly of drink. "Cécile . . ." But then she desisted — turning to a more important matter. "Cécile . . . what in God's name has happened to you? . . . the weight you've gained."

"Please do come on, Madame — I've made reservations for us."

At last Madame, almost docilely now — as if she had encountered an experience so outlandish, unbelievable, that she was prepared to throw up her hands in surrender—followed Cécile toward the rear. It only, however, imposed on her the inability to keep her eyes off Cécile's now broad posterior, her thickened ankles, and the slight waddle in her walk. Madame's tears came again and she dreaded the luncheon experience to come. What now would they talk about? she wondered. What, under the circumstances, could she ask Cécile about this apparently tragic, month-and-a-half interim? What possibly could have happened? And what of all those lovely, but now-too-small, designer clothes in which Cécile had looked so beautifully elegant, to say nothing of what terrible disaster must have befallen her to render a gorgeous woman so drastically unlike her former self of only a few short weeks ago? Still trailing Cécile as they walked, Madame could not help again observing, studying, her wearing a dark brown wool-crepe suit, with black silk borderings, and black patent-leather pumps on her feet. Yet she seemed veritably stuffed into this expensive clothing and nervous, ill at ease, about everything she said or did. But now she was leading Madame into the ornate dining room and affirming their reservations at the entry desk, from which they were then escorted across to a bright table, replete with a small vase of garnet and fuchsia flowers, for two. On seeing their ancient waiter slowly approaching the table, Cécile, seeming almost to shiver, or shudder, said it to Madame again: "I need a drink." How unlike her to say that, repeated Madame to herself. Although Cécile's voice had hardly been brazen, it had nonetheless been forced, rather too eager, and, for Cécile, passing strange. Madame did not know what to make of it. To her knowledge (though not to Paul's), Cécile had never drunk alcohol of any kind except possibly a glass, or a half glass, of wine with food— nothing more. Now, in a matter of minutes, thought Madame, she had twice stated she needed a drink. How mysterious.

City of Light

Their waiter stood over them now. Old, stooped, patriarchal, also immaculate, his thin, no-doubt-white hair dyed a sleek raven black (if faintly orange at the extremities), he wore some kind of red-ribboned decoration pinned above the breast pocket of his black tailcoat—as if in some distant, and better, era he had been rewarded (as it were, "dubbed") for the highest of cuisine services by, say, His brief Majesty Edward VII himself or some other such royal worthy. Having, after some intent palaver—all three participants speaking French— he advised his two ladies on what aperitif he thought they might enjoy, viz., a glass each of an excellent Mailly champagne. Almost at once (the ladies' minds on more crucial matters) he received their trusting approval and, with just the hint of a smile, as well as a stiff bow from the waist, he left two luncheon menus with them and slowly marched off again, relinquishing them to their own critical devices—which, with all that was at stake, neither of them really wanted. As a result, their former tension returned now with a vengeance.

"Tell me about yourself, Cécile," Madame, deftly sparring as if with an unknown opponent, said.

"I love your attire," said Cécile instead—blandly and irrelevantly. "The gray suit, pearls at the throat, and all. *Tres chic*."

Madame was grim. "Tell me about yourself, Cécile," she repeated.

Rather, Cécile ignored her altogether now. A restless, harried expression on her face, Cécile went into the purse in her lap, took from it a white paper bag containing, it was soon seen, a jumbled assortment of chocolate candies, a strange mixture of various shapes and sizes, then at once began to eat from it. Madame was speechless, flabbergasted, and finally shocked on getting a closer look at the bizarre kinds of candy images that Cécile, one after another, was now ravenously ingesting. As Madame could now clearly see the graceless pieces were deftly shaped into various kinds of chocolate human figures — figurines — of grinning, dancing, Negro minstrels or candy comedians, variously described, to her knowledge, not only as "niggerines," but "coonskins," "cotton banjoists," "sambo shufflers," et cetera — but mostly "niggerines." Cécile, still ignoring Madame, was now chewing the candies vigorously, soon pouring more of them from the bag into her palm before greedily devouring them.

"Oh, my God!" Madame, heretofore, for cause, incapable of speech, finally managed now to exclaim. "What in heaven's name are you doing with those dreadful things? And why do you hog them down like that? No wonder you're fat! Yes, yes, I see — you must carry those awful things around in that paper bag, constantly munching on them, gorging yourself, all day long, and I suppose at night too. Oh, Cécile — what has happened to you? . . . Oh, you poor dear! . . . You're in deep trouble of some kind."

But by now, looking even more manic and forlorn, Cécile had tossed three or four more niggerines in her mouth, this time, however, chewing them more deliberately, slowly, almost bovinely.

"Cécile dear," Madame persisted, though trying now to contain her own distress and alarm, "no matter how unpleasant it may be, we must discuss you; about what's come over you, overtaken your life — and why. I can hardly believe I'm talking to my own doctor here today, the person, the expert, the professor, to whom I look to guard my tenuous health, in fact my general sense of well-being. Yet here I sit trying as best I can to make some kind of sense of critical matters that clearly, maybe dangerously, affect, yes, the mental well-being, if not the possible physical state itself, of my own doctor — when it should be exactly the other way around. Yet what you plan to do, if anything, about this unmistakable crisis in your life, whatever it is, is something that has got to be of gravest concern to those close to you — which would ordinarily be your family but which, I venture to guess, you've lacked the stamina to bring in on this emergency . . . or whatever it is that so disastrously affects you. Tell me, Cécile, do you think it's your mind? — has your mind gone into some kind of strange, unfortunate decline? . . . taken a tumble, a nose-dive, or whatever? Why have you refused, all these weeks, to call me, or contact me in some way, instead of apparently avoiding me like the plague? These are strange happenings, considering our history and friendship . . . and I won't go further and bring in others also so sadly affected by your strange behavior. Do you have any idea of what has hit you, or why? Are you ill? What did you tell your husband that's happened — about your weight? And, heavens, how do you deal with the children, with Michelle especially, as 'grown-up' and outlandishly inquisitive and opinionated as she can be! — to say nothing of sweet little Zoe who loves you to distraction, beyond anything on earth. Doesn't any of this affect you? Most of all it somehow appears to be linked with your addiction, with the way you gorge yourself on these nefarious chocolate niggerines. How did you learn about them in the first place? Where do you buy them? — heavens, I've never seen them before, only heard about them. They are shockingly racist. Who would ever put you on to something like that?"

"Two friends — two new women friends," said Cécile, unabashed, "although they're both second cousins of mine."

Madame leaned forward, hearing herself say, repeating, "Two . . . *new* friends . . . "

At this juncture the waiter, still slow, snaillike, returned with their champagne and the conversation was momentarily suspended, though never resuming, Cécile was to make sure, at this specific pertinent point. Madame finally, after taking a sip of her champagne, reached tenderly across the table and grasped both of Cécile's hands. "There's something very wrong with you, Cécile dear," she said, "something that's tearing you apart. If it's not your 'new friends,' then tell me what it is — if you know. Do you hear me? — as a friend I, too, have a right to know."

Instead, Cécile warily freed her hands and, still ignoring her champagne, began fiercely plopping more niggerines into her mouth, now chewing them almost viciously, maniacally, until Madame, at last beside herself, was furiously moving her lips, talking to herself, maybe cursing. The effect on Cécile, however, strangely, was instant and mollifying. "I know you have my interests in mind, Madame," she said, "in your heart as well, and I appreciate it. But you must try to understand that my condition is something quite beyond hand-holding and advice, no matter how well-meant — more serious even than your tears."

Madame, watching her closely, thankful even for this tiny new hint of evidence, accordingly now took a different tack. She suddenly, at great effort, became what seemed almost nonchalant, uncaring, if not now all but jocular. "I apologize." She smiled, though only briefly. "This is obviously something very important to you, close to you, and I shouldn't intrude. And won't," she added grimly. "I only wish, you might spare me — also your wonderful and devoted family, your daughters — the unseemly, indeed revolting, sight of your constantly, insanely, tossing those ghastly niggerines into your poor, pretty mouth, as if they were some kind of panacea for your troubles and spleen, some cathartic agent purging your errors and hurt. Also your possibly destined ill fate as a human being, or whatever, doomed (not I, though, Cécile — I shan't be here to 'welcome' it), doomed, as I say, to honor the grisly advent of the twenty-first century with its world population doubled and no food to eat. Yet I realize you, as a prelude, may be at present heavily involved with your current problems, which I dare not devalue and be a fool. Whatever the nature of this apparently harsh, pitiless cross you presently bear, it's out to destroy you by driving you unhinged."

"I am *not* unhinged," said Cécile though biting her lip to forestall tears. "Quite the contrary. I was unhinged, indeed psychoneurotic, before, though. But no more. I have seen the light." Her eyes, suddenly enlarged now, virtually shone. "I am a different person, Madame—a new person, more intelligent, and by far a better person. The secret to it all is that I have found love of country. I love France. It's no more complicated than that. I have all along, though, but never as I have come to do now. France, the true France, composed of the French, has changed my life. For all this, of course, I have God to thank. And to think, only months, weeks, ago, I was convinced He had turned His back on me, cruelly abandoned me. I was miserable. But all along He knew what He was doing. My prayers and tears were heard after all. He has shown me the true path to my own salvation, which, I will readily confess, is somewhat different from that of the average person. God saw it all, though, and I am 'saved'—in the best sense of that term. I repeat, my life has been changed and I have God and France to thank for it. Indeed I am once again now worthy of my family."

Madame was dizzy—from confusion. She only knew she was on the verge of something, vis-à-vis Cécile, possibly of immense import. Trying now, though, to summon the remnants of at least a half-smile, she looked at Cécile and said with a sham chortle: "But those niggerines—how do they figure in all this? Whoever makes and sells them, though, don't you think, has it in for Negroes."

"Many people have it in for Negroes, Madame. There's nothing new about that. It's a matter now of containing it— being sensible and fair. Fair to France. Remember, though, we're *not* Nazis."

"I'm French too—also remember that," Madame said. "I can even deal with the niggerines. But who says I've got to eat them to make my point? All people, bar none, are bigots at times, but you don't have to wreck your body, make yourself die in the cause, to be a patriotic hero or heroine. What kind of nonsense is that, especially about one's body. And you're a doctor—*my* doctor. This is weird."

Cécile was vague on this point, finally saying, "The nig gerines have never been altogether clear to me, either. Yet they're not entirely false images, or characterizations. Have you ever known any blacks?"

Madame suddenly sat up straight and stifled her gasp but the crimson flush of her face gave her away. "Only one that I can think of at the moment," she finally said.

"Well, then," said Cécile. "You know."

Madame was apoplectic. "You're goddamn right I know! . . ." she spluttered. "He lives in my pension and pays rent to me!"

Cécile blanched a perfect white. It was clear she realized, tardily, what a mistake she had made. She was penitent now, or seemed so, although Madame knew her to be mercurial. Yet she seemed now much on the defensive, as if her mistakes had done her in. She wanted, needed, a haven, some figurative place to which to run and hide. Instead—Madame, however, anticipating, watching her like a hawk—she reached for her now-almost-depleted bag of niggerines, her only asylum of retreat, and was about to finish them off, when Madame, on the verge of a violent tantrum, half stood up. "Cécile, if you put another one of those filthy, indecent, bigoted things in your mouth I'll walk out of here and you'll never see me again!"

Cécile took a deep breath and returned the almost-empty paper bag to her purse. "You don't understand," she finally said, almost whimpering. "You don't know what I've been through. The hideous dreams. These candies have been a kind of palliative against the dreams. These two new friends, my cousins, recommended them—the nigger candies—which do help me sometimes. Why don't you have a little understanding for me, Madame? Let me tell you this: Don't ever let Negroes come into your life. It's a living hell. The dreams! Oh, God—I've even been afraid to go to Him, to God, with these filthy dreams. My two friends say that I should never do that—that it would be sacrilegious. Instead they put me on these niggerines. Fight fire with fire, they told me. It's worked sometimes. Negroes are like that in some situations."

"Oh, my God," said Madame. "What are you saying?—that your new friends, your second cousins, are Negroes?"

"Heavens, no! They are trying to *help* me. They are true French purists. They want to save our country."

"Yes, by putting you on a Negro-chocolate diet." Madame sighed, drained her goblet of Mailly champagne, and looked around for their old waiter for more. Finally, her eyes returned to Cécile, her voice plaintive, pleading—"Cécile, you must save yourself. No one can save you but yourself. You must leave these awful people you're associating with—who have you killing yourself with these so-called 'niggerines.' You must avoid them. You think that through them and God you have solved your problems. You have only made them worse. Tomorrow I'm going to take *you* to a doctor."

Cécile, observing her, was somehow strangely calmer, though quiescent, now—until they looked up to see the time-honored old waiter returning to take their food order: roast chicken and the rest, and another half-bottle of the champagne. Madame's mind, however, was on Cécile and what she, Madame, could possibly do to help her. Throughout it all Madame emitted one little sigh after another, asking herself how she could save her "daughter" from her clear torture, unfathomable as it was, over "Negroes." Now there came long lapses in their already disjunctive, agonized conversation but when later the food and more champagne arrived, Cécile, as if somehow trying to restore herself, raised her goblet and grimly gave a toast: "*Viva la France!*"

Madame looked at her, shaking her head. Finally: "You warned me a moment ago, Cécile, never to let Negroes come into one's life. What did you mean?"

"Oh, Madame, how can you ask that? Of all people certainly you should know just what I meant. It was through you, remember, that all this happened."

"What kind of answer is that?" Madame screwed up her gaunt, wrinkled face. "And why your sudden change about Negroes?"

Cécile looked at her aghast, then said nothing. Soon, however, slowly — although her mind was no longer on food — she began to put food in her mouth.

"I insist, Cécile — why the sudden change?"

"The dreams — the horrible dreams," was her only answer.

Madame was leaning across the table, almost into her face, now. "I won't ask the obvious — '*what dreams?*' — for you will tell me if you want me to know. It's up to you."

There was silence as the two ate. "I don't feel up to telling it," Cécile finally said. "I appreciate your not asking me to. So you're not getting much out of this meeting, which you threatened me about, bullied me into coming to, and of course I know why you did it. It's my recent behavior — you can't understand why you haven't seen or heard from me lately. I give you credit, though, for warning me a minute ago that if I'm at all to be saved from this beastly time I'm going through I must save myself; no one else is going to do it for me. I agree and that's what I'm trying, as best I can, to do though with unclear success—yet I try. I need your understanding, Madame."

"I think I'm giving it." Madame, masticating her food, again stared at Cécile. "Have you had any contact with Paul?" she asked. "He doesn't talk much, you know."

"Oh, heavens, no—except that he's called me, twice. I declined to take the first call. The second time he asked me if he could bring an ailing friend of his, who'd been a member of his Coterie organization, to my office for a physical examination, that the man was sick and needed medical attention. It sounded fishy to me, and I said no. I don't want to see Paul anymore."

Madame put down both her knife and fork. "What has he done to you? It must have been something very bad."

Cécile only stared over at the opposite wall and at last said nothing.

"I don't think, as well as we both know Paul," Madame said, "that you should say—especially when you know he wouldn't—that he called you up in behalf of a sick friend or colleague but that it sounded 'fishy' to you, and you turned him down. It not only doesn't sound like Paul, it doesn't sound like you. How could you have done such a thing?—and then tell about it. What have you got against him? Yes, it must have been something pretty awful." Madame's voice rose. "What was it, Cécile?!"

Cécile bent her head. "Nothing," she finally said, almost whispering it. "It wasn't that he did anything, it was who he is now."

In her confusion Madame's frown was beyond diagnosing; she was in great bewilderment and distress. "'It was who he is now,' you say, Cécile. Was he any different from the way you've always known him?"

It seemed that Cécile, also in great distress, would ponder the question forever. She finally reached for her purse and the remaining niggerines — until Madame, raising her right hand, seemed to be threatening her with death.

"Don't you dare!" said Madame.

At last, Cécile instead reached for her glass and took a deep draft of champagne, then, sighing profoundly, said, "No, he's no different — only I am."

Madame seemed ready to pounce, though her voice was low now, phony, almost wheedling. "How are you different, Cécile dear?" she purred.

"I don't know too much about it yet," said Cécile. "There's still a lot I've got to learn about everything now."

"Like what?"

"I don't even know that."

"When did you last talk with your Aunt Lili?"

"Not since she left Paris. She lives with her daughter now in Reims."

"What about your two cousins — the ones who introduced you to niggerines."

"I talk to them every day. What are you grilling me for, though, Madame? I'm a respected physician and teacher. I'm no child."

Madame shook her head sadly. "You are today, Cécile. But I've managed to learn enough about you and your present life from what you've said here at this table to enable me to indulge in some pretty fair guesses, and even better intuitions. You insist you're no child, still you know so little about the world beyond what heretofore has been your rather monotonous life. Then, through ill-fated me, you met the first man in your life who set you, body and soul, yes, on fire. And, oh my

City of Light

God, what a conflagration it turned out to be — certainly from your side of the equation. It was all brand new to you. But so it was to him also. Ah, but as it's turned out, your respective objectives have, unknown to you both, encountered a really not-unexpected fork in the road. Your cravings are very different. You, as I say, in both body and soul, craved to feast on his stunning desirability as a man, also his mind, class, character, as well as, yes, whatever else, if anything, transpired between you two — but which is none of my business. Then there was his own craving which I hesitate to try to characterize because of its utter strangeness, difficulty, its deepest profundity. It was an altogether different phenomenon from yours, Cécile, though in no way any more serious and lofty than yours. Yet it was fraught with the most telling dangers for his own sense of self. I refer to his almost pitiful yearning — it was for his stalled mission — to satisfy, conciliate, his mother's strange ambition for him, though today she rests in her grave. He spoke of it once, yet I still don't fully understand, although you yourself somehow figure in it — in a replacement role of the bizarrest type; almost fairy-tale like. Further than this I know little. Naturally, I was baffled. Also disturbed. And now also afraid — for the lovely pair of you. I feel like one of Macbeth's witches on the heath. One of them is pointing out Paul's mother. Then, Cécile dear, I see you. Then Paul. It was not a pretty sight. It was a judgment-verdict — alas, a final decree. But then you enter with those niggerines. My God!"

Cécile, hand trembling, reached for the niggerines.

This time Madame did not interfere.

A loud telephone ringing.

"Yes, you're right — I *was* sleeping," Paul said sourly. "What time is it?" But at the same moment, above the telephone, in his left hand, he squinted a hard frown at his watch: 8:05 A.M.

Cyrus Colter

"Will you go with me?" Fifi Mazisi urged. "I can't go in that place by myself and ask to go up to his room—which I'm told is a holocaust. I also hear the hotel itself is a pretty seedy affair. I need a man with me—Mango is so stubborn; he won't go; says I've been involved too long already with this Coterie fiasco. Besides, I need somebody to help bring some of the junk, including two or three big books, Ari wants in the hospital. He's restless and ill-tempered as hell, as usual."

"Of course—what would you expect?" Paul said. "He's going to be bitching about something. He'd never admit it, but it could be that he's a little worried, about his condition, whatever it is."

"I don't feel good about his condition, somehow," Fifi said. "He's adamant, though—says he's never been sick. What I think is that instead he's a chronic worrier. Now he's in the hospital, but says it's the first time he's ever been in one overnight in his life. Why, though, Paul, did you put him in a hospital away over there in no man's land, across town, so far out of the reach of us who live on the Left Bank?"

"I live on the Right Bank, Fifi. It's closer. But also, and this is the real reason, I know a doctor on the staff. I tried to call her—I don't know any other doctors in Paris—to see if once in awhile she'd look in on Ari, but . . . well, she's very busy; hard to get to; it didn't work."

"Poor Ari," Fifi said. "Although he never fully understood you, Paul, he tried his best to be loyal to you and the organization—this despite that loud-mouth phony Firestone Murphy who was always trying to influence him, to no good purpose. He would try to challenge you on some unimportant things, put up to it by old Firestone, but one could tell his heart wasn't in it. Ari is actually a wonderful, sweet, little guy, though far too excitable for his own good. But that's his nature. He was basically loyal to you. That's one of the reasons we can't let him down."

"Who's letting him down?" Paul said. "I put him in the hospital, didn't I? Then called you and told you where he was. I'm trying now to get him a reputable internist — I'm going to call this doctor again . . . I guess. I know she's good — I have great confidence in her reputation. So we shall see. Nobody, then, is letting him down."

"Let me tell you this, too, Paul — Ari is not broke. He lives up there in a shoddy section of lower Montmartre, and in a cheap, run-down hotel, but you won't have to pass a hat around for him, and, better than that, you won't have to pay his way yourself."

"Well, thank you for that, Fifi," said Paul almost in a tone of parody. "I haven't been hearing that very much lately — if, that is, you know what you're talking about; though I didn't realize you knew anything about Ari's personal finances."

The telephone became strangely silent then. "Well," said Fifi at last, "I get around quite a bit and know quite a few people, of all stripes and callings. I think I told you — didn't I — that although Ari looks younger, he's fifty-one, no less. I don't believe he's broke, either — for I know, or know *of*, a young guy or two who've gotten money from him."

Another severe telephone pause — this time on Paul's end of the line.

"Did you hear me, Paul?"

"Yes, I heard you. I just don't think I understood you."

"Hold onto your bedsprings there then. It's rumored — indeed was rumored from the earliest days of the Coterie — that Ari is gay."

"Oh shit," Paul said before he thought. "How ridiculous. Who started that canard? It sounds like something Firestone could have put out on Ari, like blackmail, to render him more of a Firestone tool. Where did you hear such claptrap, Fifi?"

"Mango first came up with the speculation."

"That figures. You call it right, though — speculation."

"Yes, until that guy — what's his name? — who was always missing a lot of Coterie meetings, then coming and making those long crazy speeches that bored everybody to death; he looked half-white; admits, or boasts of the claim, he's illegitimate (ha, Mango makes the same claim for himself, you know) — by a British lord of some kind and a Caribbean chambermaid."

"Chase."

"Yes — Jack Chase. Mango laughed and opined that Chase might be gay himself; in accusing Ari, that it takes one to know one. Anyhow, Chase is supposed to have said Ari frequented a gay bathhouse up there near that fleabag hotel where he lives and has made the acquaintance of several young French male prostitutes who in turn take his money."

"Christ, what a yarn — from both Chase and Mango," Paul said. "No wonder that the lunatic Coterie which I, the dumbest of them all, have the honor of having founded and financed, was such a miserable failure — with a bunch of people like Firestone, Chase, Mango . . . "

"Paul, please don't talk about my boyfriend Mango in those critical terms. I could resent it, you know, despite the respect you know I have for you . . . even maybe something deeper than respect. Mango — yes, an imperfect man — is my friend of quite a few years now, and I don't think it's nice of you to criticize him in my presence."

"Forgive me, Fifi — you're right; I shouldn't criticize him. I should criticize myself, though. As I look back on it, I must have been out of my mind to try to put a group of people like that together in behalf of some crazy, do-good, pie-in-the-sky effort that I never was able to think through myself, yet somehow expecting, hoping, almost praying, yes, that my followers could — Ari, Mango, Firestone, Chase, and even there at the last, good God!, James Lewellyn. I was desperate apparently."

"You were, Paul. I could see it. I tried to help you."

"I know you did. It was damned good of you."

"Mango never did like it — said I was throwing myself at you."

"Yet you criticize me for criticizing him."

"He's all I have, though, Paul — and I'm fourteen years older than he is, a man who's never had a job since he came to Paris. Not that he won't work, only he can't find a job he thinks is worthy of him. It makes me feel strange, us living like this — me being so much older than he is. Have you ever had an affair with a woman who was much older than you?"

At once there came another long phone pause. "No . . . , I guess I haven't," Paul finally lied.

"I can understand, Paul. Your mind has been on other things — higher things. On what you've wanted to accomplish — for others. It's very clear — this has been your mission, ever since you came here; in fact, it's no doubt why you came here in the first place. It's very clear to me. But I don't think many people in our now-defunct Coterie saw you as I saw you — with one possible exception: Ari. He, too, understood you. And there was no hanky-panky involved — he was as serious in his admiration for you as I was. We both recognized there was something eating you, something driving you on this mission of yours to do something really outstanding in this world for people less fortunate than you. You know, I think even that Britisher Lewellyn saw this in you — and finally went along with your begging and pleading with him to come and address the Coterie. I can only say, then, Paul, that I hope that someday the victory that, intermittently, you've longed for will finally be yours."

"Oh, Fifi," Paul said, "you are so wrong about me — you so oversimplify my condition. Who wouldn't want to be a great man or woman – like Martin Luther King, Joan of Arc, Mother Teresa, Mohandas Gandhi, and so on? Who wouldn't? But those were people not only of great vision but strength, astonishing purpose, also bravery. They were something apart – not like the rest of us. I would be glad merely to have just one small idea of theirs with the determination and fortitude to try to carry it out – that would be all I (founder, lord, and master of the great Coterie!) could dare hope for, and even that would be silly. Yet . . . yet, Fifi, there *are* times when I sit in my lonely room and daydream such dreams, and then want to cry when I realize there's nothing in the cards for me like that; that it's folly even to let my brain idle, toy with such outlandish visions. Then I get furiously angry and go out to a bar or café alone and get drunk. That's why, Fifi – despite your loyalty, and that of Ari's – the Coterie failed."

"That's also why, Paul, I feel almost as sorry for you as I do for Ari – both of you may have bad days ahead. I'm a praying woman, though, and pray this is not so."

Paul tried to laugh. "Come on, let's not get gruesome," he said. "We've got Ari to worry about. He merits our worry, too – for at heart, yes, he was faithful. Why on earth then would you listen to a lot of nasty gossip impugning his character?"

"Who said anything about character, Paul? – I didn't. Ari has it – character. No one's disputing that. But Mango has been around, seen many parts of the globe, and is no fool exactly. He believes what Chase says . . . and I'm inclined – yes, I confess it – to believe Mango. Instead, you talk about character. As I said before, that's something different. What Chase and Mango claim, and what I incline toward, doesn't keep me from liking Ari as much as I ever did – I repeat, character's not an issue here. What, alas, *is* an issue – and batten down your bedsprings again – is whether or not into the bargain Ari has contracted AIDS."

City of Light

"I knew that had to come up next," said Paul disgustedly — in the phone Fifi could hear his heavy sigh of distress. "Jesus Christ! — we can only hope it's not true. Poor Ari — it can't be. We must do something, Fifi."

"But what, Paul?"

"That's what we must find out somehow. Maybe I should try again to contact this doctor I know — perhaps she'll talk to me this time, if I can only impress on her the seriousness of the matter. I don't know what to say about her — I knew her for a short time; now she's almost turned a deaf ear. I don't get it. I must try again, though."

"I think that's wise, Paul. Only the doctors can tell us what, if anything, should be done. I'll bet those doctors out there where you've got Ari will find out what his condition is, good or bad, without even being asked to — if, that is, they haven't already. Our worry now has to be what they will do to him — or with him — if they've already tested him positive. They'll probably tell you to come get him."

"Oh, do you think so? Wouldn't that be illegal? He's not a pauper, you know — at least that's what you say. But this whole thing, if true, is horrible. I can't bring myself to believe it's true, though. I think you and Mango, and anyone else who believes Ari is gay — to say nothing of having AIDS now — will sooner or later come to recant what you think. You went to the hospital to see him yesterday, Fifi — how do you read his attitude?"

"He's churlish as hell of course — wants out; you'd think he's in the pen; wanted to know why you, Paul, a friend he's admired all along, would put him in the hospital, where they do nothing but poke him in the ribs and belly, take his temperature in the dead of night, and draw blood from him three or four times a day. I didn't comment — let him get it off his chest. But when I got home and told Mango, he said that meant they'd already come up with something, and he feared what it might be, for even the last time he'd seen him, Ari was downright weak and frail. Mango has a sensitive feel for things like that and—"

Paul interrupted—"We must do something, Fifi"—and swung out of his bed with the telephone still in his hand.

"The first thing you can do, Paul, is get in touch with the lady doctor you know who's on that hospital's staff and get her to find out what's going on—being on the inside like she is, knowing everybody, she can be a whale of a help. Then you get yourself together and at noon meet me at that run-down hotel of Ari's, The Corsair, up in Montmartre at Place Pau and Megeve. I've got his keys and we can pick up a few of the items he wants and take them to him—where we can then also have it out with him about this whole nightmare."

"What do you mean 'have it out with him'?" Paul said. "What are you going to do, ask him if he's gay? Then, if he's got AIDS? I don't think even you could do that, Fifi."

"You handle it any way you want to, then, Paul—there'll be enough mistakes made by everybody to go around. We've got a long haul ahead of us. So you ask him whatever you want—or ask him nothing, for all I care. Mango's already predicted we'd screw it up but good."

"Jesus Christ! If you mention Mango one more time I'll scream. Do me a favor and keep him home, will you, Fifi? He's a swell-headed Kenyan, while Ari's an insecure Zulu. They can never mesh—no way. By all means, then, keep Mango out of this—something, according even to both of you, is a possible tragedy in the making."

"Let Mango alone, Paul. Instead, get in touch with that lady doctor of yours, then meet me at Ari's hotel—at noon sharp—and tell me what she said. So long, Paul dear." She hung up.

City of Light

But Paul put his own phone down slowly, thoughtfully, fully conscious now of the complexity of all his woes and responsibilities. Of course no longer sleepy, he nevertheless really wanted to return to bed — as if it were some sanctuary, or refuge, awaiting him. Instead he went and took a shower — literally killing time until he was sure Madame Chevalley was up and about. He had not encountered her since her Crillon luncheon with Cécile the day before, and realized now how badly he wished to learn what had happened — having, of course, no way of knowing that her daring attempt had been far less productive than had been hoped and was, therefore, highly frustrating for her. Even Paul though now gradually grew tense, as if himself somehow sensing all had not gone well, which soon made him almost dread seeing Madame. He knew, though, this could only be a matter of time.

Shortly after 9:30, however, it was Madame who came upstairs looking for *him* — interrupting him in the middle of a letter (his quest for counsel and solace) that he was writing to Saturn. Madame, however, was demonstrably out of sorts, if not in a high dudgeon, as she entered his workroom and seated herself at the table, opposite his little portable typewriter. He easily sensed her bad mood and was distinctly curious, though also chary, about what, possibly, it portended. He observed her — her crinkled face this morning was nonetheless unduly bland, whiter than white, without the accustomed purple-and-red cosmetics applied to the high cheekbones and the short, patchy, jowl hair standing in soft, almost wavy wisps. From the steep steps she had just climbed to the second floor, her breathing was stertorous. Finally: "Have you got a minute to talk, Paul?" she said.

"Of course, Madame." Apprehensively, he was already easing into the chair across the table from her, expecting at last to get the bad news — about Cécile.

Cyrus Colter

"You may, or may not," said Madame, "be surprised to learn that yesterday afternoon — after I'd returned from the Hôtel Crillon and was going to lie down for an hour to rest my weary bones after the experience, the ordeal, I'd just been through — the doorbell rang. When I went, there she stood, smiling strangely, but also furtively — the attractive young black African lady, clad in her same, weird, crazy, red dress. But this is not the burden of the story, Paul. There, behind her, forming an unlikely backdrop, were apparently her small son — a bright, chipper-looking boy — but also this huge, this gargantuan, heavily bearded, giant of a black man, the blackest human my eyes have ever beheld, and in the prime of his life, his mid-thirties. The child had found it possible, if only briefly, to smile, but not this stygian-black Hercules, who, though not glowering, was certainly casting a dour atmosphere over the entire encounter. What repelled me more than anything, however, was that his clothes were not clean. Nor, frankly, was he."

Paul now, having recognized even more, if possible, than the totality of the picture Madame was painting, could only groan in self-pity. "Quo Vadis Jackson, yes," he at last managed to breathe aloud. "Moreover, he can't afford a telephone. So, granted, he is quite a case, quite a man." Now somehow came a mordant grinding of his teeth as he frowned. "But pay no attention to his clothes, or otherwise, Madame," he said. "Despite what you see, he is a man of highest character. He is also an educated man."

Madame finally looked away, but only temporarily. "Well, if you say it," she said, "I accept it. But what must be the feeling of my tenants here when they see me admitting this strange trio into my parlor? To them it is a near-destitute African man with his wife and son exploring the possibility of becoming tenants themselves here in, if I myself may say it,

my fairly well-kept, and highly respectable, pension. I'm de-
scribing to you, Paul, an entirely likely scenario — and also a
likely problem."

Paul, watching her, at last took a deep breath and frowned.
"I, too, then, must constitute for you somewhat of 'a likely
problem,' Madame," he said.

"Not at all. There was no problem whatever. You got
routine consideration when you came. My decision was une-
ventful and easy — for a number of reasons. First of all, I pride
myself, and rightly so, as a person utterly free of bigotry. I
also consider myself, again rightly, as an intellectual. Which,
at least to me, means I must consider people strictly as individ-
uals, not members of one group or another. I've turned away
quite a number of French citizens, some Parisians, who've
applied. On the other hand, I was most pleased indeed to have
you. I'm not making a big point of it; it's merely true. My
decisions in this context are business decisions, no other kind,
and that's why having a man appear on the premises like the
one who came here yesterday can't possibly do my establishment any good. So I frown on it and hope he won't return. In
fact, my lodgers even look askance on this young lady friend
of yours who of course has been here before and always
wearing that same, loony, god-awful, dress. And sometimes
with a monstrous, hideous, wig to go with it."

Paul bridled. "It's *not* always the same dress, though,
Madame — I'm led to believe she has a number of these dresses,
some even of slightly different lengths. She is a highly respectable person — and I'm sure very hygienic."

"I don't doubt it for a minute, Paul — if, as I said, you say
it, I accept it. Yet, despite all that, whenever she appears here
she makes no possible contribution, does me no good, whatever. I'm not saying to you that you should go tell her not to
call on you here anymore. It's just — "

Paul angrily interrupted—"Have no fear, Madame. You won't see any of those three here again. Ever."

Madame inhaled deeply—in both half-guilt and half-confusion. "I don't exactly like—or else I didn't correctly understand—what you were saying just now, Paul. Had I offended you?"

Paul paused, somewhat less sure of himself. "I don't think so," he finally said, though frowning again. "I hope, and really think, it's impossible for you to offend me. I know you well, and I don't think you have bad feelings toward me. In fact, I think you wish me well—indeed feel I deserve success; well, some success, at least. In short, I regard you as my true friend. So, no, you have not offended me. Yet, Madame, this doesn't necessarily mean you're incapable of error, either. None of us is."

"I agree, Paul, so where have I erred?"

He could not help pausing again as he studied her wizened, chalky face, before saying, "I'm not even certain you have erred, Madame." In seeming self-disgust, then, he cried out, "Oh, what am I saying, or trying to say? Maybe I mean that your lodgers err when they don't like the idea of living on the same premises with, say, people like Tosca, Quo Vadis, and even little Gwelo, who, ironically, were here not to rent rooms but to see me. They're different, sure, but no better or no worse than your present tenants. Many people might have difficulty with this, but I'm sure you don't. Human being for human being, in fact, I'd be inclined to choose Quo Vadis over any guy you've got in this pension—I'm talking about both character and brains. The same thing for Tosca, over your women here. I've got to believe you know this, Madame, but I don't have to believe your tenants do. Yet, in a way, you ally yourself—on this very moral matter—with your tenants. I do say, knowing your history as I do, your lifelong stand with those you thought were on the side of justice, that it's not easy for me to identify you here, in this very telling situation, as on the side of your lodgers, who seem, if you're right at all about them, to be out of touch with what have been your beliefs for most of your life. It's not a very pretty picture, Madame."

Madame, though still trying for restraint, was furious at what she was hearing. Finally, unable to endure it further, she held up her hand in a gesture of silencing him, yet her words instead were a long time in coming. "Paul," she said at last, "let me be truthful and tell you that, in almost the year I've known you, I've never found you so insufferable as you're being right now. You sound like a sickly, confused preacher trying to make up a sermon as he goes along. What you're saying is largely meaningless—in fact, I'm not sure I fully understand what the hell you are trying to say. The saddest thing of all, though, is that I've never known you to sound so much like an old maid. The way you've been trying to lecture me just now is, unhappily, though frankly, anything but manly. You've got to face up to it—you're a man literally searching for hard times, so that you can then bare your breast and complain to high heaven and anyone else who will listen to you. But you not only have trouble making decisions, you then conjure up all manner of bugaboos to fill in the places where your mind, sadly, has had nothing to offer in the first place. I believe your mother had a lot to do with much of this. Incidentally, Paul, I see you have her picture out on display here today. That's kind of a rarity, isn't it? I can always tell when you're in a really frantic mood—like now; out comes her portrait then—and the more you move it around (like trying to find the best direction for a radio antenna when the reception has been notoriously bad) the more agitated I know you are that day." Madame reached around the little typewriter and picked Queen Saturn's framed portrait up off Paul's worktable. "She is, yes, a very attractive woman," she said.

Paul raised both hands, saying, "She *was* a very attractive woman, Madame. She is of course no more, now. It was my great disappointment; my rebuff, really; she could be like that, you know. I've not recovered yet, but I'm working on it. She did me everlasting harm, I think, though. So it goes."

Madame spoke out of the blue: "How would she have reacted to Cécile, Paul?"

Paul studied her for a long time but said nothing. "I probably shouldn't get into that, Madame," he finally said. "Anyway, it would be only speculation on my part." He turned directly to her. "How did your luncheon with Cécile go?"

"Not well at all." Madame grimaced. "The French Nazis have got her and gone — figuratively speaking, at least. But that's not the worst news. Somehow Cécile is ill, I think. It's a tragedy." She stared out the window into the sunlight before sighing heavily. "Yes, a tragedy — this fine, lovely, sweet woman . . . and my friend."

Paul was as irritated as he was frantically anxious. "What *happened*, Madame?" he said, rising from his chair. "What did you two talk about? Did my name come up?"

Madame merely sat musing, until she said, "I almost wish I hadn't gone. Everything was so tense and strained. Oh, heavens — poor, poor Cécile. My heart goes out to her."

"Did she mention me, Madame?"

Madame ignored him; but then: "She talked constantly about dreams, her bad dreams," she finally said. "Oh, poor thing, she's been through hell!"

"Madame, Madame, did she say why she had put *me* down? I can't understand it! We were, we were . . . you might say . . . yes, collaborators — or it was even more than that; we used to take little trips in her car — just outside Paris. It was wonderful — yes, in the best sense we were collaborators. It was divine." In a blurry trance now, he stood gazing out the window.

Madame curled her lip. "Divine, ha — I should think so. Collaborators. Ah, but now Cécile has got her own theory on all that. To her now you are nothing more than a *niggerine*."

"A *what*?"

Madame shook her head. "I know the name, and I've seen the product, but I know as little as you do — except that you are the wrong color, she has decided. But that in itself, even in the tenuous way she puts it, is a complicated deal — very. She didn't say that she didn't like you. In fact, when I asked her what it was she had against you, she said, 'Nothing,' adding that it wasn't that you had done anything but that it was who you are now. At once then she wanted to start eating those horrible, disgusting niggerines again — that is, until I threatened her with death. Ah, what a shocking misfortune — Cécile is sick in both body and mind."

Paul was walking the floor now. Suddenly his hand went to his forehead in utter desperation. "Oh, I understand none of this — absolutely none!"

"Come join me, then, would you, Paul? I'm perfectly at sea." Madame somehow now tried to smile. This appeared to astonish Paul. "We must forget Cécile for awhile," she said. "If not, we shall end up as demented as she seems to be. So what next, I say. What now about your attractive African lady, Paul? I don't think you've mentioned her in the last ten minutes — ha! You did, though, for a moment address your ill-fated darling Jeannette. But Paul — my God! — we're *all* crazy. Do you realize that? . . . You, Cécile, I, your Tosca — we're all crazy, I say! Although I'm the only one who knows it. Who but you, Paul, could get so excited because Cécile has reassessed your respective positions? But then almost at once you page your poor Jeannette — at least you page her vision, from, as it were, the very stage wings of her sepulcher, apparently in order to unburden your woes on her dusty ghost." Madame now emitted a long, ponderous sigh. "Then there's Cécile," she said. "What a wonderful human being—except, as I say, like the rest of us she has a wild, a piercing, dementia, but which she sometimes tries to subdue, or else merely scatter, by just ignoring it. The same, however, is true of some of the rest of us—at least those still living. Take you, for instance, Paul—even before I introduced you to my good-looking physician that day when we all thought I was dying of a mammoth thrombosis. But my physician was soon not only trying to meet my exigency but, on having taken a second or third look at you, her own exigency as well. It appears she was not born under any of the propitious celestial bodies. Therefore I became the original broker in all this. Yes, it's weird—of course it is—and God, if there is one, please now help me. Help us all. We stand in need. Every son and daughter of us. So be it." She rose to go then.

"Oh, don't go yet, Madame," Paul said. "You haven't told me much of anything about what you and Cécile talked about." He was thinking of something else as well—his obligation to ill little Ari and Ari's selfless service to the kaput Coterie. "Madame, I must know more about Cécile, I tell you," he said now. "I need her—I need her as a physician, her expertise, her reputation. It involves a friend of mine who is ill and is now in Cécile's hospital—Lady of Paradise. It would be a great advantage for him if she were to step in and take over, advise him, and me, on what his situation is, the diagnoses, et cetera, and what specialists we should have in to see that he gets the best attention and treatment. This is the situation I called her about but couldn't get to her—she wouldn't talk to me. It's a worrisome situation. I need her, though—for more reasons than one. I therefore need you as well, to tell me about her, right now."

Paul had kept talking despite the fact that Madame's hand had long been in the air to stop him. She was adamant. "Heavenly Father!" she said. "Paul . . . you listen to me. If this happens, if you finally talk Cécile into doing this, please prepare to say prayers for your friend in Lady of Paradise Hospital. I tell you, Cécile is in no condition to assume such responsibilities. She herself needs a physician. In fact, I'm taking steps to get her medical—also, if required, psychological—help in trying to restore her own health. What you're preparing to do, though, is exactly the opposite—become a serious menace to her recovery."

Paul almost sneered. "Well, tell me what her family, her husband, is doing for her—if anything?"

"Oh, my God—if I only knew, or could get her to tell me. But what makes your plan so risky for her is the problem of just who your sick friend is and—"

Paul bristled. "He's a fine little guy, Madame! He's a former Coterie colleague of mine. So what's your problem?"

"I've tried to intimate to you, Paul, that we're dealing with a different, and really strange, Cécile now. If your hospitalized friend was a member of your recent organization, he's no doubt black, I take it. Well, that's not going to help Cécile any—as I see it. The fact probably is that her troubles right now in some way involve blacks. Even including you, Paul."

"Let me tell you something, Madame. Although you've apparently decided to withhold from me most of the information you got from your meeting with Cécile, I nevertheless have some intimations, some hunches, of my own. Remember, I knew Cécile, dear Cécile, pretty well at one time."

"And how! Lord Jesus."

"So you mark my words, Madame. Cécile will bounce back—and sooner than you think. You hinted she has weight problems. Well, that's no big deal—a sudden loss of weight, you know, doesn't spell eternal doom. Her difficulties, whatever they are, have caused her some stress no doubt. So she hasn't been eating. What she's got to do is eat more, build herself up, and thus get rid of those bad dreams you say she's been having. You should have told her this, Madame."

Madame raised her fist and struck her breast before groaning at what she considered this uninformed gibberish. "Oh, Paul – for Christ's sake!" she cried. "Cécile is *fat*! She's so fat you wouldn't recognize her! She's gained at least twenty-five pounds! Sit down there, will you, and I'll tell you some things that will blow your mind!"

Paul was awed, observing her temper with both curiosity and fear. He soon backed off and sat down again.

Whereupon Madame, eventually calming herself, told him all she knew.

Later that morning – noon impended – Paul sat alone in his room overwhelmed and bewildered by what he had heard. Somehow, though, he believed it all. To him it had the ring of truth. Yet he felt no indignation toward Cécile. Actually now, more than ever, he wanted to find her and talk, maybe assuage her. Something terrible had happened to her, he was certain. He even speculated she had not yet told Madame all. He began to think up a rash of things – tactics, maneuvers – he might resort to in order to see her again. But now somehow he began to feel strange. Soon all manner of thoughts, exotic, even eccentric, as well as familiar, began to assail his brain. And when he went into the adjacent room to shave he found himself talking to himself in the mirror. Before long, then, he began to think about what Madame had earlier said – that he, in fact all of them, were crazy. Yet, at least for the time being, these mad thoughts, ironically, seemed instead to concentrate his mind. For example, he realized now he had had no food today, that he was ravenously hungry. But almost at once then he began to think of Saturn – it frightened him. Then, weirdly, his thoughts roamed to Tosca, her incredible, long, reddish dress, plus the warlike, the hellish, dreadlocks. Yet he thought her a sweet — and, to him, perfectly erotic, indeed almost X-rated woman. However, there came not a trace of Jeannette on his mind. Ah, he told himself, Madame must be right — yes, about all of them. Demented. The lot. Certainly himself. This meant most of all that he needed Saturn. He would, he could, never deny her. It was instinctive, mechanical. He could see her lounging, on the chaise lounge, the lilac slip lucid.

Soon he had left the house. It was still sunny, bright, and his watch said 11:30. His destination was the neat-enough restaurant and bar — named only Zuchon's — located three blocks down the Rue la Chatte. But when he finally entered the place he found it still nearly empty — so far only eight patrons. It made him wonder if the establishment might be eventually headed for bankruptcy. Unfortunately he was also reminded — while on the subject of bankruptcy — that he himself was at long last on the verge of a greater familiarity with it. His father's check for the month had yet to arrive and this was no longer unusual. He himself, moreover, had contributed to the condition by informing old Zack, when the Coterie had gone kaput, that his stipend could now be cut. His father had complimented him warmly, especially, he had said, for the son's clear integrity manifested — which, he added, meant more to him than the dollars involved. Paul remembered his own self-satisfaction at the time but now even the modestly smaller checks had brought a similarly modest adjustment in his Paris lifestyle. Indeed the first item to go — paradoxically aided and abetted of course by Cécile's recent strange behavior, her apparent angry repudiation of him (if, he thought, that's what it really was) — the first item to go, then, was their memorable little trysting suite in the Hôtel Achilles in nearby Fantes. Full of nostalgia that this was so, he hated to let it go; yet, he thought, how would he later, with his checks now somewhat smaller, explain to Cécile there was no place he could take her? He could now, though, he was sure, put the matter aside as being thoroughly moot. Yet thinking of all this as he entered Zuchon's with its slim, non-spate of customers, he could not help wondering about their balance sheet and their profit-and-loss statement — at the same time that he felt a yen to reach and take out his own wallet and examine the number of franc notes in it. But he desisted. Now his watch said 11:45. How wrong he had probably been, he thought — Zuchon's luncheon trade was not yet due. Within an hour the place might be packed, for all he knew. He thought of himself, kept his hand away from his wallet, and felt better.

He wanted a drink now; glancing over at the bar he made his way back toward a lonely table well in the rear. The long and unpleasant conversation he had just had with Madame Chevalley, after she had made one of her rare climbs up to his rooms, had not only tired him but disappointed him as well; it had also made him wonder. Wonder about what? he asked himself; then made no attempt to answer. He only knew he wanted a drink, or two, he thought — possibly a viscous, 94-proof, gin martini. He was eminently entitled to it, he told himself — without even addressing now what the remainder of the day was to expect, indeed demand, of him. Suddenly, then, he was again aware of his growling empty stomach. Yet he craved a martini more than ever. Soon he had caught his waiter's eye and beckoned him over. Placing a mere drink order, however, he realized when the man had gone, had done little to prevent his mind from returning to his just-ended bout with Madame. The episode had consumed him — somewhat educated him also. She had, yes, unnerved him, he thought. He had never, seen her, experienced her, in this frame of mind. Was she to be like this from now on, he wondered. Was she already in her dotage and no one, including Cécile, had noticed it? Speaking of Cécile, he thought fearfully, he should, at least for the moment, keep his mind confined, disciplined, away from her. Things were difficult enough as they already were. One of the matters Madame had been uncommonly raw about was Tosca's, Quo Vadis's, and even little Gwelo's astounding visit to her premises—especially Quo Vadis's unseemly presence in the group. As for Quo Vadis, however, Paul's feelings were themselves not unmixed. Why, indeed, was the man so slovenly—yet also apparently proud of it? This was bad, he thought, also unnecessary, and gave a very wrong impression of who he, Quo Vadis, really was—the mind and interests, the character of the man, what he represented generally. Paul was soon in a fretful pique. He was certain Quo Vadis was his own worst enemy. Yet Paul in some respects had, on much reflection, somewhat changed his opinion of Quo Vadis, although there were still facets, intimations of the man's disposition and temperament which to date were unfathomable to Paul. Yet he had thought long about that night, that bizarre occasion, when at Quo Vadis's dreary flat they had talked about many things. He could not easily forget Quo Vadis's strange, indeed passionate, if complex (also highly arguable), views of life and the world. No matter; this was the man Madame had so cavalierly spoken of as if he had been a seedy tramp ringing her doorbell—she had apparently been that displeased, upset, even alarmed. It riled Paul merely thinking of it, and he was soon, even if somewhat unconsciously overreacting, allowing himself to get carried away, considering it as having been a personal affront. Meanwhile, he had finished his first martini and now got the waiter and ordered a second—the former pangs of hunger seeming now, strangely, fraudulently, to have subsided. This was a mistake, of course.

But now, despite his struggles against it, Cécile had returned — to his consciousness — which he thought, though, was as bad, as debilitating, as if she had suddenly appeared in person. He dreaded the thought of having to confront her, even if it was something he felt he was bound to do for Ari. But there was something else. He knew that if she had gone to the lengths she had practiced in the immediate past few weeks, against not only him but Madame as well — to say nothing of her, Cécile's, strange physical condition — she might well, yes, refuse to see him at all. Or if she did consent to let him speak to her, she, whom he assumed to be a much changed woman now, might very well visit upon him all her present craziness, misinformation, misgivings, plus her apparent wrath about something. He dreaded the very thought of such a confrontation — or any other such standoff — for he considered himself a sure loser. Yet, he thought guiltily, in such a scenario so was poor Ari a loser. He took a deep, shuddering intake of breath and reached for his drink. To his utter disbelief, the glass was empty. He had no way of escaping the fact now that during the agitation of his torturous thoughts, all the dread impasses, and wrestling with half-truths, he had somehow drained the glass. He thought ill of himself — that he was a shivering coward, and thereupon sank into a fit of deep despair. Meanwhile he flagged down the waiter again and ordered a third martini. When it came he felt much better — realizing also that, having known what he must do, see Cécile, he had earlier telephoned Fifi Mazisi and, though telling her little, had nonetheless secured her grudging agreement for their postponement of today's early afternoon rendezvous at Ari's shabby hotel (to fetch some of his books to the hospital) until a more likely date became available. Trying feverishly now to jack up his spirits, and valor, he vowed that after having a thick steak he would leave and go await Cécile — beard the lioness in her den — hang out in her outer office. But, breathing heavily now, he somehow began to feel serious again, though in physical heft actually lighter, yet his gin eyesight, strange and equivocal, now began to play games with him. As a consequence, he beckoned for the waiter and, pointing, asked for another maraschino cherry in his martini. On being informed that that was an anchovy olive, not a cherry, in his drink, he humbly gave ground and, though frowning, nodded and kept his peace. Indeed, the waiter now, somewhat anxiously, asked if he would now like a menu, to which, as if suddenly awaking, Paul smiled and replied, *"Oui, merci."* The waiter also smiled, comically, and left, as Paul reached and sipped his third lethal martini on an empty stomach. He felt even lighter now, though; pleased with himself; momentarily harmonious with the world. Soon then the luncheon patrons began to file in and the place took on a busier, more cheerful aspect. Paul could not remember when he had felt so good, so free, so easily in charge of himself. Next he began rehearsing for his afternoon task, which he was resolved now to bring off spectacularly. Now he realized he wanted a fourth martini but at once knew that if he was to be equal to his afternoon commitment he must refrain. He would therefore, after his steak, yes, leave here and go directly to Cécile's office and, even if frightened to the point of panic, wait her out until she returned from her daily visitation to Lady of Paradise Hospital (where of course he had deliberately taken little Ari), and once and for all, have it out with her. And not only about Ari (although Ari's possible plight made him wince) but about themselves — and *why*.

He sat there at his table and faced the front, the entrance door — through which now suddenly entered four women, presumably nearby office workers come for lunch. He gasped. One of them was a tall, comely, youngish, black woman, indeed quite comely, also quite black. Paul's inconstant eyes were veritably rolling now as again he gasped. Meanwhile the women were being brought back to a table not really close, yet not really far either, from his own. Before, however, they could be seated Paul rose and, eyes wide, lips quivering, whispering, stood facing them. He was trembling now. "Oh, my God!" he said, though almost under his breath — actually, as if afraid of being overheard, or of having been wrong about something, possibly an identity, utterly vital, crucial, to him. "Oh, my God!" he repeated, again softly. "Yes . . . yes, my prayers have been answered. It's she, it's she, all right! . . . Oh Jesus!" At last he almost screamed it — "*Jeannette, Jeannette!* . . . I knew I'd find you, darling! . . . and I have, I have! God be thanked!"

His waiter came rushing over now. "Monsieur, Monsieur," he said, glancing back over at the bar where the head bartender was signaling to him some very firm negatives — like, 'No more drinks for him.' "Monsieur," said the waiter, "you're creating a disturbance. Will you resume your seat, please?"

Paul staggered slightly as he stood gazing at the waiter. "Do you see that lovely lady over there? — the black lady," he said. "I know her. We were high-school sweethearts — back in the States, in Chicago." A glazed, enraptured look came in his eyes.

The waiter shook his head. "No, Monsieur. She is French — from Senegal, I believe."

"Oh, no, no," said Paul. "She's American." He was pointing now, then made a move to leave the table. "Here, I'll go prove it to you."

"Now, wait," said the waiter, more than firmly, in warning. "Let them alone. The bartender, who is the proprietor, has been watching you. He wants to put you out already, except that he knows you come in here occasionally, that you're not a rank stranger, and doesn't want to offend you unnecessarily. He says, though, not to serve you anymore drinks today."

Paul, groping for the table, finally sat down again. "I'll make a deal with you, sir," he said, and started getting out his wallet. "I'll make it worth your while, too. Go over there and tell that lovely black lady to look over here and—"

"She's already done that," the waiter interrupted, "all of them have. How could they have overlooked you, with all the commotion you were making. They knew you were talking about them, and probably figured out which one of them, too. The tall black girl was looking at you, all right—curiously, not smiling much."

Paul reached for his martini glass, only, of course, to find it empty again. He waved good-bye to it and said to the waiter, "My friend, go over there and ask her if she will look over here at me—just once." He seemed to become even more agitated now as he got a clear profile view of the girl, or woman, and became very upset, impetuous. "Look, her regal height," he said, "the statuesque tallness; it's the same; the deep, dark, opaque, actually stygian, facial color is also the same; I saw her beautiful slender legs when she came in, too—they're the same as ever: heavenly; as are her facial features, yes, strong, symmetrical, deep-dark, her slow gaze secure and cool as ever, too. Glance over there just once and lose your heart. I dare you, sir!" Again Paul seized the empty martini glass and turned it up high to his lips, to no avail.

"I must go take care of my other luncheon customers," the waiter said, "I'm neglecting them. What do you want to eat, Monsieur?"

Paul flew into a frenzy. "I want a drink, and I want a steak, and I want the woman I love, who is sitting right over there looking as saintly as she really is! I need her—I *need* her,

I tell you! I need her to save my life!" Staring at the now-retreating waiter, his jaw fell — as if a great, a universal, truth had struck him. "I need her to save my life . . . " he cried "in order that I may try to save other people's lives. Do you understand? . . . do you understand that?" But the waiter had almost reached the kitchen by now. In desperation Paul turned to "Jeannette" herself — who, talking and smiling among her officemates, was prettily chewing on a stalk of celery.

An hour and half later almost all of Zuchon's luncheon customers had come and gone — including Paul's "Jeannette," who, though, on leaving had seemed careful to keep her eyes away from his vicinity. Still later, when he had at last finished his steak, a slow process under his condition, he had not forgotten her cool and sober mien. When the waiter brought the bill he was also glad to be able to furnish Paul with additional information. "I checked it out," he said. "The black girl's name is not Jeannette at all. It's Mignon."

Paul had not heard. Bleary-eyed, he was rummaging in his wallet for money. "It was Jeannette, all right," he soon said. "Her spirit. It overpowered the whole room; emblazoned victory on my soul — my mother should have been here for the triumph. Though she wouldn't have enjoyed it. Justice has a way of righting old scores. Now, Mr. Waiter, I'm going to pay you, tip you, generously, and include enough for my final drink, a stirrup cup, so to speak."

"No, no, I can't do it," the waiter said. "You've had too much already. You're going home from here, I assume."

"Not at all," said Paul. "I'm going directly to the doctor's office. She should be there by now. Would you care to accompany me? The meeting will be fabulous, historic. I've seen the light — right here in your establishment today." He stood and hiccoughed, then began unsteadily dealing four-franc notes on the table. "Seen the light, yes," he stressed, and brought his wristwatch up close to his eyes. "Oh, I'm late already. The doctor's there by now. She is very punctual. I must go, waiter." He stood erect and tried to square his shoulders, then started the considerable distance up to the exit. Minutes later he had entered the noisy bar and grill hardly a block down the street.

By 7:20 that evening Madame, corpulent Cécile, and one of the maid-housekeepers, Bianca, all stood around his bed. "It was awful trying to bring him up those stairs, Madame," Bianca, a fifty-five-year-old Slavonian woman, said. "He fought all the way—even though the taxi driver, well over two hundred pounds, fought back."

Frail Madame was livid. "He puked up his toenails on my stair carpet all the way as well!" she said.

Cécile, outraged at their triviality, turned on them both with a shrilling order, a fiat: "Undress him!"

"Oh! . . . " Bianca's hand went to her face.

"Jesus Christ!" said Madame, and, before she thought, turned to Cécile and said: "Why don't you? You should know the territory!"

Cécile turned on her and made a face. "How awful of you—for shame! But I shall, then. I want some towels, and soap, and some coffee not too hot; and one of his robes."

"I only knew that he had *one*," spat Madame.

But Cécile now was pulling off Paul's shoes. As soon, though, as she touched him he—eyes closed—groaned. "Oh, Jeannette," he said blindly, "why did you do it, ignore me like that? Why? . . . why? . . . "

"Now we've got to hear all about his first love—Jeannette," said Madame. "Holy Jesus!" She looked down at prostrate Paul on his bed and sighed. "They can all go to Princeton, all right, yes—to Harvard or Yale, too; and the Sorbonne; to both Oxford and Cambridge. Even to Tuskegee. It's all the same, though, and nothing much can be done to help their situation. It's their fate—alikeness. Right, Cécile? This is your territory, you know. Your second cousins, who put you on a diet of niggerines, should see you now—with that big shoe of his in your pretty hands."

"Go make coffee, Madame," said Cécile, her voice vitriolic. "Bianca, find a robe; look in that closet—don't just stand there gaping, for Christ's sake! He's ill—his pulse is not right . . . Oh, God, he may have tried suicide, tried to kill himself with liquor." She bent low over Paul. "Paul, listen Paul . . . do you hear me? This is Cécile, Paul." She turned around to them. "We don't know how much he drank. It could be self-inflicted alcohol poisoning. It may be that we should get him to a hospital."

"Jeannette . . . ," Paul murmured again, softly.

Cécile bent down to him once more. "Were you expecting a Jeannette, Paul?"

Madame interrupted. "I'll tell you about some people he wasn't expecting to see—until I got on the telephone again and raised my voice to you. Now you're here. Did you bring your niggerines?" But Madame's voice was tired now, almost rasping.

Paul groaned again, then whispered to Cécile, "Don't go, Jeannette."

Cécile rose and left the bed. "Everything is off," she said to Bianca. "We've got to do it differently. Where is his telephone?—I'm going to get an ambulance over here and put him in the hospital."

Madame, seeming too tired to care now, backed up and sat in a chair. "I think you're doing the right thing, Cécile," she said at last, though sighing.

Forty-five minutes later Paul was in a private room in Lady of Paradise Hospital, four floors above Ari Ngcobo.

City of Light

Around 9:30 that night, Paul's home phone began ringing — Madame Chevalley, in her room below, could hear it. She had wanted sleep, but sleep would not come. When, then, the phone rang for the third time in forty minutes, she got out her bunch of keys and laboriously climbed up the stairs and answered it.

"I'm trying to get Monsieur Kessey," said the female voice. "He's apparently still out."

Madame knew the cultured French voice all too well — Tosca Zimsu's. "He is, yes," she replied coolly.

"Are you Madame Chevalley?"

"Yes."

"I am Tosca Zimsu, his friend — you may remember me; I've been to your house more than once."

"Yes," said Madame cuttingly. "I remember you from your hairdo — the dreadlocks."

Tosca gulped but took it. "Would you please ask him to call us — we have a telephone now. As you know, we've been trying to reach him. Could I leave our telephone number with you?"

Madame was trying to contain herself, with little success. "No, Miss Zimsu," she said. "I have nothing to write it down with or on. And I'm very tired."

Tosca, though very courteously, was insistent. "I imagine you are up in Monsieur Kessey's rooms — there are generally many pencils around."

"Yes!" cried Madame petulantly, "the ones he uses to write letters to his dead mother! Listen, Miss Zimsu, I can't help you tonight. May I hang up now? I repeat, I'm very tired. There are no pencils in sight. I'm sorry. Good night." She slowly hung up.

Next morning she was having her poached egg, toast, and coffee, when Paul's phone upstairs rang again. But by the protracted time it took her to get her keys and go up, the phone had stopped. "This is getting ridiculous," she told herself,

240

returning down to the kitchen and her cooled food. Yet she was anything but indifferent or bored, certainly not angrily displeased, not outraged, none of this, by any of last night's action—spiteful internecine wrangling, commotion—that had taken place upstairs in her pension, and which involved not only Paul but the long-delinquent Cécile. When frantically calling on her at home to come help in the crisis, Madame, shrilling all the dire details of poor Paul's plight into the telephone, was at the same time intrigued—yet also put off, riled—by her doctor's quailing hesitance, the fear, and when as a consequence Madame became suddenly wrathful, loud, the sad torture of Cécile's response to the bullying was pitiable. The root cause, of course, finally dawned on Madame. Cécile could not bear the thought—it was sheer anathema—of Paul ever seeing her in her present physical state. It was gruesome to her—she would have much preferred jumping off the Pont Neuf into the Seine. Madame understood it all now. Yet, on seeing Paul's calamitous condition, she had known better than to take chances: she called Cécile because she needed Cécile, whose presence was critical. Yet now she felt sorry for her. Her obese appearance—despite her resorting to altered, let-out dresses—was, alas, the same. The world, thought Madame, could be a rotten place. She knew this. Her own life had not been velvet—"no crystal stair."

Thus Paul, yesterday, in drowning his sorrows—at the second bar, maybe even a third—his sorrows, yes, for Jeannette Hall, yet even for Saturn, had come near, in this manic process, to drowning himself. Thus—again a miracle, even if a circuitous one—Dr. Cécile, whether she liked it or not, had now been put in full charge of his morbid ailments, both physical and psychological, alongside those of his fast-fading Coterie colleague, the faithful, redoubtable, little Sorbonne Zulu, Ari. Truly, thought Paul in the hospital later, the Lord indeed possessed mysterious ways His wonders to perform. Somehow now, as the strangest of consequences, and really for the first time, he, Paul, wished – for some reason or another, which he was not at all clear about – that he could now talk with Quo Vadis Jackson, that strangest of men. But for what specific purpose he could not at the moment make out, decipher. Their minds, however, seemed to him at times mysteriously in sync, in need of each other. He did not know why.

In the last few days, though, things had been very different for Quo Vadis – quickly, abruptly, leaving the great black giant startled, dumbfounded, rendered in no mood to talk with anyone. Things had suddenly changed. Tosca had money – modest, yes, but money – from her murdered father! Indeed, matters had come to such a sudden and unexpected fruition that he now felt somehow hurried, actually rushed, to speed up his schedule, his timetable, to at long last assume the dread responsibilities of a role he had regarded as having been named for his very own purposes by a late great Georgia man named King – the role: "a drum major for justice." He had not, however, expected to be called upon, pressed into service, as it were, so soon, almost prematurely, all forced on him by this sudden and strange, weird, almost unbelievable, concatenation of circumstances, and about which, ironically, his now excited friend, Tosca, long the beneficiary of, for what it amounted to, his ungrudging largesse, had now repeatedly sought, though unsuccessfully, to find and joyously inform her new and promising friend, Paul, of the "good," the "great," news – of money, and in doing so had precipitated Madame Chevalley's high pique about unsightly visitors invading her pension.

So now Quo Vadis suddenly had no yen to talk to anyone. He only wished to be left alone to deal with this radical change of events, this sudden crisis, in order to commune with himself, even if hesitantly, almost tremblingly; at the same time trying on his new drum major's habiliments symbolizing a new yearned-for justice, which, however, despite years of study, plus, yes, much praying, he realized now, he had somehow never completely understood. He therefore no longer wished to talk to, communicate with, advise, or exhort anyone—except himself. He was alone again now. There was only the need, indeed the necessity, for self-communion—also, alas, the need for an utter attempt, a longing, to somehow achieve rapport with an equivocal, unclear God. He, Quo Vadis, was a wholly different, a brand new, man now, he told himself. Or he hoped he was, prayed he was. Why, then, though, he wondered, did he sit alone in his darkened bedroom trembling, yes, imploring that the fatal cup somehow pass from his lips? He knew it would not. His time had come, his test, and so swiftly, so unannounced, almost ruthlessly. Was he ready? He knew he was not. Not yet. Ready or not, though, he had made a vow, a vow to himself. Now things were suddenly serious.

Chapter

Six

Paul's Lady of Paradise

He had always hated hospitals. All hospitals—ever since in Africa as a boy he had seen, and heard, his Uncle Keziahh screaming night and day in agony in that straw-roofed barn which passed for a hospital for the Kwazulu natives, subjects of their cruel Dutch masters. His uncle had had an arm lopped off below the elbow by the Dutch, having been charged with stealing a deputy commissioner's white jacket. Ari later learned his uncle had been guilty as charged but had already had little sympathy for him—the jacket was both ornate and white, entirely precluding any chance of Keziahh's ever wearing it or otherwise getting away with his act. Even the fact that Keziahh had almost bled to death in the ordeal had had a limited sorrowful effect on Ari. No matter, he had still always loathed hospitals. The mere thought of one frightened him. Yet now here he was in one and very miserable about it. He gave Paul Kessey, his erstwhile Coterie leader and benefactor, scant credit indeed for placing him here— especially, thought Ari, when there was nothing wrong with him except possibly temporary fatigue and some loss of weight and appetite.

Now here, suddenly, again, was the woman doctor — in her silver eyeglasses and starched white jacket with a stethoscope around her neck and a breast pocket full of ballpoint pens. Only this time she was merely peeping in, peering around the corner, the door, of the ward, but he knew this meant she was not, thank God, coming any nearer. But then, on second thought, this displeased him. Why did she always hesitate to come to his bedside? Before he thought, he called out petulantly, "Are you my doctor?" She seemed not to hear his strident, peevish voice and instead gazed over at the other patients. There were five beds in the room besides his own, all occupied, but she seemed to have no interest in, or obligation to, these other five, all males, all Caucasians. He alone, such as it was, got her attention, even though it was, as now, from afar. Yet, near or far, on a regular basis she had thus silently studied him — often, he thought, as if to make sure she was observing the right patient. He still wondered about this — realizing he was the only black in the room. Again her strange behavior riled him — it was almost, he thought, as if she were afraid of him, or heartily disliked him. Suddenly then, as she still stood in the doorway, staring, almost frowning, at him, he quickly raised his hand and, unsmiling, beckoned to her to come over to him. Suddenly it was also apparent to him that at one time she had been very attractive but was now overweight; also no longer young. From his recent brief experiences with her, however, he now expected no response to his beckoning. He was right, of course. Soon then she had turned on her heels and was gone. Yet he was somehow glad. Before long, then, as usual, two interns appeared and, stoically, took his temperature, pulse, and drew a blood specimen, before, unsmiling, they left. As they were leaving, though, little Ari, laughing crazily, almost maniacally, tried to detain them. "Ha, ha!" he cried. "Will I live? Ha, ha, ha! What do you think?"

The interns, at first ignoring him, finally then for a moment turned and observed each other. At last, though, one of them shrugged and smiled over his shoulder at Ari. "Why not?" he said. "Why not."

Slightly over a half hour later Fifi Mazisi arrived, out of breath, lugging a bag of books. Ari was elated to see her and at once sat straight upright in the bed with a great smile on his wasted face. "Where's Paul?" he said. Then however—"I thought he was going to help you."

"So did I," said Fifi, almost collapsing into the bedside chair. "But who can keep up with Paul these days? He stood me up again, yes, and didn't even call. So I had to go over to that crummy hotel of yours by myself to get these books. I gotta tell you, though, I was damned uneasy, really scared, all the time. Some strange folks, real characters, hang out over there."

Ari ignored the subject. "What happened to Paul? he said.

"I've called him two or three times. No one answered." But now Fifi sat uneasily studying Ari's face, having never before seen it so emaciated, before looking away as if embarrassed. "Are they feeding you all right here?" she finally asked in an attempt at levity.

"Lord, yes," he said. "So much of it I can't eat it all." He sighed then—"I never did eat much, though."

But Fifi could not take her eyes off his scant body, even though it lay under the sheet. Yet she tried to remind herself that he had always been small, actually almost dwarfish; indeed hardly greater than the size of a fourteen-year-old boy. Yet his face, though black enough, had somehow also about it a brick-reddish tinge below its high cheekbones. Yet it was a face severely seasoned and mature—indeed Fifi had only recently learned he was 51 years old. She took a worried deep breath now, but soon bent over and began taking the books out of the bag—all under Ari's watchful eye. "I've got a lot of studying to do while I'm here," he said. "You can imagine how far behind I already am in my newspaper work." He leaned over on his side to watch her. "Good—I see you brought the Du Bois book. And Léopold Senghor, yes. As I say, I've got work to do before they let me out of this place. It was nice of Paul to get me in here, though. But it won't cost him anything, not a franc—I can pay my way, all right. Besides, my organization, the African National Congress, would pay anyhow if I couldn't. But neither it nor Paul will have to, thank God. I'm going to do something nice for you, too, Fifi—you tell your boyfriend Mango that I'm not going to take advantage of your kindness, hear?"

At first Fifi tittered but soon her face grew long, contemplative. It was, then, at this juncture, that the two interns returned, but this time soberly trailed by the obese woman doctor, wearing as before the sparkling eyeglasses on her flushed, heavy, yet somehow still beautiful face.

"Look out!—look out!" frantically whispered Ari, as if a great she-lion had entered the ward. "She's back. The doctor. Oh, my Lord."

Fifi's hand flew to her mouth. "Is that your doctor? That must be the woman Paul somehow knows—and why he wanted you to come here. Ah, that's who that is, eh? She's supposed to be the one to take care of you—your doctor, yes."

Ari made a gruesome, angry face. "She's a real bitch, though," he said, "won't come near me; sends those two young doctors who're only kids, it looks like, and not worth much. She's an evil woman. But I won't tell Paul—he'd be disappointed, maybe cuss her out. Paul's very loyal like that, you know. The truth is, probably, he doesn't know her very well at all—just heard she was a widely known expert as an internist.

But those two guys with her, her young stooges, were just in here less than an hour ago; gave me a quick going over; also took some blood, as they do every day."

Fifi inwardly winced.

"But she won't come near me," Ari still complained. "Just pokes her head in at the door and stares at me. To tell you the truth, the woman acts like she's kind of crazy. It's good there's nothing really wrong with me or else I'd be in a hell of a bind. No, I wouldn't, either—I'd walk out of this damn place. I wonder where Paul ran across *her*."

Fifi, mouth open, was already staring at the three doctors now descending upon them.

It was then that Ari started his crazy laugh again, then whispered: "I'm scared, Fifi!"

But Dr. Cécile and her two young cohorts had reached them now. The taller of the two interns said to Ari: "We're back. We need more blood."

In his sudden rage Ari almost choked, speaking his French so fast it was almost phonically indecipherable—"You're not going to get shit out of me until you, all of you, identify yourselves!" He turned on Cécile. "I asked you, only an hour ago, as you were peeping in the damned door at me like I was in the zoo, if you were my doctor. And what did you do? You acted like you hadn't heard me. And soon, still staring at me as if I were an orangutan, you quickly vamoosed. Well, now you're here at my bedside—are you my doctor?"

Cécile came closer now and stood over him. "No, I'm not your doctor," she said icily. "I've merely been—at Monsieur Kessey's request—a kind of interlocutor, to see that you did get the right physicians for your symptoms, whatever these two doctors, Messrs. Tassigny and Marnix, find them to be."

"Oh, my God," said Fifi before she thought. "I thought *you* were his doctor."

City of Light

Ari turned green, or something near it. He finally swallowed and, trying to appear brave, said: "I shall telephone Monsieur Kessey at once — to discuss with him these arrangement to which, until just now, I have not at all been privy. I must try to get him at once, yes."

Fifi was alarmed, saying to him, "But I've been trying to reach him ever since yesterday — with no luck!"

Cécile looked crestfallen, then hesitant, and finally almost embarrassed. "Monsieur Kessey is a patient in the hospital here, too," she said, "since night before last."

"Good God!" exclaimed Fifi, standing up.

"But we must have the blood sample," Cécile said adamantly, and nodded to her interns, the taller of whom now exposed the needle.

On the evening of that same day Tosca, Quo Vadis, and Gwelo were at home having dinner. Tosca, in one of her more bizarre, yet attractive, red dresses, was in a radiant mood — except that she had as yet been unable to contact Paul to tell him of the "great, good" news. "I called him but he was out. And that mean old woman, his landlady, wouldn't even let me leave our new phone number for him — said she had no pencil at hand, and was also tired. Isn't that mean? I haven't had the nerve to call back for fear she might answer his phone again."

"Why all the hurry and flurry, Ma-MAH?" said cranky Gwelo. "He'll find out soon enough."

"It's his friend James Lewellyn, though, I guess, I've most wanted to tell him about," Tosca said. "That man has been heroic — oh, he's wonderful. My dear father, whom he had known at one time, would be so thankful to him, the time and effort he's given to us. But even though he has, it still would have been useless if he hadn't had your address, Mr.

Jackson, to contact me. I'd never have known what my dear, great father had done for me, for Gwelo and me—and you too, Mr. Jackson—if Mr. Lewellyn hadn't had your address here, which I'd given him originally, where he could contact us. We'd never have known anything about it. This drab, hand-to-mouth existence we've been living for months would have gone on and on until we'd have finally given up and God only knows what in the end would have happened to us. It could have been very, very bad. So what's happened instead has been a miracle from God, nothing less."

Quo Vadis, watched carefully by Gwelo, was masticating a piece of rye bread and only grunted.

"Are we rich now, Ma-MAH?" asked Gwelo.

"No, no, dear," Tosca said, "but we're much better off than we were. Just think what would have happened to us if Mr. Jackson here hadn't fed us and put a roof over our heads. I say it's all a miracle. *He's* a miracle."

Quo Vadis, stoically, took a drink of his cheap red wine and said nothing.

"Does this mean, though," asked Gwelo of Tosca, "that Grandfather could still be alive?"

"No, dear," Tosca sighed. "Nothing that wonderful. But Mr. Lewellyn, on his recent African trip, had talked to a lot of people—trying to learn everything he could about our unfortunate, our tragic, family. Yet it was less than a month after he had returned to London that he heard from one of these acquaintances, contacts, in Nigeria, to the effect that your grandfather had left me—which of course means you too—a portfolio of French stocks considerably larger than the puny securities that we knew about and sadly thought were the whole picture. Considerably larger, yes. Thank God, then, they have now turned out not to be the whole picture. So as a result of Mr. Lewellyn's efforts, his miraculous foreign contacts, and what these people told him their investigations had revealed — about what my great father had done for us, and which I've already now verified right here in Paris where the real proof is — I, we, are in far better financial shape than we could ever have dreamed we were when, as I say, we knew only about that poor little packet of minor stocks we, as best we could, were trying, with wonderful Mr. Jackson's help here, to make do with. Thinking back on it now, it was pitiful — yes, Gwelo dear, I can only say that what's happened is a miracle from God Himself."

Gwelo was poised to go to his mouth with a forkful of his boiled potato. "I guess," he said instead, "that Monsieur Kessey will also be glad when he finally hears about all that's happened. How does he figure in it, though Ma-MAH? Why have you been trying so hard to reach him?"

"Good question," grunted Quo Vadis before again upping his red-wine glass. "But I think I know the answer." Whereupon, without, though, sharing the answer, he looked away as if he alone now bore the weight of the world on his great stooped shoulders.

This made Tosca seem suddenly, uncomfortably, bereft of anything pertinent to say.

Gwelo finally looked at them both, his mother first, though. "Where does that leave things, Ma-MAH? — about Monsieur Kessey, I mean. I don't want to go back over there again where he lives. That old woman was mean to us."

"We won't have to go back, dear," Tosca said. "We have a telephone now. Did you forget?"

"No. But I don't see why you need him anyway. Quo Vadis is here. He was here when we didn't have a telephone and when we only ate rutabagas. I don't get it."

Quo Vadis grinned, and reached and patted Gwelo's hand. "But I can't always be here," he said to them, almost apologetically. "I've got to go to Caen next week, for instance. On business. I'm very busy."

Tosca looked at him, putting down her fork. "You hadn't mentioned this before, Mr. Jackson," she said.

"It's business, as I said," he shrugged. The dinner over now, he summarily rose and went to his room.

"Where's Caen, Ma-MAH?" asked Gwelo.

"A town about a hundred miles west of here," Tosca said.

"Why is Quo Vadis going there?"

"How would I know, dear? Don't ask so many questions. Let's take out the dishes, now."

Gwelo rose but his prying young mind was still elsewhere. In a mere matter of months he and Quo Vadis had become great friends. But now, since the "trio's" so-called "good" news event, he had begun to notice, or at least sense, a radical change in this giant friend's entire mood and behavior. Indeed, Quo Vadis, now so deeply and mysteriously engrossed and involved, may not himself have been fully aware of how much, certainly to Gwelo, he had changed; not, though, for the better, and in a short matter of days since the "good" news. Gwelo, though extraordinarily gifted, precocious, at age eleven now, still could not have been expected to understand the drastic forebodings at work on Quo Vadis's already fearfully agitated and thus dangerous psyche. His "family," by which of course he meant Tosca and Gwelo, as a result of James Lewellyn's "good" news, so-called—bitter Quo Vadis could see it, foretell it—his "family," yes, was inevitably, inescapably, now bound for extinction, and, for him, at this most dreadful of times—when he most needed them—his "family"—their understanding, input, their moral, maybe even tender, support. They, of course, he knew, had never had an inkling of the real, the true, reason he had in the first place taken them in. He, naturally, liked to think there had been some, much, altruism, selflessness, in his motives, his mind, indeed his heart, when he had "rescued" them; yet it had also been something far beyond that. He well knew, remembered, what he had most been concerned about, in fact driven by. It was his stark realization that he needed them fully as much as they needed him. With the dire self-commitments he had already made, and all the passion and peril inevitably accompanying them, he realized now how desperately he had needed a "family," a support mechanism, with loyal and steady instincts in his behalf, even, though unwittingly, to steer him in less fateful directions, no matter that they would know practically zero about his skewed life recently spent with a former woman of the streets, and his lofty, but also lethal, purposes, now at long last translated into "vows." But with Lewellyn's unknowing one fell stroke, he, Quo Vadis, had been rendered utterly alone, with no respectable alternatives existent. He suddenly knew this but was surprised, then shocked, frightened, and could not but hark back to Marmeladov in the tavern crying out in his pain and wretchedness to Raskolnikov: "Do you understand, sir, do you understand what it means when you have absolutely no where to turn?" Indeed, it had been only two days prior to Lewellyn's "good" news that he, Quo Vadis, along with the few other "foreign" workers, all, as himself, mere bus washers out at the Paris municipal transportation maintenance facility, had received the fateful gray-paper notification to the effect that at the end of the month, in two weeks, his employment likewise would end. In retrospect, he felt he had suddenly been metamorphosed, indeed paralyzed, into a crass stone statue — when actually only standing there, wet with sweat under his great dripping rubber apron. That evening, coming home on still another bus, he had pulled out the gray notification again, examined it minutely, then, strangely, unaccountably, brought the fragile paper up and smelled it, his bitter, vengeful imagination running rife. He was graphically aware that he was inhaling, though from afar if not in actuality — for all practical purposes, the essence — the emanation of a human being who, in addition to his other blasphemies, did not at all smell nice. It caused Quo Vadis's mind to teeter on the brink of eruption. He loathed this man who could bring about such "small" upheavals merely by the force of his distant public utterances. And now, on top of that, this mere spectral "presence" smelled to high heaven. No matter, this fact seemed to identify this trigger man and new führer exactly, somehow unequivocally — isolating the putrid aroma of *the,* one and only, malefactor of great suffering to others whom he would never see in his life, yet a creature so powerfully evil that his wicked transgressions could be detected even through one's own faltering nostrils. Quo Vadis could only liken the odor to that of a shuddering Brooklyn Bridge during a black cyclone — noisy, sulfurous, dangerous; people running. This was, then, he thought, again lifting and smelling his dismissal paper, the impure effluvium of one Monsieur Charles Poussin, the super-cool chieftain, indeed founder, of the peerless France for the French National Party, a man, Quo Vadis told himself, who had also made "vows" — his to the French people. Quo Vadis's "vows," however, had been made only to his own wrathful self. So the time had indeed come, yes. And strangely, also almost ironically, the precarious reconnoitering must now begin — in Caen.

By Paul's watch it was nearly three in the afternoon. It was also his touchy, his nettled, opinion that his physical condition had not markedly changed, improved, since coming here; yet a nurse had told him that morning that he would probably be discharged from Lady of Paradise Hospital sometime tomorrow. Actually, he thought, he felt almost as ill as when that night recently – he could not recall how many nights ago; two, three? – they had brought him here, in an ambulance, as sick as a dog; he remembered that much, all right. There was one thing, however, he could not bring himself to deal with, or even believe; that what he had been through in the last few days and nights – no matter what churlish Madame Chevalley thought and said – could all be attributed to his "liquor," his loads of gin that noon in Zuchon's restaurant when in an almost crying drunk he "saw" Jeannette Hall. In his view, though, there were things – he could not be specific about, could not enumerate – things attacking, battling, and finally overwhelming his already strung-out mind and nerves; things the likes of which he had not experienced since those sad, raucous, Chicago times when, briefly, he had been married to poor, crippled, little Agie Thomas. Nor could all this recent relentless unease and stress be traced to Dr. Cécile Fournier, even if much of it, too much in fact, could. There was also, yes, Mrs. Tosca Zimsu – he thought of her, too, as he lay there in his hospital bed in this nice private room – but Tosca, as he well knew, was but the guide, the lead-in, to a phenomenon of far more immense consequence than if both Cécile and Tosca had been weighed on the scales together. He did not like to admit – especially now that he had seen, though talked very little with, Cécile (her choice) – that this was the truth. Indeed, it all grieved him – her, Cécile's, present condition, that is; the appearance of it, her strange obesity, and what fractious, excited Madame had told him was its bizarre cause. No matter, the truth dictated that he now drastically shift his sights and face the monumental fact of the one conversation he had had that one, and unforgettable, night, after dinner (a dinner he himself had brought after paying for it but that his colossal host had so marvelously prepared); a dinner, though, spread out before them in the drabbest of dark, seedy flats,

which was the prelude — after Tosca and Gwelo, having retired
for the evening, had left the two men at the table — prelude, yes,
to a strange, rambling, intemperate disquisition by the black
giant on man's acumen, avarice, and mass cruelty toward the
luckless underclass, unequipped, as it always was, to defend
itself against its brutal marauders. The jackals, the malefac-
tors, so they were in fact, heatedly contended Paul's tutor-
pedagogue, should be mercilessly, bloodily, eliminated, at
whatever cost, from the poor, hapless populations of the world.
Thus did this self-righteous, yet also genuinely righteous, Goliath of a mentor-guru hold, for at least most of the one-sided
conversation, his listener, Paul, in thrall — even if sometimes
confused, or unimpressed, or in downright disagreement, with
the giant. At other junctures, however — especially when this
Goliath seemed incontrovertibly moral and selfless, which,
though Paul later, was, in one way or another, most of the
time — he, Paul, was hesitantly, if often confusedly, impressed
by the man. He was in fact soon a revelation to Paul — this Quo
Vadis Jackson who as a way of life fanatically believed in
absolute human accountability, the enforced variety; also, if
need be, a variety sanctioned by the most harsh punishments
possible, beginning with the knife and pistol. Yet also, for
this unique human study of a man, the opposite state of things,
i.e., doing good, drew from him, accordingly (no less readily,
confidently, freely) the inward response of lavish praise, high
satisfaction, overweening benevolence — the identical brand of
deepest humanism championed by, say, an Erasmus, Thomas
More, or Sartre. To the deadly serious Quo Vadis, then, each
alternative had its proper place. Paul, ever thinking of Jeannette Hall, to him a twentieth-century saint, this was not only
intriguing to contemplate but, to one like himself, not well
known for his reckless valor, it was no less than mesmerizing.
He longed to converse again with this incredible, huge, black

humanist, the same man who, when hardly more than a boy on a campus, had struggled—though only later to be gravely punished by expulsion—struggled in vain, yes, to memorialize his lynched hero by the bold projected raising of an on-campus status in his hero's eternal honor. Again Paul thought of Jeannette; once more then of Quo Vadis, before—grimacing sourly—he thought of himself and, inwardly mortified, scolded the lackluster culprit on suddenly now recalling that as yet he did not even wish to leave this hospital tomorrow. It shamed him. Once more he wanted to write about his plight to Saturn Marie, then remembered he had no notebook.

It did not matter, though—for there was now a late afternoon interruption. He was still frightened by this sudden daily entry in his room of Cécile—in street attire, leaving to go home to her daughters. Nor did she address him at all, merely approached the bed as if to leave some passing medical instruction but which she did not. He panicked, though—he had not shaved today.

"I thought I should come by and tell you," she said almost offhandedly, "that an hour ago I told your friend of his condition. Ari Ngcobo."

"Ari?" At once he quailed.

"Yes. We knew all along, though. The HIV virus stage is over. It's AIDS now—well advanced."

Paul took a deep breath. "Did you *have* to tell him? He's very excitable, very high-strung. Ah, poor Ari."

"He somehow knew it, had finally sensed it, but maybe only a day or two before. He seems calm now, though, resigned." She was already backing away toward the door again—until she saw his eyes. They had suddenly bulged in anger. She stopped and half-faced him.

"Go on, then, goddamn it," he said. "I can see you're in a big hurry. But this man's a friend of mine. Also a very bright guy — of highest character, too." In the bed he angrily spun over, his back to her, and faced the wall. "You may go," he said, his voice, though now somewhat lower.

"I've never known you before to be impolite," she said. "But it doesn't matter — I've ordered you home tomorrow anyway. Madame doesn't look forward to it, your coming, though, I gather."

He turned, lurched, back over to her, saying coldly, "That's no sweat, doctor. I'll get her some new carpeting right away. Then I'll get the hell out of there — so she won't again have the opportunity to insult friends of mine who've come to see me. It'll work out just fine. Before you leave, though, tell me this if you will: Madame Chevalley says you've changed — changed dramatically, is the way she put it — in a lot of your beliefs. She said this after you two had your luncheon at the Hôtel Crillon. She also said you frequently refer to bad dreams you have almost every night. She's got the idea — I don't know her reason — that it's got something to do with race, about color. Actually about Negroes, she says. Is this true? Is this the reason you've been shunning me, also, ironically, your friend Madame as well, for over a month now? She says you've put on this weight because, almost like a disturbed, unbalanced person, you've been gorging yourself on some crazy chocolate candies, which she calls 'niggerines,' that make fun of, or demean, blacks. She thinks in all this niggerine-eating, an idea you apparently got from some wacky second cousins of yours, that you've subjected your body to something that seems a little mad, manic-depressive; crazy, yes, maybe. She thinks I'm crazy, too, though — indeed that everybody's crazy. Except her, of course. Yet I don't think she's ever forgotten that it was she who originally introduced you and me."

Cécile stood staring vacantly toward the door. She had not looked in his direction. Finally, however, she slowly, as if in deepest thought, turned to him. "My husband, Georges, an able, gifted man — though at times lately somehow also capable of Torquemadalike cruelties — likewise thinks the little weight I've put on, which he hates, abhors, is a sign of my semilunacy."

"Your weight, though, Cécile — well, *it's* not 'little'. There's quite a bit of it."

"I think my husband wants to leave me. Even Michelle, my older daughter, sees signs of this. She would. It's incredible, though — all because in trying to rid myself of a demon I've put on a little weight."

"A little, Cécile? You insist on this. Oh, come now — even your beautiful ankles are swollen. I'm not worth it. I know whom you're talking about when you speak of the demon — you really mean *black* demon — you're trying to get rid of."

"Not at all," said Cécile. "Don't be so vain. It's not you, its not Georges. The demon is my life, even my daily life, which now will never change, ever. But I do think that Georges — because of my ankles, also by girth — wants to leave me. If he walks out I'll kill him. If he walks out, I'll kill you, too." She slowly, very slowly, almost as in a daze, turned now and left without ever once looking back.

After a few minutes Paul turned his face to the wall again. "It's not my fault, Saturn," he said. "Things are breaking up, coming apart, all around us here. I didn't do it, Mother. I'm not to blame."

Next day — a bright, sunny midday — Madame Chevalley, at home, was engaged in a pastime she did not often any longer pursue. This was not because she had lost interest, far from it, but that now, at age 78, in the twilight of her existence, it too readily brought, to say the least, a strange unpleasantness; while a source of nostalgia, true, it also raised questions, personal speculation, as well as a rash of misgivings, about what she had done with her life. What she was actually doing at the moment, then — seated in her pleasant, cleverly furnished bedroom — was looking through old family pictures, both portraits and snapshots, some of which, because the ladies often wore large hats, a few of them even with amorphous veils, and frequently long, heavy dresses, still much amused Madame. Suddenly now she came across a snapshot of her first husband, Maurice, a handsome young man, shown on a tennis court, racket in left hand, and wearing a jacket and high, starched — Herbert Hoover — collar in the hot sun. Madame smiled again, knowing that nevertheless Maurice would want a cold stein of beer, maybe two, when they reached home, then sex, much sex, wildly varietal, too, all of which the young Natalie found thrilling. There was a catch, however. Even at that early juncture in the marriage she had not yet fully made up her mind about its longer range efficacy. True, she loved his young manly good looks, his comical flamboyance, and above all, most crucial to her at the time, his politics — bold, activist, far-left — as well as the *outré* sex, yet she had somehow lately come to question whether his good tennis, good politics (although in the face of his solid bourgeois family), and all the thrilling sex, were quite enough. She doubted it. What were his credentials, thus potential, for the long haul, to head up, provide for, a family of his own? Therefore, she made the decision to become more or less adept, finally expert, at avoiding pregnancy until, she thought, she could better read the immediate future about Maurice's success, or lack thereof. The fact was that he had already had three fairly promising jobs within eighteen months even though two of them were in the highly volatile French tourist industry. As a consequence, young, but hereditarily (her lawyer father) shrewd and strong, Natalie began to wonder if there might not soon be still a fourth, even fifth, job coming up for Maurice. In short, for all intents and purposes, the marriage was doomed, and two years later she married Claude Cruys, the musician, the testy Paris Opéra contrabassoonist — who liked nothing so much as telling of the two occasions on which he had played for Arturo Toscanini. Natalie, however, actually admired Claude, his serious professionalism, even despite the hauteur and quick umbrage, and was proud to be married to him, although, alas, after a time — not quite three years — she could not help but feel, intuit, that her feelings toward him were not entirely reciprocated. She was devastated, grew panicky, and took every measure she could conjure up to try to ward off what was all too clearly a very unsettled course — i.e., separation, then finally divorce.

Still sitting in her bedroom before the dresser mirror, a hapless lap full of antediluvian pictures, Madame found herself in utter distress, dismay, and was soon enveloped in a kind of angry, childish sorrow. She had made so little of her life, she told herself, and now, inevitably, was soon to die. She so wished now she had taken at least some of her father's conservative advice — not necessarily political, but merely parental, familial, indeed loving advice. One outcome would surely have been children, maybe a house full of them; she would not now be so direly, cruelly, alone, so minus anyone at all who really cared for her, wished her a relatively sane, content, unruffled end to her life. She had once, a year or so, even just months ago, thought Cécile might in her kindness, even at times tenderness, become a surrogate in this role, in essence come to her rescue, but now this had all become a nightmare. Cécile was beyond understanding. True, it was clear by now that Cécile was susceptible, indeed almost allergic, to any form of self-error, *faux pas*, blunder, that might, helter-skelter, happen to come her way. Despite her meritorious background, the generations of good family, her degrees and pedagogy, Cécile could only be regarded a misfit. Look at her debacle with Paul, thought Madame. Of all the misfits, yes, in the world, these two would have to, would be fated to, find each other — and, of all people, via *her*, Madame! It was proof that the world was an absolutely unaccountable place. Yet, truthfully, she, Madame, had not set out to introduce them. It was a freakish accident.

Then, again, inevitably, reviewing the welter of her life, she suddenly burst into tears — all as she still helplessly observed herself in her bedroom mirror. Finally, in her desperation, she called out to her long-deceased father: "Oh, I'm sorry, so sorry, Pa-PAH! Had I only taken more of your advice!" She reached for his picture now and held it up before her weak, rheumy eyes. "I failed you, Pa-PAH, after you had been so kind, so loving to me; to us all. Now I must face the final consequences. I have only death now to confront and I am glad. Forgive me, forgive me!" She was sobbing profusely now — when the doorbell rang.

The crying stopped — as if she had been guillotined. She stared in the mirror as if some impossible happening had occurred. Finally she found her throaty voice. "Oh, hell," she said disgustedly, getting up. "What nuisance is that?" She reached for a Kleenex to wipe her teary eyes, then blew her nose. At last she began a slow, deliberate traversal of the parlor and was soon at the front door peering myopically through the glass. "Oh, my God!" she groaned then, already wheeling around to duck out of sight. Yet, her hot anger overpowering her, she returned, wildly threw the heavy latch and jerked open the door — to Tosca Zimsu, gloriously decked out in one of her long, almost street-length, crimson dresses, plus her dark-sorrel-dreadlocks hairpiece reaching almost to her attractive hips.

City of Light

"What do *you* want, Miss?" said Madame in a curt, bristling French, though self-conscious of her aged, tear-streaked face. "I'm busy — I cannot receive callers."

"Oh, lady, if I could just enter for a minute I could explain — it is important," Tosca said in her impeccable French.

"Explain what, Miss?"

"I'm a Mrs., Mrs. Madame, not a Miss," Tosca said very politely though unsmiling. "I have an eleven-year-old son at home."

Madame bristled. "And at home do you also have a telephone yet?"

"Oh yes, Mrs. Madame — I have been using our new telephone to call here to Monsieur Kessey's telephone but no one answers. That's why I came on this short visit to you again. I did not bring my family this time because we apparently displeased you before. But today could just *I* please speak to Monsieur Kessey if he is in?"

"Monsieur Kessey is not in. He got so drunk the other day we had to call an ambulance and put him in the hospital."

Tosca's jaw fell. "Oh, mercy!" she finally said. "No wonder I have not been able to reach him. What hospital? Is he very ill?"

Madame, still barring her entry, frowned indignantly. "He was ill enough — that is, as I say, drunk enough — to vomit all over my stair carpeting. When he gets out of the hospital and returns, I'm going to put him out."

"Oh, that would be fine, Mrs. Madame," said Tosca. "We could invite him then to come live with us — when we move into a better, larger, place. That will be very good — you will be rid of him then. I'm sure he got drunk only because he's unhappy. You don't know — he is a very serious and deep-thinking man. I hope he and I, and my son, will now become staunch and long-time friends. It is a great opportunity for all of us."

Surprised, Madame viewed her curiously—almost as if she, Madame, had not heard correctly. Inadvertently, then, she stumbled back from the door. Eager Tosca then pushed it farther open and entered. Soon—Madame still bewildered—they were seated in her little parlor uneasily observing each other. There followed a long silence, which, however, Tosca finally broke by removing her dreadlocks and draping them neatly across her knees, as if to give them a rest—before asking if she might have a glass of water. Madame, in exasperation, waved her in the direction of the kitchen. "I'll bet you," she said, "Monsieur Kessey won't come live at your place. I'm sure it's not as nice as his quarters upstairs here—you've visited him up there, so you know that I'm right."

"Oh, you don't know that, Mrs. Madame," said Tosca, "for I shall be moving out of the flat where we are now and into a better one. In fact I'm going to start looking for one when I leave here—except, though, after I've been to that hospital to visit Monsieur Kessey and see if he is being taken proper care of. I shall also, of course, tell him the great thing that's happened to me and my family since he and I last talked. He will be surprised and gratified—but *very* surprised." Tosca now put her big wig aside and left for the kitchen. "What hospital is Monsieur Kessey in?" she said over her shoulder.

Again Madame ignored her. Soon, however, Madame called to her even though, in the kitchen, Tosca was out of her line of sight: "What 'great thing,' as you call it, has happened to you and your family? You sound almost like a highly enthusiastic child about it. If it happens to be a little money there's surely one thing you can do. You can buy that whale of a big brother of yours some shoes. His big toe was sticking out of one of those he was wearing that day he was here with you and your son. Good God!"

City of Light

Tosca returned with her glass of water though ignoring this slap at Quo Vadis. "So, Mrs. Madame," she said, "if you will kindly give me the name of the hospital where Monsieur Kessey is recuperating I shall go there immediately and have this very important meeting with him." She had not sat down. Instead, after drinking the water, she retrieved her dreadlocks from the sofa and again carefully draped them on her head, rendering her indisputably pretty.

"I don't think you should disturb Monsieur Kessey," said Madame. "He may not feel up to seeing you. You should wait till he's out — till he comes home."

"He has no home, Mrs. Madame," Tosca said. "You've put him out — you said so; or are going to. He needs *me*."

"So *you* say," said Madame.

"You wouldn't stand in the way of our getting together, would you, Mrs. Madame? He needs me, I say. You should be willing to help us — especially since you're not going to let him stay here anymore. I can help him. You're not going to. Besides *I* need him too — because of my son, who should have another clean-cut father — his own wonderful father is no longer alive. The large man you saw here with us, Mr. Jackson (who, by the way, is *not* my brother), though a fine person, is inadequate to the task. I'm almost certain that in time, though, Monsieur Kessey would be, especially now that there is, yes, money. You can see it's the big object involved in all this, nothing more, nothing less. So I must look far ahead to the future, even if Gwelo is presently only eleven, and act now — you must surely understand that, Mrs. Madame. Did you have children?"

Madame winced, almost recoiled, as if suddenly hit by a sharp pain, a spasm. Finally, however, she raised her stubborn chin and, for what seemed ages, gazed forlornly out the window. But then she turned and coolly studied Tosca. "Monsieur Kessey is in Lady of Paradise Hospital," she finally said, and stood — signifying the visit had ended.

It was much later that afternoon that Quo Vadis Jackson was alone in his bedroom discarding, throwing things away — almost as if he were leaving to take up residence on some other planet. His strange state of mind, however, was such that he could not possibly have been sure about himself or known why he was doing all these crazy things. Things did indeed seem to change, although, contrariwise, he was planning to go absolutely nowhere in the near future — except to Caen, and there for only part of a day. Why, then, he asked himself, was he now so infernally busy rummaging through his accumulation of books and papers; even, such as they were, his own glorified, stilted writings? It was as if he were, say, planning a return to the States for good, a reuniting with his wife, Glade, and her three outlaw brothers? No, he insisted to himself, there would be no major changes in his life, even if he would now have to get out in the streets and try to hustle up a new job of some kind (which he knew, though, would not be easy, and he with money for only about a month and half's rent). His mind, however, was somehow inert, not registering; plus the face that any inclination he may have had to worry about things was, for the moment at least, suddenly blacked out when one of his old writings, a term paper, turned up in a stack of other dusty papers he pulled out of a drawer. He had done the assignment for young black associate professor Hollis Tate down in Gladstone College and could still recognize Tate's handwriting across the top of the first page of the now-brittle, musty, old paper. First he saw the grade he had received — "A." Then: "Well done, excellent, throughout, Quo Vadis. Yet see what I have to say on pages 9 and 10." Quo Vadis turned forward to page nine somehow eagerly, although he still remembered Tate's helpful admonitory strictures as if they had been written yesterday instead of thirteen years before.

"Remember, this was the 18th century," wrote Tate. "Derek Kutyba, the century before, had caused much of the then-present strife by his stubborn materialism, which was now anathema to the 'idealists' of the 18th century, led of course by the great Irish thinker Bishop Berkeley who could not abide the 'materialists.' This is especially pertinent for us — Negroes — today. We must never forget the great force and efficacy of the teachings of Jesus Christ, the *original* 'idealist' — who, re-member, was *our* Negroes' savior. This is still a fine paper, though, Quo Vadis — by far the best I've had from you. Keep up the good work." Quo Vadis paused, then somehow wanted to smile, but did not know why; there was nothing funny about it. Maybe, he thought, it was because this was all so irrelevant. His mission now as in Caen.

Ten minutes later he heard a key in the front door of the flat and assumed it was Tosca arriving with Gwelo. Then, however, he heard the somewhat overly tranquil, maybe weak, voice of a man — who seemed to be asking Tosca an insistent question or two. Quo Vadis was in a quandary about this and, rising, stood in his bedroom doorway in clear view now of the front door, waiting. Then it hit him — the man's weak voice was Paul Kessey's. The front door opened, and Gwelo, Paul, and Tosca trooped in.

"Hello, Mr. Jackson." Tosca thus greeted Quo Vadis in a hesitant, feeble English as she bolted the door.

"Hello," Quo Vadis said to them all. "Please speak French if you like, Mrs. Zimsu. I think maybe I can understand it about as well as I can your attempts at English. We are both cripples in this regard."

"I'm hungry," said Gwelo, an algebra book under his arm.

"So are we all, I suspect, dear," Tosca said. "We shall do something about that, though, after a bit. But first I want to tell Mr. Jackson what all has happened today and . . ."

She had, however, looked in vain at Quo Vadis, whose mind now seemed elsewhere, in a kind of stupor, or dazzle, as he nonetheless looked in Tosca's general direction, then over at quiet, sickly Paul who appeared looking around for a chair. "Much, much, has happened, yes," finally reaffirmed Quo Vadis. "I . . . somehow know that, I guess."

"Why can't we go *out* and eat?" said Gwelo, who seemed recently to be gaining an inch or two in height each six months or so; yet still resembling his comely mother whose own height, figure, and build continued normal, even more than ever attractive, despite her recent trials and fearful challenges. The trials and challenges, however, had not left Gwelo unaffected; he stayed restless, often perverse and demanding, regardless of his mother's sympathy yet her far-seeing insistence on discipline as well. "We can't eat out yet, Gwelo," she said, "because I haven't received any kind of hard cash, any check, yet from our sudden new good fortune. I've first got to go through the required red tape and lawyers to begin to get it, but that won't take long. So keep your shirt on, Gwelo dear—God has been good to us. In the hospital today I told Monsieur Kessey about this wonderful thing that's happened to us and, although he's been sick, and is still sick actually, he was extremely pleased for us. I need not of course have to tell you how glad Mr. Jackson—our heaven-sent original savior—has been for us in this dispensation from heaven we are experiencing. God will repay him for his tremendous humanity, mark my words. There are great things in store for Mr. Jackson, and no one alive deserves it more."

"Do we have food in the *house*, then Ma-MAH, if we can't go out?" said Gwelo, sprawled now in a chair against the wall.

City of Light

He wore a cheap lightweight greenish sweater Quo Vadis had bought him—bearing the baffling black lettering on the chest: The Centurion. Paul, seated feebly, drowsily, on the dingy sofa, had been trying to decipher, decode, it.

"Yes, we have food in the house," replied Tosca. "But first I want to tell Mr. Jackson what happened today." She sat down on a heavy wooden stool opposite Quo Vadis. "I of course, as you know," she said to him, "went looking for Monsieur Kessey today on *very* serious business, I need not tell you—after four days we had been unable to reach him by telephone. With great reluctance, then (I had virtually to make myself do it) I went to see his landlady, as you know a curious, irascible, old woman, but whom apparently everyone else, with greatest respect, too—no bawdy-house nickname—calls 'Madame.' She didn't want to let me in at first but finally did so, then ended up reluctantly telling me Monsieur Kessey was ill and in Lady of Paradise Hospital. Of course I went there right away—only to learn they were already getting ready to discharge him, send him home."

Gwelo had left to go foraging for any food knickknacks in sight in the kitchen, while Paul now feebly stretched himself out on the fetid sofa and was listening, though sleepily. Soon Quo Vadis again interrupted Tosca: "Can you slow down a little again, Mrs. Zimsu—it's not easy for me to follow that fast French of yours; forgive me for asking again."

"Not at all, Mr. Jackson," said Tosca. "I'll try harder. But the moment I saw Monsieur Kessey, I, no doctor, knew he shouldn't be going home. I was alarmed—and curious about who made this careless decision. I began talking to him as he lay there in his bed. Part of the time he seemed out of it altogether—mumbling and groaning. I asked him what pained him, and he said his stomach. Am I right, Monsieur Kessey?"

"Yes — it was my stomach," said Paul. "In fact it's my stomach now."

"Then Monsieur Kessey told me something I didn't know he knew yet," Tosca said to Quo Vadis. "He said he probably had no place to live any longer, that Mrs. Madame was angry with him for coming home intoxicated that day and vomiting on her carpet; that she may ask him to leave. This only verified what she told me today."

Quo Vadis turned to Paul quickly. "Are you guilty, sir?"

"Yes, I am," said Paul finally, having raised himself on his elbow in seeming pain.

"So if this, her intention, is true," Tosca said to Quo Vadis, "he has no place to go, even tonight — on top of all his other troubles — Mr. Jackson. It's very disturbing — plus discharging him from the hospital prematurely. It's very mysterious — I don't understand any of it. Maybe I should call that old woman about his lodging."

"No, no, let me handle that," Paul said. "I can go to a hotel tonight."

"We could put you up here," Quo Vadis said, "but there's absolutely no room — unless you want to use that sofa."

The sofa's stench settled that question for Paul. "No, I can go to a hotel," he said. "But I think I'll call Madame first, to make sure."

"But at the hospital, Mr. Jackson," Tosca said, "I was so upset that I went looking for Monsieur Kessey's doctor, who, I had learned, was a woman, a Dr. Fournier. I had an awful time trying to find her, although I was assured she was still in the hospital. So I went and sat at the entrance to the small space she apparently uses for her hospital office. But the longer I waited, the more I began to think about what Monsieur Kessey had said, that he had gotten sick from drinking too much . . . "

Quo Vadis, smiling, interrupted — "That's no capital offense, I hope."

". . . and then he had come home and gotten sick on the old woman's stairs carpet. That's when apparently old Mrs. Madame had gone and called her doctor, this Dr. Fournier, who finally came but soon had an ambulance come and take him to this hospital, Lady of Paradise, where she is on the staff. But why would she discharge him so soon after that — a couple or three days, I understand; Monsieur Kessey doesn't remember exactly; he was so sick — but why so soon when he's sicker now than when she put him in? That's what Monsieur Kessey worries about, too." Tosca turned to Paul for confirmation but he was lying rather helplessly on the sordid sofa, his eyes open, though, but his back no longer directly to them; he at last said nothing, however. "Monsieur Kessey also said this," Tosca went on endlessly, "that Dr. Fournier had him take some strange-looking, huge, dark-purple pills."

"Strange-looking to whom?" said Quo Vadis. "Mrs. Zimsu, don't you feel you're carrying this thing a little too far? You're saying now she's poisoned Paul. Oh, come now — have a heart, also a mind."

Paul feebly raised himself on an elbow and looked at Quo Vadis. "I'm afraid of that woman," he said.

Quo Vadis guffawed. "Which one?" He slapped his knee hilariously.

"It's no laughing matter, Quo Vadis," Paul said. "She may be out to get me."

Quo Vadis bent double with laughter. "*Which one?*" he cried.

"I don't think that's very nice, Mr. Jackson," Tosca said, "Or funny."

"Why would he be afraid of his doctor?" asked Quo Vadis. "She had never seen him before in her life."

Frightened, flustered, Paul tried to affect anger. "She saw my skin color, though!" he said, much too loudly.

Quo Vadis perked up. "What's that mean?"

Tosca innocently came to Paul's rescue. "Why badger him like that, Mr. Jackson? He's sick."

Quo Vadis was contrite. "I beg your pardon," he said. "Both of you."

Paul feebly swung his legs around off the sofa. "Would you be kind enough to call me a taxi, Mrs. Zimsu?" he said. "I'm going home."

Again Quo Vadis guffawed, though half-seriously. "Which home?" he said. "The old woman's, Madame's? Or back to Chicago—where you probably belong; where your father can look out for you."

"Oh, Mr. Jackson! . . . that's cruel," said Tosca.

"No it's not," Paul said, unsteadily standing now. "I'm fair game—especially to someone like Quo Vadis, himself probably deeply in trouble." He looked calmly, not unkindly, at Quo Vadis.

Quo Vadis ignored him, however, and turned to Tosca. "He's right, Mrs. Zimsu. Nor did I tell you that next week I'll no longer have a job out at the bus barns. They fired a bunch of us—us 'foreigners.'"

"Oh . . . is that so?" said Tosca, genuinely taken aback, though also quickly recovering. "You'll get something else, though, Mr. Jackson—and, I'll bet, soon. Meanwhile, God be praised, Gwelo and I are still here with you—you have nothing to worry about. Except maybe yourself. You never show it, Mr. Jackson, but you're actually a real worrywart. You have nightmares, too. Gwelo heard you in your bedroom the other night on his way to the bathroom. You were apparently chasing a train you'd just missed. 'Stop, stop!' you cried, apparently running alongside it. 'Stop!—let me board you. This is the train to Caen, is it not? I must be in Caen today — *today*! This afternoon — for sure! WITHOUT FAIL!' You were loud, Mr. Jackson. Gwelo could hear you easily although your door was tightly closed. Do you see what I mean? You've got to get a hold on yourself, Mr. Jackson."

Quo Vadis heaved a heavy sigh. Finally he turned again to Tosca. "Would you like to go call Paul's taxi now?" he said. Then he retired to his room until frail Paul had gone — gone to find out whether he still had a home at Madame Chevalley's.

Next morning, Saturday, after breakfast, Quo Vadis had gone out, and Gwelo was helping Tosca do his and her laundry in the bathroom. Cagey, alert Tosca noticed it of course — that her son was unusually quiet, introspective, as if thinking hard about certain things, though many things in general as well, including his own life, his future, his mother's life too, past and present; yet, most of all, about their very present joint, and equivocal, existence. No matter, he was not talking about any of this, only tacitly washing, scrubbing, their clothes on this small washboard which his at-the-time-near-destitute mother had purchased on the day they had moved into Quo Vadis's dark, dingy flat at his extraordinarily humane invitation.

Finally their colloquy, in French, could no longer be deferred. "Mother," said Gwelo, "why do you bring Paul here? — even when, like yesterday when you came by my school with him to pick me up, he is sick. *Je ne comprends pas.* What is he in your life? The first time you brought him he had even bought the groceries for our dinner. Then he would sit looking at you a lot, especially when you would get up merely to go across the room or into another room. He would look at you from behind. *Etrange.*"

The water in the bathtub was steaming. Tosca had reached again for her bar of soap to lather one of her strange-looking red dresses, but now she put the soap back and looked queryingly at Gwelo—who, though wearing overalls, was barefoot—but then she picked up the soap again. "I don't know, dear, exactly how to speak about that subject, of Paul," she finally said, "because I never want to mislead you, but always tell you the truth."

"Is he your boyfriend?" asked Gwelo. "Because I know Quo Vadis is not. You almost cringe if Quo Vadis gets too close to you. He saved us, though, you say. *I* say, yes he did—whether he takes baths regularly or not."

Tosca stood up straight and bravely exhaled. "I would like for us to form a closer relationship with Paul, dear," she said.

At this the socks Gwelo had been scrubbing with a brush somehow dropped back into the hot water. "I guess I'm not surprised," he finally said. "I know what you mean—marriage. How old is Paul?"

"Twenty-nine."

"The only reason," Gwelo said, "that I can think of why you would want to marry him is that he has money; *some* money, at least."

"No, it's his father—his father has the money," Tosca said. "Paul, though, is the only child. His mother is deceased, and it is highly unlikely, because of his advanced age, that his father will ever remarry, dear."

"Where did you find out about all this?" inquired Gwelo.

"Fifi Mazisi told me. She could be sweet on him herself—although she didn't tell me that, of course. I have eyes, ears, and a brain, though."

"Paul's twenty-nine, you say," persisted Gwelo. "What has *he* accomplished—on his own, I mean?"

Tosca shilly-shallied. "Goodness, what questions you can ask for a child," she finally said. "He's got a lot of things in the back of his mind. He thinks a lot. In a way, deep down, he's a do-gooder. He doesn't care anything about money. I think that's to his credit. There is no doubt in my mind whatever that Paul is a man of the highest character. I was once fortunate enough to have married one other such man, your wonderful father, and I'm not sure God has vouchsafed me the good fortune to have another. Paul represents class. And I think—I *know*—that you and I represent class. I also know what you think of Quo Vadis—you almost idolize him, as well you might, for he has just as much character as Paul."

"He's got more, Ma-MAH!" Gwelo's young face—smooth, dark nut-brown, earnest—lit up in furious defense as he swallowed hard to crush, subdue, his emotions. "He explained to me one day, when we were walking down the street, what it is in life that makes a good person. It's the person's understanding and determination to do all he can to protect the less fortunate, even the less gifted, people from the bad, very bad, people—he calls these bad people roving hyenas—who constantly take advantage of the little people, those unable to fend for themselves, protect themselves, and make their lives, even until they die, often at the hands of these hyenas, terrible, just terrible, Ma-MAH. That's what Quo Vadis stands for. He hates these hyenas. What does your Paul stand for, though? Oh, how can you compare the two!"

"Someday, Gwelo," said Tosca, "when you get older and learn more about the world, you will understand better what I'm talking about."

"Oh, even Quo Vadis said that to me. And we were *agreeing* on every point he was trying to make. Goodness gracious—I'm eleven years old and can read and write. I don't have to wait until I'm fifty years old to understand and agree with what he's trying to tell me about life based on his own experience that's so much broader than mine. So Ma-MAH, please don't tell me to wait until I get older to understand

something that's *now*, right now, clear as the light of day to
me. So if you want to marry Paul, go ahead. I have nothing
much against him—he hasn't done anything to me—but please
don't try to get me to compare him with Quo Vadis no matter if
Paul bathes a dozen times a day. I'm sorry to talk to you like
this, but you're my mother, who, by all the hell you've been
through for me, has placed some obligation, at least, on me to
grow up *fast*, so that I can be of whatever service I'm capable
of being to you—such, then, as not showing a lot of happiness
when you tell me you want to marry a man who gets drunk,
pukes on his landlady's carpet, then gets you to bring him here
from the hospital so he can stretch out on Quo Vadis's sofa and
play dead. Ma-MAH, what in the world got you interested in a
guy like this?"

Tosca had finally taken all she could or was going to. She
hurled her red dress back into the hot suds and, fire in her eyes,
began yelling, screaming, at Gwelo: "Damn it, you little fool!
It was *you*, your welfare, your future, that got me interested 'in
a guy like this'! And I'm a fool to stand here and let you talk to
me like this! The decisions I make from here on will be made
according to what *I* think is best for me—not you! Sure you're
precocious, gifted—with a mind, though, given you by your
father and me—but you're only eleven years old and hardly dry
behind the ears from my own womb-labor mucuses and fluids
running down your face, your head, as they emerged from me!
I will take no more of your damned childish chatter, your
phony adulthood! That's *that*!"

Gwelo was devastated, destroyed. Now displaying his
true age, he was crying almost as a baby would, great, swelling, shining tears—while at the same time seizing his mother
first around the waist, then the neck, trying, it seemed, to
climb into her arms, all the while yammering like a stray, lost
calf. "Oh, Ma-MAH!" he bawled, almost roared, still trying to

climb up her body, her bosom, like a baby Sumatran orangutan with its mother in the forest. "Oh, I'm sorry, I'm sorry, Ma-MAH! Forgive me, please forgive me! You are all I have, all I've ever had. It was Quo Vadis—yes, he's the one who told me to always be kind and mannerly to you, for I couldn't imagine all you've been through for me. He even told me what those men, those terrible men, those marauders, in Copti, probably did to you after they had killed father and grandfather. It was Quo Vadis, yes, who told me all you had done, been through, for me! How courageous, how absolutely brave, you had been as my mother, he said. I see now, ever so plainly, what all along you were trying to do for me in the case of Paul—and at the expense of having to marry that man, that handsome Chicago nobody. All for me! Oh, forgive me, forgive me, Mother!" Shining tears were streaming down his face.

"Shut up, Gwelo," Tosca, herself, though, not unmoved, said, "and go bring the rest of those soiled clothes in here."

Gwelo almost jumped to comply.

The remainder of the day before, however, a Friday, had been a trying one for Paul. He had left Quo Vadis's flat in the taxi which Tosca, after Quo Vadis's reminder, had called for him and, still weak from his dull stomach pains, was on his way "home," although he had no way of knowing, since his vomiting fiasco, how Madame Chevalley would receive him, if at all, as a continuing resident in her bright, pleasant pension. But as the taxi entered the final street on the way to Madame's, he realized he had not long to wait to find out. On arrival, then, as he paid the driver and was climbing out, he was, in addition to his plaguing physical discomforts, aware that somehow, strangely, he was overly nervous, also cautious, as he got out his keys and approached Madame's front door—cautious as well he might have been, for Madame had company.

Cyrus Colter

He finally opened the door. Madame, in her quaint little parlor, sat on the sofa facing him, but the other woman — there were but the two of them — sat in the big chair with her back to him, yet, his breathing at once wildly accelerating, her identity was to him beyond mistaking. God! . . . it's Cécile, he thought, and wanted to turn and run back out the door. He had not before, though, seen the masculine glasses the woman wore; they were heavy, thick-lensed, and a burnt umber in color. And she was not quite fat, yet sturdy, almost husky, and very near Cécile in age. Yet she seemed tall; taller than Cécile. No, he would not run back out, he thought, he would run upstairs to his rooms. This, then, was the direction in which he had started — until he glanced out of the corner of his eye at Madame and saw her deadly frowns — at him. Had she evicted him? He judiciously paused, then again glimpsed, furtively, in her direction, only once more to see her penetrating eagle eyes on him. Moreover, the strapping other woman had at last turned in her chair to get a better, fuller, look at him. At once she gasped, as if, from descriptions, recognizing him — or thinking: "That must be him! Oh, my God. Yes, yes — because he lives here. Why else would he be on these premises? Ah, so this is him . . . the bastard!"

Paul, too, was sensing things. Also his knees had weakened. He speculated he had something on his hands here far worse than any Cécile. In fact, he wished for Cécile — for this strange Amazon of a woman now sat literally scowling at him.

Madame had also now, though, all of a sudden become highly nervous. Yet she sat quietly for a moment, as if trying to regain her composure, then spoke at last, though still in a faltering, throaty voice, her wan, white, pinched face troubled, scared, but finally firm, even resolute. "It can hardly be believed," she said in French, "that you two, in this great city of some two-and-a-quarter-million people, could ever meet."

City of Light

She passionately then smote herself on her fallen, withered breasts. "But *I* accomplished it—this contact—even if it was sheer luck, happenstance. It happened, though—somehow because of the availability of my own house here; but also, alas, because of certain careless, unfortunate information—the identity of the male lover—that has, even if almost innocently, leaked out to persons in whose possession it can, unless desperate care is taken, become more than hazardous; indeed deadly. Your happening to be here at this particular moment, Monsieur Kessey, can be important, to say nothing of critical." Paul gave a great inward sigh of relief. "The same is true of you, Madame Leverrier," said Madame Chevalley. "In fact, you may have realized it and called to come and investigate, as you have. Actually, now knowing you—knowing who you are and what you really stand for, the shocking hate that you and people like you, carry in your minds—I shan't even introduce you two at all, for it would only make things worse, more than ever churn the already-violent waters of all these tragic happenings. I've a moment ago stated your respective names. That's enough. I shall merely, then, tell each of you who the other is."

Madame Leverrier, her ruddy, mannish face—which also exposed the slightest mustache—now purplish, engorged, jumped to her feet and almost hurled a forefinger at Paul. "I already know who he is!" she bellowed. "God help us all! God save our country!"

Madame Chevalley was oblivious. "Will you please take a seat here, Paul?" she said, pointing to a chair at her left. Sternly, Paul ignored her.

"Paul," she persevered, "I may as well tell you. Yolande, here, or Madame Yolande Leverrier, happens to be the older of the two second cousins of Cécile's whom you've, through me, heard so much about. She's the one who induced Cécile to begin eating those horrid, ghastly niggerines that have now resulted in Cécile's present illness, obesity, her sad, sad, self-destruction. What a frightful calamity for us all."

Paul, stunned, was already groping—for somewhere to sit down. He finally went to the chair Madame had before pointed out to him. As he sank down mercifully, for a moment he gazed at her mournfully—before he then suddenly, for no apparent reason, began to yell, almost bellow, at Madame Yolande Leverrier: "It's not the only frightful calamity, though!" he cried. "Your slippery, insidious, second cousin, Dr. Cécile Fournier, my physician in the hospital, has tried for days to *poison* me!"

"No, no!" at once cried out Yolande hoarsely, her tinge of a mustache quivering. "The poor girl, whom we all in the family so love, adore, is, I'm afraid, no longer quite in possession of all her sanity—for she was trying to *help* you, you heathen, black wretch! She sought to minister to you—actually to cure you of the curse, of Satan himself, the hellhound of drink. You apparently had tried to kill yourself with it and she had come to your rescue—poor disturbed, unbalanced lady that she is! It's a dreadful pass she's come to—trying to help the likes of you. She cannot possibly be sane! And now you claim she was trying to poison you, when actually the medicine, those large purple pills, she was giving you was the direct opposite of what she had been advised to take herself—the graphic chocolate images of the very devil's legions, who, you among them, were out to sully, despoil her. We, yes, were trying to rid her mind, certainly her heart, of all your evil. She, on the other hand, yes, was trying by this other medication to save you, keep you from going through what she had been through. Don't you see that, you African cur!" Yolande had ominously confronted him—now almost as if on the verge of attacking him.

City of Light

Madame Chevalley angrily stood up. "Now, that's enough, Madame Leverrier!" she said, starting toward the robust Yolande as though to protect Paul from her. "You've had your say, now you must go. Indeed you've said *too* much. You're an extremist — a bigot on the loose. But I'm glad to have let you come here when you called — you've cleared up some things for me. How, though, did you ever learn Monsieur Kessey was said to have at one time been involved with Dr. Fournier? You realize you must be wrong about that," she lied.

"Oh, come now," rudely sneered Yolande. "What I do realize is that you realize I'm not wrong about it — because you must by now realize that it was Cécile who told me. She had already paid a tremendous price, in anxiety and fear, for her lapses, her horrible sins, in the form of the most hideous dreams. Nothing she did could stop them — no wonder her mental condition is what it is; plus her later distraught worry that the word might get out, get leaked, yes, and her husband find out. Oh, my God! — he would kill her, massacre her, if he knew. But he *won't* ever know — if it's left up to my sister and me, her loving second cousins. This terrible secret is sealed not only in our minds but our hearts."

"I'll bet," scoffed Madame.

"We love Cécile," said Leverrier, "even if not her cold, highfalutin family who've always thought they were so high and mighty, so much better than anybody else. But never sweet Cécile. She was a model of kindness, almost deference. We wanted so much, beyond anything, to help her when, in her mania and wild seizures, she came desperately to us for help. And we did help her — soon she was back at her office and the hospital routine. The only thing was that she began to gain weight — because she had become addicted to those sweet-chocolate players, those black scourges lashing her, and much more. She pored over a dozen medical books, but no relief came. That's when you, Madame Chevalley, took her to lunch at the Hôtel Crillon—which, though, only made matters worse for her. So you have nothing to feel so great about."

In his chair Paul, his eyes closed, was reeling from side to side, before then he began to whisper to himself, crazily.

"So don't you see how we feel about her?" said Yolande. "We must somehow, some way, nurse her back to health, to her old, wonderful, beautiful self again." She suddenly wheeled now and stared stilettoes at unwell Paul before, with her interminably long forefinger, again pointing him out to Madame Chevalley. "There, there!—*he's* the culprit. And should be made to pay for it with his life. Under our new French government, sooner or later sure to come, he *will* pay, too—into the bloody basket of the guillotine with his head! And even in the same old location as of yore—the Place de la Concorde. *Viva la France!*"

"But let me warn you," said Madame Chevalley, though almost cowering. "Cécile is no bigot. Don't count on her—for you won't be able to make one out of her, no matter how hard you try. Now, good night to you, Madame Leverrier."

At this moment Paul jumped out of his chair, pulling desperately at his hip pocket for his handkerchief, then pressing it hard to his nose—which already, suddenly, was bleeding profusely. He ran for the parlor powder room.

"Ah, do you see?" said Madame Leverrier, on her way to the front door. "Someday you will learn, Madame Chevalley. You have just witnessed Cécile's life-saving medicine at work. The poor, misguided girl is still trying to help this debauched American-African who, though, swears she is trying to poison him—great God!—which is something that should be left to *me!*" She went out and slammed the door.

"That fascist bitch," spluttered Madame, having followed her in order to lock the door—before then scurrying to the door of the powder room, where she knocked. "Paul . . . Paul what happened to you?" she said. "Is your nose still bleeding?" She knocked again. "Is there anything I can do?"

Paul finally opened the door, a fistful of white paper toweling, wet, soaked through, with blood, in his hand. "It's slowing down, I think—the bleeding," he finally said. "I don't know what happened—it was all so quick. It may be stopping now, though."

Meantime, Madame was peering in behind him, again to assess the damage, to see if there was any blood on the floor or elsewhere. She saw none except on the paper towels and on his hands. "What do you think happened, Paul?"

"I don't know. I've been feeling lousy, generally, though."

"Did Cécile tell you anything, give you any clues, before you left the hospital?"

"No. She just discharged me, got rid of me, that's all. The only thing she said was that if her husband tried to leave her, as apparently he's been threatening to do, she'd kill him. And kill me, too, she said."

"Oh, she's just talking," Madame said. "Just dreaming things up. But what a terrible thing to say," she added, after some reconsideration. "What else can happen? What a terrible state of affairs things have reached. Can you imagine her telling those awful second cousins of hers all her business? How dangerous—my God! Poor Cécile—who knows what she'll do next? She's in bad shape—I worry about her. I worry about you, too." Madame stepped back from the powder room door now, though pointing to the wastebasket, saying, "Get rid of those bloody paper towels and go up and take a slow hot tub bath. Meanwhile, I'll fix some food. I also have some mail for you—I noticed too there was a letter from your father."

Paul looked at her quickly, strangely, as if almost frightened. Finally, though, he came out of the powder room and began slowly climbing the stairs.

Madame, watching him, was worried. She was also curious. Before going in the kitchen to begin cooking, she went into the foyer and telephoned Cécile at home. When Cécile came to the phone she seemed in better spirits than Madame could have imagined. She soon learned why. "Georges just got back in town," Cécile said, "back from Moscow. You should hear him tell about that place. It's scary. The whole country is in utter collapse, sheer chaos. He fears terrible things can happen—the old-line Bolsheviks could start a bloodbath and, after frightful slaughter, take the country back. As it is now, the people are literally starving."

"I'm worried," Madame said, her mind elsewhere.

"I know, but there's little or nothing we can do about it," said Cécile. "Georges vows he'll return to Russia, and I think he means it. He just got home this afternoon and is exhausted, though the gleeful children will hardly let him rest. But he says the best thing about his travels is coming home to Michelle and Zoe. I laughed (but didn't think it funny) and asked him what about me. He was serious and said he assumed that was understood, a given. I felt better—for about a minute." She tried to laugh. "I know why, though, he feels better toward me now. I've lost twelve pounds, maybe fifteen—I haven't weighed myself for a couple of days. But it's so much nicer with Georges in a better mood—not like he's been recently, a real bastard; dangerous and threatening; that's when I really fear him and can't sleep. It's been unpleasant, Madame."

Madame said nothing for a moment; finally, though: "I'm worried, Cécile," she repeated. "I'm worried about Paul." There was more silence in the phone. "He's ill, Cécile. Why did you discharge him from the hospital so early?"

Cécile could almost be sensed bristling. "Who says it was early?" she said.

Madame sighed. "I did, I guess. Excuse me. Yet one doesn't have to be a doctor to see that he's ill. A few minutes ago—he hadn't been home here very long—he began bleeding from the nose; he bled quite a lot. He's upstairs now taking a bath while I fix him some food. But he's ill."

"And I'm *not*—anymore—Madame. I've passed it on—to others. As I say, I've lost probably twelve to fifteen pounds and will soon be losing more each day. I've, yes, passed my troubles on now. I'm healing, Madame—healing myself."

"Healing yourself by poisoning Paul, yes—I get it." Madame's voice dripped scorn. "Well, kindly listen to me as I tell you that you may not be quite healed yet. One of your highly esteemed second cousins, Yolande Leverrier, just left here—after, I might add, becoming angry and slamming my front door so hard it almost shattered the glass."

Cécile audibly gasped.

"She had called earlier and asked to come see me—about you, Cécile. I wonder how she got my phone number."

Cécile was stammering. "You're listed—you're listed, you know."

"No, I'm not. My business—my house—of course is listed, but my name is not. When I answered, though, she asked for me, by name. She told me then that she was your cousin and that she'd like to come see me—about you. Hesitating, I finally said yes—and she came. What did I learn? A God's plenty. All about your family, for one thing—including the lowbrows (for which branch she and her sister appear to qualify) as well as the highbrows; that is, you and Aunt Lili and all the other hifalutin Pierre Laval collaborators of your family down to the present 'savior' of France, Charles Poussin. I won't go into any more detail than that right now. But the most awful—unbelievable—thing she told me was that you told her and her sister about you and Paul. Holy Father!"

There was a long, tense pause, during the interminable length of which Madame soon began praying that the unstable, unpredictable Cécile might not let out a bloodcurdling scream of horror, terror — well within earshot of her husband, Georges. Nothing happened, though, until Madame then began to hear a fearful whispering, *sotto voce*, in the phone. Cécile: "Oh . . . oh, this is *horrible*! Madame! I can't believe it! I was taken advantage of — because of my hopeless mental and physical condition. It was during the most dreadful period of my whole life. As I've said, I couldn't sleep, eat, or sometimes even go to the bathroom. It was the nightmares — terrible, cruel, maddening, degrading — almost every night. I thought finally I would die — I *wanted* to die. I had no one to go to — Aunt Lili had moved to Reims. So it was then I thought of Yolande and her sister, Margot. They had always been nice to me — except when they would occasionally suggest that I go to FFF meetings with them and hear Poussin, or, if he had to be elsewhere, some of the other big-time speakers, like Marin Valois, or Hector Duquesne. The mere mention of Duquesne's name makes me shudder, for he was somehow in most of the awful dreams I was having. So I was always able to beg off going with Yolande or Margot to any of these meetings — besides, I had no real interest in them. I thought those people beneath me. My father would have agreed — he was always chary of public policy made by too much input from the populace. Nevertheless, I was driven to talk to someone whom I thought would be sympathetic to my woes in general but never, *never*, in particular. Yet in the latter I failed and it brought my . . . "

Madame heard an interruption over the phone. Cécile was talking to someone else there at home: "Go tell him, Zoe, that I'm talking to Madame Chevalley. She is a longtime patient of mine, but, more important, she is a very close friend. And tell Michelle it's perfectly all right for her father to inquire about whom I've talking to so long, but it's certainly not all right for *her* to do that. All right, dear — go along, now."

Cécile came back: "You can see, Madame, I can't talk any longer. Be assured, though, that when I went to see my two cousins — even as vulnerable, helpless, as I was — there was nothing further from my mind than letting them pick my brain. But almost as if they had plotted it, they went about everything so politely, so lovingly, indeed even innocently, that, in my miserable and pitiful state, I, alas, ended up pouring out my very heart to them, begging for their advice and assistance. Oh — God being my judge — that's how it all happened. I realize I'm now in a *terrible* predicament, Madame!"

"*If*, that is," said Madame, "we're dealing with two un-questionably dishonest people — as indeed we have every right to believe they are. So if they're really out to get you, they've *got* you. Now. It smacks all over the place of plain and simple blackmail — ah, yes, blackmail over a black male. Why else would Yolande have wanted to come talk to me? Maybe to find out anything at all they might be able to use later. She even asked once if I'd ever met your husband. That doesn't sound good. I acted as if I hadn't heard her and apparently she wasn't prepared to risk asking it again. Yet there's another imponder-able factor about this scruffy incident: Her manner, also her manners, were anything but ingratiating the whole time she was here — especially after poor, sick Paul had arrived in the middle of our conversation. She soon fell to calling him names, refer-ring even to his color, his race. Had he not been ill there's no telling how he might have taken it, what he might have done. The question is, though, would a blackmailer have acted this ugly? I don't know. It would have to be a very experienced one, however, I'm inclined to believe — or else one dumb as hell."

There now came the second telephone interruption — apparently brazen, insistent Michelle insisting her mother end the conversation and return to their rare family gathering. "You heard," Cécile said to Madame. "I've got to go. May I call you tomorrow?

"Yes," finally said disgruntled Madame. "But I want to say this, and listen carefully: By noon tomorrow I want you already to have Paul back in the hospital. But I also want you to entirely withdraw as his physician and I'll see to it that the office there assigns another doctor to him. No ifs, ands, or buts. I'm in charge here now — if you know what I mean."

Cécile could almost be heard sighing in the telephone. "Someday, Madame," she said, "You will come to understand how I still feel about Paul. Good night."

As he languished in his hospital, Ari Ngcobo had not been observed smiling for at least a week. Today, however, was different. There were not only smiles but occasional hilarious laughing, coming, though, not from him alone but from three of his old ANC buddies, colleagues, who had flown all the way from Gambia in northwest Africa to Paris to visit him, word having reached them via the grapevine (Fifi Mazisi, who else?) that he was hospitalized and very ill, ill with the dread disease which, on the plane coming, they had preferred not even to mention. They had known him for a decade and a half, had worked with him much of that time in various African outposts, and, from random bits of evidence over time, had come to suspect what his sexual preferences were. This did not faze them. He was, yes, a valued colleague in the mutual cause of African freedom, and they had not only respected but revered him. It was therefore now, under the circumstances, one of Ari's happy days. He well knew there would be few, if any, more.

It was near noon. The hospital ward was sunny, as usual astir with personnel, and the three jolly men, visitors, were seated around his bed. "Ari, old *mon*," said John Ndola, "the first time I ever saw you in life – Lord, how long has it been? – you were playing tenor sax in a five-piece band in a scrubby little bistro in Freetown. In Sierra Leone, yes – on Calmar Street. *Mon*, you were playing the hell outa that thing. . . . People were hollering, waving their arms, and stomping their feet. It was quite a joyful rumpus!" They all laughed, and Ari, in bed, propped up on pillows, his face drawn, leaden, wasted, was trying his best to participate in the hilarity. The speaker was a tall, rangy, Angolan, wearing a neat red shirt without a necktie. "You loved that music, Ari!" Ndola went on. "You should have seen yourself – the horn looking bigger than you; and you up there – ha! – wincing, ducking, wobbling, the horn warbling like a February robin redbreast. Man oh man! And the people going wild. Ah, but pretty soon, in the coming months, something happened to you. You got bored, it looked like; very serious, too; wanted to do bigger things; for blacks, for Africa – which meant you wanted to finish your education; but we thought you was educated already; really brilliant, the way you talked about, bragged on, your homeland, and how in the last century the Zulus, your people, had fought to defend their lands against the marauding Europeans – ah, but failed. the whites had guns, we had spears. This affected you deeply and made you determined to go to France, to Paris, and continue your education at the Sorbonne."

Ari heaved a heavy sigh, turned his face away, and stared at the blank wall. "Yeah, my friends, but I never finished it," he said at last, ruefully.

"But you did come on to Paris, Ari," said Zumbo Par, the eldest of the three visitors, a bald mulatto, native of present-day Botswana, Fifi Mazisi's homeland, "and you never looked back. Now, you got to admit that; give yourself credit. So you left the Sorbonne – I remember you saying you made almost straight A's at Lagos, so what could the Sorbonne do for you? Ha, you were feeling your oats, wasn't you? But we all know what was in your mind—you was hell-bent on starting a paper; now, wasn't you? An ANC newspaper right here in Paris! Ha, even if it is a tabloid. But still going strong."

"You're not kidding, Brother Par," spoke up Trek Kaarta, now a landowner in Zimbabwe. "We never did understand, though, how you came to give it that crazy name. *Realité*. It's not an African name at all. We always said you couldn't figure Ari out—always coming up with something 'way out'."

Ari turned to them and smiled wanly. "You guys never failed to give me the support it took, though," he said. "But I fear for the paper now."

The three visitors quickly, furtively, glanced at each other. "I don't know *why*," John Ndola finally spoke up, faking it, ill at ease. "And the people at ANC have sent you this new man to take over until you come out of here."

Ari was already shaking his head, distastefully. "He's no damn good—he has no guts. Afraid of his shadow—especially of the FFF."

"Hell," said Zumbo Par, almost too boastfully, "if you don't like him we'll tell them to send somebody else. That's no sweat."

Ari seemed unassuaged. There was an uncomfortable lull around the bed.

Whereupon, at that moment, Dr. Cécile Fournier entered the ward and, frowning, soon approached Ari's bed. "Please don't tire him," she demanded at once of his visitors. "How long do you plan to stay?"

Trek Kaarta bridled. "How long *can* we stay?" he said. "We've come all the way here from Gambia, in Africa. We practically just came in the room." He tried to smile then. "We just beat *you* here."

City of Light

"Right," said Zumbo Par.

She ignored them and went to the bed—as Ari suspiciously watched her. "How do you feel today?" she said, placing her hand, almost tenderly, on his forehead.

At once he looked around at his friends, in mock astonishment, yet unsmiling. "Well, I'll be damned," he said at last, weakly. "She's my doctor, but it's the first time she's ever touched me. I guess I should say, Hurrah!" His frail voice, though, hardly carried the words.

Cécile turned to the others. "Would you be kind," she said, her face somber, "and promise to leave in thirty minutes. He can take a nap then. You could return during his dinner and stay for an hour if you like." She left then.

No more than thirty minutes later, however, she had returned—reconnoitering: Had they done as she had asked them, left Ari alone? she wondered. She saw now that they had left and was quietly gratified—he was sleeping. Yet in a way she regretted this, too, ever so slightly—his sleeping—for she had wanted to tell him his good friend Paul, his former Coterie leader, was once more a patient in the hospital here; four floors up again and in another private room. She went to the bed and stood over Ari as he slept; he was snoring very softly, indeed making hardly any noise at all, his deeply browned (from his illness) visage, not quite black anymore but of a charcoal-reddish hue and now sadly withered unlike even a Benin African face—the lower lip just scantly quivering as he lay insensible, as if stupefied, suppressed, in his all but death-anticipating yet lightest of slumbers. She still stood studying him. Blacks, Africans, Zulus, Negroes, even her chocolatized *niggers*, the latter doing their handsprings, singing, dancing, cakewalking, these, yes, and all their like, their tribe, whatever, were indeed, she thought, an altogether unique, a different, species; and likewise indifferent to the surrounding world's own bafflements, fears, and hesitancies all within their full view, even as that same world's unvarying hatred forms its ranks to encompass them in order to extirpate the entire race. This was somehow not good, she felt in her heart. Had God anything to do with this? She was not sure. But what, for example, were the faults of this little Zulu lying here before her—almost as asleep as he would soon be in his coffin. Whom had he harmed? No one, she thought at first. Then, on reflection, plenty; many, many—all of those, as it were, who had cursed the day he and his strain of creatures had been born into the world. He had harmed them, yes. She thought of Hector Duquesne. But was God apprised of Duquesne's presence? Of what he stood for? She could not bring herself to say yes or no. She only felt it was not good. It lingered in the mind too long. She did not understand it at all—like Duquesne professed to do, or like her two second cousins, Yolande and Margot, did. And . . . and Aunt Lili? Cécile shuddered. She only knew she herself had, more than once in the past hellish weeks, asked God about this conundrum, but He had only acted as if He had not heard her. Was His utter silence, of itself, of some critical moment or meaning? Had He, in His infinite wisdom, elected to stand completely aside? She had so often, even during her upbringing, heard others speak, speak in awe, and profound satisfaction, of what they called "God's work." Was this grotesque phenomenon of Aunt Lili, Duquesne, of the second cousins—ah, even Paul himself, somehow the unknowing, unmeaning, instigator of the crisis—was, yes, the phenomenon properly classifiable as "God's work"? Did God, then, draw any distinction between the Paul Kesseys of the world, on the one hand, and the chocolate cakewalkers, among others, portrayed to her in the niggerines which Yolande and Margot had prescribed (as penalty for her alleged misprisions) to the very point of her brown-candy addiction, on the other hand?

City of Light

Why then also could not God have drawn the same expansive dividing line between, say, a pack of brutal black Le Havre stevedores, on one hand, and little Ari here, in *extreme* extremis, on the other? Did not Paul and Ari, in their Coterie organization days, stand for the same things — devotion, zeal, ready sacrifices, for the betterment of a people? God, she was sure, took into account all such developments. Yet, unconnectedly, it had been claimed by some that she had, in addition, tried to poison Paul — because in the hospital she had administered to him a regimen of dark purple tablets which, even if substantial, indeed large, very large, and predominantly containing nitrate of potassium, KNO_3 (saltpeter; for they at the time had not experienced a tryst in six weeks), the decision, the choice of treatment, that she had made would in the end redound to the improvement of his general physical well-being, to say nothing of her own health as demonstrated by her ability now to break the niggerine addiction and thus begin loss of the gruesome, ghastly pounds that had brought on her such shame and misery. She was therefore, as both a physician and woman, sure her resolution of the deadlock was sound, correct, and good. Sighing now, she glanced down at Ari again. Wide-eyed, wide awake, he had apparently been watching any movement of her lips as she soliloquized. Though not understanding her perturbation, he still seemed frightened. What had she been talking to herself about? he may have wondered. Was he the culprit? Was his number up? Had his time finally come? Was he at last being called upon to, as it were, give up the ghost? Now he was finally, suspiciously, moving his eyes in her direction. Then he put the question to her out loud: "How long? How long have I got? I feel lighter in weight already, sometimes almost floating, and now have only token pain. Is the time here?" He held his steady gaze on her starched white uniform with the pencils and pens protruding from the breast pocket and a clipboard in her uneasy grasp.

"I don't know if the time is here," she said. "Only God knows that."

He tried to shift his wasted legs around for greater comfort but finally desisted, merely observing her; though, yes, seriously, honestly, with mixed approval. "Is that the best you can do?" he said at last. "Is that all you know? Remember, you're a physician. Yet you're so dependent on Him. How sorry I feel for you. I do hope your life continues smooth and continuously happy. I hear you're rich and have a wonderful husband and family who adore you. Think of it—you may never know unhappiness. But you must learn who *not* to thank for that—eh?"

Her pretty face troubled, she began backing away. "Your visiting friends will soon be returning," she said. "I've told them they may stay an hour this time if they like."

"Why would you require such a thing of them?" he said, his weakened voice now hoarse. "What difference can it possibly make—how long they stay. They've come all that distance to spend a few hours with me—don't you have any grasp of reality? You ordered them away so that I could sleep, but what difference does it make whether I sleep or not? Think of these things, Doctor—and I'm not being snotty or morbid. Maybe it would indeed help you—if you occasionally talked things over with your 'Almighty' God."

She did not reply but soon left in deep thought. Next she was standing at the elevators waiting to ascend four floors and now took out a stick of chewing gum, unwrapped it, and began chewing it vigorously. What she really craved, though, was a niggerine, especially when, on arriving up in Paul's private room, she was aware of how tired she was. She would go home, she thought, after checking on him briefly.

City of Light

Paul was duly in his bed, reading *The New York Times*. He put it aside, though, when she entered and seemed now to view her agreeably, understandingly, enough. She, however, treated him offhandedly, almost brusquely.

"How is Ari making out?" he finally said.

"I don't know, actually." She was gazing forlornly out the window now. "About as well, though, I surmise, as you'd expect. He talks rather freely about his imminent death, but it's not as close yet as he thinks. I feel sorry for him—he's still got a lot to go through, the really rough part, before it's over, but he seems unaware of it. One bad feature is that he doesn't believe in anything. Certainly not God. He's somehow very bitter."

"Why do you say 'somehow,' Cécile? You speak of his bitterness as if it were an anomaly. It's not."

"You mean because he's gay?" she asked—almost eagerly.

"Of course not. He's not bitter about that—although it looks like he did do little to protect himself, frequenting those crummy bathhouses up there in Montmartre where he lived. It had to be only a matter of time before the axe fell. That's tragic, of course—tragic enough for any drama, even a soap opera. The real tragedy in his case, however, is that he'll probably be dead before his fifty-second birthday without having achieved any of his goals as a black man. Indeed he was unable—he'd admit it—to make *any* kind of difference in the lives of blacks anywhere, anywhere at all. Yet this had been his whole life. His mind was perpetually full of ideas—most, or at least many, of them harebrained—which he thought would begin to turn the tide. Now here he is—he knows the bald situation—dying at age fifty-one, with otherwise many potential years of his life still ahead of him, and none of his goals accomplished. That's why he's bitter, Cécile, and there's no 'somehow' about it."

"As I've said, he doesn't believe in God, either." Cécile was disturbed, also resentful, over the fact.

Paul shrugged. "Neither did my mother, much — come to think of it. But a lot of people in this world get bad breaks from God. You and I, for instance."

Cécile turned pale and looked around her as if about to flee.

"You surely must know," said Paul, "what brought about all this havoc you and I have recently been through. Someone apparently brought to your attention a fact you well knew beforehand — that you were having a knock-down, drag-out affair with a Negro. So what did you do? You panicked. The fact heretofore that you have a very successful husband and two darling daughters had never fazed you — quite. You enjoyed our suburban trysts as much as I — sometimes I think even more than I, if that's at all possible. But suddenly then something happened. Do me a favor, Cécile dear — incidentally, I don't use that word of endearment lightly or frivolously; it's not acid, either; for in many ways it's still in my heart — but, yes, do me a favor and sit down in that chair there and tell me why you and I stopped communicating. You even dropped your longtime patient and friend Madame in the crisis. Or — wait, let me back up and state it this way — first, what, if anything, did *I* do that helped bring all this on, except, that is, finally show up with the wrong skin pigmentation? Now, Cécile, stop standing there first on one foot, then the other, and pull that chair closer here so that we can talk about what happened to us — and why. Please, now, just do what I've asked you." His eyes, though, were ablaze.

Cécile froze. Soon she gave him a skeptical, fishy look, before staring a long time out one of the windows. Paul's room, though not really large, was well appointed; indeed, a pretty room with three windows and heavy dark-green and russet damask draperies. He of course could not have afforded

such a get-well chamber and wondered who, at the time of his
entry, indeed both of them, had signed the room price guar-
anty for such an attractive setting. It was, however, on his
part, no great brain test, or feat, to draw for himself the
almost-infallible conclusion about both the identity and coin-
cidence of his benefactor, her role, her boldness. Had she
thereby, though, unwittingly, made a pimp of him, he asked
himself, and as quickly brushed off the thought as not only
preposterous but silly, enfeebling. Nevertheless, he thought,
bless her, bless her. Actually, it forced his mind back — back to
the little town of Fantes, to the Achilles Hotel again, the wild
but sacred wallpaper of Palm Sunday, and made him ravenous
for her. Why was this so, he asked, scolded, himself. Hadn't
she been enough trouble for him already? It couldn't be — or
could it? — the fact of her spectacularly improved appearance
alone, he thought, although she was indeed once more good,
no, heavenly, to look at, even now, this minute, in her ritzy
professional garb with the stethoscope around her pretty neck,
the sparkling silver glasses low on her undeviating Caucasian
nose. Watching her furtively out of the corner of his eye, he
was soon beside himself, both hands spasmodic, shaky, his
gaze tottery, disoriented. He could also see, however, or at
least divine, that she was still clearly undecided about his
overture to come have a seat and, incidentally, by weak impli-
cation, discuss themselves, their recent lives apart, their mutual hunger. Her hesitant, equivocating face was not flushed a
cherry red. She was on the brink, he knew — the brink of
surrender. Already, in white pajamas and maroon robe, he had
spun out of the bed heading, dashing, for the door to close it,
though it had no lock. He too, though, was on the brink —
unmindful of any earthly thing, desperation his lot. Yet Cécile
was saved. Somehow, from somewhere, in the subterranean
recesses of her Cambon ancestry, she summoned the will to

challenge the precipice, step back from its dizzying allure, just before, though at its very edge, recognizing, remembering Duquesne's shocked, livid, deranged countenance as the pistol went off in his face. She wanted to scream again — until, inundated by guilt, she thought of Michelle and little Zoe, their utter love on that infamous night.

"Return to that bed!" Cécile suddenly ordered Paul, her voice an angry, frightened tremolo. He obeyed at once, his mien contrite, penitent, almost sheepish, the maroon robe closed now and tightly belted. "It's already past time for your medicine," she added with the same harsh authority. As he got back in bed she took up a new remedy, a bottle of deep-purple medicine on the end table and began looking around for a spoon. As he reached for one and gave it to her, he noticed her trembling hand.

"Here, give it back," he said then. "I know how to take this terrible stuff, though I'm ashamed to admit it. What is this poison you've been plying me with both times I've been here?" He took the half-full bottle from her and held it up to the light. "What is it?"

"Nitrate of potassium," she said. "That's one of its names. Saltpeter to you."

"What's this do for me — or against me?"

"It helps keep you stable. Go ahead — take three spoonfuls."

"Helps keep me stable! What's that mean, Cécile? I'm already stable."

She made an ugly face. "You're anything but that — you're a rogue, really. An outlaw. A potential one, at least. Also a pitiful, confused, ne'er-do-well. Then there's your color, of course. You frightened me a moment ago. I don't know what to do about you — or us. Oh, Paul . . . " Tears had welled in her eyes. "But I haven't helped you any. I'm sorry about that, I'm so confused. Now you're a patient of mine. Oh God."

City of Light

"I thought Madame had banned you from ministering to me, being my doctor, anymore," he said.

"That's a joke. Madame had tried, and failed—though she doesn't know it. I handled that. My husband—at my behest—gives far too much money to this hospital, and has over the years, got to have some say, through me, when matters arise involving me and my service here."

Paul seemed hardly listening. He was, rather, looking hard at her—marveling at her almost-fully-recovered appearance. It was a miracle, he thought. "Say," he finally asked, "what was it you said this medicine you've been giving me is supposed to do?"

"You wouldn't be asking if you'd been taking it as I asked you to—regularly, faithfully. You *certainly* wouldn't be acting as you were a moment ago. I've told you—you scared the life out of me. I don't exactly like to think that you would have raped me. Yet there *is* the thing about your color, you know—I was worried about that. I was just mixed up, I guess—but scared, too."

"Shit," Paul said. "You looked like you wanted to be scared. By a black man, of course. Maybe you yourself should get a bottle of that . . . that saltpeter you've been feeding me." He began laughing now, but it was strained, and soon loud, almost maniacal. "Black rapist, eh?" he said. "That's your thing now, is it, Cécile dear? You may even be thinking, right now, about our favorite little place, little city—Fantes. Ha, remember?—and that crazy, bleak, wallpaper in our flashy but modest little suite where on the north wall we couldn't help seeing Jesus riding that poor little mule, going into Jerusalem. Palm Sunday, yes—entrance of God into Valhalla. You may even be thinking about that damn noisy bed in our suite, where one day I thought there for a minute you were raping *me*. Honest, Cécile, dear! The bed was that noisy—remember?"

At once Cécile, though frowning, mortified, nevertheless wanted to argue the point — but only about whether or not
the bed was noisy. Nothing more. She shook her head vigorously, saying, "It was not noisy at all. In fact, it was rather
quiet — quiet enough, certainly. It chirped a little sometimes,
like a wren would, or even maybe a finch, but it wasn't noisy."
She was soon somehow emotional, though; sad, maybe nostalgic, her eyes again thinly glazed with tears. The memories,
yes, possibly — before she now reverted to her prior adamance.
"But the bed was *not* noisy!" she said.

"You couldn't hear it, Cécile dear," Paul remonstrated.
"You always drowned it out."

"What do you mean by that? . . . " Cécile bristled.

Paul was racking his brain for a kindhearted answer —
when the lull was breached by the arrival of a newcomer. A
handsome Negro lad, hardly yet an adolescent, had stuck his
head in at the door. Paul saw him and froze. Bad news had
arrived, he realized. He was in for it now, he knew. His heart
sank. But the boy, ignoring them both, was frantically preoccupied in an eager, scattered conversation with someone still
down the hall. "Here it is, Ma-MAH!" he cried. "We were
going in the wrong direction. This is his room — he's in here.
His doctor's here, too."

It was only a matter of ten seconds, then, when Tosca
Zimsu arrived at the door where her son Gwelo stood now as if
on a singularly prestigious guard assignment. He was delighted
with himself. His attractive mother, regal in her lengthy red
African dress and ferocious dreadlocks descending past her
shoulder blades, was also delighted with her son as she briefly
placed her hand on his shoulder. "Good work, dear," she said,
then unceremoniously entered Paul's room.

Cécile's shock was not unexpected. Her mouth was open
as she turned, almost accusingly, to Paul, who, though, had no

immediate explanation because he was now being smilingly, enthusiastically, greeted by Tosca. "Oh, we finally found you, Monsieur Kessey!" she said. "Gwelo did, that is. But it hasn't been easy locating you — from the very beginning. I found out you were in the hospital from your Mrs. Madame. I had been telephoning you to break the good news that we've moved into another, a better, flat. She said, though, you were back in the hospital. I was *very* sorry to hear that. So was Gwelo."

Paul, managing to clear his throat, interrupted her. "Mrs. Zimsu," he said, "this is Dr. Fournier, my physician." He then added, to Cécile, "This is Gwelo, Mrs. Zimsu's son." Cécile, neither smiling nor frowning, nodded, yet seemed in another country.

Tosca, however, was smiling widely. She stepped forward and extended her hand to Cécile — *"Enchante, Docteur.* I do hope you will help Monsieur Kessey to be able to leave the hospital rather shortly. We are good friends."

Paul, who had arisen, now almost staggered before finally retreating in order to ease into a chair, all the while on the verge of forlornly shaking his head.

Cécile, if possible, seemed more speechless than ever, then, pausing to view again Tosca's immaculate, but wild, red dress and the dreadlocks wig, turned to Paul almost challengingly.

Tosca, as if oblivious — which, though, she certainly was not — also turned to Paul. "I think, Monsieur Kessey, you will like our new place much better than the old one. First of all, it's not dark. And Gwelo will have his own room. A third bedroom — for someone — even has twin beds."

Cécile, her face drawn, white as a sheet, was already attempting to leave. "I'm sorry but I must move on," she said, glancing at the door, then resolutely, though not curtly, adding, "I'm pleased to have met you both." Gwelo, though, sensing something direly amiss, stood silent as a stone statue.

"Thank you, Doctor," Tosca replied, though already turning again to Paul. Cécile, still pale, but now desolate, also burning angry, hurried out the door, Paul glumly watching her. "May we talk?" Tosca said to him now. "I would like Gwelo to be in on it too if you don't mind."

Paul irritably shrugged, drew his robe closer about him, but could not camouflage his complicated temper. "OK," he finally said, though his ire was obvious.

"Quo Vadis is acting funny," Tosca said to him. "I don't know what's wrong with him. Neither does Gwelo, and they are very close. Gwelo thinks, though, Quo Vadis is worrying about something."

Paul, edgy, fatigued, was sitting on the bed now, as Gwelo stood watching him. "I think," Gwelo said, "it's because he didn't want to move—he's not head of the house now."

"I think it's more than that," Tosca said, turning to Paul. "It would be a great help, Monsieur Kessey, if you came to live with us."

Paul stared at her incredulously. "Oh, I couldn't do that," he said.

"Why? I'd think you'd want to get out of that place where you are—with that old mean woman who does not like blacks."

"Ma-MAH," said Gwelo, "I told you there wasn't room for anybody else."

Tosca frowned and waved her finger negatively. "That biggest bedroom has twin beds," she said. "He and Quo Vadis could sleep well in there. I think Quo Vadis might welcome it—he enjoys his conversations with Monsieur Kessey."

Paul, though smiling now, after a fashion, was also shaking his head. "No, that's out of the question, Mrs. Zimsu," he said, soon laughing.

City of Light

"I tell my mother," Gwelo said to him, "it's not necessary that you come live with us in order for you two to be 'friends.' That's something that depends on how you feel about her. I wouldn't like my mother to be 'friendly' with a man who doesn't like her — or who might not even respect her. I think she's too eager about all this — even if it is eventually for my benefit. What do you think, Monsieur Kessey?" Gwelo was grim.

"There's that other matter, too," sighed Tosca, finally sitting down in the chair by the window, "about Quo Vadis. Strangely, something has recently, within the fortnight, occurred to me that so often now keeps returning. It worries me. No, maybe it's not worry — it just raises a lot of questions. As you certainly know, Monsieur Kessey, Quo Vadis is a great man — great in the sense that he hurts, his heart bleeds, for the trials, the hard lives, the disappointments, of the common people ('the downtrodden,' as he calls them). Thinking about these people, really, he apparently gets some kind of uplift, or levitation, coupled with a maudlin sense of pity for them. And maybe for himself, too. Then he philosophizes about it, brings out his books and reads way into the night — even when he had to get up early to go scrub those city buses — trying to enlighten himself on what, if anything, can be done to help 'the downtrodden,' yes. Of course the matter worries him, greatly agonizes him, really, but also somehow fascinates him. I think he sees himself, potentially, in the role of Hero. It's heady stuff, you know. He also, though, as I say, worries about it a lot. He was supposed to go to Caen this week — I don't know what for — and has been busily preparing for it; then something must have happened; he didn't go. He only sat in his room, pored over more of his books and papers, and drank red wine — as if trying to free himself of some high nervousness, as if, no matter what, he had come out of a most singular, if not dangerous, experience unscathed. He doesn't even talk as much to Gwelo as he did, and that's unusual; just grunts his short answers to Gwelo's question. He's deeply worried about something, Monsieur Kessey. I tell him that being out of a job is not the end of the world, that he had fed Gwelo and me when we were destitute, and that now he has a home with us just as we'd had one with him. He smiled and thanked me — this huge great midnight-black creature of a good man — and said everything was going to be all right. I wasn't all that impressed, though — his demeanor didn't match his talk. So, I can't help it; I worry. He's a proven friend of mine, and of course of Gwelo's, too, and, as I say, he's somehow a very great man. Many of the things Gwelo has learned from him remind me of some of my own childhood schooling experiences — right here in Paris where my parents would bring my brother and me from Copti. For the most part we had wonderful teachers. Along with the subjects we were taught there always came expressions of what throughout our lives would be our obligations to others less fortunate than we. The teachers knew of course that many of us were children of fairly well-to-do families and needed to be reminded that not everyone had been so blest. But apparently, in the South in the United States, Quo Vadis, though of a poor family, was taught at black Gladstone College the same things we were taught — about our obligations to the unfortunate. It's ironic, then, is it not, that it was here that he again fell prey to the very ideas he'd thus been taught (humaneness, charity, caring for the 'downtrodden,' etc.) and was expelled for it. We may therefore be seeing in him today some of the effects of that damning experience. It may even, in his case, have added a further — also possibly queasy, ugly, dangerous — stricture to his teachings, namely: hold those, who have deliberately, or even recklessly, brought on the suffering of the 'downtrodden,' to, if need be, a lethal, deadly accounting. Who knows, then, Monsieur Kessey, what Quo Vadis's believes are today? I don't. I worry about it, too."

"Let's go, Ma-MAH," said Gwelo. "Monsieur Kessey is sick in the hospital and needs his rest."

Paul smiled again. "Thank you, Gwelo," he said. "Also thank you both for going to the trouble of tracing me, looking me up. I haven't got my strength back yet, but I shall, I hope, in a couple or three days. Don't ask me what's wrong with me. I don't know. I don't think my doctor knows, either, though."

"What!" cried Tosca.

Paul laughed. "I hope, though, somehow to survive." He became serious then, though he still hesitated. Finally, however, after another pause, he said: "Mrs. Zimsu, wouldn't it be a little better for everybody if you just tried to refrain from speaking so freely about what you refer to as our 'friendship'? I think Gwelo here a moment ago spoke very intelligently to the situation of our relationship, showing a knowledge of the general concept far beyond his years. I compliment him."

Tosca had sat up in her chair. "What concept are you talking about, Monsieur Kessey?" she said, looking him in the eye.

Gwelo cut in, however. "Monsieur Kessey, I thought your doctor wasn't much for all the talk about 'friendship'—as if such talk meant something else. Like marriage. You could tell by her reaction she was displeased. Maybe she was thinking about your health."

"You know, I noticed that, too," said Tosca, now in a deep study. She turned to Paul. "I take it, Monsieur Kessey, that your general health is good, is it not? Dr. Fournier did seem slightly upset—about something. Was it your health?"

"Not at all, Mrs. Zimsu," said Paul, though now in a severely weak and nervous voice. "She's just a conscientious doctor, and an excellent one, who therefore cares very much about the hospital progress of her patients."

"How nice, how very nice," said Tosca. "She did seem extremely devoted to your well-being, Monsieur Kessey." Gwelo, though, already had his mother by the arm and was gently leading her toward the door. "God bless you, Monsieur Kessey," she called over her shoulder, her long, reddish dress slightly fettering her footsteps, the black-brown dreadlocks flouncing around on her shoulders. "We shall be seeing one another again soon, very soon," she went on. "Gwelo and I shall see to that—and don't worry about any inconvenience to us. Always remember that we, too, very much have your welfare at heart. We are your friends, Monsieur Kessey, and always shall be."

"Come along, now, Ma-MAH," said Gwelo." They had reached the door. "He understands you by now, all right. I'm *sure* of it. *Relax* now, Ma-MAH!" Soon they were outside awaiting a descending elevator.

Paul, breathing heavily, was already back in bed. Soon his hand went under the pillow and came out with one of his five-and-dime notebooks and a pencil. Feverishly, then, he began whispering to himself, even before he had begun writing. "Dear Queen Saturn, my love . . . " he began.

Chapter
Seven
Cécile's Baptism

Her name was Canary.

That was the only label they knew her by — her very few friends and hangers-on, such as she had. This tag sufficed, however — some of them even called her "Midget," because of her tiny size; she weighed around a hundred pounds, seldom more, and was barely five-feet-one-inch tall. Few cared about any of these matters, though, especially the abundance of her surnames, apparently having little interest in her reams of personal, also intractable history — for example, though still in her early thirties, she had already had four last names, viz., "Moten," received at birth, in Barbados; then with three recorded marriages endowing her with as many different monikers, which, however, she herself often had difficulty remembering. She was also a woman at times strange to observe, unless you had seen her a number of times before, for her dark brown yet freckled complexion made her face ever mobile, adaptable — even when, if infrequently, she was silent, morose. It was still, though, not quite a facial twitch, but one more of certainty, especially whenever she found herself railing at her huge, erstwhile, or at least inconstant boyfriend. There were, moreover, other exceptional features of her presence—the stubborn Negroid hair, say, the not-unattractive breasts, even the cheap brass necklace she wore and often slept in. She kept the hair, though, closely trimmed, actually almost cropped, just as would have a Negro man—particularly the man she for months now had called, even if spasmodically, her "boyfriend." *His* surname was Jackson. She also called him, at times when they were on fairly good terms, i.e., when not fist fighting, literally, "Quo-vee"—for "Quo Vadis."

Today was a grim, rainy Sunday, near noon, and, up in Canary's tiny, almost bare flat, she and he were in bed together—she at last relaxing on his huge left shoulder and drawing on a postcoital cigarette. Quo-vee had been there since 9:30 that morning—but with troubles on his mind that no forenoon sexual congress could quite ever assuage.

"Do you feel better now, though, Quo-vee?" she inquired. "You sure should—with all that grunting and groaning you carry on in bed." She laughed—"I can't be *that* good, now, can I? What would your friend, your roomer, Miss Tosca, and her kid, think if they could have heard you?"

"This time next week I won't have a job," Quo Vadis said—obliviously, seriously. "That's a helluva come-to."

"If I hear that one more time out of you, I'll scream," said Canary. "I know you're a religious man. Then why don't you pray?"

"What the hell, I pray all the time. But in this situation somehow God doesn't do much. So far, He's really let me down—didn't furnish me with any of the courage I needed when I was supposed to go to Caen and hear Poussin speak. Did you read the papers? Caen had one helluva rally for him. People came from all over—sort of like, but smaller, a Nuremberg rally the Nazis used to have. Poussin is a poor speaker, they all say, but apparently he stirred the hell out of them at Caen."

"You better be glad the Lord didn't in fact give you the nerve to go—those damn French Nazis would have lynched you, big and black as you are. They couldn't mistake you—and, in addition to that, your French is so lousy they'd know right off you was from the States. That would be bad. If they didn't lynch you they'd sure run you out of town. The truth is, God was looking out for you, and you didn't know it."

"The truth is," mimicked Quo Vadis, "I turned chicken, lost my guts, and stayed home. Again the truth is I was scared shitless, and God probably knew it. Besides, you understand, He's got a lot of other things on His docket other than any gathering of the FFF at Caen. I have no excuse, though—I should have been there anyhow. I really wanted to hear, and see, Poussin. The papers, yes, said he aroused the hell out of them—spoke of the great changes that were soon to come over France. Yeah, I should have been there to hear all this to try to figure things out, find out where he's coming from, what's on his mind—and on mine, too. I tell you, though, what was on *my* mind—I was scared to death. Ah, how sad. I could at least have gotten in touch with Paul Kessey and asked him if he'd like to go along with me to Caen. What a shame, though—I'd already told him there were a lot of things I could teach him about straightening his life out. He doesn't know what he wants to do with his life, you know—has so far screwed it up good. Even during the few times I've been with him he can't help talking about his dead mother—can't seem to function when in spirit she's not there to tell him what he should do, and why. So I told him I'd help him get his mind on track, show him something about what his mission in life should be, and so forth—if, that is, he would take Tosca off my hands. But he didn't act like he thought that was such a great idea, even if he didn't come right out and say so. Yet look at me, supposed to be his great adviser, and afraid of my own shadow. Let's face it, Canary, I'm all fucked up myself — actually almost as much as Paul is."

In the bed Canary now rose on her hip, propped her chin on her hand, and badgered him. "*Est-ce tout?*" she asked. "Just because you wanted to go check out what Poussin is saying, and because the FFF is after your job, so, you lost your nerve, is that it?"

"Speak English, will you?" Quo Vadis said. "But I don't think you really know what's on my mind — you smell something that's not there. I merely wanted to size this fascist bastard up, hear him speak, see what he looks like, and so forth."

"Well, to hear you yelling all the time against him, you'd think you was getting yourself ready to go ambush him, shoot him with that big blue-steel pistol you've got at home. Meantime, though, whatta you think those French fascists are going to be doing? Eating ice cream? No, they're going to be ringing your bells like it was Notre Dame — before you end up in a morgue." She swung out of the bed now and threw on her see-through kimono. "I'm going to go make some coffee, *Reverend*," she grinned. But then, turning to view his huge hulk still in the bed, she became serious and soon perturbed, saying, "I was ribbing you, calling you 'Reverend'; but no fooling, Quo-vee, does it ever both you that you spend so much time talking about God, praising Him, and touting religion, at the same time that you're doing so many things, and liking it too, that we've just been doing here in the bed this morning, have been engaging in for months now really, all things that are sure unreligious."

"*Ir*-religious," Quo Vadis said.

"Whatever you call it, you — we — do it. Your alibi is that it's all necessary for healthy God-fearing people. You said it, I didn't. I know better, though — I was in the business. But you rescued me, and, ha, then at once began praying over me, before in less than a week's time you started screwing me. All, mind you, though, in the name of God. Whatever you do—that's sinning or righteous—you always lean on God. Quo-vee, honey, to save my life, I can't figure you out. Sometimes I think you're the biggest phony God (your Boy) ever put on this earth. At other times, though, when you go so damn far out of your way to help other helpless people, folks like me, and like that Tosca and her son, who're desperate for help, but who can't do anything to pay you back, I can't figure any reason in the world you do it except out of the kindness and mercy of your big old weird funky heart. Yet then you turn right around and give all the credit to God and leave nothing for yourself. It's not only damn peculiar, it's crazy. *You're* crazy, Quo-vee. The only thing I can think of that might possibly explain it is that you're scared as hell of God. He's put a fix, a hex, on you and you can't make a move without Him. That's what *I* think."

"And I think you talk too much," Quo Vadis said, yawning. "Tell me, how would you like to move back in with me?"

"I wouldn't like it a bit. Besides, if you're gonna be out of a job, what will you be using for money to pay the rent? Another thing, it's almost insulting of you to ask me back—when you all but put me out of your flat in order to bring in Tosca and her son. Again, of course, you laid it all on God. But I didn't believe it for a minute and still don't."

Quo Vadis heaved a heavy sigh and sat up in the bed. "By that time, though," he said, "you had a job, could sort of fend for yourself, but Tosca was in bad shape, destitute, and with Gwelo on her hands. It was bad, real bad, when she told me about it in that little one-horse fruit-and-vegetable market where she'd found work three days a week. I really felt sorry for her and her kid."

"How long was it before you started screwing *her*?"

"Ah, why would you say that, Canary? . . . that's not nice at all; she's a very upright woman, with a clean, cultured, and educated background. That's bad for you to say that."

"Where, then—tell me the truth, now, Quo-vee—does that put *me*? I'm not upright, huh?"

Quo Vadis, failing with an answer, wearily brought his huge legs around and sat naked on the edge of the bed. "Why are you so rough, almost bitter, on me? We've all had enough trials and hard times to go around without trying to do one another in by accusing him or her of low esteem for the other. Life is too short and dishes out too much hell for us to be that way, unkind, to each other."

"I don't give a damn what you say, Reverend, I know when I'm being used—and whether God's in on it or not, I couldn't care less. And I'm not jealous. I only know when I'm being had and don't like it. No, I won't move back into that sorry midnight-black flat of yours and start paying the rent. Sure, I get lonesome living alone, just like the next woman, but that don't mean I'm going to be a fool and move in with a broke deadbeat." At once she winced with remorse as she said it—and as he sat staring mournfully at the floor. "Oh, forgive me, Quo-vee," she said. "I also talk crazy sometimes; you're not the only one. Talk about crazy talk—do you ever think back on how, and when, we met? Ha, crazy *no*-talk. It was in early—bad—December, remember? Cold as hell, and in Paris's first real snow of the winter. And do you know who introduced us? *You* did. A Friday evening—seven or eight months ago now. I was standing a little down the street from, get this, the swank George the Fifth Hotel—like I'd lost my mind or something; *me* gonna pick me up a millionaire in front of the George the Fifth Hotel. Ha! And I accuse *you* of being crazy. So it goes, though."

Quo Vadis, still sitting in the raw buff on the edge of the bed, finally pulled the sheet up over his great girth and heaved another strange sigh as he continued staring lugubriously at the floor—uttering not a word.

"It was then you came along," Canary said. "You was the biggest man I ever saw in life, and the blackest; a God-almighty giant; an African Goliath. Right away—I remember it—I was proud of you. Ha—talk of crazy! Yeah, I wanted somehow to meet you, get close to you, snuggle up. You was so big you could have been in a circus. And, Lord, sex was the last thing I was thinking about. I was thinking about you, what I thought you represented—and what I *wasn't* thinking about was some damn pimp. I've never let one come near me—I threatened to cut one's gizzard out one night. But you—well, it was because I felt so alone out there freezing my little ass off in all that snow and cold. I had nobody, nobody in the world, to look after me, or give a damn about me at all, my only protection being the knife in my purse. Then as you got nearer to me, and finally saw me, you looked twice, did a double take, real quick, almost like, though, you'd suddenly seen your poor freezing mother, or sister, waiting for you to come along and save them or something. In the next couple of seconds then you slowed your walk but no longer looked at me, though I knew then you had business on your mind—monkey business—even though I knew I didn't look like somebody out hustling, though I was. It didn't matter—I was scared to death; I'd never even heard there could be a man like you, so big, black, and scary. So, no fooling, I really wanted to be nearer to you—yet at the same time wanted to run like hell. It's a helluva feeling. Then you merely came and stood right beside me. I thought I was going to faint, though you hadn't said a damn word. Just stood there. I was scareder than ever then. At last, though, in about a minute and a half, you finally turned to me and, in your strange pelican voice—high sometimes, low sometimes, both, though, queer, scary—asked me if I'd like to go with you to a bar somewhere and have a drink and get warm. By then I was shivering so in that little dog-ass light coat of mine — it was the only coat I had, though — that my teeth were chattering like the bill of a yellow-billed magpie. I was so cold I forgot all about being scared of you. Yet, all the while, I was giving you out of the corner of my eye one fishy look after another — until I finally said yes. But I was glad to say it, and we left. Later, after we had had a couple of drinks and got warm in the bar we got some food and took it to your place. But you were a perfect gentleman — never tried to lay a finger on me; didn't even act like you wanted to. I was thankful — I felt lousy; could feel a cold coming on. Then when I opened my purse to get some Kleenex I saw my big, long, pocketknife, a wicked switch-blade, in there. I'd never had to use it in protecting myself, only threatened to, but every time I looked at you I kept wondering what your real story was — because, as I say, you were all business; kind sometimes, yes, but mostly matter-of-fact. Yet I started liking you after that. Do you remember any of this, Quo-vee?"

"Of course," Quo Vadis said. "How could I forget it? It was God — He was working right alongside me. We were in that dingy flat of mine now, and I felt righteous. I wasn't thinking about screwing — I was thinking about doing God's work. I want to make this clear, though — the fact that a man and a woman screw is no big deal. It's a perfectly natural condition given us by nobody less than God Himself, and that often they're not married doesn't mean God's going to bring the world to an end, shut it down, and all the people like us in it. God doesn't operate that way — He's much wiser; and also has compassion. The only backfire we got out of that cold night, yes, was that you had caught that damn bad cold. But I kept you at my place and doctored you — until you felt pretty good again. Then I invited you to move in with me. All God's work, you see."

"Yeah, but don't get too carried away, now, Quo-vee—remember that . . . "

"Don't interrupt me, Canary, honey. I was carrying out God's command when you almost had pneumonia. He stepped in and your illness stepped out. He also prompted me to have you move in with me. You know why? He wanted me to start lecturing you on changing your life and getting a job. So for over a week that's all I did."

"Lord have mercy," said Canary, "you sure are right; you did nothing else for two or three weeks. I thought I'd never live through it—you gave me no rest. I finally went out and eventually got the job, too—if that's what it can be called. Chambermaid in a crummy little hotel. But you got what you wanted—got me off the streets. And I'm still off and mean to stay off. So, Quo-vee honey, I do owe you a lot."

"And God," said Quo Vadis. "Don't forget Him."

"But, as I started, tried, to say before—when you wouldn't let me talk—that you shouldn't get carried away, Quo-vee. That's what I was trying to remind you about—do you remember that within two months after I got my chambermaid's job, and was already living in your flat, (and all that went with it, if you know what I mean, though I'm not complaining) after all that, as I say, and within two months, you, God's greatest do-gooder, had run into this stranded African woman, a widow, and her smart little son, and forgot all about me. I can't help but believe, either, that God was in on that, too—you claim He was running everything. Well, anyhow, you came and said to me that now that I was more or less established, you meant had a job, that it would be nice if I could get my own little flat, or even a room somewhere, so you could carry out God's wishes to provide temporary shelter for this widow lady and her son who were destitute, in a really bad way, and needed God's help, and yours. So I had to start looking around and finally

landed this den of rats and cockroaches here where I still live —
and where, now that you yourself are out of work, you may
soon be joining me. What do they say? That what goes around
comes around. Right, Quo-vee?"

Quo Vadis, still naked under the bedsheets, solemnly
nodded his head in assent.

"I do, though," said Canary, "feel sorry for the widow
and her son — they'll be on their own again. But all of us have
been on our own at one time or another. That's the way the ball
bounces — or the cookie crumbles. Right?"

Quo Vadis, glum, also pensive, now rolled his gigantic
limbs and torso around off the bed and began to pull on his
shorts, saying, "But meantime, Tosca, the widow, as you call
her, has had some strange, but what she calls 'good, very good'
news, which I'll tell you about later. But it changes things
around — quite a bit — where I'm concerned. I don't know what
the outcome will be. I only know that Tosca and Gwelo will
soon be out of my life. And that's whether Paul Kessey comes
through on what Tosca and I both hope he will — marry Tosca
and take her and Gwelo back to the States."

"Good Lord!" said Canary. "What happened?"

"Tosca has come into some money, she says — and I believe her — money not known of before, from her dead father's
estate. Now she and Gwelo are getting ready to move into a
nicer flat, nothing fancy, but it wouldn't have to be to outstrip
that hellhole of mine."

"Yet it's the same hellhole you're trying to get me to come
back to. Well, I won't. Why don't your Tosca friend take you
with her to her new place, especially now that it's you that's got
the money problems. You took her in once, didn't you?"

"Her place — which I haven't seen though she's told me
about it — has a bedroom they've set aside for me. But I've told
her, and it's the truth, that I have different plans."

"I get it now — plans to take a new girlfriend into the old place. Well, Quo-vee, it won't be me this time. Sorry."

Quo Vadis finally grinned. "I found out, though, she also wanted Paul Kessey to move in and share the bedroom supposed to be mine. That woman is nothing if not the world's greatest enterpriser. She's a wizard. Yet what luck she'll have in trying to marry Kessey remains to be seen. I understand — through Gwelo, my main man, a wonderful kid — that Paul has refused to move into the new place. Yet you can't tell what he might do later — he never made up his mind about anything in his life. Still he's somehow a nice guy. But he's never yet to my knowledge shown up with a woman whose trail he's really on. So I have no idea what he does for female companionship. That, though, of course, is none of my business."

"But there's sure no doubt what *you* do for female companionship," Canary said. "Ask me. My back stays sore for a week after I've been to bed with you. I try as best I can, though, not to make a big deal out of it — you've been a good guy most of the time, and also took me (ha, you and God, that is) off the streets. I'll never forget that — I could have been dead by now, you know. I mean to *stay* off the streets, too." She inhaled deeply, sadly, then and looked away. "If I can, if I can," she said finally, in an anguished voice.

But Quo Vadis bristled. "What the hell do you mean — 'if you can' — after God took all that time to straighten you out, then get you a job (even if it isn't the best there is) that has kept your head above the water until you can get something better. I've told you again and again it's all God's work. Don't you play with God, girl."

"I've been waiting for that — I knew it would come," Canary said. "You yourself had nothing to do with it, right? . . . God thought it all up — getting me off the streets — then went on and carried it out. Huh? You just stood by and watched; is that it? Ha, and took your pay out from me in pussy. Am I right? Quo-vee, I repeat, you gotta be the world's strangest man—a good man; yes, a very good man; a sweet man even (when, that is, somebody hasn't riled you up so you're ready to kill two or three people), but a man that will never be able to understand himself, any more than the people around him, who claim to know him, will. Ah, and that can be downright worrying, maybe even dangerous, to such a man—who almost has to be thoughtful and careful about what he says or does, who's gotta think everything out first before he acts, because he never knows what he can do, or what he can get away with, and what he can't; but who just believes God will somehow take care of everything, all the dangerous darts and curves the man's got to make yet not go over the cliff. I'll tell you, Quo-vee, God had His hands full when He made you, and everybody who knows you hopes God knows what He's doing, that He can look after you, and bring you through OK." Canary finally looked at Quo Vadis now. He was smiling. "What are you grinning at?" she frowned.

"At you," he said. "Girl, you should have been a preacher." He was pulling on his socks.

She, though, was already on her way out of the room.

"If you won't come live with me," he called after her, "may I temporarily move in here with you—until I can figure out what's ahead for me?"

Canary returned, her face grim. "You know damn well I can't say no," she said. "I'm too beholden to you. But no sex, Quo-vee. Hear? Absolute no more sex. Is that a deal?"

Quo Vadis sighed glumly before at last nodding affirmatively. "No more sex," he said. "It's a deal."

"And there's something else," she said. "You've gotta climb in that bathtub every day. Agreed?"

Quo Vadis looked stunned, hurt. "Why, of course, baby,"

he said. "Why wouldn't I? I did this morning, didn't I? — as soon as I walked in the house."

"Yes, you did," said Canary, "after I suggested it, twice. Is this agreed, though — along with no more sex?"

Quo Vadis took a deep breath and reached down to put on his left shoe. "Agreed, sweetie," he finally said — wistfully.

Paul's second stay in Lady of Paradise Hospital lasted six days. His new (or additional) physician, a middle-aged man who, though, looked younger, and who had a French name so difficult Paul had yet to try to pronounce it, had, as earlier vowed by irate Madame Chevalley, been brought into the case ostensibly as a consultant, but actually for the purpose of monitoring irregular, quixotic (Madame's brash opinion) Dr. Cécile's professional treatment of the patient. Madame, nevertheless, was confident she had come through on her threat to Cécile, though unmindful that Cécile was unfazed and still in overall charge of things merely as a result of her adroit use of family (husband Georges's) donor, or philanthropic, clout with the hospital, the effect of which was to reduce the new and affable doctor, as well as Madame herself, to the role of virtual figureheads.

This new man, however, during a daily hospital visit, on the fifth day, told Paul he had decided to let him go home the following day; discharge him. Paul was elated — until later that same afternoon the august Dr. Cécile herself paid him a visit to inform him, in what he later considered a rather high-handed manner, that she had "countermanded Dr. Dupuytren's decision" to discharge him.

At once Paul, sitting by the window with an American magazine in his hand, was disappointed, upset. "What's going on here?" he said. "Last time you tried to hasten my discharge, but this time you apparently want to slow it."

Cécile's stare was cold. "It's a medical, a professional, decision," she said, in a tone of finality. "*My* decision."

He gazed at her but finally said nothing.

"Another thing," she said. "You owe me money. I was the one who arranged to get this pleasant private room for you; signed the papers."

"I imagined as much," said Paul, shamefaced. "You'll be paid the very day I get a check from the States, no later — which should be in ten days or less." He fell glum then, dispirited, aware of the humiliation and disgrace involved. He would no longer look at her.

Soon, though, she was standing over him, a slight but bitter smile on her face. "If at the moment," she said, "you happen to be pinched for cash — there's also word going around that your wedding is coming up and all — I'll be glad to give you all the time you require; it's no problem at all." Suddenly then, though, he saw her hand trembling, just before she reached in the side pocket of her starched white uniform, took out a smallish paper bag, and poured into her left hand the contents remaining — a half-dozen chocolate niggerines. At last, as if she were achieving some kind of bitter retribution, as she stared him fully in the face, she now tossed the wretchedly symbolic candies far, far back in her mouth; but at once then seemed frightened.

Paul's eyes jumped. He almost reeled. But then froze in his chair. "Well, Goddamn!" he said at last. "This is horrible. Oh, Cécile, how can you do this? We thought — especially Madame — that you had finally kicked this awful, this insane, and bigoted habit. Poor Cécile — what has come over you? I'm going to call Madame the minute you leave here. What a calamity. And you were so beautiful. Now in a couple of weeks you'll be big as a house again — and all because of your sudden, insane change toward blacks; that's got to be the reason, the only reason. What a pity—Cécile, we know now you're an authentic screwball, and all because of this sudden, mysterious, ambivalence toward blacks. How did it come about so suddenly? What happened?"

"You're wrong," said Cécile, her eyes alight. "It's no longer an ambivalence. It's truth now."

"Good God," Paul uttered.

She said nothing, only morbidly gazed past him out the window as she now busily, heedlessly, masticated the mouthful of niggerines, in the process almost smacking her dainty red-lipsticked lips. "What do I care?" she finally said. "Think about *that* as you stand at the altar beside that African woman wearing her dreadlocks and long red dress."

Paul, his mouth open, could only look at her, at last forlornly shaking his head.

She suddenly laughed—"Who will be your best man? And will I be invited to be a bridesmaid?"

Paul could only stare at her, incredulously. It was at this point, then—a clear, yes, situation of *deus ex machina*—that a hospital orderly entered the room with a pitcher of ice water and placed it down. "Thank you," confused, befuddled Paul finally said to the young man and reached for a glass off the end table. "Would you please pour me some?" he said. "I'd appreciate it." When the orderly had obliged and left, Paul, murmuring madly to himself, then fiercely grimacing, quickly stood and dashed the glass of ice water in Cécile's face. Her mouth flew open with a great gasp. Taking one mammoth, frantic, inhaling gulp of fright now, and horror, then self-pity, she yet managed to stifle her scream before running, sobbing, from the room.

The following day, day six, came quickly to Paul although he had slept hardly at all during the night. Early that morning, however, kindly, agreeable Dr. Dupuytren came to tell him there had been a slight mix-up the day before about his, Paul's, departure date; but that it had all now been straightened out and that today Paul, after a routine examination following lunchtime, would be leaving; but also, Dupuytren informed him, Paul's original physician, Dr. Cécile Fournier, had somehow yesterday become indisposed, and it was unlikely she would be on duty for the remainder of the week. Paul fully understood this and winced.

When left alone in his room again his anxieties and tensions — most of all his guilt — loomed larger and larger. At last he became furious with himself, which soon brought him to realize how much he hated himself. Why, he asked for the *nth* time, was he like he was, how did he get to be himself, what had most contributed to his sorry mental state, the whole composition of his faculties, indeed his bewildered view of life itself. His whole career so far, it readily appeared to him, had been nothing more or less than a series of crises — even when as a child he would try, though with varying success, to frolic, gambol, at his mother's knee, for she seemed often unimpressed, having perhaps her own quota of deep concerns merged with all her other fancy designs, until her inevitable bafflements returned in the form of her own even deeper crises. Could these sickly traits, vexations, auguries of un-happiness, have been transmitted at his birth? If so, was there nothing one could do about such things, except bemoan one's fate — about which, he knew, he had had considerable experience. Thoughts of Cécile, coupled with yesterday's, and to-day's, guilt, returned to him now, multiplying even further the cramps of his culpability, plus his chronic low self-esteem. He knew what he had done to Cécile yesterday was unpardon-able, ugly, coarse. Even his father — certainly, when riled, no paragon — would have been furious with him. It all then merely constituted one more crisis in the life of the son he was sure his father had never understood and was scarcely ever likely to. More than anything else now, though, he wanted to leave this dismal hospital.

It was therefore less than five minutes after his breakfast had come and he was eating that, of all people, smiling, dressed-to-kill, Fifi Mazisi put her head in at his door. He was of course surprised but very glad, actually elated, to see her. Her presence, he more than speculated, had to be an improvement over what he had lately been mentally experiencing. Laughing now, even clowning a little, Fifi tiptoed into the room and over to his bed in the guise now, the role, of food inspector, soon literally bending over his plate in order to smell the food. "Damn it, Paul, I'm too late," she said. "Why didn't you save me some of the scrambled eggs?" She retreated to pull up a chair.

"I'm not a mind reader, Fifi," Paul grinned. "You show up at the damndest times. Here, take this piece of toast."

"I was only kidding," she said. "I ate at seven o'clock this morning. Tell me, how is Ari—bless his heart."

"About the same. No good. I went downstairs and saw him yesterday for a little while. He's alert, though—in fact, still talking his fanny off. But he's failing, Fifi."

"Sad, sad. I'll go by and see him on my way out."

Meanwhile Paul had been watching her. "Say, you look very good today—foxy, smart. Jesus. That dress—I didn't know you liked blue, sky blue. Did Mango buy you that?"

Fifi laughed. "Are you kidding? I'd have fainted if he had."

"You're real chic all right, smart, today. Wow."

"I'm chic and smart *every* day," said Fifi. "The only thing is, some people don't notice." Eyeing him, she pulled her chair closer. "How long are they going to keep you here, Paul? But you've got a very nice room."

"Hoo-ray." Paul grinned again. "They're going to keep me until *this afternoon!*"

"Lord, didn't I know it – or feel it?" Fifi cried. "I'm just in time. Something told me not to put it off any longer." She tried to pull her chair even closer. "Paul, I've come to ask you a favor."

Paul, putting his fork down, watched her now – apprehensively.

"Tosca's been calling me, you know," she said. "She told me she and her little boy even visited you here."

"That's true, yes," said Paul, waiting.

"Why, then, couldn't she herself have come again – if she wanted a favor from you – instead of calling me about it, twice? Hell, I don't know why. Tosca is strange. As you're aware, though, a lot has happened to her lately. She's got a hold of some money and has rented a different flat – and, as if you didn't know, has been pressing both you and her giant friend, Quo Vadis Jackson, to move in with her and her son. But big old Quo apparently told her no. I don't know what you've told her."

"The same thing," Paul said.

"But now for some reason – maybe something entirely different – she wants you (or *Quo* wants you, is probably closer to the truth) to have a meeting, a talk, with him. He's been badgering her for some time to set it up, get you two together. I didn't even know you two guys knew each other that well. But Tosca says he's insisting on seeing you. She doesn't let on, but I don't think she herself knows what he's got up his sleeve."

Paul, though eating, was watching her intently.

"So, you know me," Fifi said, "I took the bull by the horns."

Paul, though never having taken his eyes off her, was gawking now, if not faintly alarmed – almost as if he, knowing

Quo Vadis, feared that something surprising, or critical, maybe even a little creepy, impended. But at once he aroused himself. Yet this brought on a spate of irritability. "Okay," he finally said. "So you took the bull by the horns, did you? But what did the bull do—turn around and shit on you?"

"No, no, not on me, Paul. But possibly, even if later on, he did it on you. We shall see. So what I did was bring Mr. Quo Vadis with me. He's cooling his heels—I'm sure extremely impatiently—downstairs in the lobby."

"What?" cried Paul. "Well, that's where he'll stay. I'm not up to seeing anybody today. Not even you any longer."

"But you listen to me, now, Paul. Remember, I'm a responsible person—at least at one time you must have thought so; I was your second-in-command in the old Coterie days, and by your own designation. So I have this hunch that this is not just some frivolous brainstorm that Quo Vadis, this enormous and dangerous specimen of humanity, this black colossus, is toying with—this most extraordinary guy who, even like little Ari, reads big, thick books written a century or two or three ago; this would-be scholar, yes, but who smells like he bathes once a year, you'll find to be very interesting." In her excitement Fifi had almost risen from her chair, then, though, as if some monumental joke had struck her, she suddenly broke into a loud, shrill laugh. "Paul," she cried, "if you've got any sense left, and I know you have, plenty, you'll see and talk to this man of the mountain—before he comes up to this pretty, private room of yours (how'd you get it?), picks you up, and hurls you through the big window there!" Fifi was still laughing—her face, though, almost shocking, stricken.

Hapless Paul was continuing to gawk—trying to study, masticate, the implications of what he had just heard and witnessed. Fifi was crazy, pitiful, he finally concluded. No matter, he proceeded at once to take a different, more legitimate, tack. "Listen, Fifi, are you sure you have the credentials to preach to me, much less practically threaten me about Quo Vadis and his brawn. You don't comment on his brain, though — which may be fried, helter-skelter. I know the man better than you do. I talked to him at length one night after dinner at his flat, when Tosca and her son were living there, and I know something about what kind of human being he is — and that's making allowances for my own preparation to engage in conversation with him, a man so undeniably brilliant in some things and woefully unglued in others. No matter how all that may be, though, I'm not up to talking with a Quo Vadis today or with anybody like him. In fact, not even with you, Fifi, and you, throughout, have been my proven friend. But please now don't push me any farther. I can't take it, and won't."

Fifi, looking at Paul, gave a heavy sigh. "Yes, Paul, I understand you," she finally said. "You are right. And you're speaking today with such authority. I like that. But, you'll admit, you haven't always done it. I only wish you had. The Coterie might still be with us today."

"I did the best I could," Paul said. "But that's all history now. Yet I haven't given up, completely."

"What do you mean? 'Completely.' That's not a very nice thing to say. I don't like to hear you talk like that."

"I can only say, Fifi dear, that, yes, I've not given up. I still have some time ahead of me. So please don't write me off, yet."

Fifi sighed again, at the "yet," but finally smiled. Then it hit her and she jumped up. "Oh, my God, I can't keep Quo Vadis waiting any longer! Paul, Paul, you've got to, this once, let me go bring him up. There's something on his mind that makes him insist on talking with you. Please go along with him, and with me!"

Paul groaned. "Oh, for Christ's sake. Go ahead and bring him up." Another groan. "Poor me, poor me."

Cyrus Colter

But Fifi, in a great hurry, had already left to go down to the lobby — where, alas however, she found that furious Quo Vadis had long since gone.

Later that week: "The *splendor* of it all!" was the possible excited, yet fair, comment one might have made in characterizing just the parlor itself of the apartment. The "splendor," yes — though there was no gigantism; the parlor's size was yet normal and of no issue, even if at first it may have loomed a somewhat larger room than it actually was — but for which there may have been cogent reason — if, that is, one entered, or even approached the fascinating perspective of the parlor from its willing foil, the not-too-lengthy Egyptian gallery close outside and leading in from the main entrance to the total room, the whole apartment. Indeed the predominancy of this strange controversial gallery affair was achieved by its gala ceiling, yet somehow also the staid walls — or rather the wall-*paper* on them — on which one saw graphically portrayed much Egyptian history, as well as the great timeless figures, Pharaohs, who made the history, some harking back to the Hyksos dynasty (circa 2,000 B.C.) and other similarly depicted worthies, such as Ptolemy I, even the vaunted Apis bull, and, both stiffly brandishing scepters, the queens Nefretete and Cleopatra. This stunning "outside" display, then — of these walled images, et al. — may have caused, at least some dinner guests, say, both pro contentious gallery as well as con, to truly feel that magnificence of the parlor "inside" had been woefully upstaged even before it could ever awe, be seen, much less experienced, by visitors. What so few, if any, of these suppositional guests knew, however, was that the thriving, handsome man, age 45 now, heading up the whole impressive and expensive dream of a household, or household of a dream, though tall (enough), "blond" (hair, even if often dark at the roots), and French, had

City of Light

nonetheless, in his veins centuries on centuries of this ripe and virile Egyptian blood and culture – all of which, from his earliest childhood, he had heard extolled from a proud father long since deceased. The son's name? One Ptah Serapis Georges Fournier – Paris scientist-engineer. Fournier, too, though, was himself a father now – of two lovely, vigorous, high-spirited girls, one, however, Michelle, far more vigorous, insistent, challenging, though perhaps (yet only on the surface) less sweet, than the younger one.

It was now a late Saturday morning, though the sun, momentarily, painstakingly, sluicing in at the chic, royal-chartreuse, half-curtained, casement windows of the parlor, seemed equivocal, at times even partially cloud-obstructed, and lending an already semiconfused aspect to a morning now fast nearing noon. Georges Fournier, wearing a red sweater, and in such oblivious concentration of mind on the task at hand that, perforce, he whispered to himself as he worked, sat in his study – a bright, well-kept, but sequestered offshoot of the parlor – where since ten o'clock he, whispering, yes, had been feverishly plying not one but two computers. His wife, the doctor, though, had left before nine, ostensibly, ritualistically, on her way to Lady of Paradise Hospital. This, however, was not her aim.

There came a hesitant, almost reluctant, knock on Fournier's study door now. His whispering ceased. He knew it was not a servant – only one, or both, of his daughters would dare interrupt him. "Come in, dear," he called cheerfully, though in an excessively throaty, almost harsh, French. *"S'il vous plaît!"*

Gingerly, the door was opened by now semitallish Michelle, clad in flaring brown skirt to the knees and lighter brown cardigan jacket, all in apparent imitation of the cowgirl regalia of the old American Wild West, her attractive russet hair, as Buffalo Bill's, falling hardly short of her shoulders.

Her father was laughing already. *"Hi-ho Silver!"* he cried.

Michelle, though, was not smiling—merely closing the door carefully behind her. "Pa-*Pah*," she said, her French almost whispered, "Zoe is in the bathroom, but she'll come looking for me as soon as she finds out I'm gone. I wanted to talk to you alone, for just a minute—first to thank you for putting off your trip to Berlin next week so that we could try to find out if we can do something for Ma-*Mah*. She needs help—our help, your help, don't you think?"

"Oh, can't we talk about something more pleasant," said Fournier, "like your birthday coming up next week. Thirteen, you'll be—it's incredible. Time is ruthless, isn't it? Our little Michelle fast becoming a young woman."

"But Pa-*Pah*, if I hadn't asked you not to go to Berlin—because of Mother, which of course she knew nothing about—you wouldn't be here for my birthday Wednesday. We miss you so much when you're gone like that. The house is empty then—that's what Ma-*Mah* says, although she doesn't say much else about it; but I know she feels it. And she still has those awful dreams sometimes—they haven't completely stopped, especially since you mentioned to her (it sounded almost like scolding to me, Pa-Pah) that she had 'put on all those pounds,' as you called it. I don't know what else you've said to her about it. But, Pa-*Pah*, don't you think those things hurt her some?"

"Oh, I kid her a bit sometimes, nothing serious—ha, I told her one night that if she got fat on me I was going to walk out on her. You can imagine how that went over—like a lead balloon. She said that if I did she'd kill me—she wasn't laughing, either. Your mother can act very strange sometimes."

"What you don't know, Pa-*Pah*, is that she's been eating a queer chocolate candy she gets from somewhere—I don't know—that I think has had something to do with her weight going up and down like it has. I don't know what's happened to her lately, but for some reason she's going through a very stressful time. That's why I hope—Zoe does too—that you can be with her more, be with *us* more. Day before yesterday some woman telephoned here saying she and her sister are cousins— second cousins, she said—of Ma-*Mah's* and that they would like to make an appointment with you. They want to talk with you. I told her this was impossible—that you were a busy man and were out of the country a lot. She got mad and hung up on me, Pa-*Pah*."

At that moment came the next, expected, knock on the study door—at which Michelle turned livid with ire and frustration.

"Come on in, Zoe honey," called Fournier, laughing. "We've been expecting you, haven't we, Michelle?" Michelle was glum, silent.

Little Zoe, in skirt and sweater—she had lately turned age nine—entered at once, a fiery, hurt expression on her pretty face. "Why have you got the door closed, Michelle?" she demanded.

"We're planning some bad, very bad, things we're going to do to you, Zoe honey," laughed her father, "like not taking you anymore to the Mozart piano recitals you love so much, or the soccer games, either. How's that?"

Zoe frowned a glance at Michelle but soon then calmed down and spoke of their cook: "Mina is fixing lunch. That's what I came to tell you both about." (Michelle sneered.) "We're going to have salmon," said Zoe, "and boiled potatoes, also fresh asparagus. Pa-*Pah,* you may have white wine if you like."

"Well, thank you, dear," Fournier said, though preoc- cupied, hardly smiling, now. "How nice of you to come tell us. Now, why don't you kindly dismiss yourself and let me talk a few more minutes with Michelle here." He finally smiled — "For all you know it may be about you. Have you considered that?"

"You were talking about Ma-*Mah*," said Zoe accusingly, though with also an innuendo of triumph, as she was already retreating toward the door through which she had just entered. "I don't want to hear it. It's too sad."

Fournier gasped. "What do you mean by that, Zoe?" he said.

"I mean it's too sad, Pa-*Pah*," said Zoe. "And there's nobody to help us out — Michelle and me. You're not here, Pa-*Pah*."

Fournier, mouth agape, stared first at Zoe then Michelle. He seemed lost, bewildered. "You see more of your mother than I do," he said at last, though falteringly. "What do you think is wrong with her? . . ."

"We don't know, Pa-*Pah*!" Michelle said, deep anguish in both her face and voice. "We don't know where to find out. She won't tell us."

Fournier shook his head helplessly. "Why did she gain all that weight there for awhile?" he finally said.

"We don't know." Michelle, though, was thinking hard, even if haltingly. "It happened . . . it may be . . . well, at the time when she was eating all that chocolate candy. But maybe she's stopped that. I'm not sure."

"No she hasn't," said Zoe. "I saw her eating one or two of those things yesterday. Not all that many, though, like she was at first — when she gained the weight. Just a few now. Maybe the weight won't come back."

"What are these things *like*?" Fournier asked, frowning deeply. "You say they're chocolates . . . is that like chocolate *drops*?"

"I never saw them — up close," Zoe said. "When she'd see me watching, she'd stop."

"I saw them good," Michelle said. "One time. I went in all her purses. They *are* like chocolate drops, a little, Pa-*Pah*. But chocolate molded into people, human beings, and all the time like they were jumping around, or dancing, their mouths open laughing, heads thrown back in big noise and fun, strutting back and forth, hands on each other's shoulders, men and women. They're all Negroes."

"*What?*" said Fournier, aghast. "*Negroes* . . . how can that be? What can it *mean*? She wouldn't be carrying Negro candy around in her purse, Michelle."

"It's not Negro candy, Pa-*Pah*. It's chocolate candy *about* Negroes, their clowning, laughing, and dancing, making fools of themselves. It's candy that puts Negroes *down*, Pa-*Pah*! That's what Mother's been eating and getting fat on. It's awful."

"Why do you say it's awful?" Zoe complained. "The Negroes and Ma-*Mah* don't have anything to do with each other. It wasn't the Negroes that made Ma-*Mah* fat. It might have been different if it had been only one Negro. Michelle, you don't think straight sometimes. What do you know about Negroes anyway? I'll bet you've never seen one."

"I've seen them on television, dunce!" fired back Michelle. "That's more than you have. Anyhow, Ma-*Mah* wouldn't know anything about Negroes—that's why I can't understand why she'd be eating chocolate candy about Negroes. She's never seen one, except possibly one or two on the street somewhere."

"You told me one time, Michelle, that Pa-*Pah* is part Negro."

Fournier threw his head back in howling laughter. "Now, that *does* it!" he cried. "Where on earth did you get that, Michelle?"

"From you, Pa-*Pah*. You showed us a black man among all those Egyptians out there in what you call your ancestral gallery. I even saw Ma-*Mah* out there one day looking at this same man—who lived two thousand years ago maybe—while all the time she was chewing her Negro candy. Could that be some connection, Pa-*Pah*?"

"I remember none of this, Michelle dear," said Fournier, rising. "Let's all go see." Whereupon they left and went into the vaunted, colorfully impressive gallery from which one next entered the imposing, though less colorful, parlor. "Now show me, Michelle," he said as they entered this strange, pictorial, in its muted colors almost ethereal, "gallery of our histories." "Where, Michelle?" Fournier said eagerly.

"Pa-*Pah*, where did you get that red sweater, please?" interrupted Zoe. "It's not very dignified, you know."

"Zoe," scolded Michelle, "will you please try to remember why Pa-*Pah* has brought us to his gallery? Fundamentally, it's to see if you have any Negro blood in you—which, in turn, might explain why Ma-*Mah* has this thing going about Negro minstrels, dancers, singers, vaudevillians, what have you, as long as it's Negro, so much so that she resorts to eating chocolate candy celebrating them, even if it's in a kind of put-down manner. What would you do if you found you had Negro blood?"

"What *could* I do?" said Zoe. "But what difference would it make anyway?"

Her father behind her put his arm down around her shoulder. "My dear, it would make a *lot* of difference. Thank God that you'll never have to worry about it. I'm very disturbed that your mother's *name* even could ever—and due to her own fault or carelessness—be mentioned with such a dreadful route, even if only temporary, that she has chosen to take, such as becoming addicted to this ruse (it may even signify the danger of something worse), this fraud of infernal *nigger* chocolates. We—*I*—must talk to her. I was only kidding the other time that I mentioned to her, just that once, the abominable thing, her weight, that she had let happen to her. Think of it—when before I would remind her she was the most beautiful woman in Paris. Now this. Well, let's go—we can view the gallery another time. I'm in no mood even to review my swarthy ancestors. I'm *French*, you know. Come on, my dears, let's go have lunch. And may I really have a glass of white wine, Zoe? Someday, you'll be able—you too, Michelle—to have one, *one*, with me."

Michelle, though, was pensive, disturbed. "Pa-*Pah*, you were angry, very angry, just a moment ago . . . when you were talking about Ma-*Mah*. I've never seen that side of you before, Pa-*Pah*, even though you tried to hide it."

"Neither have I seen you like that," said Zoe. "Something made you *furious*, Pa-*Pah*—when you were talking about Ma-*Mah* losing her beauty by gaining that weight, yes, eating her Negro chocolates (you called them 'nigger chocolates') just like that was something awful. What made you so angry? Was it Ma-*Mah*, or was it Ma-*Mah's* 'nigger' chocolates?"

Fournier made no reply.

"Come on, Zoe," said Michelle, "let's go get ready for lunch."

Zoe finally, quietly, followed her.

Almost at once Fournier returned to his heretofore-beloved, unchallenged gallery—and its slightly famous entrance to the grandiose, yet regularly upstaged parlor. The parlor, alas, he thought, had never quite been able to preempt, then hold, his attention. It had always been the Egyptian gallery, yes, unique, strong, scrupulous, though also beautiful, which had to this unhappy day held him in thrall. Soon now he was wholly absorbed in it and all it had stood for, again whispering to himself, recounting its mysteries, even vagaries, of race and color. Yet he had always until this very day, alas, felt safe, solid, true, with what this gallery had told him. About race.

The gallery's "race" had been a shibboleth, a truism. Now, though, he no longer felt this former certitude. What was all this talk from his know-it-all daughters about his very own wife — the erstwhile "beauty of Paris" — to the effect that, by her own unbelievable behavior, she had cast unwitting doubts about herself, and *him*self as well, and of course their two remarkable children. Chocolate Negroes — *niggers* — making even her *belly* fat! He could not, he told himself, abide the thought and remain sane. What was happening to the world, he whispered, then continued whispering, until, twenty minutes later, he came to. It was Mina, the cook, who, unctuously, somehow deathly afraid of him, had come to tell him his daughters awaited him at luncheon. He followed her toward the dining room then, saying nothing — until at last asking her, again almost in one of his strange whispers: "Mina, when do you expect Madame Fournier?"

Mina seemed almost shivering from fright. "Not until dinner, sir," she finally said. "Before going to the hospital to see her patients, she now spends most early mornings in that little Church of the Blessed Ascension over on the Rue Blomet. She is again very devout these days, sir."

"I'm not here to discuss my private life," Dr. Fournier said. "I'm here as your attending physician — to make *your* life as comfortable as is possible under the circumstances."

"I know that," Ari said. "I appreciate your efforts — which are far different from what they were when we first started out. What made you change, Doctor? What made you more humane? But, on second thought, I withdraw that question — it might require of you something you just said you weren't here to do; that is, discuss your private life. Something made you change, though, Doctor. You may have, at one time in your life, or maybe even recently, been in situations where you yourself wished you were dealing with humane people. You may have awakened to the fact, early on or recently, that it makes a big difference." He was tiring now — his voice had descended almost to a whisper. "Yes, it can make a difference, Dr. Fournier — in fact, it may have made the difference in you. It may even have made a difference in *me* — and that's a big order — for I have much to hate this world about, if I may say so. But I have no way of knowing what activates *you*. Although you're a seasoned medic, and an outstanding one, I'm told, did it ever occur to you that, nonetheless, you're still a human being? — capable of all manner of reckonings and obsessions? Who knows? — maybe you've been utterly fascinated, absorbed; yes, even obsessed, with the fact of my coming death. You and I both know it's coming and damned soon. I, however, have become attuned to that fact, you see — the fact that this week, or next week, or maybe by the end of the month, I shall be no more. Can you think, or envision, yourself, *ever*, in a similar situation — where you knew, were damn certain, this was the final month of your life? Of course you cannot, for that's not at all the situation in your case, not at all even germane to your present life. Yet that doesn't mean you're impervious to my fast-fading state of existence — quite the contrary. For if there is anything starkly visible about you, it's your deep sensibilities. It's not necessary that my state, physical or mental, has any connection at all with yours — and, happily, it doesn't — for you to have jittery moments, like now, or utter absorption, indeed, yes, obsession, terror-stricken obsession, with my own hapless condition. Proof of this is the mere appearance of your face — right now — its blanched, terrorized look, as if you this very moment stood before a stern judge who is about to impose on you the ultimate terminal penalty. Even I, with what awaits me, am frightened to look at you as you are now."

Ari was right. Poor Cécile, her face truly ashen white, somehow now jerked her body straight upright at the side of the bed and, in her fury, seemed almost to hiss at him. "What are you possibly thinking about!" she shrieked. "You yourself at the border, the very brink, of death, can only try now in your misery—brought on in great part by how you came to have this illness, to drag others down with you! How absolutely horrible, atrocious! . . . reprehensible! And I've never talked like this to a patient—or anyone else—in my whole life! but I'll hear no more of your ghoulish talk and derision! You're sick in more ways than one! How awful, how *cruel* of you!" She was crying now. "And all because your number is up! Well, mine is *not*!" Tears flying, she stormed out of the room as the other patients gaped.

"Poor, poor, Dr. Fournier," sighed spent little Ari to himself. "Doesn't she know *all* our numbers are up? . . . "

How he missed them, he thought. Tosca and Gwelo. But they were gone now—to their own tidy little flat. So it was, though, he told himself—and how it had to be. He, Quo Vadis, sat alone in his sordid kitchen chewing a heel of stale French bread. His beleaguered mind, however, was now soon elsewhere. No longer now with a God to consult, no vast intelligence wielded by the Deity to prompt him, he felt sorely weakened, if not enfeebled, as from day to day he contemplated the awesome talk, the "project," he, as a harsh duty, had set for himself. But now he and God were on the "outs," permanently so, he sadly reminded himself, yet he was bitter about it. No longer was he willing to blame himself for how he had earlier, in talking to others, anyone who would listen, boasted of, almost paraded, God in their faces. But now he would no longer take this rap on himself, from himself, he vowed. He bristled now. He had *believed* in God, he furiously whispered to himself, near tears (a rarity for him), as he insisted that this at the proper time would stand as his air-tight defense in his own behalf on Judgment Day. It was *God* who had let *him* down, he said aloud to the now-gangrenous empty flat. It didn't matter a whit that he had woefully, desperately, appealed to Him for guidance, then, it was hoped, for sanction, of the hazardous enterprise he, Quo Vadis, had fashioned and put before the Almighty, who, even if burdensomely occupied with other pressing obligations, even crises, had inexcusably ignored his please for ratification and support. Inwardly, he, Quo Vadis, had been hurt, to say nothing of humiliated; therefore he must now, already had, in fact, severed the ties according to which he had so long now lived his life and formulated its theory, its creed. What, though, was he to do in this zero hour? he asked himself. Who was there, in his present extremity, he could turn to? He had already, thrice, been unsuccessful in reaching the only man in whose judgment, whose steady mind, even if hesitance, he felt a "gutfull" confidence. This man was Paul Kessey, of course, who, though, surmised Quo Vadis, may still be recuperating in Lady of Paradise Hospital from a frightful drunk and near-last contest with the "valley of the shadow," etc. Quo Vadis, however, from personal experience, considered this often to be the messiah of the heavy thinkers, and therefore drinkers, of the world. It was indeed, on occasion, the badge of necessity—even of honor. He must go, then, nevertheless, and try to see, commune with, this strange man again—about the "project," the "mission," indeed the very "valley of the shadow." This time the final action, the reckoning, site would not be Caen. It would be closer to home than that. It would *be* at home—Paris. Quo Vadis could not help shuddering. So now, strangely, he began undressing, there in the kitchen, soon, stark naked, leaving his fuming, miserable clothes in a reeking heap in front of the cooking range. He left, then, to—of all things—go run a tub of hot bath water. Surely his earnestness about what now lay ahead was no longer in doubt.

An hour and a half later he was across the Seine, over on the Right Bank, talking into a street pay phone—where he was not long in learning from Lady of Paradise Hospital that his quarry had been discharged and gone home yesterday. Palpitations at once set in. He realized now he, in order to see Paul, would first have to run the gauntlet in the person of that petulant old woman he, with Tosca and Gwelo, had had to face on his first, and so far only, visit to this unpleasant, inhospitable pension-place. Nor was he to be disappointed. Madame, when she saw, and recognized, him, stopped in her tracks and, frowning, pondered whether she should even acknowledge his presence, although knowing he had without doubt come to see Paul—who was presently upstairs dashing off page after page of half-querulous, half-endearing, correspondence to Queen Saturn. "YES?" cried Madame through the closed front door. Her harsh voice-tone told even more than her sour frown. Then she saw his great dark brown jacket, also his green necktie, and tan drip-dry slacks, even the passable black loafers pinching his feet, and wondered what was "afoot." She opened the door. Quo Vadis bowed ever so slightly but did not smile. "Is Monsieur Kessey in?" he asked.

"Yes," said Madame in English. "He is here. But he returned from the hospital only yesterday and is resting. Could you come another time?" Her voice was cold.

"No I could not, Ma'm," Quo Vadis said, not forgetting his manners, slight as they were. "If you will kindly tell him that Mr. Quo Vadis Jackson is here and that I've come to consult him on the matters he and I discussed recently at my house, I shall be very obliged."

City of Light

Madame finally nodded her head, compliantly, but stalled on the question of whether to ask him in at this point.

He spoke quickly. "I shall wait out here, if I may."

Yet she left the door ajar, went to the stairs, glumly, and called up to Paul, repeating exactly what she had been told – as Quo Vadis came near to smiling his thanks to her even before Paul's hasty, and affirmative, reply. Whereupon herculean Quo Vadis, already inside the door, brushed past Madame and serenely mounted the stairs, which were already creaking under his great weight. Yet, on the fourth step, he turned, gave the minutest of bows, and continued up.

Paul, in pajamas and a robe, greeted him warmly – yet quizzically – before leading him into the workroom where he motioned him to a seat at the table opposite himself.

"Sorry to learn you've been under the weather, Paul," Quo Vadis said. "Hope my visit is not a nuisance, or worse, to you. The talk we had at my flat the first time you were there has often, very often, returned to my mind. First of all, it included my bringing up the plight of Mrs. Zimsu and her son to you. While she's had the recent temporary good fortune of having some family money turn up for her, her more basic, heavier, problems are still unsolved. For one thing, the boy badly needs a "father," in quotes.. I have – during the little time, from my more awesome interests, I have been able to give to Gwelo – I have tried to play the role as best, under the circumstances, that I knew how. The results, though, have been irregular – although both he and his mother, a fine woman if there ever was one, have overdone their praise of me, plus their thanks – but I have been able to do very little in a *fundamental* way. I regret that, of course, for Gwelo, if given the right upbringing – and I don't mean mollycoddling him, which his mother, though, is not guilty of, seeing the dangers – most surely will Gwelo then make a great mark for himself, as well as for his wonderful mother and his great African ancestors; for *all* of us. You can see that, Paul. You've got to try to help these two very exceptional people."

Paul, being careful, wanting to throw him off the track, suddenly decided to curl his lip, derisively, at him — which he did. He thought this the better way to camouflage what had been his, Paul's, true feelings about "dear" (his own thought) Tosca, almost, in truth, ever since he had first laid eyes on her — that first day at noon as she stood with Lewellyn in the restaurant queue. Nor, though, was he driven — entirely — by her unknown, to her, sexual attraction, for it was something which had grown on him gradually but steadily. Now, however, unbeknownst to anyone but himself — certainly never to Quo Vadis — his Tosca-attitude had taken to growing not by leaps and bounds but certainly enough to have forced him to take the strange, yet almost metaphysical, matter up with Saturn, where it was now, unfortunately, in full tilt. It was indeed well beyond the trifling issues with which he must these days deal. So, certainly, because of Quo Vadis's passion to have something done in Tosca's and Gwelo's behalf — now that their rescuer would be withdrawing from the scene — he must today, here and now, be most cautiously dealt with. This Paul intended to do — yet somehow felt less than a surfeit of confidence. No matter, he still remembered Quo Vadis's edict: Do something, Paul Kessey, for Tosca and Gwelo, these two outstanding and deserving people. Paul wanted to ask simply: "How?" And he finally did — still playing his Machiavellian role.

Quo Vadis, however, seemed to have been waiting for the question. "For one thing," he said at once, "when you return to the States, you can take Tosca and Gwelo with you."

Paul became more canny than ever now, indeed almost coy. "And get into all kinds of entanglements with the law, eh?" He laughed.

"Not if you're married," Quo Vadis said.

"Whom would I be married to?" But Paul knew his face gave it away. He tried to frown now, but that was no good either—until he looked at Quo Vadis, whose ungenial look was so authentic one expected it to produce a growl any second. "Good Lord," Paul said in a hurry, then laughed, "are you talking to *me* about Tosca? . . . ha, ha, ha."

"How you find anything in that to laugh about puzzles the shit out of me," growled Quo Vadis this time. He stood now and looked helplessly around Paul's workroom, finally pulling open a table drawer to no avail. "Where do you hide things?" he said. "You got anything to drink—I'm not talking about water—in this *study* of yours?"

But Paul was smiling again. "There's a few beers there in that little fridge," he said, pointing to a corner across the room.

"Oh Christ—not beer!" cried Quo Vadis. "Have mercy on me—I can't use it. It starts my piles acting up again, terrible. I have to sit over a bucket of scalding water. No, thanks. Sorry. But speaking of marriage, who else would I be talking about but Tosca? But you laugh. Christ."

Again Paul quickly gathered his wits about him. "You forget something, though, Quo Vadis," he said slyly. "Tosca, I believe, is no longer the marrying kind. You're the one who told me why—or strongly hinted at it—that night in your flat after dinner when Tosca and Gwelo had gone to bed. Remember? You hinted at the real possibility that Tosca, during a terrible uprising in her country had for days been gang-raped by victorious troops and marauders—who had already shot her husband and her father. This, yes, came from you, Quo Vadis."

Quo Vadis, again fast losing his temper, spluttered something indecipherable as he stared at Paul. Finally, though, he relented and once more looked around the room. "May I repeat myself?" he asked. "Have you got any whiskey or wine around this neighborhood? Don't tell me you don't drink, Paul. I know better. Liquor is what put you in the hospital."

Paul rose unsmiling. "Let me go downstairs," he finally said. "I don't think Madame has anything but she might be able to get something from one of the other residents. So let me go see." He went out.

Whereupon Quo Vadis took the respite to visually survey the room and its contents. He glanced at a few of Paul's books and was unimpressed, then at the small typewriter, and a big English dictionary alongside it. At last his eye caught a notebook. He picked it up and, curious, began to read: "Mother, I keep telling you, that I need none of your advice about my women friends. Good Lord, our bitter fiasco about Jeannette should have told you that. So *please* hold off on your implied advice, your steering. *Of course* I like Cécile! Where in the world did you sense the idea I've somehow downgraded her? But Cécile is married, I've told you again and again. This can be a potentially dangerous situation—how many times have I told you this? Besides, I've never *really* known what she thinks of me—she's older than I; has, with her husband, got money; she's highly sexed, true, but that doesn't at all tell the whole story about Cécile. I don't know what that story is, though. I only know she's disturbed—and I don't necessarily mean mentally—but by things in life she's never been able to understand, though she never talks about it. Actually, I don't think she likes anything about this setup, this world—excepting her children, of course—and maybe trying to find the *real* values available on this planet, even about the screwed-up way its run. Being a doctor, she sees a lot of bad stuff, helpless suffering, often on the part of people she can't at all, as a physician, help. So they just die as she looks on. Mother, I like the woman, a whole lot—but I'm afraid not as much as you do *for* me. How can you, by your subtle silence, encourage my relationship with a woman — white, while I'm black — who, for all we know, may like nothing about me except sex. I don't really believe this — if I did I wouldn't like her as I actually do — yet it's something to think about. She's a fine, tender, and at heart a caring woman — even despite the fact she has some strange relatives who tend to be fascistic. But not Cécile — I'd never believe it about her. So, yes, I admire, and like, her. Yet I'm somehow not driven by the same forces you apparently are — which I can't really get to the bottom of, either. It's weird. Is it because she is white that you somehow prefer her? I can't believe that tells the whole story where you're concerned — it's too simplistic. You're more complicated than that.

"Meanwhile, Saturn dear, I've met here in Paris an African woman, who is a few years younger than I but has an eleven-year-old son who is a veritable whiz kid. His mother, however, a really good-looking, well-educated, sexy woman, 'likes' me, but for one reason only — she wants me to marry her and be a 'father' to her extraordinary son. She is a widow. She hasn't said so, but I'm sure she wants me, after I've married her, to bring her and her son to the States to live. I've been thinking a lot about this, Mother. I really like this woman, though not a soul but you knows about it — certainly she doesn't."

"*Oh!* . . . this shit is awful! *Awful!*" cried Quo Vadis. Breathing stertorously, hardly any longer actually aware of where he was, he dropped down in the closest chair, the open notebook still in his trembling hand, and stared vacantly out the window at the beautiful afternoon. "Jes*us* K. Christ!" he finally murmured, then again held up the notebook before his eyes, yet, squinting, seemed no longer able to read it. "Good God Almighty," he whispered at last, having apparently forgotten about his recent unilateral break with the Deity. "Paul Kessey's lying like a dog! He likes this married white woman far better than he does poor Tosca. This motherfucker's crazier than a bedbug. And writing all this shit to his dead mother that he told us all about that night—that's where he got it; she must of been crazier than he is. Wow! Somebody ought to put a pillowcase over his head and lock him up before he kills somebody. Ah, but never mind. I can use *him*. I do believe it— if I go about it right. That Hitlerite Poussin wouldn't know what hit him, would he?" Quo Vadis slowly then, yet almost as if mortally afraid of it, again lifted the notebook, turned away the pages he had already read, and resumed.

"It's true, Mother—from my behavior in her presence that Tosca would never believe my actual, my really good, feelings toward her. I'm sure she thinks all I want of her is to go to bed with her, while the truth is I deeply admire both her mind and her character no end. Maybe I could even get accustomed to some of those African clothes she wears, together with those awful dreadlocks down her shoulders. I tell you, Saturn, *it can happen*—IF you will only take a greater interest in the welfare, the tastes, above all, the needs of your son who worships your memory as well as your spectral presence. It would be wonderful for me at this critical juncture in my life— a life that's so far produced little or nothing, though I've certainly tried hard enough—if I could have some input from you. Mother, where *do* you stand in this crisis? I needn't remind you you've always participated in the crucial decisions and events in my life. You know this—including the sad Jeannette affair, or catastrophe, or tragedy, you name it; as well you might. Let us, then, here avoid all those heartaches. You know the pitfalls. *Color* is the name. So why would you seem so stubborn about Cécile—taking her side when, for all we know, she might not want you to. I've told you twice now about Tosca but I get no signs, hints, even, no initiative or feedback of any kind, nothing at all to indicate I might be on the right track where Tosca—not Cécile—is concerned. No, it's always vague, noncommittal. There's not even an inkling, or an innuendo, that you would more than likely have me go in direction A rather than direction B. How in the hell, Saturn, can I be expected to cope with things involving my very life and future? Meantime, I'm to take the punishment, the penalties, the risks, indeed the possible horrors, attendant upon your remotest, and most aloof, decrees. Cécile vs. Tosca. Both great and good women. Yet Tosca would faint were she to know my true feelings. Maybe, though, so would Cécile. But what am I to do, Saturn? I've never, never, crossed you, have I? How could I ever? You are the *Queen*. For me, you rule by divine right!"

Quo Vadis's utter spell was broken by Paul's voice. Paul was coming up the stairs but talking back down at Madame. Quo Vadis, though still in a daze, quickly tossed the five-and-dime notebook he had been reading as far away on the table as possible, short of its going over onto the floor.

"No problem at all, Madame," Paul was saying. "The janitor sent one of his guys down the street to Arachon's—got a cold jug of Rhine wine for us. No, no Madame—thank you, thank you. I've already tipped the guy." The next moment Paul entered the workroom with the cold white wine. Strangely, indeed unnaturally, Quo Vadis's stygian face was a wreath of horrible, unspeakable smiles. He also seemed a nervous wreck. "Well, what have we here?" he said, rubbing the palms of his hands together in phony glee.

"It's about time," smiled Paul. "That's the first time you've smiled since you arrived. Remember, you came here for certain of your own reasons—to sell a bill of goods to *me*. Right? Then why, before I left to go send for something to please your dry throat, were you so rude, almost insulting, to me in my own quarters? You are a strange man, Mr. Jackson." All the while Paul was pouring Quo Vadis's cold, white wine.

"You may be right, Paul," he said. "I've got many things on my mind—important things—and I may have been a little crude." He raised his wine in a silent toast, or mere gesture. "A little crude, yes."

"How can one be a *little* crude?" But Paul returned the wine gesture and sat down. "We were talking about Tosca and Gwelo," he said.

Quo Vadis almost stood—as if he had been frightened. "Oh, no, no," he said. "Let's let that rest for awhile. It's a matter that's entirely up to you, anyhow. I know you'll do whatever you think is right, Paul. Indeed, you have that reputation. But it's my present feeling that that issue—of you, Tosca, and Gwelo—will somehow solve itself."

Paul was surprised—and confused. He started to speak, perhaps remonstrate, but was not allowed to.

For Quo Vadis had suddenly changed. He had become deeply grave. "I came here to see you today, Paul," he said, "on a matter we once discussed—that evening in my flat. Simply, it has to do with the duties, the responsibilities, of men fit to live in a society worth its name." Paul had eased into a chair. "Other people," continued Quo Vadis, "do not have these responsibilities. The reason is simple. They lack not only the ability but the vision to assume these great societal duties. I learned this years ago. I've spoken of it before. There was, yes, this young black man, named Cager Lee, down in Gladstone College located in a little town in southwestern Tennessee by the (Wagnerian) name of Valhalla— though incorporated well before Richard Wagner was born— this young black man, yes, was born and reared on a poor sharecropping farm in eastern Virginia. His father, like mine, was a 'nobody'—a penniless dirt farmer with a shack full of kids. That's the kind of environment that Cager came from, and that's the kind that I came from." Quo Vadis's great black

City of Light

mass of face and jowl was frightening to look at as, in deep emotion, he placed his huge right fist across his chest as if swearing an oath. Paul had finally become so involved he put his wine glass aside and scooted forward on the edge of his chair, the better to listen, before again being insulted. Quo Vadis's voice rose: "There were no rich, bigshot, Cadillac-driving fathers in *these* families, Paul!"

Paul bristled. "What's your point?" he said. "My father never owned a Cadillac in his life and would shoot one of your ears off if he ever heard you say so. He and his family, down in Georgia, had gone through the same hard life as the families you're talking about. But my father had brains! Get it? BRAINS. They do make a difference, you know."

"Paul, Paul," said Quo Vadis, "don't you think I know that? Hell, yes. But brains aren't enough in what I'm talking about. I'm talking about three things: guts, commitment, and vision. I dare you to bring this thing home, Paul—to your own case. That's why I'm here today—to find out what you're made of, what makes you tick, where you stand. There's a man in this country of France, Charles Poussin, by name—you've heard me speak of him before—who, if he completely gets his way, is going to hurt thousands of people, actually millions, and especially people like us. But who is trying to do anything about him? A few, a few people like me, and that's all. Where are you, Paul? I'll tell you—in some damn saloon getting drunk and finally going to the hospital. *That's* where you are, Paul. But tell me, doesn't it make you feel shitty. Or how does it feel to be a person, a *man*, so-called, like you. Let me ask you, do you have high esteem for yourself? Take a minute and think it out. I've already told you—I did so that night at my house—that I can help you. I have extremely high esteem for myself. And I'm no dumbbell—I don't get all upset when I don't take baths as often as some people. So what. The things I'm interested in are not going to be made better if I bathe a dozen times a day. In fact, I don't bathe as often as some people more-or-less as — not a protest — but like a badge, or a ribbon of some kind, even as a Purple Heart maybe. Anything that makes me know I'm really better than most. You know why? Because I care about people — about my fellow men and women. That's the highest calling a man or woman can ever have. But in your case, you're almost willing to tell anybody who will listen of your low esteem for yourself — you of course don't say it in quite those bald terms, but you're willing to at least strongly hint at it. It worries the shit out of you, Paul — that's the actual truth of the matter. Am I right or wrong?"

Paul, his handsome face in turmoil, was literally threshing about in his chair. It was clear he was in agony. "You see," he said, almost pitifully, "I'm not alone, don't think alone, don't act alone, in these matters. I'm blamed for them but a lot of the time I'm not guilty."

Quo Vadis knew. He had just read Paul's five-and-dime notebook. Yet he leaned forward and said, "Meaning what, Paul?"

"Oh, hell, I don't know *what* I mean half the time," Paul said — in sorrow and disgust.

"Paul," Quo Vadis said, quite coolly now, "I'm planning to move against Poussin very soon, and I need your sharp ears, eyes, and mind. You must come with me. You must forget about all those unhealthy ties you just so pitifully acknowledged and suddenly become your own man. It's my belief you can do it. You can free yourself — become a man, and a *free* man, in one bold stroke. Tell me, would you like to be a man?"

"I am a man," said Paul. "But, like you — although you'd never admit it — I'd prefer to be a different kind of man than I am. How on earth, though, could *you*, of all people, bring about this change? It could never happen and it's presumptuous of you, highly so, to ever claim it could — where *I'm* involved. You and I are, very basically, different types. You're still talking about Poussin, for example. Tell me, point-blank, what you meant a minute ago when you said you were planning to move against him and very soon. Did you mean kill him?"

For the first time Paul witnessed Quo Vadis on the defensive. Even, finally, when he did try to speak to Paul, he stammered. "Who said anything . . . about killing anybody?" he asked. "*I* didn't. Unless scaring him to death, that is, can be called murder or assassination. He has got to be shown, though, that he's being watched."

Paul forced a grim smile. "Come now, Quo Vadis — what happens if he thumbs his nose at all attempts to frighten him, what then?"

Quo Vadis, angry now, rose and poured himself more wine. "That contingency would have to be addressed if and when it arose, not before," he said. "What I'm looking for now, before anything gets under way, are standby recruits. That's one of the reasons I'm here today. But I can tell already, by your snotty questions, that no one could ever interest you in a project like this. If you can't see, and at once, anything in it for you — good-bye, get somebody else, kiss my foot. But so it goes."

"Stop the charade, Quo Vadis," said Paul. "If all these efforts you're talking about, like scaring Poussin into giving up, and all that crap, failed, you'd be the first one calling for his life. Or not calling for it but taking it. Then you insinuate that people who're not anxious to get implicated in a murder are uncaring cowards. Next time Poussin is scheduled to make a Paris speech, let me know, will you? I may, or may not, go with you to hear him. It can be damn dangerous."

"For me, Paul, yes," Quo Vadis said. "You, though, can almost 'pass.'" He got up to leave then. "The other reason I came to see you is that I'm out of a job — thanks to Poussin and his people — and it's not going to be easy for me to get another one. But you speak far better French than I do, and I thought because of that you might be able to help me find something."

Paul groaned. "I ought to be out looking for work for myself," he said. "Lord only knows what I can do to help you, Quo Vadis. But I'll keep thinking about it and trying."

Quo Vadis nodded glumly, threw up his hand, and started toward the door and the stairs — but then stopped. "I don't have your telephone number, Paul," he said. "Would you give it to me?" He fished a pencil stub out of his pocket.

Paul recited his number. "What's yours, Quo Vadis?"

"They took my telephone out, Paul. I couldn't keep up with the payments. I don't need a phone anyhow — especially after Mrs. Zimsu and Gwelo left. In fact, I'm going by their new location from here."

"Tell them I asked about them," Paul said.

"Sure, I kinda hate to go by there, though. I'm going to have to ask her for a small loan."

Paul could only look at him, unable to think of any reply or comment, and said nothing. He saw then, though, Quo Vadis suddenly, bitterly, grinding his teeth — at the same time, though, somehow trying his best to laugh. "Paul," he finally said, "I may be on the phone to you sooner than you think. It won't be — it can't be — long before Poussin comes to town." He waved and left then.

Chapter
Eight
A Solution

I t was a fortnight later now, a period, a hiatus, however, during which much had happened, and today, July 14th, was Bastille Day. Still, notwithstanding that the afternoon, near two o'clock, was sultry and overcast, no rain had yet fallen on the Champs-Elysées down which the grand, crowded, military parade was now moving — consisting of glorious marching bands, huge tubas, clashing cymbals, flying tricolors; the eyes of solemn-faced men and women of the armed forces fixed straight ahead down toward the Rond Point as they proudly marched; followed by the ceremonious ranks of top-hatted dignitaries; the robed clergy; and always, stationed along the curbs, the watchful, ineluctable gendarmes. Surely a magnificent sight to watch, up and down the whole vista of the Champs-Elysées, by the shouldering public throngs — among whom, perhaps not surprisingly, were Tosca and Gwelo Zimsu.

"Look at the blackies, Ma-MAH!" proudly cried Gwelo, pointing to a few scattered French Negro troops in an artillery regiment passing. "If I weren't going to be a lawyer, and then a politician, I'd like to be a general!"

Tosca's mind, however—despite the din of all the band music and cheering—was elsewhere. She had failed in getting Paul to come with them, had even failed in getting from him a plausible (to her) excuse, unless, that is, she considered his telling her he instead had to go to the hospital and sit for a while with Ari to be one. Had Ari's condition worsened? she had asked. No, Paul told her—he was merely lonely. Tosca thought this almost an affront and—here at the height of all the fanfare, ostentation, and pandemonium of a Bastille Day parade—remained preoccupied, unhappy, actually peeved. What she did not know was that little Ari was not only lonely but now—indeed for the same fortnight period, yes—had been without his favorite physician.

Now the slightest of drizzles had a last begun, and a few of the few who had come prepared hoisted umbrellas. Not many of them, however, knew, or would have cared, that well south of them, across the Seine, there was yet another, though drastically different, also of course smaller, assembly gathering, soon to take place—but in out of any rain, even if, as was the case, it was to be held in that drab, now-old Monnaies Auditorium building nestled at the end of the once-bustling Rue Branfoure. Monnaies was originally, at the turn of the century, a lesser Paris opera house, yet one where occasionally both Patti and Caruso had sung. People were still entering the hall now—only a few of them seedy-looking—and taking seats on the smallish (for a former opera house) main floor where, however, there appeared to be, certainly, no less than 500 of them already present. The closed balconies above, though, were dark. But those seated below and waiting were conversing among themselves, though in what seemed a peculiarly dour manner; others talked urgently, even excitedly;

a few smiled; none laughed. On balance it was a somber, serious meeting-to-be. Yet so far there were only three or four people — and clearly underlings — up on the well-lighted stage, but who, busybodies, were constantly coming and going, arranging things. Everyone else, however, sat waiting — restlessly.

Soon there did occur, though, some slight, seemingly inconsequential, action up front now. Location: third row center, almost in touching proximity of the old orchestra pit's brass rail, where a couple, man and woman, newcomers, were being obliged almost to climb over others to reach a few as-yet-untaken seats midway down the row. Seated people were having to stand in order to accommodate the two new arrivals — except, that is, for one conspicuous, if strange, seat holder, a lone, blond, mammoth man, not old, not young, who appeared at first, however, to give ground grudgingly, until seeming then to remind himself of some overlooked factor which apparently counseled caution, heed, even cunning; whereupon he rose and stepped back, smiling, until the couple were able to push past him to the available seats beyond. The blond giant who had obliged them wore sallow kid gloves on his great hands; his bright-yellow flaxen hair, though at the moment in considerable disarray, reached almost to his shoulders; indeed, it was a somewhat alien foil for his unseemly blunt face, especially when, as now, leavened with what might have passed for some greasy ivory cosmetic; the nose, moreover, was not merely pudgy but somehow flat and flush, as he sat, tense, from his inner fear almost trembling, and stared hard, yet expectantly, up at the stage.

But almost before he knew it three well-dressed men, in their late thirties and early forties, stepped out of the wings onto the stage and headed for the speaker's lectern. There two of them took seats while the third, perhaps the youngest, faced the microphone and the audience before clearing his throat and speaking, of course, in French.

"*Bonjour*, Ladies and Gentlemen. How gratifying it is, beyond all words, actually, to see so many of you out today. Yet we up here on the rostrum can also see, or at least sense, that big question mark on all your minds—'Where this afternoon is our leader?' Well, we can certainly tell you where he is *not*: Charles Poussin would not be caught dead over there today on the Champs-Elysées gawking at all that phony pomp and circumstance at the taxpayers' expense trying to celebrate a France—thanks to them—that does not exist anymore. France, yes, was indeed great at one time, and not only just during the era of a Napoleon, from which we did, however, achieve the masterly Arc de Triomphe at the end up there, the top, of the, yes, beautiful Avenue des Champs-Elysées, but even before, as well as since, there have been all those other symbols of the genius of the French people. But then, alas, something happened—happened to the French people themselves. They were infiltrated!—that's what happened to them and is still happening. But it required a Charles Poussin to diagnose the trouble and lay it bare before the French people—or at least before those of them who had the intelligence, or even the interest, to grasp his fiery message. The message was simple, just as it still is today, namely: France no longer exists for the French. Or to state it another way—again credit Monsieur Poussin—France today exists for everybody *but* the French. Actually, it's not France—rather, it's Babel with its thousand different voices, only a few of them French, but everything bedlam, that has now won the day, though not without our leader's outcry in the country's behalf, Ladies and Gentlemen. 'But why isn't he here today as you talk?' you ask. My answer is merely that he hasn't felt up to it. His health is not good— which, though, is something, we hope and pray, will soon reverse itelf, change for the better. As many, or most, of you know — because of his fanaticism in the struggle — he suffers from a heart condition, and it has been acting up recently. Yesterday, then, his doctors would not approve of his coming out on this occasion and making a speech; he was just not equal to the challenge, but only for today; I don't have to tell you he's not a quitter. Still, rest assured, he made the necessary provision for someone else to appear on this stage in his stead. I'm sure there is no doubt in your minds who that person is — indeed he is the man our leader himself has designated as second-in-command of our organization, the FFF, and who, Ladies and Gentlemen, sits right here behind me. He really needs no introduction to you. Throughout, he has been Monsieur Poussin's walking shadow, so to speak, and is here at the leader's direction. Therefore, knowing both these men, I'm certain you don't feel in any way demeaned or mishandled. I am, then, happy to present to you again our other tried-and-true leader, a spellbinding orator, and absolutely fearless man — Monsieur Hector Duquesne!"

There was applause, though it did not shake the ceiling beams, yet our huge blond-haired man, still seated down in the third row front — up close — seemed gasping for breath as he gawked and shook his head. The golden hair helter-skelter halfway down his shoulders, he seemed literally gasping for breath as he sat staring up, in utter disbelief and anguish, at the bold, defiant Duquesne marching to the lectern and microphone. He had read much about Duquesne, almost as much as he had of Poussin himself, and had watched his audacious, repellent, hammy, FFF antics on television. But he knew Duquesne was no Poussin. There was too much of the braggadocio, angry melodrama, insistence always on a semblance of flair, even courage (which, truthfully, he was not without), yet not the basic intelligence of a Poussin, nor his singleness of purpose, above all no sick Hitlerian dedication — and therefore the danger — of the quieter, older leader. He — call our thinker "X" — knew this and now, suffering, realized his pitifully hasty efforts of the last two or three days (as well as the humbling raising, borrowing, of the requisite funds for the disguise), all this had turned out to be useless. Now, mouth open, he could only sit emptily staring up, *up close*, yes, at the wrong man, with a sinking, sorrowfully wretched, disappointed heart. What he actually wished to do now was get up and leave. He was afraid to risk it, though. He felt insecure enough — matters had finally, if disastrously, peaked — as it was. His only recourse, then, as he saw it, was to later try again, at the next open-house party gathering, when then the setting would be normal, habitual, the proper FFF people present and on stage — up close. Yet he could only sigh. This, though, was the way it had to be, he told himself; his only resort. Unless, that is, he chose to abandon the project altogether by which, alas, he had originally designed a prospectus to serve his own very special will, his needs; as it were, yes, his mission; his mission to make himself whole; a fantasy he had experienced only once in his entire life — when, that is, years before, as a raw student down in Tennessee at Gladstone College, he had dedicated his mind, heart, and soul to the mission for which his idol, Cager Lee, had far earlier made the supreme sacrifice. He, then young X, during this first real challenge of his life, one which, though, alas, he had in the end lost, had nevertheless undergone something he had never felt before or since; that is, until feeling the first heady glimmers of this present undertaking. During his crisis down at Gladstone College he had experienced something he could at the time not possibly have described. But today, on his way here to the opera house, he had once more — across the many years — felt, yes, the "glimmers," indicating he had again embarked on his mission of old. It was the mission, as a human being, to make — render — himself whole. No more, no less. But it was *he* — X — who must be the achiever, the consummator of the feat; the feat it would be, he knew, for he had only, this second time, encountered its presence, yes, in glimmers. Otherwise, throughout his existence, his life had been anything but whole; rather he had lived in what can only, though feebly, be described as living in psychically dissimilar portions, divisions, even subdivisions, fragments, indeed fractions, of himself — *one's* self, as it were. But it had recently become his nervous aim to bring about change; change through correlative doings. He had thus sought to convince himself — of endeavors seeking their natural relationships — on the way, yes, to the *whole* life. Yet — a prerequisite — it must involve, positively, humanely, the lives of others. He had already made this move, he was glad to be able to tell himself (as Hector Duquesne's loud, livid voice came at him off the opera stage, even if unlike Caruso's) and he had come here today to, yes, consummate it. Consummate it on behalf not only of himself but, it was hoped, on that of a small, even a tiny, segment of afflicted humanity. Yet his was a solo endeavor now — he hated to have to remind himself. There was no one else. God was dead. The noble hoax was over. But could life actually go on like this, he asked himself, still skewered by doubt. Who but God, or His designate — like himself formerly — could ever find time to take up the cudgel, on behalf of some poor nobody, who like himself, was merely trying to eat and have a roof over his head, by, say, standing all day, wet ankles deep in blistering liquid detergents scrubbing great city buses, but then to have even this non-job snatched away under dire threats to the city from the new Gallic fascists, the FFF. It was all pure mayhem, thought X, somehow now on the verge of trembling. Who but himself, though, had arrived here today at the opera house to enforce justice with his heavy pistol in his pocket? No one. God was dead. Even he, X, however, had been thwarted—temporarily. But he would return and thereby be made whole. No more fragments or fractions. It was his covenant with himself. Again he wanted to rise and leave. Again he ruled against it. He was conspicuous enough already, he knew. Somehow again, though, strangely, he found himself trembling. He did not know why. He only wished that God had not died.

Meanwhile up on stage embattled historian, Duquesne, flailing his arms and perspiring through his shirt, was baying like a hound at a juniper tree. "Enough is enough!" he cried out to them. "Don't forget what happened to King John at Runnymede!"

"*God is dead,*" whispered Quo Vadis, tears in his eyes.

Next morning.

"You haven't eaten your toast, Gwelo," Tosca complained, observing her son as they sat at the kitchen table.

"You didn't put enough butter on it," Gwelo said. "It's almost dry. Doesn't make any difference, though—I don't feel very good anyhow." He reached for the jam.

The furnished flat they had moved into was not as large as Quo Vadis's place, but it was nicer—that is, cleaner, lighter, more cheerful; though the furniture was only passable.

"Did you like the parade yesterday?" Tosca asked.

"Oh, yes," Gwelo said. "Very much. I wish Quo Vadis had been with us. Do you think he'll get put out of his flat?—is that why he came to borrow some money Tuesday?"

"I didn't ask, of course," Tosca said. "I really don't know what his situation is now. It can't be good, though. He acted so embarrassed—coming to ask me for money. It was very hard for him. I felt sorry for him."

"Does he know anybody in Paris besides us?"

Cyrus Colter

"He never says, but I know he must. He probably doesn't want to get into that—the people, or person may not be of the best background; especially if it's a woman. That baffles me, you know. I can't imagine he'd dare come to us to borrow money if a woman were involved. But he did ask if I knew a place that sold wigs. Then he tried to laugh. I didn't laugh, though. But then I thought I should have. Later, however, I tried to liven things up—about money—by telling him, the truth, that I still had my little three-day-a-week job at the fruit-and-vegetable market. Maybe I shouldn't have told him that either, though. But when he started asking me about fancy things like wigs, and about facial make-up—remember this was Mister He-man talking—I thought I'd better remind him that I and my son were not millionaires yet. But, you know, Gwelo, I may have been misreading him—our minds may not have been meshing. Why would Quo Vadis, after I'd lent, or given him, really, the money he'd—very ashamed, humiliated—gotten up the courage to ask me for, why would he then, sort of incidentally, or like it was only an afterthought, ask about wigs, blond wigs, and also, I can't quite remember his exact words, some kind of thick, maybe light, or chalky, flesh coloration? Why?—if a woman weren't involved with him in some kind of idiotic brainstorm he was having? Quo Vadis is a strange man, Gwelo—it's hard, very hard, to tell where he's coming from. The only thing you can be sure about is the *he* thinks that he's doing good. Some might differ with him on that but *he* thinks he's doing God's will. And he hadn't been drinking—I'm sure of that. We've seen him drunk. This time, sober as a judge, he was mostly trying to laugh a little, but he'd have made a terrible actor. First, as I say, he was deeply humiliated—coming asking us for a handout, when only weeks before it had almost been the other way around. But he *wanted* that money—felt he needed it; that it was crucial . . . for some reason. Quo

City of Light

Vadis had worries that day, Gwelo—I can't bring myself to believe anything else. Well, whatever it was, I hope it comes out all right—for he's *very* religious."

"Quo Vadis is a great man, Ma-MAH," Gwelo said after drinking some milk. "He believes in the rights of man. What are the 'rights of man,' Ma-MAH? He told me this, though—one day when we were out walking—that every man and woman has certain rights and they should not be tampered with, except on pain of death. He said that. He believes it, too. *I* believe it also, Ma-MAH."

"Wouldn't it be wonderful," Tosca said, "if Paul had feelings like that—humane, uplifting feelings, caring for people. Quo Vadis tried to talk him into adopting a different outlook on life but I don't know if it ever made an impression. Paul is a strange man also—you must know by now. He doesn't like to talk about serious things much—unless it's about his deceased mother. Yet he figures definitely in our future—yours and mine—and we must keep him there. There's too much at stake—I'm talking about *your* future, Gwelo."

"Ma-MAH, I actually think talk like that is embarrassing. Don't you ever feel that way? It sounds like you'd do about *any*thing to boost my future. I don't want that, really. Besides, I don't absolutely know for sure what it is I want to do in life. I change from month to month. Yesterday, watching that great, beautiful parade, I wanted to be a general—remember I told you? Next week it will be something else. Don't—please don't—promise to do anything for anybody in my behalf. It's simply because you don't know yet (because *I* don't) what life holds for me. That's what Quo Vadis used to tell me—about life and death—quoting his old grandmother testifying in church, her saying: 'You don't know the day or the hour when the Son of Man approacheth.' I guess that's from the Bible somewhere, I don't know. So take it easy, Ma-MAH—don't overdo things."

364

Tosca was insulted. "You may try to *sound* like a grown man," she said, "but you're a long way from being one. Next minute here you'll be crying like a baby about something, anything, I might say that offends, or maybe scares you. Don't worry, I can handle myself all right. And I can handle you, too. I can even handle Paul—I think."

"Paul can never be a Quo Vadis," said Gwelo stubbornly, shaking his head.

To which Tosca, sighing, finally made no reply.

"I'd call Quo Vadis," Gwelo said, "but you said they cut off his telephone or something when he got fired from his job."

"They did. But we can take the Métro and go over there. He'd probably like that—I'm sure he hasn't gotten used to not having us around."

"Hey, let's do that!" Gwelo said.

An hour and a quarter later, when, on a clear, beautiful day, they had left the Métro and were approaching the Rue Val d'Or and the drab building housing Quo Vadis's flat, Gwelo somehow now became silent, pensive, perhaps reminiscent, too—until at last he said, "Suppose Quo Vadis is not home, Ma-MAH?"

"We'll just go in and wait for him—read some of his books."

Gwelo almost stopped in the street. "Have you still got the keys. How come?"

"He wouldn't take them back," Tosca said, "told me to keep them, that I might need them. I don't know what he meant by that."

"Ha!—he meant it for just some situation like this."

"We'll ring the bell first, though," said Tosca, prettier than ever as she continued walking slightly ahead of contemplative Gwelo—her customary long dress, red yet somehow multi-colored, the faithful African shibboleth she had self-pledged never to yield, plus her inevitable dreadlocks to the shoulders, all made her a fetching sight to see, oblivious, fleshly, sensual, and all, despite her would-be cold self, a petulant mystery to Paul Kessey. When, finally, they, mother and son, arrived at Quo Vadis's building, Tosca, Gwelo at her heels, entered the lobby and pressed the buzzer, ringing Quo Vadis's flat on the second floor. After some moments then and no response, she rang again — though with the same result. She turned to Gwelo and smiled — "You predicted it, dear. But I'll wait a moment and try again. If still nothing happens, out will come my keys." Her eyes twinkled.

Gwelo, as before, was somber, quiet, soon stone-faced, also making sure his eyes avoided hers.

Tosca pressed the button now, but, as if expecting no answer, went in her purse and, brought out her set of Quo Vadis's keys. "Let's go up," she said peremptorily, herself now, though, earnest, even if stoical; maybe also concerned. Almost at once she unlocked the lower door to the stairs, and they were soon ascending the dark, dour steps they both knew so well. Neither was talking now. Soon letting them in the familiar flat, Tosca, remembering all, swallowed hard — though they did not, tears could have come easily. Gwelo, still refusing to look at her, hurried to the kitchen at once. "He didn't even eat breakfast," he decreed, as if blaming his mother. "He's not here." He ran to Quo Vadis's bedroom. "The bed's not made but that doesn't mean anything — he seldom ever made his bed. He's not here — he hasn't *been* here."

"Gwelo, will you please shut up and calm down!" cried Tosca. "You don't know whether he's been here or not. But suppose he hasn't — so what? You're eleven years old, but you act like a six-year-old. Let's go back to the living room, sit down, and catch our breaths. Then we'll go bring some of Quo Vadis's books out of his bedroom and read and talk until he comes. Now quiet down."

Cyrus Colter

Two hours later, near 1:30, Gwelo was fast asleep on the stale old living-room sofa, as Tosca, sitting in a chair, was reading a book authored, it said, by a prominent Australian sheep farmer named Cooker Drusilla. Its title: *Man's Responsibility to Man.* She had found the book among many others stacked on Quo Vadis's bedroom floor and had chosen it primarily because of the thoroughly, almost cruelly, marked-up pages by Quo Vadis indulging in his frequent arguments, hot disputes, with Drusilla's theories on the subject of what persons are entitled to what responsibilities and from whom, depending on one's wealth, or lack of it; and the length of time, the span, of one's need for gratuities; that some would-be recipients were entitled to more generous consideration depending on his/her ability and the likelihood of the help to improve the person's life to the extent that no further assistance is indicated or even desired. "No, no, no," Quo Vadis had angrily scrawled in the margins. "Even these borderline cases should be suspect, put to the bottom of the list; their needs are actually minimal, if worthy at all. The ideal recipient is one who, by birth, environment, heredity, what have you, hasn't had a chance in life, and *never will* have a chance— never, never, never! It's been ordained that way. So why shouldn't we be willing to contribute to even one day's, or night's, pleasure, say, to some poor man, woman, or child, whose life since birth has *without letup*, been a living hell! But you, you cruel man, who has the gall to write books, more than one book even, would never give a quarter, much less a dollar, to such an unfortunate person, on the grounds that the first thing he/she would do was run in a saloon and buy a drink. *Of course* that's what he'd do, God help him, if he's got any sense, for when he gets sober it'll be the same old grind again, until his number is up, and he wins a highly deserved death in hell. My God, Mr. Author, have you no compassion, mercy, to advocate better things in your beautifully published and expensive books? Be assured, though, I paid not a nickel for this sad book — I filched it from a bookstore." Tosca, reading, was far more impressed by the various pages, page edges, footnote spaces, as well as those across the tops of pages, that Quo Vadis had put to service in recording his blistering diatribes against author Drusilla's way of jump-starting proven, worthy beneficiaries but no others, so that she, Tosca, soon found herself taking no sides on either position. Yet her heart overflowed with admiration and affection for Quo Vadis, remembering that she herself and her son, though mercifully not among those written-off people Quo Vadis so pitied and defended, had nonetheless benefited from his selflessness and good works. No matter, she put the book aside, looked around her, yawned, then glanced in Gwelo's direction. He was watching her. She did not know for how long. He sat up now. "I feel funny," he said. "Did somebody knock?"

"No, dear," Tosca said. "You were dreaming."

"Let's go," Gwelo said. "Quo Vadis is not coming."

It was at this moment that the erratic bell from the vestibule sounded in the room. "There he is," Tosca said excitedly, jumping up to go answer.

"Why would he be ringing the bell — he's got keys." Gwelo, too, though, was standing in the middle of the floor now.

Tosca was talking loudly into the speaker. "Hello? . . . Hello — is that you, Quo Vadis?"

"I'm *looking* for Quo Vadis." It was a woman. "Where is he?"

"We don't know," Tosca said. "We've been waiting on him for some time. Have you seen him?"

"No. Who're you?"

Tosca hesitated to answer. "Will you tell me who you are?" she finally said.

"I'll bet I know who you are, all right," the woman said. "You lived there, with your son, for a while. I ought to know — I was living there myself until he put me out to make room for you two. Your name is Tosca. Well, if Quo Vadis is not there, there's no use for me to come up. If he comes, tell him to call Canary. He's going to move in with me when they put him out of there — which won't be long. Yet I probably won't put him out like he did me."

Tosca was stuttering. "Will you . . . will you come up and talk to my son and me? We're concerned about Quo Vadis. We're not sure he was even here last night. When did you last see him? Will you come up?"

"Remember, Tosca, I don't have a set of keys like you have. You'll have to buzz me up if you want me."

"Sure — I'll do it right away." Tosca did.

Gwelo had been standing so closely beside her she felt she would lose her balance. "Who's that?" he demanded.

"Some woman Quo Vadis knows — she's coming up."

"For what?" Gwelo said.

Tosca turned on him. "You go back over there and sit down! I don't want to hear a peep out of you. We're trying to learn what we can about Quo Vadis. If he didn't come home last night, maybe he stayed at her house. I want to talk to her."

Canary was already knocking.

But when Gwelo saw how actually frightened his mother was on her way to the door, he jumped to accompany her — "Here, Ma-MAH, let me open it."

But Tosca's hand was already on the doorknob and she was speaking, her voice, though, a hollow tremolo. "Canary, is there anyone with you?"

"Of course not," replied irritated Canary. "Who besides your son is with *you*?"

"Nobody!" yelled Gwelo fiercely.

City of Light

"Oh, no one," echoed Tosca, already opening the door and astonished to see that Canary was hardly taller than Gwelo, conforming to how the few people in Paris who knew her described her — as a "midget," for she weighed scarcely a hundred pounds. Also the deep brown of her somehow plump face was not so pronounced as to overshadow the few freckles scattered across her cheeks.

"Hello," said Tosca, smiling and still speaking French as was Canary. "Won't you come in?"

Canary, none too pleasantly sizing her up, finally stepped in — not unaware, however, this was the woman, even if herself innocent, who only months ago figured in her, Canary's, polite ouster from this same dingy flat. "This is my son, Gwelo." Whereupon Canary and Gwelo grunted at each other. "Please sit down," Tosca said. "I'm so glad you happened to come while we're here. We've been waiting and hoping Quo Vadis would come home. Have you seen him, or do you know where he might be?"

Canary had sat down and was taking out a cigarette. "He was by my place day before yesterday — looking, he said, for some big safety pins, also tan shoe polish."

Tosca frowned helplessly. "What did he want with those?"

"I haven't the slightest idea," said Canary, lighting the cigarette then, talking, letting it go out. "I asked him that — what was going on. He said it was none of my business — he laughed a little, but I didn't like the laugh. Quo Vadis has changed quite a bit, to tell you the truth. He used to be nicer, politer — when he was more religious. He took religion very seriously — prayed a lot; thought in the end God was maybe going to fix everything up. Then you brought that guy, Paul somebody, by his place here and after dinner those two still sat at the table way into the night, Quo Vadis told me, bragging. But that long talk that night I don't think helped anybody. He

called Paul two or three times afterward, trying — you know
Quo Vadis — to get him to take his life more seriously; that is,
according to the way Quo Vadis would think it was more
serious, which of course finally got around to God and religion. He quizzed Paul into telling him about a little guy Paul
knew, an African, a Zulu, who is in the hospital dying of
AIDS. Oh, Lord — Quo Vadis, the do-gooder, naturally, got
interested right away. Honest to God, you'd think Quo Vadis's
life itself was pure as the driven snow, but I gotta tell you it's
not. He's a great guy, he wants to do the right thing, but he's no
saint — I can tell you that. Well, anyhow, what does he do after
hearing about this poor guy in the hospital dying of AIDS?
Why, he starts getting all the information, background, on the
little fellow — named Ari . . ."

"We've heard about him," said Gwelo, unenthralled. "He
studied at the Sorbonne — for a hot minute."

"Let Canary talk, Gwelo," scolded Tosca.

"Well, your son really put his finger on it, though," Canary
conceded to Tosca. "The smart little guy who was also a journalist for certain African causes, did go to that university here, the
Sorbonne — but for way more than any 'hot minute.' Still it would
have been better, for Quo Vadis, if little Ari had never heard of
the Sorbonne. But that's life. They don't believe in nothing over
there at that place, you know — including God. They say, 'Who's
God?' Well, apparently by the time Ari left, though — far short of
graduation, it's true — he had learned plenty, I'll tell you. Too
much. If you don't believe it, ask Quo Vadis. Wow. Quo Vadis,
the protector of mankind, the righteous sinner, had heard, I
guess from Paul, that little Ari "didn't believe in God" — but
nevertheless was getting ready to die. And he, Quo Vadis, was
thunderstruck; rolled and tossed for nights. So in less than a
week's time, unknown to Paul, he paid an uninvited visit to the
little Zulu in Lady of Paradise Hospital. Wow. Strong stuff.

City of Light

When Ari saw his visitor he didn't know what to make of Quo Vadis — he looked like a black mountain, which he is, but still without a lot of fat. Ari laid there and listened to him for a while — trying to figure him out, find out why he'd come. Finally Quo Vadis told him why — that he'd come to introduce him to the Almighty Living God. At once Ari raised his withered right hand in a signal of grave offense. 'I don't care to discuss that — it's a private matter,' Ari said. 'It was kind of you to come but this is all the time I can give you.' Ari had put up one hand but now Quo Vadis threw up both of his giant paws and began to plead, also advise. 'But, oh sir,' said Quo Vadis, 'you may soon — God forbid — be called upon to meet your maker. But you're unprepared. I merely ask you, before it's too late, to acknowledge Christ as your savior and thus save yourself from those awful, those blistering and searing, the eternal roaring fires of hell!'"

Gwelo tittered.

"'But it's not at all too late for you to be saved,' Quo Vadis told him. 'Merely confess Christ, through God, to be your rescuer, your redeemer.' Quo Vadis said he'd never in his life seen anyone react like little Ari did then, all the time struggling to pull himself up in the bed to a sitting position. But when he finally had managed this he started cursing to high heaven, using all kinds of the worst, violent, dirtiest, most vulgar language there is. 'You are the biggest, blackest man I have ever seen in my whole life. I myself am as black as you but I am small. But don't you know that both of us were put here for one purpose only and that is to fulfill the black role of helplessness; to be kicked around by any white man coming along; our women, too! There is no race in the annals of history that's been made to suffer as we have! None. Soon I'll finally be beyond all that, though. I am glad — not sorry at all. You talk to me about hell's fire. Well, I've had fifty-one years

372

of it already. Then you come in here lecturing me as if I'm a child—a dying child at that. Of course I'm dying—I'd have been gone long before this if I'd had my way. You speak of God, like He was at the newsstand just around the corner. But there's no such entity—not even up there in the clouds. Do you hear me? *There is no God!*—you big ignorant son-of-a-bitch! Even if there was, it's surely been proved often enough that He wouldn't give a f . . . about either one of us. I hope the time comes in your life when this is proved to you in no uncertain terms—when you get left in the lurch, high and dry, by your great God. You'll know then what I'm talking about. God, even if He did exist is not for us. But we don't have to worry about that—for to us He's not worth a s . . .!' Oh, the foul language he used, Tosca, was dreadful. I wouldn't dare repeat it here in front of your son."

An uneasy, bewildered silence ensued.

"Quo Vadis, though," Canary finally said, "even looked scared when he was telling me how he turned and ran right out of the hospital; that when he was going down in the elevator he could still hear Ari ranting and raving, maybe at the doctors and nurses this time. It's a little comical when you think about it, but Quo Vadis, though he don't always know it—because he's so serious about his beliefs—he can be very funny to be such a good guy. So he got a heck of a scare from poor little Ari. Ah, but think about what it was that he was so scared *of*. It wasn't all Ari. It was that he now began wondering if Ari could have been right, or even half right, about what he said about God and blacks. This really started worrying him. If he didn't have God standing behind him, supporting him in all these big deals he had on his agenda, like the protection and uplift of poor people's lives, especially blacks—plus the other side of that coin which meant practically crucifying the awful crooks and hyenas sucking the blood of the unfortunate people unable to

defend themselves (how many times have I heard these charges
out of Quo Vadis's mouth!) — if he didn't have God backing him
in all these things, yes, there was no way he could feel comfortable, to say the least, in all these undertakings. No way. He'd
even tried to get Paul interested in all these out-of-sight ideas
and plans he was making. So if there was no longer any God in
the picture, what was he going to do about all these things on the
drawing board he and God had been working on? How could he
function? How could he even *try*, without God's backing?
Take the Caen situation — all over now. He had made very
serious preparations to go to Caen and try to hear, actually
take a hard look at, those crazy FFF people who're out to drive
all non-Frenchmen, especially blacks, out of France. Apparently, though, something had happened to him — he'd lost his
nerve, begun to start finding excuses, got cold feet. But when
he came to realize this, it really upset him, sent him into deep
misery — almost like the blues. Even I could see it — it was that
plain. Here's what had upset him, though: that he, of all
people, since talking to that dying little Zulu — who, by the
way, I hear is not dead *yet* — had begun to lose his faith in God.
This was the really bad part — God had meant everything to
Quo Vadis, even if the big guy had gone on sinning a lot; and
always will — you hear me? — as long as he's alive. Yet God was
real for him just the same. You know, it's not always what
we're successful in doing, but what we really want to do, even
though we fail a lot at it. I always have to think of myself, my
own life, for instance — all the troubles and close calls I've
had — that if . . ."

"What is your field?" asked Gwelo.

"Gwelo!" exploded Tosca.

"Let him talk," said Canary. "He can learn a lot from me.
But if I didn't have God to talk to, consult with, about some of
the pinheaded things I do, or try to do, I couldn't make it in

this life. This, you see, is Quo Vadis's real problem. He got to thinking about this little screaming dying Zulu sissy up there in the hospital — on the very *edge* of death — and still calling not only Quo Vadis all those awful, those filthy, names, but God Himself! Wow. That takes a *lot* of nerve. Quo Vadis realized this, and it floored him. He began to wonder then if this little guy, no bigger than a minute, and on his way shortly to a sure death (between you folks and me — I don't think Quo Vadis necessarily much likes the idea of death, you know) he began, as I say, to wonder if Ari didn't know some things *he* didn't know; that he, Quo Vadis, had maybe been wasting his time, and also trust, on God. That was when he began to mope, stay to himself a lot, read those damn big books he's got in there — wondering what he should do. He apparently had a crisis on his hands right there — or thought he had. Or then it may have been that he had some really crazy, maybe even dangerous, things planned — all in the name of God, for God's Own glory, as we say — that Quo Vadis was depending on God to be kind of looking over his shoulder, helping him to figure out everything: things like how to keep your thinking cap on; protect against failing and going down like the Titanic; dying; in other words, things like that. Who knows? But if it turned out that he now no longer had the faith and confidence in God like he once had, even until recently, before he made the blunder of going to see balmy, raving, little Ari, if he felt differently now, less sure of himself, even less sure of God, than he'd been when beginning to make his plans originally, that could have started the downhill problems, worries, for him. He's worrying, you hear me? You can see for yourself. I think Quo Vadis is in some kind of bind, if you ask me. . . ."

The doorbell rang. Canary and Tosca jumped to their feet, both using almost identical words: "Oh, my God, it's Quo Vadis!"

"Why would he ring?" said Gwelo for the second time. "He's got keys."

But Canary and Tosca had already run to the door and thrown it wide. "Quo Vadis, Quo Vadis! . . .is it you!?"

A man's voice came up. "I have a package for Claude Conde."

The two women, simultaneously, groaned.

Gwelo, now on the scene, called down — "You want the *third* floor" — and closed the door.

The three of them returned to their seats and, saying little, if anything, waited until inevitable darkness approached — when it, and hunger, sent them off then, finally, to their respective homes and agonies.

Friday following.

He had called her at the hospital — which was strange; something he had almost never done. She was in her little cubbyhole of an office going through the usual patient documents and earlier hurried notes to herself. The day was sunny and hot, the air conditioning cold, too cold, so she wore a white sweater. What she had most noticed about Georges's voice had been its dry, grating quality. It was not unpleasant, only slightly alien; not palpably nervous, yet somehow husky and unready; strange in its hesitation. Nor was there the slightest hint of levity.

"He knows," Cécile told herself. "He may even know that I know he knows. He knows," she repeated, and with her right hand went rummaging down in a bottom drawer for a niggerine, something she had not touched in over a fortnight. Her weight was almost normal now, and once more she bordered on the beautiful. But why did Georges want them to drive up to their country place — sans the children! — for a whole weekend? Didn't he know that his daughter Michelle, in her anger for being left out would tear the Paris apartment asunder. And that sweet little Zoe would cry her eyes out? "But he knows," encored Cécile. "Indeed, even poor little Ari had seemed to sense something if only by the process of trance, or somnambulism. Her erstwhile patient—whom, remorsefully, she had been in to see this very morning—had at one earlier point dissolved her in tears about her suspected, or at least intuited, tragedy. But she had forgiven him. Now her husband wanted to take her up in the country—possibly to *murder* her? She did not laugh, though she told herself she should have, she merely shuddered. Should she go, without the children, to the country with Georges? She had put him off, told him she would let him know. The reason? She first wanted to consult yet another erstwhile patient—his name, Paul Kessey. She reached down again, took the niggerines, including the one she had not yet put in her mouth, and threw them all in the wastebasket—though having doubts about this inept symbolism. Then, however, she called Madame Chevalley and invited herself to dinner at Madame's that evening—*if*, that is, Madame could produce her tenant Paul, whereupon Cécile would furnish the food and wine, have them sent over at once. Madame was so stunned, unbelieving, excited, and moved that she wept outright over the telephone. Indeed Cécile herself was almost moved to tears. For so many things—slights, insults, ice water thrown in faces, temporary threats, selfishness—seemed somehow to have been forgotten on all sides. Old friends, even erstwhile lovers, would convene. Nothing more, nothing less.

She therefore went home and telephoned the food and wine orders that were to go to Madame's, then leisurely bathed, took a short bed rest, and proceeded to dress as if she were going to a gala party. Her daughters, especially Michelle, were both excited and curious, Michelle also envious as she asked why her mother had dressed as she had, merely to go to dinner at

City of Light

Madame Chevalley's. Georges, arriving almost as Cécile was leaving, may have been the only one in a position to answer that question. He, of course, even if able, made no such effort. He still, however, had the dry, alien throat when he talked and was otherwise indecipherable. Cécile felt strange, nor under the circumstances free of fright certainly, yet, more than anything, aware, paradoxically, of a deep sense of exhilaration—all as she waited for the garage man to fetch her pretty car.

But then when she was finally outside and, in an almost girlish excitement of expectancy, had pulled away from the curb, another car, a new, small, black Mazda, parked three spaces to the rear, its lone occupant, a heavy man wearing a cap, steering with his right hand and with his left already reporting to someone on his cellular mobile telephone, pulled away behind her, though carefully keeping his distance. Cecile, however, unmindful in her perfect ebullience and hedonism, had been busy turning on her car radio. The music happened to be vocal excerpts from *Carmen*.

Earlier, across town at the pension, Madame's sudden awareness and happy dither—resulting from Cécile's astounding phone call—while arousing Madame's enthusiasm, alas did little to make her forget her fragile health, a fact Madame had sought to hide by having cried out upstairs to Paul that Cécile was coming to dinner this evening, and, as Madame put it, to see *him*. It was Cécile's price, had laughed Madame, of underwriting the night's festivities.

Yet what did she want, or what were her most inner motives, if any, wondered Paul. No matter, he was elated—even though he speculated now in retrospect, whether he shouldn't have played harder to get, told Madame he was unavailable this evening, had another engagement, or something, anything. He also knew, though, Madame would have known he was lying, that he wanted more than anything to be present, otherwise Madame would have held it against him almost for life. Therefore, realistically, he knew he could only be sensible and cooperate.

But after the passing of an hour it became evident to him that Madame was turning out to be a possible problem. She was not only already in a high state of nerves but was acting crazily in other ways. He could hear her fussing to herself about how little she had to wear. He partially attributed this to Cécile's often strange effect on others. Here was vintage Cécile, all right, displaying another of her peculiar ways, her unpredictabilities; also the consequent tensions for everybody connected with her, tensions, however, no one had quite successfully analyzed. She was therefore, to all, an enigma. These were Paul's then-present thoughts. Up in his rooms, having just showered, and now shaving, Paul could not avoid still trying to figure out a future inconceivable to him, though one which certainly included him, together with the so many immediate issues also presently puzzling to him; all this as he now stood viewing his moody, lathered face in the mirror.

Nor in this unyielding context could he possibly avoid thinking of Tosca. Poor Tosca and her problems. Was it these, actually, which had most fazed him? He had never had this exact feeling for Cécile—but how could he have had, with their lives so different, he scolded himself. For him, he bravely, also forthrightly, told himself—for him, yes—both these women were utter dead ends. In Cécile's case, in fact, considering the attendant danger, he was all too well aware the term, dead end, could carry literal connotations for both him and her. On the other hand—Tosca. Her personal problems, yes. The money exigencies, her son's scholastic future, and, of all things (he shuddered), her appalling, otherworldly, abhorrence of personal sexual intercourse! He shivered. Both these women, yes, presented problems—ah, to say nothing of himself, his poor self. Yet Cécile, with no intentions whatever, was sincere, credulous, and exciting. Also pitiful. Also he adored her — in his way. This, however, was by no means *love*. Of this he was sure. For he *knew* love. What, then, of Tosca? She, he knew, was just as complicated, also of equal integrity to Cécile — but possessed inspired brains and a graceful intellect. No matter, neither of these most extraordinary women could ever hope to tilt his sickened soul as had his Queen of Heaven. Paul stared in the mirror and, thinking of Saturn, yet swallowed his tears. It was no revelation at all — he, yes, was truly her first, last, and only "child," he told himself. He wondered, though, what this really meant, even if he felt he would never know. He only knew she was the Queen — the Queen of his soul.

As Paul put his shaving materials away and brushed his teeth, he suddenly became aware he would have to help Madame prepare the dinner — salmon and shrimps, however, would not be difficult, at least not beyond attainment — and he could readily do much of it by merely following her instructions. Moreover, the grocery and wine merchants had already delivered their merchandise, so he excitedly looked forward to seeing dear Cécile in a setting of good food, good wine, and friendly, hospitable surroundings. Besides, in such a cordial, talkative environment he and Madame might well learn from serious Cécile what had *really* happened to her during her hectic absence. Nor would there be the curse of a monstrous hospital to turn everybody into ferocious dolts. He somehow felt actually blissful now. He also soon recognized how he badly wished for, and needed a drink. He tried then, though, to take his mind away from it. He donned his jacket and went downstairs looking for Madame. He found her, alas, not only already in a state of nerves but acting crazily again even if in other ways. It suddenly then came to Paul that she had been drinking. She soon confessed she had placed the half-case of Domaine de

Cyrus Colter

Grandmaison Cécile had sent in the "cooler," and had shortly before drunk half of a bottle. Then she laughed, rather foolishly, Paul thought—before he himself went and took charge of the remainder of Madame's bottle. Soon he too was in a much lighter mood—including now one of an intense expectancy. When would Cécile arrive, he pestered himself, as he sat nervously on a high kitchen stool and sipped the lovely white wine between great, nervous smiles.

"Why is it, Paul," asked Madame, "that we are acting like children?"

"I think it's because Cécile is coming," Paul said, laughing, then finishing off his glass held it aloft. "Hip, hip, hooray!" he cried.

Madame, however, had somehow become grave. "Why is it, though," she asked, "that she thought up this idea of coming? What happened, Paul?"

He looked at her intently while searching his mind. It was then that the doorbell rang. He laughed hilariously—"Hey, let's ask *her*!" Just then, however, his telephone upstairs also rang. He stood, confused.

"Go ahead," Madame said. "I'll get the door."

He left and went upstairs as Madame went up front. When he finally said hello into his bedroom telephone the easily recognized voice answering surprised him. It was Tosca. "Oh," he said.

"Hello . . . Paul? Is that you? This is Tosca."

"I know it. How are you, Tosca dear?"

"Oh, Paul, I don't know! Have you seen a newspaper?"

"No."

"I got a call today from a woman I met only very recently—a friend of Quo Vadis's named Canary. She says *Le Figaro* carried a story this morning that a tremendously huge black man, a giant, was found horribly beaten and knifed to death, disfigured terribly, and all probably before he died, tortured for days, yes, no doubt, then dumped in a dark alley way over in the Lyonnais district. The police are looking for help in identifying him and getting any clues."

"Jesus, that sounds bad," Paul said. "How are you involved, though, Tosca?"

"Gwelo and I think Quo Vadis hasn't been in his flat for days. This woman, Canary, thinks the same thing—she was probably seeing a lot of him at one time, living with him even; she almost said it. Gwelo and I are worried sick. So I thought you might be willing to come with us—look at the body in the morgue and see if might be Quo Vadis. I don't tell Gwelo, but actually I fear for the worst. *Figaro* said he may have been trying to pass for a white man—wearing a lot of crazy stuff, a blond wig, for instance, and painting his face and neck white. Oh, heavens, Paul—this is terrible. Could you please come go with us? I know I've called you on short notice. You might be busy. I'm sorry, of course. I'll just have to go, then, I guess, and take Gwelo along, for it will very soon be getting dark, and see for myself, if possible, what has happened."

Paul tried to appear cool and judicious but he was neither. "My problem, Tosca," he said, "is that I'm not free this evening. It's a dinner, and I've got to help prepare it. The person of the house is an elderly lady—also not very well—and I've got to help her."

"Yes, I see," said Tosca, "that must be your landlady, Mrs. Madame. Of course you couldn't leave under those circumstances. I'm sorry to have had to disturb you like this. I have a duty here, though—I'm sure you can see that. And Gwelo is very upset—Quo Vadis was almost a father figure to him, so I've had no alternative. Excuse me, now—I must go."

Paul, completely cornered by her skill and mastery, began rubbing his jaw with his free hand and trying to figure out a way at least to backtrack. "No, no, Tosca," he finally said, "you and Gwelo stay put tonight, at home right where you are—I have your new phone number—and let me try some things. A guest coming to dinner tonight is a physician, one of wide experience, who must know many of the people, police, coroners, and other officials, who are undoubtedly involved in all this. I'll ask her to advise us; maybe later on tonight she might go with me to the police and the morgue, I don't know. I can't guarantee this, but I can talk to her."

"Thank you, Paul—she must be the alluring, eye-filling lady who was your doctor at the hospital that day when Gwelo and I came to see you."

Paul hesitated. "Yes, Tosca, you're right," he said. "Dr. Fournier. It will really be a tragedy if this turns out to have been Quo Vadis—he came to see me recently, a dynamic guy, with a great heart. But I'll call you later tonight; try not to worry. It may turn out that it wasn't Quo Vadis at all."

"Good night, Paul. Thank you so much."

Paul returned downstairs to find Cécile in the kitchen conferring with Madame about the stove. "Oh, hello, Paul," she said when he entered and extended her hand which he took with both of his. "You're to be my second-cook tonight, Madame says. Where is your apron?" Everyone laughed, though Paul was worried, thinking of Quo Vadis. Yet he had seldom seen Cécile so beautiful although her weight had not quite yet returned to normalcy. "You look beautiful tonight, as always," he said.

Madame, laughing, stepped between them. "Paul, Paul, go open some wine! Let's drink to the prodigal daughter. Oh, it's so good to have you back, Cécile. Hurry, Paul!"

"Let's do the food!" laughed Cécile. "I'm starved. May I have an apron, Madame?"

Paul was already back with a chilled bottle of Cécile's Domaine de Grandmaison, which he served all around. "Ah, how my dear father loved this wine," Madame said. "My toast to you all is: 'Joy to the world!' And it doesn't have to be Christmas." They drank.

Paul's toast, next, was to Cécile. There was slight sadness in his tone. "To a great lady."

"Why are you sad, Paul?" said Madame.

"Oh, he's not sad, Madame," said Cécile. "He's just serious. I love that. I am serious, too. Now, let's cook before I keel over."

"Oh, thank you, Cécile," said Madame, "for undertaking these chores. I'm a terrible cook, always have been. I'll go up front and put on a record for you, Cécile dear, and turn the volume up so that you can hear."

"You haven't asked me, though, Madame, what I'd like to hear," Cécile said, as Paul tied on her frilly apron for her.

"I don't have to ask you, dear," said Madame. "I know. Cole Porter."

"Oh, bless you," cried Cécile, but gluing her eyes on the open oven so that they would not forget the main chore.

Paul, looking far away, as if instead of in a kitchen, they were all out on some vast rolling meadow in the month of May, drew more censure from Madame. "Paul, my friend, this is no funeral. *Cécile* is here."

Cécile turned gently to her though speaking in almost the desperate tone of a plea: "Madame dear, he may not feel like laughing, or even smiling, tonight. Isn't that a prerogative we all have? Then let us make the most of it. Please go put on the Cole Porter — that may liven us up." Cécile laughed. Paul was still mooning at his great May meadow.

Dinner was a great success. Paul had drunk more than his share of the wine and likewise was now doing more than his share of the laughing. Cécile, her pretty face somehow starkly drawn, would not let her sorrowful eyes go near him and talked exclusively to her loving friend Madame.

Cyrus Colter

Madame, now sober as a judge by her wary choice, missing not a pinpoint of the drama, or whatever was presently taking place in her dining room, elected to engage Cécile in conversation about Cécile's experience with her second cousins, also the niggerines, and the FFF generally. "Cécile dear," said Madame, "please tell us what you can, or feel like telling us, about all that's happened to you since we were all last together. Are you a French fascist?"

Cécile was cool, undisturbed. She showed not a whit of reluctance to talk. "Of course I'm not—I'm not any kind of fascist. I am very pro-French, though. That's, then, how all this furor got started. Actually, it goes back to my dear departed mother, a wonderful, sweet woman, and what she told my sisters and me about the great war, ending in 1945, against Hitler and the Germans. Mother had learned many things about that war, but, alas, not until it was all over and the truth began to come out. The dear woman never recovered from what she learned. But my father, a most decent man, had known all along what was happening. He couldn't have done anything about it, though. Part of the time he was a French soldier, an officer, and later a German prisoner of war. Among what was happening under the Nazi occupation here were the terrible atrocities that were being committed against French Jewish children, kids right here in Paris, for instance, and by the Paris police. Remember, too, that I myself have two sweet children at home in bed right now. But those French children, who happened to be of the Jewish faith, were herded into stinking trains, even boxcars, and sent to the death camps in Germany and elsewhere. Herded not by the Germans, though, but by the French, the Vichy French police. Of course the children were never heard from again. This catastrophe was never discussed in our house after the war—and had certainly not been before. I wasn't even born. I knew that my father's sister-in-law, Aunt Lili, had been a hardliner during the war. But she suffered the penalty — her husband was shot by a French firing squad after the war. But we all somehow felt sorry for her — I myself and my sisters were taught to be compassionate, though in that situation it was highly questionable. The two second cousins were something else — they turned out to be almost criminals — but not before I, in those terrible weeks not long passed, told them, in the most unguarded moments of my sheltered life, things they should never have known." Cécile hurriedly, swiftly, glanced at Paul then let her eyes dive to the tablecloth.

"Oh, heavens," said Madame softly, "Poor, poor, Cécile."

"As a consequence I then began to rethink what loyalty to one's country meant — when it was laudable, when it was not. That's when I left the fellowship of people like the second cousins — to whose company, anyway, I had been largely driven by the most terrible, nasty, appalling, horrible dreams any woman ever had on earth. Yet it all changed me, retaught me, showed me what it should be like to be a human being on this earth, this planet — and that, above all, we *are*, every one of us, human beings and should treat one another accordingly. I returned to my family then, to my dear children, much the better, I hope, for the unhinging experience I'd had."

"Ah, bless you, dear," said Madame in almost a whisper, or a prayer. Paul looked across the table at Cécile proudly, fondly.

Now Madame began to stutter. " . . . Cécile dear," she finally said, "could you now tell us about the niggerines. I, for one, never understood the role they were meant to play. Would you, then, please . . ."

Upstairs Paul's telephone was ringing again. He stood, almost as if aroused from a dream, and finally said, "Excuse me, please," then hurried upstairs.

Cyrus Colter

He had feared the worst even before picking up the telephone. It was indeed Tosca again, now in tears. "Oh, my God, Paul! . . ." she said. "It *was* Quo Vadis! It's horrible! I still can hardly believe it. Canary just now called me. She had taken it on herself to go to the police and tell them she might have known the big dead black man written about in the newspapers. The police picked her up right away and took her to the morgue. Apparently, according to them, some of the FFF thugs had kidnapped him as he left their big meeting at the old opera house that day, having finally recognized him as a black man and therefore an interloper, and taken him to what turned out to be a makeshift torture chamber. This must have been a terrible thing for Canary to learn, and even more so when in the morgue she saw that pile, that great hulk, of bloody flesh lying there on the tilted slab. The police said the torture by the murderers was probably to get him to talk, reveal information they thought he might have and that they wanted—apparently they weren't looking for money. So the police think he may have refused, and that's when the torture was resorted to. It went on day and night, until his strong, massive body gave way and he finally died. Most of his teeth were gone by this time, his left leg had suffered a massive compound fracture that they said must have produced a bucket of blood. And, strangely, Canary said, there's some white paint still on his face and neck that the police think could maybe have been an attempt by him, yes, to pass for white. At the end, his body must have been a fright to see. I think I said most of his teeth were broken up, and an eye had been put out. Finally the savages, white savages, took his vast, punctured body and dumped it in a dark back alley. Canary said, though, that the mutilation was so great that it was only Quo Vadis's pitch-black color, and the bulllike structure of his body, that made her so sure, even early on, that it was he. Then she confessed to something else that, even had these other

387

signs failed, would have assured her beyond any doubt that it was Quo Vadis. She gave in and confided to me what we had suspected, even known, all along, that she had been his mistress during a couple of periods in their lives, had lived with him. So, finally crying, she admitted that the absolutely sure bit of evidence, that had put an end to any possible doubts she still might have had, had been the frightening sight of Quo Vadis's great, long, huge penis. She said after this there could never have been any uncertainty in her mind. So before she left the morgue to be taken home she gave the police my name, too, with Gwelo's, and our address and phone number. I was glad to hear this, though, for Gwelo and I of course would be glad to do anything we could to assist the police by telling them all we know about Quo Vadis in both good times and bad. It also just occurred to me that I must make sure to give the police your name and number, Paul. You can be at least of some help to them—for you and Quo Vadis, while not longtime friends, had had some deep talks, as I've reminded you; and I'm sure you had your own slant on him and what he wanted to do with his life, also what and whom he disliked or even hated. There's also the matter of who is going to claim his body, when the police see fit to release it, and arrange for his burial; also for the notification of kin, if any; he said he had a wife, you know; a woman named Glade, if I remember correctly. Also, what about his books still in that old flat where we lived and which makes me shudder to think about. But there's the problem of burial too, Paul. What shall we do about that?"

Paul seemed drained, tired, and thinking about what was taking place downstairs. Where should he be—here or down there? Where, though, did he want to be? he asked himself. He knew what Saturn's fiat would be on that. Downstairs in a hurry. And Cécile looked so heavenly tonight—no wonder; in better times her husband was said to have boasted she was the most beautiful woman in Paris. Paul also wanted now to go back downstairs — even if Cécile might still be talking about, explaining, her niggerines. But he heard Tosca talking: "What do you think, Paul? — about Quo Vadis's burial?"

"No burial, Tosca dear," Paul admonished. "Cremation."

"Oh, Paul — I've somehow never liked the idea of cremation. It's so final."

"It's the death that's final, Tosca. Don't confuse it with burial in the ground, which is mostly froth and trivia, though doing the deceased — it's thought — a favor, when actually you're merely consigning him or her to rotting."

It brought a pause from Tosca. Then he could almost hear her sigh. "Well," she said, "I'll let you go now, return to Madame Chevalley and Dr. Fournier. You of course now won't have to ask the favor, which you originally had in mind, of Dr. Fournier — that is, to go with you to the police." Then he could hear her sniveling in the phone. "Oh, poor Quo Vadis! . . . I feel so terrible," she said. "So does Gwelo. We know the horrible truth at last! . . . Oh, that fine man! Good night, Paul."

"Good night, Tosca." He hung up and hurried back downstairs. Discussion of the niggerines, if it had taken place at all, was now concluded, and Madame, who had resumed her wine drinking, was now babbling to Cécile about winners of the current motorbike races. Cécile, though, quiet, pensive, somber, was veritably drilling him with her eyes. Madame, swaying slightly, asked, very seriously, of Paul, "Do you know of this young guy, from down in Avignon, who seems to be winning all the races, practically *all* of them — his name Chiappe? He's a real daredevil — people are crazy about him, his bravura, the defiance. He merely shrugs and gets out another cigarette, laughing that cigarettes will get him first. He's defiant, yes!" Madame was swaying again — she herself defiantly. Paul sat down beside musing, reflective Cécile as he smiled somewhat condescendingly at Madame, whose chin now, however, was often on her chest.

Meanwhile Paul was inquiring of Cécile about her daughters. "How sad," he whispered, "that I have seen neither of them, ever. You know this, of course."

Cécile first glanced at sleeping Madame before laughing, "I'm afraid Michelle might view you with some superciliousness — that's her thing, you know, bless her heart. But little Zoe would literally *adore* you."

Madame opened an eye. "Say, who's adoring whom in this village?" she laughed. "I'm sleepy as hell but just hate to go to bed — because I've had such a perfectly idyllic evening, thanks to you, Cécile my dear. And you of course, Paul. If before I leave you two I were to go in the kitchen and brew you a pot of de café, would that then bring me your kind permission to retire for the night? Damn it, must I tell you my age first?" She struggled with her laugh. "But you folks can still sit here and gab as long as you like, with Paul's only chore being Cécile; that is, to walk her to her car when you've talked to each other to your hearts' content."

Cécile seemed pleased. "Assuming Paul agrees," she said, "I say fair enough!" She laughed. "And into the bargain I shall make the coffee."

Madame, tired but smiling, proud, came around the table, kissed Cécile, patted Paul on the shoulder, then continued down the hall to her room, undressed, and went to bed at near 11:20. Ten minutes later Cécile and Paul had quietly left the dining room and begun tiptoeing their way upstairs.

It was later, shortly after 1:00 A.M., that the lovers emerged from Madame's house and out onto the wide thoroughfare of the Rue Tiedeur — Paul accompanying Cécile a half block down the lighted street to her car. At the first moment at which they were identifiable, especially Cécile, the jet-black Mazda which had trailed her here started its motor and, tailpipe spewing cobalt fumes, pulled swiftly away from the curb opposite Cécile's Citroën and sped away into the night, leaving behind it the beautiful yellow sports car containing the lone man at the steering wheel — but who now was already climbing out. Cécile and Paul had almost reached her car, and she was getting out her keys — when from across the street and under the streetlight they heard the door of the yellow car violently slam. Cécile turned, saw Georges crossing the street toward them, and emitted a bloodcurdling scream, as Paul, at her elbow, stood transfixed with mouth agape — for he too had seen the large pistol. Georges, less than ten feet from Paul now, was already shooting — point-blank but, symbolically, at his groin, three times, and unable to miss. "OH!" Paul uttered, going down with the second shot, writhing, groaning, trying with feeble hands — also symbolically — to protect his genitals, eyeballs wide under the lights intermittently moving back and forth in their sockets like those of a dying calf. Cécile, screaming, till her lungs seemed bursting, was falling, sprawling, on top of Paul to protect him, now drew, again point-blank and deliberately, the remaining three pistol slugs into her brain, the spurting, almost spraying, blood finally running down into the sewer outlet at the curb. Her skirt was above her glaring white thighs and waist now and the panties she would ordinarily have been wearing — but hardly minutes ago victims of the haste of departure from Madame's second floor (in Paul's arms Cécile had gone to sleep) — had instead been stuffed in her purse, which now, though, lay in her still-hot blood along the Rue Tiedeur's curb and the sewer's entrance. Georges, crazed, hyperbolic, as if stricken with rabies, lips moving yet not uttering a sound, merely stood bent, stooped, over her, in vain clicking the empty pistol at her gory head. *Click, click, click.* Finally, though, he tossed the pistol into the curb conduit filled with the moving blood. At last, then, he followed the trail and stood leaning against the lamppost – awaiting the police. Paul still lay trembling and groaning before trying to raise his hand and point, as if sadly, outrageously, protesting Cécile's missing clothing, her public disgrace. This, then, was the rancid tableau first the gendarmes, followed by the medics, found on arrival.

Later, when Paul's ambulance had left for the nearest hospital, Cour Carree, he was not only fully conscious, despite the grave possibility his heinous groin wounds were fatal, but insisted on wildly talking, preaching his sudden life views, tutoring, lecturing to all, including the speeding ambulance driver and his cohort-medic, the latter in the rear trying against great odds to minister to this strange lunatic patient he had drawn tonight. Paul's now high-voiced preachments, the discourse and exhortation, were somehow delivered not only with the voice but with twirling, jabbing fingers, flailing elbows, all with is wildly radiant countenance on fire. It was apparently the history of his off-beat and portentous life he sought to convey – in Websterian bombast yet total English – to the two hospital employees who understood not a word of what he was trying to say. "Calonne," said the medic to the reckless driver, "we should take this poor bastard directly to the nuthouse – even if he is, for life, fresh out of nuts – and have him locked up. You can't get around it; he's insane."

"Hell, so are you, Tujean," said Calonne, turning a corner on two wheels. "So am I. The world's insane."

Meantime Paul raved on: "Listen, listen, people! I've been talking to Queen Saturn! You've heard of her, I'm sure. She is a goddess, actually, a Cithaeron goddess, actually. I am her *son*! I shall be dead before daybreak, and I want to inform her of this, get her ready, son-to-mother like, for henceforth together we shall be living a different and far better life. Did you hear that, Mother? . . .Can you hear me? The deep and sorry aspects of my life have finally caught up with me. I have some high forfeits to pay. Even as in your case, but for us both now, the reckoning of Judgment Day is at hand"

"What did I tell you?" Tujean called up to the driver Calonne. "He's gone—his mind. He thinks we're priests, and he's confessing. It'll probably be his luck to live another forty years—shitting in his pants."

Paul, his face grimacing, scowling, was trying to sit up as the pain, eviscerating him, brought tears to his eyes. "I owe you so much, though, Queen Saturn," he tried to say in his agony. "You showed me the way of *true* beauty—beauty not only of body but of heart, soul, spirit, a rare bequest indeed, for which I shall repay you well when once again now, like Oedipus and Jocasta, we shall be reunited." The pain was searing now, the bleeding profuse.

Tujean, the medic, kneeling beside him, said: "Are you all right, Daddy? . . . Hurts a little, eh? We'll be there in about five minutes. They'll knock you out with the drugs, and you'll sleep like a baby."

Paul seemed not to hear him, his mind channeled elsewhere, as he loudly announced to the world: "God save the Queen! . . . whom I dearly love . . . and soon now expect to see and take in my now-passionless arms without any longer the slightest torment of guilt! Amen. Amen, I say!"

Six weeks later Paul was alive. Still in a serious condition, but alive. Cécile, of course, had died instantly on the Rue Tiedeur. Paul's father, old Zack, in panic, shock, crying, had come at once. But now, after the first weeks of cursing out everybody in sight—surgeons, anesthetists, interns, nurses, food handlers, and, indeed, most of all (after hearing medical opinion to the effect that Paul would live), his son. But now, after his first trials with French alcoholic beverages, he at night returned to his fine hotel, ate dinner, after which in his room got on his knees and prayed vociferously, before then climbing into his lovely bed and crying himself to sleep. His only fresh and fulfilling experience had been Tosca Zimsu, who came each day, occasionally with Gwelo, and did more than anything or anyone to keep Zack functional. He felt deeply in her debt and adored her. There was a hitch, however. Not knowing Tosca's acumen, her mind, and enterprise, to say nothing of her generally unrecognized eagle eye, Zack dreaded the day he would be called on to tell her something she had known even before he had caught his Concorde flight out of New York for Paris a month and a half ago. It was that his son, whom he loved beyond reason, was now a eunuch for life. For Zack, yes, it meant saturated pillows of tears every night. Also—another relevance—his attitude, feeling toward Fifi Mazisi, also a regular bedside visitor, was the exact opposite of that which quiet, tender (but wide-awake) Tosca enjoyed.

When, early on, Paul had been told Cécile was dead, he began, for the next fortnight, to make funny, crazy noises unlike anything the hospital staff had ever heard from a patient. It was like the baying of a lone wolf—there was somehow a vicious sadness, or often something resembling a rebel yell that would then die out yet with frequent overtones, all followed by a spate of the foulest effusions of obscenity and blasphemy. Then he would cry, before trying to make excuses to his mother the Queen whom he claimed was without doubt a partisan of Cécile's. How would Saturn react to the downfall he could well be charged with, despite his own "loss of life" — literally. Then he would defiantly break wind in the bed, causing his distracted father to shout his tears. It was bedlam, and then Tosca would go out and sit alone in the floor's foyer. Not once, however, was she seen joining in the tears. She appeared full of sympathy, an assuager for old Zack, but watching every move even a hospital orderly might make.

This, she told herself, was her, and Gwelo's, crusade to lose. She was even averse the time she spent reading the newspapers Zack bought which, except for the few American and British papers, he could not read. Tosca's one exception was her wish to keep abreast of Georges Fournier's coming trial, the outcome of which, of course, Tosca knew, was a foregone conclusion. Michelle and little Zoe, both of whom had been sent to live with a well-to-do sister of their father's in Rennes, were as lost as if wandering in the wilds of Borneo. Little Zoe hardly knew her name anymore as benumbed and dazed as she was. Michelle would not eat, or ate very little, wore strange, unkempt clothing, and swore she would return to Paris and become what she called a "street walker." Then, alone, she would go sit out in the park and sob.

In the sixth or seventh week at the hospital Zack, more than ever, began to confide in Tosca. "He's getting stronger," he said of Paul. "He's not quite so mean, either."

"He sleeps better, too," said Tosca, in a long red dress and her dreadlocks down her back. "When do you think he can travel, Monsieur Kessey?"

"Hell, I wouldn't know," Zack said. "But it's high time he was getting some strength. I can say that and not be a doctor. It's nearing two months now — poor guy. But the surgery was a flop. You know that, of course." His saddened voice faltered. "A perfect flop. They can't do anything for him, can't help him, can't save him — at least that particular part of him. You weren't aware of that, were you? That puts a different spin on things, doesn't it?"

She paused. "Yes," she said, almost whispering it — her mind alert.

"You haven't said so, but I get the feeling you and he were pretty tight there at one time. You don't have to comment on that, but I do so admire your integrity."

City of Light

"Thank you."

"I was first aware of this when I asked you why you wished to marry my son, You told me the truth — that it was because of your son. I liked that. But you don't know why I *most* liked it — you may be the one (God, look down on us; help us!) the one who can save Paul, as much as he can be saved after this hell's fire and brimstone he's been through. He's mixed up — has always been. His late mother before him, a good, an intelligent woman, was herself mixed up. They were very close, though — in a way — but she bossed him around a lot, plagued him, some think tried to run his life. I don't believe that. But it must have been hell for him sometimes. So even with my support — and it's been pretty regular, if I say it myself — he still, psychologically, has had a rough time of it. Yet you may be able to help him some simply because of your integrity. His former landlady has called me twice at the hotel. She's sold her place now and gone into a retirement home — her health's not good, she says — but she thought the world of Paul. I told her you come to see him pretty regularly. She wasn't surprised at this, said you'd been stuck on him for quite some time, and said you were all right. Of course, the death of the other lady, the doctor, put the Chevalley lady out of business for keeps. She's going to be a witness at that terrible man's trial. I hope to have Paul back in Chicago by that time, though — he's been through enough. Oh, I'm so glad you've come into his life — for whatever reason — and I know he'll come to appreciate you."

Tosca looked at Zack askance. "He appreciated me before, Monsieur Kessey," she said. "He just didn't talk about it — not even to me. He liked me not only because of the person I am, but because of the person he is. He's that way."

"I'm so glad to hear that, dear. How well said."

They had been speaking softly to prevent their voices from disturbing Paul, though they could never quite tell when he was asleep. Much of the time he lay on his back with his eyes closed. But suddenly, then, if some remark were made with which he did not agree, he might open an eye and look with displeasure at the speaker. Today, however, he had been listless, unobtrusive, hardly at all responding to others' remarks or even their presence. It was near two o'clock one afternoon when a senior nurse entered the room. In the presence of both Zack and Tosca Paul asked the nurse if he might have a ruled notebook and some pencils. Tosca perked up immediately. The nurse said she would contact an orderly and have the items sent up. Tosca's dissatisfaction was clear now. She leaned over to Zack. "Oh, Monsieur Kessey," she whispered, "do you think that's the proper thing for Paul to do at this early point in his recovery?" Zack looked at her blankly. Meanwhile, Paul on his back in the bed could hardly have heard her, yet his interest in her whispers may have been what now caused him to lie there quietly with his eyes, as usual, closed and monitor developments. Why would Tosca be whispering to his father the moment she heard him, Paul, request pencils and paper? he asked himself. Both eyes still closed, he waited, soon letting his breathing rise to make a sleeper's sound. "I don't get you, dear," he heard his father say to Tosca. "We must talk about this sometime, Monsieur Kessey," whispered Tosca. "Maybe soon." "Why, of course," whispered Zack. "About the pencils and paper, do you mean?" "Yes, yes," Tosca murmured. "Very well," said Zack, *sotto voce*. Paul was "snoring" now.

Next morning he tried to get his writing done before either Tosca or Zack arrived. "Saturn dear, the plot thickens yet gets weaker," he wrote. "You and I are not dumbbells. We see things. There's an effort afoot here to keep us from communicating. You'll hit the ceiling, though — especially since you've now learned of your Cécile's sickening tragedy — when you learn the identity of the ringleader. My reaction, however, is nowhere near that of what yours might be. When Cécile was alive I needed all three of you, including Tosca. Dear Cécile — God rest her immortal soul — is no longer with us, of course. Adjustments must therefore be made, but honorable adjustments — for the deceased as well as for the living. You are *not* of the deceased, Saturn. This must always be clear. Cécile, though, now is no longer among us in a rational sense. You are, though, yes; I am; but so is sweet Tosca. You must remember now that I need Tosca. It's *she* who is the ringleader, Mother! But that I need you (and always shall) is to be taken for granted, of course. Yet I also need dear Tosca — more than ever now, in my present and irreparable state. She is the only woman who would want to marry me in my condition, and there's a reason for that, but it's a long story. We're, however, being thrown together by tragedies she had no part in making. This is inarguably true — and it's no feather in my cap. Yet it may somehow also be true of me — if, that is, one is a determinist. Cécile and I encountered each other through Madame. It was an accident. That's all. My plate is clean. There was no volition whatever involved — by Cécile or me. So, then, what is the present situation? It's this. We have in Tosca and me two people who, for weal or for woe, need each other. It's that simple. Therefore I *must* have your blessing. Oh, Queen-of-the-Night, you *must* hear my plea! You must stand by me."

At this juncture Zack walked in. Paul quickly pushed the notebook under the bedsheet. "How are you this morning, Father?" he said.

"I've felt better, Paul," said Zack. "I'm to meet with all, or most, of your doctors this morning at eleven. They haven't summoned me — I've been summoning them for two or three weeks. They're a busy bunch, though — besides I won't be understanding much of what they say anyway. I should have asked

Tosca to come with me, to translate, but between us two this is sort of a family affair, and I'd like for you and me to know what the doctors have got on their minds before outsiders are briefed."

"Tosca is no outsider now, Father. She's very much of an insider—don't you think?"

"Is that what you want, son? It's fine with me. If she comes before I'm supposed to see the doctors I'll be glad to take her with me. I'm hoping, though—really—there won't be much to this meeting. Except that I hope they tell us to get the hell outa here and go home. That's the briefing I look forward to. Say, what was that you were writing when I came in—that you pushed under the sheet right quick?"

"Oh, I jot things down that I might forget otherwise," lied Paul. "No big deal."

"Tosca doesn't take to the idea much—of your keeping a notebook. That big black guy who was tortured and murdered by those fascist thugs—whom they never did catch, I hear—got a hand on some of that stuff you were putting in your notebooks, things addressed to your mother, and about other people, including Tosca, et cetera. This guy told Tosca you were as crazy as a bedbug."

Paul threw the covers back and seemed about to leap out of the bed—before the pain said no—as he asked: "Did Quo Vadis actually say that? . . . my God, that's terrible. It's slander. I never thought he'd do a thing like that—not Quo Vadis."

"Well, Tosca apparently gets nervous, too—when she sees you with one of those pad-and-pencil deals. You don't want to scare the girl to death."

"You like her, don't you, Father? I'm glad you do. So do I."

Tosca, in her red dress and dreadlocks, walked in, then, smiling. "Did I hear the name Tosca?"

"Yes, honey, you did," said Zack, "and it was all complimentary. Besides, you've walked in at the very time we need

you most. The doctors have agreed to see us at eleven." He
looked at his watch. "That's little over an hour from now.
What we're hoping for is that they're going to send us home —
all of us, Tosca dear, including of course you and your fine
boy. But you must go with me, dear, so I'll be sure of all they
said. Will you do that?"

"I'll be glad to . . . ," Tosca finally said, though somehow
apprehensively. "I wonder what they'll say. It'll probably be
more than about going home, Monsieur Kessey. It may be
about what Paul's life — and ours — will be like in the unknow-
able future. Especially if he continues to write those mash
notes to a person, a lady, who was his mother, and your wife,
sir, for that's not a very wholesome situation to have around a
household which wants to be happy (as much, that is, as the
situation will permit) and also a place in which a boy such as
my son will have chance to grow, and learn, and be a productive citizen wherever he happens to be."

You don't think your boy would have that kind of chance
in our home? — is that what you're saying, Tosca?" Zack had
stood, but Tosca had sat. "I'm not sure I'm following you,
honey," he added.

Paul was trying to sit up on the side of the bed again. He
was deeply frowning, though saying nothing. It could be seen,
however, that he was in physical pain.

But Tosca was trying to reply to Zack. "No, Monsieur
Kessey," she said, "I'm not sure that's what I'm saying. Frankly,
I don't know what I'm saying — or even want to say. Poor Quo
Vadis Jackson, less than a week before he died, came to borrow
some money from me. I didn't know it but the money was to be
used for all that fancy white getup he wore to the FFF meeting
that brought about his terrible death. I was glad to lend him the
money for I had no idea of what the consequences would be.
But he and I sat and talked awhile and he told me some really

disturbing things. On the day he was talking about, he had gone to see Paul to try to enlist him in the anti-FFF cause that Quo Vadis was so wrapped up in. But when Paul left the room for about ten minutes, Quo Vadis saw one of these notebooks Paul writes in. It was lying on his worktable. Quo Vadis picked it up and read as much of it as he could before Paul returned. Quo Vadis was flabbergasted. He couldn't believe what he was reading."

Paul, jerking around, was trying to stand now. "That stinking blackguard!" he cried. "How dare he! Those notes were sacred! They were to my dear mother! . . . *Oh!* What a terrible thing for Quo Vadis to have done! Father, why don't you intervene! She was your dear wife! Why don't you say something, Father? Don't sit there and let them defame me in my attempts to commune with my own mother!"

Zack's face was sad. "You mean 'communicate,' Paul," he said.

Paul, now standing directly over him, looked as if he might attack him. "I mean nothing of the kind, Father! I was communing—*communing*—with my mother. There's a difference!"

The handsome hospital room was quiet as death now. Soon Paul, his shoulders in spasm, was sobbing like a baby. "I have *always* tried to commune with my mother!" he said. "She wanted it, encouraged it. We communed with each other. We still do. And we always shall. Forever, yes!" His shoulders still spasming, the loud, groaning sobs could be heard out in the corridor. Again the room was quiet as death.

Tosca knew now what the coming meeting with the doctors would merely provide—corroboration of Paul's condition: derangement, paranoia, psychopathy, lunacy.

Even Zack saw that something gravely in addition to heavy, near mortal, pistol wounds beset his son, his only progeny, now. His reaction, though, was strange for him. He could not bring himself to believe, no matter the evidence, what so clearly faced him. He thought he knew Paul better than anybody on earth. It couldn't have been Paul putting on this "show," he told himself. He also remembered what he had been told about Paul's behavior in the ambulance the night (morning) of the shooting. Thinking he was dying, as most who saw him that night thought, he performed like an inmate of an insane asylum. None of the hospital staff thought it even worthwhile to ask him questions, even if those pertained to the facts and circumstances which had surrounded Paul's ordeal, for they expected nothing rational from him. He was "in orbit," as one intern had put it, though, exclusively, addressing (exhorting, sermonizing, moralizing, hectoring) his mother. Zack now remembered these staff allegations from his first encounter with the hospital personnel. Most, though, thought it idle to spend much time on the subject, feeling there was only a small chance for the patient's recovery. Zack's attitude now, therefore, took on the stature of, not weakness, not weeping, not even self-pity, but of strength and inquiry. His first decision was unequivocal: He would take his poor boy home—now. "How would this be gone about, though?" he asked himself. What was needed? *Who* was needed? He at once thought of Tosca, though with an urge to shake his head sadly. She seemed now anti-Paul, he thought, and he knew her, correctly, to be a strong woman. Nevertheless, he would again talk to her. The two of them were still in Paul's room, though Paul was quiet now, perhaps really sleeping, having been given quieting injections by the staff—also a pat on the brow by his father.

Zack looked at Tosca. "I must talk with you, now or later," he said. "But of course at your convenience. It's about what we do now. Or are you interested in doing, or trying to do, anything? Have you given up? I haven't, Tosca. I'm not the type. I don't believe you are, either, given the right situation. Yet, for you, is this it? Are you backing up, throwing up your hands?"

"I don't know, Monsieur Kessey," Tosca said. "Why don't we go to the doctors' meeting first. Maybe there won't be anything left to talk about; maybe there will, too. But if there is, I would want to go home and return with my son, Gwelo. The issue then, you see, would very much involve him, and therefore, for me, no unilateral matter. Does what I say make sense?"

"Yes, it does—that's why I *need* you," Zack said with great emphasis.

Tosca made no comment. Instead she went to the bed and tried to adjust Paul's head more comfortably on the pillow—also to test the extent, if one existed, or the depth, of his slumber. Now it was nearly eleven, whereupon she and Zack soon left for the doctors' counsel.

That evening, near six o'clock, Zack sent a taxi to fetch Tosca and Gwelo to his hotel for dinner. It had been raining most of the afternoon, the traffic was heavy, and Zack in the hotel lobby awaiting their late arrival, had a miserable time holding fast and not ordering a "high-stakes" martini, to him, an expert, the most formidable gin drink extant. He kept his seat in the high-backed chair and watched the revolving door of the lobby for his guests. Tonight his mind was a conglomeration of attitudes: wrenching sadness on hearing the truth about his son's mental condition; a queer relief from a father's torture at watching the helplessness of an invalid son; satisfaction at having played a model role in doing all that was humanly possible to save his son; and now his role in trying to guide and oversee the workings and duties entailed in the rationed time left for Paul—ah, he thought, and for himself.

He could hold off no longer. He went into the bar that was in full view of the lobby entrance and ordered the "high-stakes" relief he knew so well. He soon sat ruminating over the drink, wondering what the imminent meeting would be like. Looking out, before the urge for a second drink befell him, he saw the long red dress, then the shoulders of dreadlocks. He signed the bar check and went out to greet Tosca and Gwelo. He could not understand it, but he now felt some kind of lift — fully appreciating, however, that, to his knowledge, there existed no grounds for it. He also noticed people looking at Tosca in her African attire and headdress. This somehow amused him. "Hello!" he said to them — especially to Gwelo, whom he had seen infrequently and who, in the coming discussion, would doubtless be consulted to the extent his sweet but hardened mother indicated, or permitted. "I haven't met you recently, Gwelo," Zack said, "but I've heard a lot about you and your great high-school work. I salute you, young man."

"Thank you, sir," said Gwelo, in a new suit and holding his mother's wet umbrella away from him.

"Follow me, will you, folks?" Zack said. "Nice evening for ducks, is it not? Ha, ha." When they reached the dining room entrance the *maitre d'hôtel* and the busboys alike viewed Tosca's garb with in interest that was varied but cordial enough. The good table they were shown to, however, was the result of Zack's lingering handshake with the *maitre d'*. So, given the stark circumstances, everything seemed to be going well. Then . . .

As Gwelo shook out his linen napkin and spread it across his knees, he observed to Zack: "Monsieur Kessey, you can't always depend on what doctors tell you. The fact that they said today at your meeting that your son may have only a year to live in his present insane condition doesn't mean that he won't outlive you, sir."

"Gwelo!" gasped Tosca. "Who's asked you for your opinion and anything yet? Where are your manners?"

"OK, Ma-MAH," said Gwelo, though with scant contrition in his voice.

Zack leaned toward Tosca. "May I order you something from the bar, Mrs. Zimsu?" he said.

"Oh, no," Tosca laughed. "I'm a teetotaler, though not necessarily proud of it. Believe me, I'm not a killjoy. And, Monsieur Kessey, why don't you call me by my first name as you do in the hospital? Is it because of Gwelo? He won't mind, will you Gwelo?"

"Monsieur Kessey is trying to be a gentleman, Ma-MAH," said Gwelo. "What's wrong with that? — especially when we know he is someone who has accomplished a lot. And aren't you a millionaire, too, sir?"

Zack saw and annexed the opportunity. "Of course and much more. A mere millionaire today, though, is a nobody. I sold my business once, then bought it back — I loved it so. You come with me to Chicago and I'll make something out of you overnight." Zack was already waving at a bar waitress for a "high-stakes" martini. Immediately Gwelo asked for a Pepsi Cola and a cup of tea for his mother.

"Ma-MAH apparently didn't hear that about the millionaires in Chicago," Gwelo said. "If I weren't an earth-saving activist, Ma-MAH, I'd take him up on it. I bet I'd like Chicago anyhow, though. Besides they've got one of the great universities in the world — out there on their Midway."

"Now you're talking, Gwelo," said Zack. "I ought to be a trustee out there but they never asked me. So I give my money to the United Negro College Fund. But I'm glad you like Chicago. I think, though, Mrs. Zimsu has some reservations."

The waiter came now with the menus. By the time the food orders were given Zack, now sadly thinking of Paul, had become quiet, introspective, also slightly tired of Gwelo's talk. Zack's latter attitude, however, vanished in a hurry when Gwelo said to him, seriously, "You would like my mother to marry your extremely ill and now permanently insane son, who, besides, I hear, has no money (except what you give him) and no means, certainly now, after all that's happened, no means of making a living for a wife, my mother or any other woman. I have a remedy for that, though, sir, which, of course, I've never discussed with my mother. It is that instead of her marrying your unfortunate son she should marry *you*, Monsieur Kessey."

Old Zack's mouth fell open and he couldn't get it closed. Surprisingly, though, Tosca was shocked; she did not, as could have been expected, begin screaming at Gwelo. Meanwhile, Zack's mouth was still open.

"No, Gwelo, that wouldn't work, dear," Tosca finally said, still, though, with no screams at him. "Monsieur Kessey wouldn't be interested in anything like that — my goodness."

Zack finally found his voice. "Let me see if I rightly understand what's going on here," he said. "I have an objective for my sad, unfortunate son. You, Mrs. Zimsu, have an objective for your son, who, all agree, has a very bright future and is not yet twelve. I have money, which I made, though, by some of the hardest work, use of my brain, constantly trying to cope with all manner of race prejudice, and also myself not averse, on occasion, to cutting a corner here and there to keep from going under. And I made it. But I'm also an old man now, yet, God knows, I had wanted Paul to come out of the university rarin' to go, to carry on what I had beaten out my brains to accomplish, taken all kinds of laughing and pranks from white folks, also my share of insults, all this so Paul could come out and hit the ground running. But it didn't turn out that way. He wasn't interested. He wanted to read, follow athletics, run after the girls at school, and, most of all, sit across the room and gaze into his mother's eyes. Sure, she would act embarrassed, and like she didn't like it, but she was *crazy* about his attention. Weird maybe, unusual, kind of funny, too, but they had this thing going that they couldn't deal with. Wasn't anything wrong with it—just a boy and his good-looking mother in love with each other. I watched it—they didn't know, of course—intrigued. They both thought, despite what I'd done, that I was a little out of things, maybe a little dumb. But, you know what, I consider myself dumb as a fox. I look at you two, for instance. I've especially studied Mrs. Zimsu here. Gwelo would kill anybody—*anybody*—who insulted his mother. And his mother would damn near marry the garbage man to get her son launched on a great career. And do you know who loves it, who thinks it's terrific? Zack Kessey, that's who." He turned to Gwelo. "But I wouldn't marry your mother if she was the last woman on earth. And I'll bet you, Gwelo, there's no man who respects her more than I do. Even you. But *I* would never marry her. I don't need her. It's my dying son— whom I love with all my heart—who needs her. And I think you're a little flip, maybe a bit calloused, to say what you did— that your mother should marry me. Now, let's get down to the nut-cuttin' (excuse me, Mrs. Zimsu). Are you interested in marrying my son and going to the U.S.A. to live or not— otherwise we can adjourn this conclave *sine die*."

"Don't do it, Ma-*MAH*," Gwelo said. "We can make it."

Tosca finally turned on him, with a vengeance. "Make it on *what*? Don't make me laugh!" She turned then to Zack. "I need more time to think about this, Monsieur Kessey. I'm sure you wouldn't be so cruel as to make this our final conversation on something so crucial to all of us, including poor Paul." She was losing control, getting teary-eyed, her voice caught up in the momentousness of the "conclave." Of all people now, even Gwelo was sniffling. "You are rushing me," said Tosca to Zack. She too now was sniffling. "I need more time, Monsieur Kessey! You're taking advantage of me."

City of Light

Despite all his recent sorrows, Zack came very near to smiling. "I wish I had *you* running my business," he said sourly. There was silence as time ticked on. Suddenly he almost stood. "SAY, it just occurred to me! That was no idle, no dumb, remark I just made. Lord, have mercy on me and my poor, dear son. But I see you're still on by side, Lord." He spun around to Tosca. "Mrs. Zimsu," he said, "just let *me* paint a picture for you. The doctors there today spent almost the entire time painting the grim, hopeless picture of Paul's illness, his near fatal gunshot wounds, which they say will never really heal, as well as his new affliction (or not so new). Insanity. It was grim—how was I to keep from crying. I couldn't. I was thinking of my dear boy, as any father would. But it just occurred to me—who's thinking of me! WHO?" He was beating his chest with his fist. "*Nobody's* thinking of me, that's who! And I'm older, by far, than anybody, including the doctors, connected with this woeful affair. Think of that. I'm not going to tell you my age. I don't make a habit of doing that—for business reasons—but I'll tell you this, I'm no spring chicken. Just imagine, then, what would happen if I were to keel over right here, right now? What would become of my business that I've spent a long, rugged career in establishing if the Lord called me in, say, tonight or tomorrow? I've got a will, of course, bequeathing, naturally, almost everything I've got to Paul. But you saw it, you heard it, I just had what they call a phantasm, or a thunderbolt. You were sitting right there. It almost knocked me down. But it didn't dim my eyesight. I see my big main office in Chicago with you in it, Mrs. Zimsu. I see my own private, palatial, inner office, with its three private secretaries, who deal only with me on matters affecting company policy and strategy and then go tell my board members what I've decided. Ah, but take the situation when the Lord has lifted my sights—yes, to higher duties and responsibilities up there with Saint Peter and his angels. *Think* of it, my friends! Well, *I* just thought of it when I was, yes, just a minute ago, almost struck down, like Saint Paul on the road to Damascus, by this thunderbolt of an idea. So up in heaven with all that angelic host" — (Zack was not laughing, not even smiling) — "whom do I look up, or down, and see sitting at my desk, conferring with my three secretaries, checking things out, talking about any sloppy people we've got to fire, how much money we give to the NAACP, the Urban League, the United Negro College Fund, and the others — even some of the hustling jackleg preachers (the kind who will *surely* have a harder time with my pretty, smart-as-hell, lady successor than they've ever had with me) whom, yes, do I see there behind my fine mahogany desk issuing the orders, just before she has to be rushed, chauffeured, out to O'Hare to make the plane for an important meeting in New York . . . yes, you know whom I see. What, or whom, are *you* laughing about, Gwelo? Didn't you just say to your mother a few minutes ago: 'Don't do it, Mother.' Now you're laughing. I don't know what at. This is the most serious matter I've ever faced in my long life, Gwelo — I don't know about you. Just suppose in less than a year after I take my boy back to Chicago, I die and go on to my maker, what happens to Paul — no matter how much money I've left him. Who will look after him, be kind to him, have him taken out for car rides, read to him maybe, watch television with him — treat him as the dear, fine human being he is, no matter that he's demented. You know whom I'm looking for? I'm looking for somebody — man or woman, black or white — who has some . . . some . . . some *lovingness*, yes, that's it, some lovingness in their heart, and is, of course, a person of integrity. Those are the specs, yes, I'm looking for; that I must have. I must, I must — I must have them! It's my boy, my only offspring, I'm talking about."

City of Light

But Gwelo, listening to Zack, and, as a result, now suddenly having seen in his mind's eye a lovely sky of brand-new, glorious vistas before him, was soon grinning, beaming, from ear to ear, even itching to clap his hands and cheer—as if Zack had just described for them a virgin, untried, promised land. Gwelo had changed in only those few convincing minutes.

Tosca, however, was serious and silent—staring hard, somehow, into her empty plate. Then the good food came and they were all soon eating with relish, though, also now, with a minimum of conversation, for everyone was wrestling with the problem at hand, the enigmas pending before the "conclave." Gwelo did, though, now, with great effort, manage to hide his elation, exaltation. He kept watching his mother, trying to read her mind, hoping she would do the "right" thing—that is, as he now, belatedly, saw it. Although the food was there and she was slowly, contemplatively, eating, Tosca sat absorbed, not quite bemused—until Zack, with apologies, ordered another drink for himself, belovedly referring to it as my "high-stakes pacifier." Then the dining room orchestra began to play—as Tosca still sat slowly eating and anguishing about her and Gwelo's unknown future, their fate.

Next morning, even a little before nine o'clock, Zacharias Hamilcar Kessey was in his son's handsome hospital room wondering what this, still another, day would bring. Paul smiled widely when he saw old Zack and put out his hand as though he were greeting the president of the United States. Suddenly then his eyes took on a strange celestial glare before he smiled again as if his face were photographing heaven. "The Queen is dead!" he said now, though sadly. "Long live the Queen!"

Zack came closer to the bed. "Ha, what queen are you referring to, old timer?" he asked, smiling. "Elizabeth the First?"

"No, Dad. Queen Saturn. You don't know of her yet. Ah, but you will. The *world* will." Paul's eyes were glittering.

Zack, still smiling, closed his own left eye and squinted up hard at the ceiling. "That stumps me, son. Saturn, you say. . . . When did she reign? And where?"

Paul studied Zack's face. Then his lips moved mysteriously as if he might soon have an answer to the questions. Finally, though, he shook his head. "You know, I've never been very clear on that, Father," he said. "I know she took a strong stand in Cécile's behalf. Cécile hasn't been in yet this morning, has she?"

"No, she had to go out of town, son," Zack said, his whole body quivering.

"She's a wonderful person, that girl," Paul said. "Also high-principled to a fault." He then reached in the drawer of his bed stand and, feebly rummaging, finally brought out a small, crumpled news clipping apparently from some long-ago Palm Sunday. It depicted a likeness of Christ astride a donkey entering through the gates of Jerusalem. "When she returns, Dad," said Paul, "tell her I have something for her. Here." Again feebly, he handed Zack the *Le Figaro* clipping. "Give her this. She'll remember. Ah, look at that terrific hotel wallpaper in the room — isn't it crazy? I want to see if she really remembers it all. What a lovely, sweet girl — or woman, I should say. Saturn really went to bat for her, though, but now dear Tosca is in the saddle and that's probably better for me — she's mentally strong, steady, knows what she's doing." Paul sighed. "Ah, but I don't most of the time. She's also African, remember that. That's a definite plus. But I myself am African — and don't forget, either, that I am the founder, former director, and general strategist of the famous Coterie organization here in Paris. You remember all that, Father — you should; you financed it. You are a great guy, Dad. I and my Coterie folks all meant to do great things for ourselves as well as for Africa. But then something happened. Oh, I was so sorry about that. A lot of it had to do with me — my lack of whatever it takes to be in charge of things, to lead. Right? But you didn't run out on me, Father. You bit your lip and hung in there. I'll salute you till the day I die. No man alive ever had a better father than I, I'll tell you that, by God. No, sir. Ha, but back to Tosca, bless her heart. She's another Saturn, in a way — an honest-to-God leader. If we can talk her into taking over the helm of this ship, we'll do OK. I'd bet money on her."

"We're working on it, son." Zack was so distraught he could not look at Paul.

"Could you pour me a glass of water there, Dad, if you don't mind?"

Zack complied and, fighting tears, used the opportunity to leave the room for the adjacent corridor — just as Tosca was arriving. She saw his distress and immediately came and, consolingly, patted him on the arm before stealing over and taking a quick peep into Paul's room. "He seems chipper enough this morning, doesn't he, Monsieur Kessey. And he's had breakfast. How do *you* feel, though, sir?"

Zack could not answer her for staring at the clothing she wore. Nor did she fail to notice his surprise, almost astonishment. She wore a bright tangerine silk dress, in length reaching hardly past her pretty knees, and blue patent-leather pumps as foils for everything. No long, red, Copti dress anymore; no dreadlocks, either. Zack had never seen her look so different, and so chic. He was amazed — actually dazzled. "Jesus-whillickers," he said. "How beautiful you look! I've never seen you dressed like that, Tosca dear. It certainly becomes you."

"Thank you, sir. Maybe it will all help keep my mind off certain things. We must not tell Paul, but one of his friends, little Ari—I can't remember his last name—a charter member of Paul's Coterie organization, died yesterday here in the hospital. I only learned about it last night. It's rather sad. But he had AIDS. They hadn't expected him to live this long, though. His body will be flown back to Africa. He was a Zulu."

"That's too bad," said Zack, "but you're right, we wouldn't want to tell Paul about it. It would serve no useful purpose."

"But now, Monsieur Kessey, I want to tell you about something else—something I hope will be more pleasing. Gwelo and I decided last night when we got home that it was time now for me to turn my life around—and of course his, too—and prepare to go with you and Paul to the U.S. I'm sure Gwelo will be happier there—you could tell, when the three of us were having dinner last evening, by the way he changed his mind, how he reacted to your beautiful, your really glowing, description of how things could be for us all there in Chicago, how, too, by our dedication, we could make a much better, maybe truly happy, life for poor Paul—whom we all love."

Tears had already come to Zack's eyes. "Oh, Tosca dear, how I love you for saying that. It is so beautiful of you. And I could understand almost everything you said. And also *why* you said it. It was your graciousness, your goodness, that did it all, for you've been pondering this matter, I understand, for a long time. But let me tell you one thing, dear, that when a minute ago I saw how you were dressed, what a change you'd brought on yourself, my heart went to my throat. It seemed God was talking to me. I was almost sure you had made your decision. And, sure enough, I had it right, didn't I? Oh, Heavenly Father—thank You, thank You!" Zack was going in his pocket now for a handkerchief to wipe the tears. "Oh, Tosca honey, you'll never know the great load you've lifted off my shoulders."

"Thank you, Monsieur Kessey," said Tosca. "I am very happy—you deserve everything good. And so does dear Paul.

City of Light

So we must begin now to chart our course — it is never too early for that. You may recall, for instance, our discussion about Paul's asking the hospital personnel to furnish him pencil and paper that he uses to accomplish what he apparently feels, or hopes, is some kind of communication with his deceased mother. That could become, you know, Monsieur Kessey — if not soon attended to by us — something of a stumbling block in our forthcoming strategy to bring Paul around, calm him down, set new, fresh, sights for him in his present and unfortunate mental condition. You can probably enlighten me, sir, on the background, the history, of this seeming pen-propensity, if not fondness, on Paul's part to have these long, involved, written pleas, or admonitions, or maybe just pep talks, to his late mother — before then throwing away all these letters, so-called, or even cuneiforms, they might be named, and starting all over again. I've discussed this, at some length, Monsieur Kessey, with the hospital personnel. They seem, however, not in the least disturbed — they even smile — about this strange practice of Paul's. They challenge, or correct, me when I say his missives are always meant for, addressed to, his mother. They contend they're often addressed to a creature he identifies as 'Augustine,' a huge fish — a dolphin, actually — with whom, so they say, Paul has terrible altercations, wrangles, including his accusations that Augustine is set to entice Paul's mother from him and he often threatens to kill this dire oceanic aggressor. The hospital people smile but, Monsieur Kessey, I don't think it's funny at all. We shall be trying, then, to help Paul, rescue him, start him out on new paths, return him to the world he knew. That will be our mission. Do I have your support, Monsieur Kessey, and especially your best wishes?"

Zack could only shake his head in a complete absence of understanding. "Of course I wish you the very best, dear. We are talking about my son, my only child, you know. But I'm completely baffled by what you tell me. It's true Paul and his mother had a strange association—they were daffy about each other—but I certainly don't mean that in a foul, dirty way. Yet, though in different ways, and to different degrees, they loved each other. But she wasn't quite as fierce, or as impetuous and uncontrolled, as Paul—a very strange man (I started to say 'young man') but he's not anymore. And he's now come to a terrible pass; poor, poor, fellow. Yes, of course, I wish you well, Tosca. And—you are such a wonderful lady—I hope you, you as a person, will derive something from this wary, uncharted undertaking that goes well beyond your son's education, or your getting a free plane ride to the U.S.A. with us, or your no longer now having money worries, none of this. I only hope you will derive something from it that will apply to only you—you as a person! *That* is my prayer, Tosca dear."

Tosca only gazed long at the floor. Her eyes were dry, yet she seemed in a very emotional state. She turned finally then—to old Zack. "You are a good, a wonderful, man, Monsieur Kessey. I had a father like you a one time—a man of decency and honor. Then terrible things happened to us—our family. But then I met your son—under the most bizarre, unbelievable circumstances. It was not long then before he could not control himself, in a sense; wanted very much to get to the physical side of my nature. I of course rebuffed him. Yet he did not entirely change his curious, though not entirely demeaning, ways toward me. And I watched his every move. Why was that, you wonder. It was because I had begun to like him. Like *all* of him—insults and all. As you know, both my father and husband were killed, murdered, in an entangled, horrible war which overran our African country. It was a terrifying, dreadful insurrection. I was gang-raped, until I suffered temporary blindness, by the wild, marauding, so-called troops of the enemy. I was lucky to come out of any of it alive—and even with a baby son, sired by my husband. I thereafter hated the sight, physically, of any man who lived. Men were anathema to me! Your son, Paul, included. For a time. But then I somehow began to bemoan my fate. I knew I was attractive, actually pretty at times, and I soon cursed myself for the life I was leading — and all this was aside from the starvation constantly threatening my son and me after we somehow escaped to Paris. It finally came to the point where I longed just to be a housewife again — with a good husband who could love me — spiritually and physically. So before I realized it, and in my innermost, hushed, ashamed, consciousness, and other faculties, your son now was constantly on my mind. Yet also on my mind for the high purpose of insuring that my talented son got an education commensurate with his natural gifts, which are considerable. All the time, however, I had your son in mind. Yet I was putting out all this guileless, undefiled fanfare about my willing sacrifice for my son, Gwelo, and my hope to be able to make even more (not for myself, but for Gwelo). I needn't go on, Monsieur Kessey — you can easily guess the rest. I've had my heart set on going to the States with you and Paul for some time now. Gwelo has of course figured in my plans — I've truly wanted to do the very best for him — but your son Paul has figured even more importantly, materially, than anyone, or anything, else. So there you have it. I therefore hope you'll still be able to say you wish me well, for, if you permit it, I'm going to take Paul to Chicago and nurse him back to health — God being my judge and helper — *for myself*. Tell me, sir, if you still wish me well."

Old Zack was practically floored. He was tongue-tied as well. He scratched his head of white woolly hair now before he spoke. Finally: "Are you telling me, Tosca, that you're going to the States with Paul and me to somehow improve his health to the degree that, eventually, he can become a really viable husband, one who can fully function, in bed or else-where, as he could have, say, a year ago? Is that what you're saying, dear?"

Tosca took a prolonged and deep breath. "I guess that's what I'm saying," she finally said. "Or at least what I'm trying to say — although I know it can never happen. I also know that what I'm saying doesn't make sense. The truth is, though, that I just want to be a woman agaiı.. ı want someone, I guess, who will look out for me, fend for me, but who also respects me, sees some good qualities in me. Is that wishing for too much, Monsieur Kesscy?"

"Ah, my God," breathed Zack, before then saying, almost to himself, yet audibly, "This only heightens the tragedy. My God, my God."

"Then you don't want me to go home with you, is that it?"

"I don't know what I want you to do, Tosca."

"Does what I've just told you, confessed to you, make me less serviceable to Paul?"

"I don't see how either one of us can answer that. I don't know what service you're talking about. What I had wanted — though sort of like pie in the sky, I guess — was someone with integrity whom I could trust, depend on, to look after Paul when I'm dead. That's how I saw you, that's what so elated me about you. But now you tell me you have wished, after you marry Paul, that some kind of normal sex life could eventually be looked forward to. Well, Tosca, that can never be. You yourself must know it can never be. So now comes the rub that scares me. I'll be dead — and, ha, as we used to say down in the country: 'dead and in hell' — I'll be dead, yes, very soon and Paul will be alone in the world. He won't have any money worries but, I fear, other problems. Although you know he can never be a normal husband to you, there's no guarantee that despite this you might not get disgusted with him eventually and begin mistreating him. Oh, that's a nightmare to me, Tosca. I'm sure you can understand that and sympathize with me. Yet I don't have anybody but you. The question is, can you be depended on?"

"The answer is 'yes,' Monsieur Kessey." She had spoken at once. "I know I can be depended on."

"How do you know? It's as simple as that. How, Tosca?"

"I will have a home, money, a husband, and a son. That's a life I would hardly ever have had the good fortune to claim if I hadn't encountered first Paul, then you. So I have all the incentive in the world to do the right thing, Monsieur."

Zack was already shaking his head negatively. "That's an inadequate answer, of course," he said. "But, I realize, there *is* no adequate answer. The only thing we can do, I guess, is give this thing a try. I, Paul's father, have no alternative. You, as I see it, don't have much of one yourself. I guess we must just go forward with it. I'm doing the best for my son I know how. You, as I look at it, are doing the best for yourself and your son that you know how—or that you're likely to be able to do. So, as I say, Tosca dear, there's nothing left for us except to go forward." He shook his head again: "Ah, life is a rocky road. But now let's go in and see how Paul is doing. I'll bet he's sleeping."

They went in and Zack was right. Paul in bed was snoring— legitimately now. Tosca went over and placed the back of her hand on his cheek. He made no move except to open both eyes. "Hello, Paul," she said, not smiling.

Paul smiled, however. "Hi," he said. "Hey, you better not let my mother, Queen Saturn, see you wearing her clothes like that. I remember the first time she wore that dress. She and Dad went off to a party and left me at home by myself. I got even with her, though—I hid a pair of her golf shoes from her. She couldn't find them and blamed the hired help until I finally came up with them. Ha, ha, ha!"

"Shame on you, Tiger," old Zack laughed. "That wasn't a very nice thing to do, now was it?"

"It's going to be worse than that if I ever catch her again making eyes at Augustine. I don't like that. She knows it and shouldn't do it—although I have no bias against dolphins as such."

"Paul," said Tosca, "I've got news for you. At least I hope you will consider it good news. I and my son are going to Chicago with you and your father. I look forward to it. I'm going to be your new friend."

Suddenly Paul was trying to rise on his pillows with his elbows. "Hey, that's pretty good news," he said. "Is that why you're wearing Saturn's dress? Come on, now." He looked at her and gave a tiny, whimsical smile.

"Forget the dress, Paul. As I say, I'm going to be your new friend."

"I'm going to be *your* friend, too." He laughed. "Ha, if Saturn, that is, will look the other way. Ha, ha, ha!" He turned to Zack then. "Dad, I hate to have to break this news to the Queen. If you only knew her better you could do it for me. I hate to start a big row. Already she may have sensed what's happening. She'd blow a gasket if she knew her clothes were also involved. She has a long memory, you know. But so it goes—that's life. Change must come—we get a new president every four or eight years, don't we? Then she's got Augustine to fool around with—don't forget that."

Old Zack started crying. Actually boo-hooing. Getting his handkerchief out, backing away to a chair, he plopped down and was soon almost hysterical. Tosca finally went over, put her arm around his shoulder, and tried to calm him, but it took some time for his crying to stop.

Even Paul became sympathetic. "It's too bad, of course," he said, "but it's inevitable. Change is always evitable." He put out his hand now, wanderingly, as if he wished to make contact with another hand, in this hour of sadness and change.

City of Light

Tosca saw it, left Zack, and returned to Paul to hold his nervous, withered hand. But he was shaking his head, as if there were aspects of life even he could not fathom, much less control. He looked up at Tosca, almost appealingly. "I do hope, though, Sweetie," he said, "that before we leave, you can change into another dress — otherwise it seems cruel, like you're rubbing it in. My mother deserves better than that. You don't have to do that now. *You* are the Queen. As Dad always says, that's the way the ball bounces; the way the cookie crumbles. Indeed, dear, already your predecessor may have sensed what's happening, or what I was going to do, for only a week ago she and I went to a beach on the Atlantic. Lord, she looked so lovely — in her totally white bathing suit, with her marvelous legs supporting the libidinal grooves and curves of her body." He turned to Zack, who, wet handkerchief yet in hand, sat quietly sniveling his tears. "Oh, Father! — you should have seen her! She was utterly *maddening*! Ah, Saturn."

Zack began crying again, almost bawling, no longer able to control himself. Tosca looked alarmed now.

Paul's voice, however, seemed stronger than ever. "She was in fact so beautiful," he said, "that we had hardly gone waist-deep in the ocean when three great dolphins came zooming in over to her! They were, of course, courting her. Then I spied, and immediately recognized, the one in the middle of them. That bastard! — I'd have recognized him in *hell*! It was her lover, Augustine! Oh!"

Tosca, though frightened, was nevertheless standing over the bed and still holding Paul's trembling, agitated, left hand.

"At once then," cried Paul, "one of the damndest dolphin fights you ever saw in your life broke out among the three of them. Over her! But you know who won that one, I'm sure — old Augustine, of course. The moment he returned, then, her majesty the Queen leapt up on his back and, sea foam flying every which way, they sped, hurtled, away! So, yes, early on, the Queen had already evened up the score with me; me who had been the culprit of her frustration and defeat. But, alas, she was gone now. Forever. Somehow, though, in all the threshing, wet melee, she managed to turn and wave a weak, certainly anything-but-triumphant, good-bye to me! . . . her face long, stern, cold now. Then everything was over. It was the last time I would ever see her." Paul sighed. "So it goes, yes—our fractured lives."

Old Zack, already lunging, moaning, in his chair, now began crying bitterly, indeed childishly. "Oh, my God!" he pleaded, "Help my boy! *Help* him, Lord! Help *me*!"

Paul, absolutely oblivious, inert, seemed hardly any longer aware of where he was—as if, also, he did not, or could not, even hear his father anymore. He seemed only trying to pull himself up higher in the bed, as if positioning himself for one more unknown but herculean effort. Tosca, her pretty face long, sad, perturbed, but without a tear, was doing what little she could to help him. But soon then he *addressed* them—it seemed really that formal: "When I was in college we studied a poem written by a man named John Stewart Carter. It was titled "Mr. De Paolis and the Shades" and was about life and death. It was about nothing else—just life and death, yes. It may have seemed to some to be about other things as well but"—Paul thumped his chest—"*I* know it was only about those two things. One stanza, which I shall never forget, went like this, verbatim:

So tongueless shades cry out to us—
from misted mirror above a knob
    marked "Waste"—
to ride again the dolphin's back
through no enameled sea
but crowded deep in far-refracting
     glass
they ask the anguish of our choice.

City of Light

The pall that had fallen and still now rested on the room would remain. That night, far into the night, Paul, alone, though somehow now content, indeed almost euphoric as he slept, did not once feel the jarring death pangs, the last surgings of a toilworn heart, before he shuddered once then breathed his last. It was finally over. When next morning the hospital orderlies entered the room, they found only peace on his face. It was as Macbeth said of Duncan's body: "After life's fitful fever he sleeps well."

Three days later, then, Paris was at high noon, and the handsome chartered jet awaited its turn far out in the take-off line at Orly airport. The flight crew and attendants numbered eight but the passengers only four and one of them, alas in effect a stowaway, was sequestered in a neat catchall cabin just behind the plane's right wing as its occupant lay reposing in a beautiful, closed, silver-gray casket covered with roses. But soon then the plane, having been given clearance, lifted slowly, almost funeareally, off Orly's west runway headed for the States and Chicago.

Old Zack sat quietly but was grim. "Paul looks terrific, darn near sweet, doesn't he?" he said to Tosca beside him and tried to smile but could not.

"He does look sweet, Monsieur Kessey," Tosca said.

Gwelo, alone across the isle as if banished, stared straight ahead, refusing to look out the window. He had not been on a plane since his fleeing, despairing, shattered mother had brought him to Paris. Most of the experience he did not remember and now he was scared.

"Ah, Paul is so handsome," said Zack to Tosca. "He's a heck of a guy with women, you know."

Tosca gently patted his hand then gazed out the window at the distant tremulous white clouds over Chartres. "Yes, he is, Monsieur Kessey," she said.

"I hate to think of the past," Zack said. "He was a good boy. He did the best he could. Life was just too tough an assignment for him, that's all."

Tosca quietly sighed and patted his hand again. "Yes, Monsieur Kessey," she said. "But now we must look ahead, sir. Don't you agree?"

Zack seemed, almost frantically, searching his mind for the answer.